Kya Mordrayn's eyes blazed with hatred. Protected by the Mythal's aura, she had survived the baelnorn's cleansing fire unscathed. The archmage lifted her long reptilian arm and pointed a talon at Kestrel's heart. "Think you that I will allow one scrawny chit to undo a plan decades in the formation?"

A thin green ray shot out from Mordrayn's talon and raced straight at Kestrel.

Based on the best-selling computer game from SSI!

FORGOTTEN REALMS

More books about the Forgotten Realms

THE HALLS OF STORMWEATHER

Enter the mean streets of a city where
everything has its price and even the
wealthiest families will do anything to survive.

❖

DEATH OF THE DRAGON

Ed Greenwood and Troy Denning
Azoun of Cormyr, in the twilight of his years,
is still a shining hero to his subjects. Yet his beloved
kingdom has never faced so many ominous foes.

❖

ELMINSTER IN MYTH DRANNOR

Ed Greenwood
In centuries past, the great mage Elminster
lived among the elves of Myth Drannor. There,
in the face of treachery and passion, he helped
erect the Mythal that would protect the secret
kingdom down through the years.

Carrie Bebris

Based on the original CD-ROM
game story by Sarah W. Stocker
and Ken Eklund

POOL OF RADIANCE
Ruins of Myth Drannor

©2001 Wizards of the Coast, Inc.

Distributed in the United States by St. Martin's Press. Distributed in Canada by Fenn Ltd.

Distributed to the hobby, toy, and comic trade in the United States and Canada by regional distributors.

Distributed worldwide by Wizards of the Coast, Inc. and regional distributors.

Cover art by Brom
First Printing: November 2000
Library of Congress Catalog Card Number: 00-101965

9 8 7 6 5 4 3 2 1

UK ISBN: 0-7869-2688-0
US ISBN: 0-7869-1387-8
620-T21387

U.S., CANADA,   EUROPEAN HEADQUARTERS
ASIA, PACIFIC, & LATIN AMERICA   Wizards of the Coast, Belgium
Wizards of the Coast, Inc.   P.B. 2031
P.O. Box 707   2600 Berchem
Renton, WA 98057-0707   Belgium
+1-800-324-6496   +32-70-23-32-77

Visit our web site at **www.wizards.com/forgottenrealms**

For Alex and Katherine

Acknowledgments

This book would not exist without many people who generously shared their time, knowledge and encouragement. In particular, I wish to thank:

My husband, for aiding and abetting my dreams.

My parents, who demonstrate their unconditional love and support in more ways than I can count. And my sister and brother, for the same.

My grandfathers, whose lifelong love of reading and learning are an inspiration, and who helped me grow up believing I could do anything I set my mind to.

Shannon, who helped keep my home life from falling to pieces when I was on deadline.

Sharon Antoniewicz, Susie Just, and Georgann Suszka, from whom I learned much about storytelling. I miss our Tuesday nights.

Many friends at Wizards of the Coast, including my editors Bill Larson and Peter Archer, and FORGOTTEN REALMS® authorities Steven Schend, Dale Donovan, and Ed Greenwood, for their encouragement and patience in answering endless questions.

And finally, the Pool of Radiance computer game creators, especially Sarah Stocker, Jon Kromrey, Ken Eklund, and Chuck Yager, for making me feel like part of the team—and for giving me such wickedly fun villains with whom to torment my protagonists.

BOOK ONE
Up From Under

CHAPTER ONE

"That one's mine."

Kestrel inclined her chin ever so slightly toward the richly attired stranger ambling through Phlan's busy marketplace. Her practiced eye had taken only a minute to single him out of the throng. Was he a rich trader? A visiting nobleman? No matter. She'd never been fussy about her victims' professions, just the size of their pocketbooks.

Ragnall studied Kestel's choice and nodded his approval. "Want any help?" The thrill of the hunt glinted in the rogue's clear blue eyes.

"Nope." She worked alone, and Ragnall knew it. The fewer people she trusted, the fewer she had to share the spoils with—and the fewer could betray her. Besides, the greenest apprentice could handle this job solo. The graybeard was an easy target. He'd been careless as he purchased a gold brooch, chuckling to the young female vendor about the weight of his money pouch when he'd accidentally dropped it. Kestrel was more than willing to relieve him of that burden. The brooch too, with any luck. "I'll meet you later at the Bell."

Ragnall's gaze had already shifted to a middle-aged woman overburdened with parcels. "If you're successful, the ale's on you."

"If?"

They parted. Kestrel dismissed Ragnall from her mind, concentrating on the task at hand. To Ragnall, several years her junior and born to a respectable family, thieving was a game. To her it was serious work.

She followed her target through the noisy bazaar, weaving past haggling merchants and ducking behind vegetable carts as she maintained her distance. When the man stopped to purchase a sweetmeat, she paused several stalls away to admire an emerald-green silk scarf.

"It matches your eyes," said the seller, a young woman about Kestrel's age. She draped the scarf around Kestrel's neck and held up a glass. "See?"

Kestrel made a show of studying her reflection, actually using the mirror to keep an eye on her mark. "It does indeed," she said, combing her fingers through her wayward chestnut locks. She sighed. Someday when she'd made her pile and no longer had to work for a living, she'd grow her hair out of the boyish but practical cut she'd always worn. Though she doubted she'd ever wrap a fancy scarf around her neck—it felt too much like a noose.

In the mirror, the gentleman finished paying for his treat and moved on. Kestrel handed the looking glass and scarf back to their owner. "Perhaps another day."

She considered "accidentally" bumping into her target as he savored the confection but elected for a less conspicuous method this afternoon. She'd been in Phlan several months, and already some of the Podol Plaza vendors recognized her. Too many obvious accidents like that and everyone would know her for a thief. She couldn't afford that kind of attention. Though the local thieves' guild operated openly, she had not joined it. The guild required its members to lop off their left ears as a sign of loyalty—a practice she considered barbaric. She planned to leave town before the guild pressured her into joining.

The nobleman stopped thrice more, admiring a jeweled eating knife, studying a plumed helm, testing the fit of a leather belt around his considerable girth. The latter he purchased. By all the gods, was he going to spend the entire pouch before she could get to it?

At last, an opportunity presented itself. The gentleman paused to watch a brightly garbed performer juggle seven flaming torches while singing a drinking ballad and balancing on a wagon wheel. Good old Sedric. She really ought to give the entertainer a commission for all the distractions he'd unknowingly provided.

She approached her target's left side, eyeing the bulge just under his velvet cape. Casually, she bent down as if to secure her left boot and withdrew a dagger from inside. Sedric finished the ballad, caught the last torch in his teeth, and hopped off the wheel. The gentleman raised his hands, applauding heartily.

With a quick slice through straining purse strings, the moneybag was hers. By the time her victim noticed the missing weight from his hip, she was long gone.

❦ ❦ ❦ ❦ ❦

Kestrel had learned—the hard way—that after lightening a gull's pockets, it was best to get as far away as possible from the scene of the crime. She slipped down an alley, her leather boots padding noiselessly in the soft dirt, until she could no longer hear the din of the marketplace. A few strides more brought her to the grounds of Valjevo Castle. No one would bother her here as she counted and stashed her newly acquired coins.

The once-proud stronghold, like the city it had protected, was ruined by war and later corrupted by nefarious inhabitants. From what Kestrel had heard, a pond known as the Pool of Radiance had formed in a cavern beneath the castle. Thought to confer great wisdom and leadership on those who bathed in its waters, the pool instead turned out to be an instrument of evil, used by the power-hungry creature Tyranthraxus to advance his self-serving schemes. Though Tyranthraxus had been defeated and the pool had evaporated into a mundane hole in the ground, the castle remained empty and undisturbed despite improved prosperity in the city. Most residents yet feared to tread anywhere near the pool's dry basin or its ominous environs, so few ventured this way intentionally.

Kestrel, however, came and went with perfect ease. The thief had grown up in the streets of a dozen cities, and it took more than a ruined castle to scare her. She'd never encountered trouble there and found the deserted cavern a convenient hideout. Though cutthroats and a few common creatures also enjoyed the isolation from time to time, generally the once-menacing cavern was safer than most city streets.

Safe enough, at least, that she had hollowed out a cavity beneath a pile of fallen rocks to use as a cache for the coins and other items she acquired. As she thought of the small hoard that waited for her within the castle, her fingers drifted to the nobleman's money pouch at her side. Her stash of treasure was growing steadily—just yesterday she'd added a walnut-sized ruby to the hoard, courtesy of a quintet of sixes in a game of Traitors' Heads. She wouldn't use those dice anymore, however, until she left Phlan. She'd never live to roll them again if anyone discovered they were weighted.

It wouldn't be too much longer before she could leave petty thievery behind, and the dangerous, seedy lifestyle that went with it. When she had enough coin she'd live and travel in style, supplementing her savings with an occasional high-profit, low-risk heist. No more dockside inns with flat ale and lumpy mattresses, no more tramping from city to city on foot, no more risking her neck for a few measly coppers, no more wearing the same clothes until she itched. She'd secretly ply her trade among a better class of people while enjoying the easy life. The one she and Quinn had always imagined.

She entered the castle bailey and negotiated its once-formidable hedge maze. When Tyranthraxus had been defeated, a wide swath had been cut through several rows of the sawlike leaves, black flowers, and poisonous six-inch thorns, but in the years since then the hedges had grown back enough to warrant caution. She ducked and sidled her way through, careful to avoid even the slightest brush with the menacing vegetation.

Once past the maze, she relaxed her guard. She approached the white marble tower, half-ruined and defaced with sinister-looking but now impotent runes, and circled to an ebony door marked with an intricate carving of a dragon. Standing in the spot she'd marked twenty-five yards from the door, she withdrew a dagger from one of her boots and gripped it in her left hand. Though she could throw a dagger accurately with either hand, her dominant left provided more force and deadly aim.

She hurled the blade at the entrance. The dagger stuck in the door with a solid *thunk*, landing dead center between the dragon's eyes. Foul-smelling yellow mist issued from the dragon's mouth—another lesson she'd learned the hard way. If not for the potion of neutralization she'd happened to carry on her first visit, she'd never have lived to return.

After waiting ten minutes for the poisonous cloud to disperse, she retrieved her dagger and opened the door onto a landing in the main room of the ruined tower, which lay open to the sky all the way down to the subterranean cavern. Birds, bugs, and spiders made their homes in the nooks and crevices of the interior tower walls. Despite the fact that rain could fall freely inside, the pool basin below had always remained dry.

She nimbly padded down the black iron stairway, alighting at the bottom and heading toward her secret cache. She stopped abruptly when she heard voices.

Bandits. She couldn't quite make out what they were saying, but she could see them through the rubble, not fifty paces away. She quickly slipped into the shadow of a large unearthed boulder. How stupid she had been—approaching so carelessly, without even glancing down into the cavern! Fortunately, the intruders appeared not to have noticed her.

A tingling spread along her collarbone. It was a sensation she had experienced only a few times before, always a forewarning of serious danger. While others felt chills up their spines, hers apparently traveled up her spine and continued across her shoulders. Previously, however, the heightened perception had alerted her to perils more extraordinary than a handful of brigands. When her intuition kicked in, it usually meant something very, very bad lay in wait.

Her instincts must be working overtime today. Nevertheless, they'd saved her life before. She glanced back the way she'd come, assessing the possibility of a silent retreat.

Too risky. The iron grillwork stairway was far too

exposed, and she'd been fortunate to escape notice the first time. Stifling a sigh, she turned her attention back to the bandits. If she couldn't leave, she might as well see what these visitors were up to—and make sure they didn't get too close to her cache.

There were three of them, young men with a week's growth of stubble on their faces and a lifetime's worth of maliciousness in their dark eyes. They hadn't observed her because they were arguing among themselves over a sack the largest man gripped tightly in his fist. As their voices rose in anger, she caught snatches of their conversation.

" . . . said we'd split it evenly, Urdek!"

"That's right. A quarter for each of you, a quarter for me, and—" the large man, Urdek, flashed a stiletto—"a quarter for my friend here."

Kestrel silently shook her head. There truly was no honor among thieves. Urdek's betrayal illustrated precisely why she worked alone.

The two smaller men produced daggers as well. One of them approached Urdek, muttering something Kestrel couldn't make out. Urdek swiftly kicked the dagger out of his opponent's grasp, sending the weapon flying to the ground with a wet *splat.*

The sound caught more of Kestrel's attention than the ensuing fight. She shifted her position to get a better look at the ground where the dagger had landed. It lay in a puddle of muddy water. Tiny rivulets of brown liquid streamed into it from the direction of the dry pool.

Which was no longer dry.

She gasped. In one rainless night, the basin had filled with amber fluid. Its surface lay smooth as a mirror, not a single ripple marring the stillness. The water caught the late afternoon sunlight, seeming to infuse it with a golden glow. To someone unfamiliar with its history, the pond appeared almost serene.

Almost. Around its perimeter, nothing grew. The moss and weeds that had begun to spring up around the dry basin had withered and fallen to dust. Shriveled, skeletal husks lay dead where just yesterday thistles had flourished. The lifeless band of earth extended two feet from the rim of the pool, nearly reaching the scuffling bandits.

Kestrel turned her gaze back to them. Urdek had killed his weaponless comrade and disarmed the other. The smaller man tripped as he backed away, landing near the dead man's dagger. He grabbed for it.

And screamed.

At first Kestrel thought the puddle's liquid burned away the skin it had touched, but the stench that drifted toward her soon revealed otherwise.

The man's flesh was rotting off his bones.

As she and Urdek watched in horrified fascination, the tissue and muscle of his hand turned green, then brown, then black in the space of seconds. Finally it disintegrated, exposing a skeletal claw.

The rot continued up his arm, to his torso and the rest of his body. Putrid hunks of flesh and decomposing organs fell into the dirt, until finally the decay crept up his neck. White hair sprouted from his head; the skin on his face withered. His eyes dried up and shriveled until they became nothing more than two gaping sockets.

The once-human creature lurched to its feet, still clutching the dagger. Its scream of pain now a murderous cry, it advanced on Urdek.

Kestrel turned and ran as fast as her nimble legs could carry her, not caring how much noise she made.

❧ ❧ ❧ ❧ ❧

"Now can you tell me?"

Kestrel lowered the shotglass back to the table and

shuddered—whether from the liquor or the memory of what she had witnessed earlier, she couldn't say. She shook her head at Ragnall. "One more. At least."

"You'll regret this in the morning, you know. I've never known you to drink firewine before." Nat's firewine, the Bell's house liquor, was said to be distilled from wine mulled in the inn's washtub. It was also said to pack a nasty wallop. Despite his warning, Ragnall signaled to the barmaid for another shot.

Kestrel regarded her friend. At least, Ragnall was the closest thing she'd had to a friend in a long time—the fair-haired scoundrel had never betrayed her, which was more than she could say for most of her acquaintances.

The only person she'd ever really trusted in her life had been Quinn, the old rogue who had found her in a burned-out house when she'd been barely old enough to walk. Quinn had raised her as a daughter, at first trying to protect her from the shady side of his life but eventually teaching her everything he knew. At the age of seven she was winning bets from unsuspecting tavern patrons by throwing daggers with amazing accuracy. At nine, her mentor had deemed her old enough to dabble in minor illegal activities like picking pockets. By twelve she was learning more lucrative—but also more dangerous—skills.

Then Quinn had died.

That had been ten years ago, and she'd survived on her own ever since. All she had left of him was the knowledge he'd passed on to her and a custom-made club he'd commissioned. The compact steel baton was easy to conceal, but with the flick of a wrist it telescoped to thrice its size. She'd lost track of how many times the weapon—and Quinn's training with it—had saved her life. While daggers were her weapon of choice, the club sometimes proved more practical.

Though there had been times when she'd wished for Quinn's advice or guidance, years had passed since she wanted to talk to him as badly as she did tonight—not as a master thief, but as the only parental figure she'd ever known. The scene at the pool had shaken her more than she thought possible.

Quinn was gone, and she was an adult now. She pulled her thoughts back to the present conversation and Ragnall's admonition about the firewine. "I'll be fine," she said. "You know I could drink you under this table if I wanted to."

"I know," he conceded. "I've witnessed it."

Kestrel rarely drank to excess. In her profession, it was too risky not to be in full possession of one's faculties. She didn't intend to get drunk this evening, just dull the tingling in her collarbone. Though she'd fled Valjevo Castle hours ago, the sensation hadn't ceased. If her adrenaline didn't stop pumping at this rate, she'd be too exhausted to leave town in the morning.

Which is exactly what she planned to do. Phlan could keep its creepy Pool of Radiance and the undead creatures it spawned. She was moving on.

The serving wench returned with the liquor bottle. She refilled the shotglass, which Kestrel immediately emptied and slid forward for more.

"Slow down, Kes—you'll make yourself ill." Ragnall turned to the barmaid. "Bring us two tankards of ale instead."

Kestrel made no objection. The firewine was burning a hole in her gut anyway. "And some bread and cheese," she added.

She looked around, taking in the atmosphere of Nat Wyler's Bell one last time. Though she'd called it home for several months, she wouldn't miss this dingy little corner of Phlan. The common room had a hard-packed dirt floor and rushes that hadn't been changed in years. The tables and walls were scratched and scarred. At its best, the fare was mediocre. Her corn-husk mattress upstairs was in desperate need of restuffing. The inn's main appeal—its *only* appeal—was that Nat minded his own business and encouraged the serving girls and other patrons to do the same.

No, she wouldn't miss the Bell, or Phlan as a whole. It was a place, just another place. By next week she'd be in a new one.

The food arrived. Kestrel tried to eat, but the doughy bread stuck in her throat. She washed it down with the ale, but it sat like a lump in her stomach.

"So tell me what happened." Ragnall lifted his own tankard but set it down without drinking, his blue eyes narrowing. "He didn't hurt you, did he?"

"Who?"

"The old goat in the market today."

"No!" Kestrel snorted.

"What is it, then? I've never seen you quite like this."

She stared at him a moment, debating. Would he think her crazy? On the other hand, what she'd witnessed today might *make* her crazy if she didn't tell someone. She quaffed more ale and leaned forward.

"The Pool of Radiance has reappeared," she said in a low voice.

Ragnall's eyes widened. "You know this for a fact?"

"I saw it suck the life out of someone today—rotted his flesh right off his bones."

He leaned back in his seat and let out a low whistle. "After we parted at the market, I heard a few rumors, but I didn't put any stock in them."

She frowned. "What kind of rumors?"

"Stories similar to yours. I guess several people—the number increases with each telling—have disappeared since last night, and others speak of undead creatures wandering the city. Like I said, I thought they were just bogeyman tales to keep children in line, but supposedly Elminster himself arrived tonight to investigate."

"Elminster? How did he get here so fast? Or even hear about this?"

Ragnall shrugged. "How do wizards do anything?"

How indeed? Kestrel disliked spellcasters, considering them more treacherous than the sneakiest assassin. They were always muttering under their breaths, moving their hands in strange gestures, collecting odd substances. They gave her the creeps. Just when a body least expected it, they'd blow something up or send objects flying through the air. Or worse—set traps, like the one at the tower, that unleashed their sorcery long after the spellcaster had left the scene. She still bore a scar on her left wrist from trying to pick an ensorcelled lock three years ago.

"You going to report what you saw?" Ragnall asked.

"Yeah, right," she said. "That's what I need—to solicit a wizard's notice. No thanks."

"I hear there's a reward."

That got her attention. "What kind of reward?"

"One hundred gold pieces for a genuine firsthand account." He broke a hunk of cheese off the wedge. "That's what I heard anyway. Don't know if it's true."

A hundred gold pieces. Kestrel had been debating the wisdom of trying to retrieve her treasure from its hiding spot near the pool. If she couldn't get to it, the nobleman's money pouch was all she had in the world, and any additional coins would make a big difference. Even if the rumors of reward proved false, perhaps she could convince Elminster that her tale was worth paying to hear.

She stood, immediately regretting the quick movement. A wave of dizziness rocked her. That firewine must have been more potent than she'd thought.

Ragnall extended a hand to steady her. "You all right?"

She nodded. The dizziness passed, but her head remained cloudy. "Fine. Where did you say Elminster was?"

"Meeting with the Council of Ten." He snorted. "As if the blowhards who run this city could have anything useful to say. Why do you ask?"

She drained her tankard, tossed a few coins on the table, and fastened her cloak around her shoulders. "I'm off to see the wizard."

⚇ ⚇ ⚇ ⚇ ⚇

Kestrel groaned and rolled over. She was going to kill whoever had stuffed her mouth with cotton. And glued her eyes shut. And now shone a lantern in her face.

Someone was sitting on her head.

Slowly, she forced one eye open. Then the other. Then both. Then squeezed them shut again.

She was back in her room at the Bell, lying facedown on her lumpy mattress. Sunlight poured in the window, sending darts of pain shooting through her eyes. Her head hurt so badly she feared her skull might explode.

Damn that firewine. And damn Ragnall—for being right about it.

By minuscule degrees, she pried herself off the mattress and into a sitting position. When the room stopped spinning, she glanced down. Relief flooded the tiny corners of her brain not occupied with processing pain signals. However intoxicated she'd been, she'd at least managed to pass out on top of the money pouch, preventing anyone from stealing it while she slept. Her thieves' tools also remained undisturbed, as did the club secured to her belt. Her twin daggers, of course, remained untouched, one hidden in each boot.

No one else was in the room. Either Nat hadn't rented out the other two beds last night, or the lodgers had risen and left. Either way, she was grateful for the solitude—she didn't think she could bear the sound of even a whispering voice. The murmurs rising from the common room below were bad enough.

She crept over to the washstand, her body stiff from having slept in her leather armor. She splashed cold water on her cheeks and looked into the glass. Deep creases from her mattress webbed the skin on the left side of her face. She must not have budged all night.

What time had she returned to her room? She recalled drinking with Ragnall downstairs and his talk of Elminster. After that, she couldn't remember anything specific. Had she really gone to see the old mage? Blurred images of a mysterious bearded man floated through her mind, but they could just as easily be remnants of a firewine-induced dream.

She pulled together her scattered thoughts and tried to clear the fog from her head. For someone who had planned to travel many miles from Phlan today, she was off to a poor start. From the strength of the sun, she judged the time to be close to noon. She needed to obtain provisions for her trip, collect her treasure from its hiding spot, and hit the road. Or the docks—she really ought to decide where she was going. Sembia, perhaps? Cormyr?

An hour later, her pack stocked with food and other supplies, Kestrel strode toward the castle. She'd considered leaving her stash behind and coming back for it later, but greed had gotten the better of her. Who knew when she'd return to the Moonsea? Her travels might never bring her here again. In the meantime, the thought of those riches just sitting beneath the rocks rankled her thief's soul. The idea of starting over—of having to wait that much longer before living a life of ease—sank her heart.

Already her collarbone tingled. She ignored the sensation. She knew she headed toward danger, but she also trusted her ability to avoid it. Just get in, get the goods, and get out. That's all she needed to do. Stay away from the water and be alert for any stray puddles.

As she entered the tower, she saw three figures near one end of the pool. She could tell from his uniform and standard-issue chain mail that one was a member of Phlan's city patrol. The guard was a large man, at least six and a half feet tall, with a pair of the widest shoulders Kestrel had ever seen. Beside him stood a knight in full plate armor, the scales-and-warhammer symbol of Tyr emblazoned on his tabard. He wore a sword sheathed at his side and a warhammer strapped to his back. A paladin, she assumed. He was about half a foot shorter than the guard and of a more average build. The third figure, a slender woman, wore brown leggings, leather knee-high boots, and a dark green cloak. She leaned on a wooden staff, listening to a conversation between the two men. The woman's hood shadowed her visage and the fighters' helmets obscured theirs, so Kestrel could not get a good look at any of their faces.

Silently, Kestrel berated herself. Of course, she should have guessed that in light of yesterday's events the pool would draw investigators or gawkers today. She glanced around for evidence of the ill-fated brigands but saw no sign of them. Their bodies, if anything remained of them, must have been disposed of while she'd snored her way through the morning.

She assessed her surroundings. The cache lay on the other side of the strangers, but their focus seemed to be on the pool itself. If she moved very quietly and kept to the shadows as she circled around, she might manage to reach it without arousing the group's notice. The exposed stairway was unavoidable, but if she didn't take a chance she could grow old waiting for the trio to leave.

"Lord of Shadows preserve me," she muttered. She crept to the stairway and slowly descended, hugging the wall to make as much use of the thin shadows as possible. When she reached the bottom, she started her cautious circle toward the rock pile. As she padded, she eavesdropped on the party's conversation.

"So Elminster thinks this has something to do with goings-on in Myth Drannor?" the guard asked. "What does the ruined elven capital have to do with us?"

"From what he explained to me, he has suspected for weeks that someone has created a new Pool of Radiance there," the woman said in a hushed tone. "Now with Phlan's pool reawakened, he's all but certain. Even as we guard this site, he's trying to contact a party of adventurers he sent there to investigate. If they do find a new pool, they will destroy it—and whoever created it."

"You sound sure about that," the paladin said. "Those ruins have a reputation for eating adventurers alive."

"These are not ordinary adventurers," the woman replied. "Elminster hand-picked them, and they bear the Gauntlets of Moander—artifacts created specifically to destroy such pools. They will succeed where lesser parties would fail."

Yeah, right, Kestrel thought. She'd heard her share of tales about thieves lured to the ancient elven city hoping to find untold riches in its ruins. She'd heard very few tales of thieves who'd actually returned. Elminster better have sent a score or more adventurers into that den of doom.

She made it about halfway to her goal before her foot slipped on some rubble. Damn! To Kestrel's ears, the tell-tale scuffling sounded loud as a thunderclap.

"Who's there?" the guard called out. All three of the figures now peered in her direction. "Show yourself!"

Kestrel paused, torn between trying to elude them and attempting to brazen it out. Before she could make up her mind, the hooded woman raised her hand, palm facing Kestrel's direction, and murmured some words the thief couldn't understand. A spellcaster! Kestrel turned to escape whatever sorcery was about to be hurled at her . . .

. . . And a moment later found herself unable to budge.

She tried to fight the magic, but her body refused to respond. Her feet, arms, even her mouth could not move. She was stuck in a half-twist, half-crouch, helpless to defend herself. Heart hammering, she watched the trio make its way toward her.

The paladin reached her first, assessing her from head to heel. "A thief, by the look of her," he said with obvious distaste. "Identify yourself!"

The sorceress approached. "She can't speak until I release her from the spell."

Gods, but Kestrel hated wizards! She'd not only lost control of the situation but of her own body. How long was the witch going to keep her like this? What did she plan in the meantime? Her vulnerability made Kestrel want to scream.

The paladin nodded toward the guard's short bow. "Train that on her." When the guard complied, the knight of Tyr unsheathed his long sword, pressed the tip of it beneath Kestrel's chin, and met her gaze. His eyes were as gray as his steel and just as cold. "Don't try anything foolish." He lowered the blade but kept it drawn.

She wouldn't. If the paladin didn't cut her down first, Phlan's guards were known to be quick to release a bow-string. Accurate with their aim, too—though at this range, the fighter could be blind and still hit her. Kestrel's agility and weapons couldn't help her now; she would have to rely on her wits.

The wizard spoke a command word, and Kestrel's body sagged. The rogue caught herself from falling and stood upright to face her captors.

"Who are you and what are you doing here?" the paladin demanded.

She considered lying but decided a modified version of the truth might ring more genuine in the holy warrior's ears. "My name is Kestrel, and—"

"Kestrel!" The guard lowered his bow. "You're late!"

"I—I am?" She glanced from one member of the trio to the next. The paladin still regarded her warily, but the mage appeared suddenly guilt-stricken. The guard actually looked as if he were greeting an old friend. Did she know him—all of them—from somewhere?

"Er . . . yes. I *am* late," she stated boldly. "I apologize. Profusely. Didn't mean to keep you waiting."

"We weren't so much waiting as concerned," the guard said. "I thought maybe you arrived before us and something happened." He removed his helm, revealing coarse blond locks, a square jaw, and a neck thickly corded with muscles. "My name's Durwyn. Like you, I volunteered to stand watch here."

Volunteered? When in her life had she volunteered for anything? A sense of dread swept her. "Just . . . um, when did you volunteer for this duty, Durwyn?"

"Last night. Elminster told my commander that you and two others would be here today."

Damn and double-damn Nat's firewine! She'd actually gone to see Elminster and now couldn't remember what transpired. What in the world had she gotten herself into?

The paladin cleared his throat to draw her attention from Durwyn. "Tell me if you would, Kestrel, what you were doing skulking about if you indeed came to stand guard with us?"

A fair question, but his tone chafed nonetheless. The inflections of his voice suggested noble birth. Holy warrior or not, if he thought she'd tolerate arrogant condescension very long, he was sorely mistaken.

She lifted her chin. "Spying on you, of course. You don't

20 • Carrie Bebris

expect me to put my trust in people I know nothing about, do you? I was trying to judge what sort of folk I'm to work with."

"Honest ones. Which, I imagine, is more than we can expect from you."

She bit back the retort she would have liked to let fly. Paladins of Tyr, if indeed that's what this knight was, were known for their self-righteous sense of honor and justice. Rogues avoided them like the gallows. "You mind tossing me your name between all the insults?"

"Corran D'Arcey, Defender of Tyr the Even-Handed, and third son of Baron Ethelred D'Arcey of Sarshel."

So, she'd guessed correctly. A paladin of Tyr *and* a blue-blood. She held his gaze without blinking, determined to show him that his titles did not intimidate her. "I'll just call you Corran for short."

"And I'll just—"

"Aren't we supposed to be guarding a pool here, Corran?" she asked.

The rebuke silenced him for a beat. "Yes, *we* are," he said tightly. He sheathed his sword and strode back to stand nearer the water.

In the awkward quiet that ensued, Durwyn shrugged and followed him.

Kestrel was disappointed to be left standing with the sorceress and not the guard. Durwyn seemed kind but not particularly bright—the perfect source to pump for more information about what she'd gotten herself into. The spellcaster, on the other hand, made her nervous.

The mage, who had not yet spoken to Kestrel, drew back her cowl. By her gold-flecked blue eyes and slightly pointed ears, Kestrel guessed her to be of partial elven descent. Moon elf, judging from the bluish tinge to her ears and chin. "I am Ghleanna Stormlake," she said. "Had I known your identity, I would not have thrown that spell."

Kestrel could not tell whether Ghleanna's words held contrition or criticism. Was she supposed to have strutted into the tower declaiming her name?

"Apology accepted," she said, whether one had been offered or not. Then, deciding Ghleanna could prove informative, she added, "I should have arrived on time."

The mage's lips formed a half-smile. "Elminster told me you might have a . . . headache . . . when you awoke."

Kestrel felt her face grow warm. She'd not only been drunk but also obvious about it. No doubt the wizard had taken advantage of her compromised state to coerce her into this volunteer duty. She thought of the conversation she'd overhead as she arrived in the cavern earlier. "Elminster seems to tell you a lot of things."

"I am one of his apprentices. When he left this morn to investigate tidings from Shadowdale, he asked me to keep an eye on events here in Phl—"

A crackle of energy suddenly rent the air. Not ten paces away, a floating, glowing ball of white light appeared. It expanded, forming a window in its center as sounds of ringing steel and battle cries filled the air.

"A gate!" Ghleanna exclaimed.

Corran and Durwyn rushed over. "To where?" Corran asked.

The window elongated to the size of a door, allowing brief glimpses of the combatants. A besieged fighter stumbled into view, overwhelmed by an unseen opponent. "By all that's holy, help us!" he cried.

"That's Athan—one of the adventurers Elminster sent to Myth Drannor." Ghleanna cried. "They must be in trouble!"

The border of the gate flashed and hissed, like a flame being extinguished. The window winked. When their view returned Athan could no longer be seen. The sounds of battle continued, mixed with cries of the dying. Just outside visual range, a terrible moaning commenced.

"We must aid them!" Corran started toward the gate.

"Are you out of your mind?" Kestrel asked. No way was she stepping into some sort of magical portal. If the sorcery didn't swallow them up forever, they'd only be spit out into the middle of whatever was happening on the other end.

"We're not supposed to leave our post," Durwyn said.

"This is more important," Ghleanna answered. "If Athan's band fails, all Faerûn could be lost! Make up your own minds, but I am going." She stepped into the gate. It flashed violet light, obscuring both the mage and the Myth Drannor scene from view.

"She's crazy," Kestrel declared.

"No—she's honorable and committed to a greater good," Corran retorted. "Something a rogue wouldn't know anything about."

She glared at Corran. "So follow her, then!"

The gate hissed and sputtered, its light turning pale blue, then a sickly green. The window began to shrink.

"I will—and so will you!" So quickly she couldn't react, Corran grabbed her by the arm and dragged her into the gate.

She shouted her objection, but the sound was swallowed up by a vacuum. She found herself surrounded by black nothingness, the extradimensional space seeming to stretch to eternity. Corran still held her arm in an iron grip. Involuntarily, she grabbed his elbow just to have something solid to hold onto. They floated, propelled only by the momentum with which they'd entered. Far in the distance, she could see the battle scene in Myth Drannor taking place through a window.

A window that was closing.

They were going to be trapped in here! A frightful rumbling surrounded them as the window ahead wavered. Suddenly, the space didn't seem so vast anymore. In fact, it felt close. Her chest tightened as she gasped for air. The rumbling repeated, accented by flashing golden light from either end of the portal.

Corran turned toward her, mouthing words she could not hear. She didn't need to hear them—they were the same words running through her own mind.

The gate was collapsing.

CHAPTER TWO

Helpless, Kestrel and Corran bobbed along, unable to speed their progress toward the shrinking exit. They were near enough now that they could see the broken cobblestones of the street where Athan's band fought, but at this rate they'd never reach it before the window closed.

Kestrel's mind raced. They needed something, some fixed object, off which to push.

Or pull.

It was a long shot, but it just might work. She shrugged out of her backpack and brought it around so that she could dig through it with her free hand. In the wan light coming from the exit, she groped through the contents until her fingers brushed against a metal claw.

Corran saw her withdraw the grappling hook and nodded in understanding. He maneuvered her ahead of him to give her a clear shot at the window, then shifted his grip to her waist to free both her arms.

She'd never made such a long throw before, but they were running out of time. She cast the hook. Unencumbered by air resistance, it sailed through the exit and caught hold of an upturned cobblestone. Thank the gods!

She began to pull herself forward. Corran released her and also grabbed the rope. As the portal rumbled and flashed orange light, they desperately pulled themselves hand over hand, the rope trailing behind them as they reached the exit. They tumbled through. Kestrel rolled to an abrupt stop, striking a solid object.

A body.

She sat up, quickly assessing the scene. Three more bodies—all of them motionless—lay sprawled in the street. A band of five orcs scavenged two of the corpses.

They'd arrived too late.

"Get your filthy claws off them!" Ghleanna shouted from behind her. She turned in time to see the mage lift her hands and send three bursts of magical energy speeding toward the snouted humanoids.

The orcs dove to the ground, but the missiles corrected their course and hit three of the creatures. One orc, struck in the head, died instantly. The other two suffered chest wounds but managed to climb back to their feet, axes in hand. With a cry of retribution, all four remaining orcs now rushed Ghleanna.

Kestrel rolled out of their path, yanked a dagger from her boot, and threw it. The weapon caught one of the orcs in the neck. Her victim sank to its knees, but with a series of inhuman grunts, it struggled to its feet. Tightly gripping its short sword, the beast staggered toward Kestrel. Its eyes held the expression of a mad animal.

Kestrel bent to reach her second dagger. A second hit would finish off the humanoid. Before she withdrew the blade, however, the orc collapsed.

She glanced around to see whether any of the remaining orcs approached. Corran, who'd landed several yards away when he tumbled out of the gate, had engaged two of the beasts. The skill with which he deflected the orcs' blows bespoke the superior training of a nobleman. He fought with controlled, precise strokes that countered his opponents' brute swings.

A thunderclap boomed so loud that it shook the street. Kestrel spun to discover the sound came from the gate, which now wavered violently and glowed flaming red. The rope attached to her grappling hook still trailed inside. What would happen to her tool if the portal shut with the rope still inside? The gods only knew when they might need it next.

A quick glance toward Ghleanna, who was releasing another volley of sorcerous missiles, indicated that the mage held her own for the moment. Kestrel grasped the rope and tugged.

It was stuck.

She pulled harder. The rope remained taut, but she could feel vibrations along it, coming from within the gate. What was going on inside?

A moment later, a familiar figure tumbled through and landed at her feet. Kestrel yanked the rope out of the portal. Within seconds, the gate shuddered and imploded, disappearing from sight. At the same time, the sounds of combat ceased.

She offered Durwyn a hand. "I thought you weren't going to leave your post?"

He grasped her arm and rose. "I got lonely."

She looked toward Ghleanna and Corran, who had dispatched the last of the orcs. "I can think of many places

I'd rather seek company than here," Kestrel said, turning back to Durwyn. "We're lucky we even made it."

He nodded toward her grappling hook. "I saw you and Corran ahead of me and grabbed the rope as soon as I could. That was quick thinking on your part. I never would have made it out in time."

"None of us would have." She harbored a bellyful of resentment toward Corran. How dare he force her into that malfunctioning magical gate, nearly killing them both? She shuddered to think of her fate had she been trapped inside during the final implosion.

Durwyn joined Corran and Ghleanna, who were checking the fallen adventurers for signs of life. Kestrel hung back. As she coiled her rope, she thought about how much she wanted to wrap it around Corran's neck. Instead she stowed it and the grappling hook in her pack. She retrieved her dagger, noting her surroundings as she cleaned it.

They'd arrived on a street lined with buildings in various states of destruction. Even in its ruined condition Kestrel could see that Myth Drannor had once been a city of incredible beauty. The wood, stone, and glass buildings of the former elven capital had been constructed as extensions of the very trees that sheltered them, wondrous feats of architecture that enhanced nature even as they altered it. Spires soared toward the sky, prompting Kestrel to raise her eyes. In doing so, she discovered a network of bridges that spanned the trees.

Now many of the bridges were destroyed, and the buildings below looked like an earthquake had violently shaken them. Broken spires lay in fragments on the ground, their jagged stumps rising no higher toward the stars than did human constructions. Collapsed walls exposed the rooms they had been meant to protect, inviting creatures mundane and malicious to make their homes within. Statues of exquisite elven maidens lacked limbs or heads and stood watch over dry fountains choked with moss and debris. Weeds and thorns overtook the gardens. Rubble littered the streets.

A feeling of sadness, unfamiliar but genuine, washed over Kestrel. Something more than a city had been lost here.

At last she approached the others.

"You certainly took your time coming over," Corran said. He gestured toward the adventurers. "They're all dead—if you care."

"Good thing we almost killed ourselves getting here, then," she responded. "You had no right to force me into that portal."

"You would stand idly by while others suffered?"

"This isn't my problem."

"You did volunteer," Durwyn piped up.

Was he ganging up on her too, now? She fixed him with a withering gaze that caused the burly man to step back a pace. "My commitment began and ended in Phlan," she said.

Corran shook his head in disgust. "Don't you have the least concern for anyone besides yourself?"

"I saved your arse in that damn gate, didn't I?"

"Enough!" Ghleanna, her expression strained, stepped between them. "Corran, she's right—you shouldn't have forced her to come. Kestrel, now that we are here, can we at least search for clues to what happened?"

"Sure," Kestrel responded, her gaze remaining locked on Corran. She'd settle this later.

The adventurers appeared to have been dead for hours. Ghleanna hypothesized that time had become distorted in the malfunctioning gate, suspending the travelers in limbo much longer than the few seconds usually required to journey through one. The party also looked to have suffered wounds the orcs could not have inflicted.

"I believe their opponents wielded magic," Ghleanna

said. "Look at those deep burns on Allyril, the party's sorceress. Ordinary fire doesn't burn skin quite that way—I suspect lightning bolts. The cleric over there seems to have had the life drained right out of him, as does Loren. Athan is missing. I—I fear he was disintegrated altogether." She cleared her throat and looked away.

Corran uttered the opening words of a prayer for the ill-fated band's souls. Kestrel, never one to take much interest in religious observances, rolled her eyes but remained silent during the invocation. As she waited, paying little attention to the words, she noticed a smooth rectangular bulge under the cloak of the man Ghleanna had called Loren. When the paladin finished his prayer, she bent over the body to investigate.

"Have you no respect?" Corran hissed.

"What? I thought you were done."

"You would steal from the corpses of fallen comrades?"

She clenched her jaw, fresh ire rising within her. If Ghleanna or Durwyn had reached for that object, he wouldn't have said a word. "I thought we were investigating what happened here." Pointedly turning her back on him, she unclasped Loren's cloak, slipped her hand into its inside pocket, and withdrew a slim book. She opened its leaves, quickly skimming the pages. "It's a journal."

Corran reached for it. "Let me see."

Kestrel snatched the volume out of his grasp. "I can read." She flipped to the end, hoping the last few entries would prove the most informative.

Elminster was right, the last page read. *A new Pool of Radiance exists somewhere in Myth Drannor. The pool's creators know our mission and already send agents to stop us, even though we have not yet learned who's behind the plan. Fortunately, we still have the Gauntlets of Moander, and once we find the pool we shall use them to destroy it. Mystra—and Fate—willing.*

Kestrel read the passage aloud. When she finished, Ghleanna turned to Corran.

"I saw no gauntlets when we examined the adventurers," the mage said, a note of panic in her voice. "Did you?"

"No, but we weren't looking for them, either," he said. "Let's check again."

Their search yielded several vials of bluish liquid, a plain, battered silver ring sized for a woman's hand, an assortment of weapons, and numerous other provisions—but no Gauntlets of Moander.

"Well, we will just have to tell Elminster what happened and let him worry about it," Kestrel said. She turned to Ghleanna. "So go ahead and do your thing."

The mage regarded her quizzically. "My thing?"

"You know," she prompted. "Conjure up one of those gate things so we can get out of here." As much as she hated the thought of trusting another magical portal, twilight approached, and she was even less enamored with the idea of spending the night in this haunted city overrun with the minions of some unknown foe.

Ghleanna was silent a moment. "I cannot do that, Kestrel," she said finally. "I have not the power."

"What do you mean?" A sick feeling spread through her insides. "We're not stuck here, are we?"

"You're welcome to try to find your way out of the city and walk home," Corran said. "As for me, I choose to take up this party's mission. The cause of good cannot afford the time it would take us to reach Elminster. We must instead pick up where these fallen worthies left off."

Kestrel stared at him. The paladin really had an overinflated sense of his own honor. Fallen worthies, indeed. Did anyone actually talk like that?

"Yes, we must!" Durwyn exclaimed.

She closed her eyes. Of course Durwyn would follow

the knight. He was lost without a commander, and apparently he'd settled on Corran as his new one.

"I'm glad you both agree," Ghleanna said. "I would have taken up this quest alone if I had to."

Kestrel sighed. Was she alone possessed of sense? "Aren't you all forgetting a few facts?" she asked. "Our foes already defeated the original party—we're fewer in number and less prepared. Even if we do manage to find this new pool, what are we going to do when we get there? Skip stones across it? The bad guys have the gauntlets."

"But we have the advantage of surprise," Corran said. "They won't be expecting a new party so soon. We can figure out the rest as we go along—we haven't even read the whole journal yet."

She bowed her head, rubbing her temples. They were insane. All of them. They would end up dead, and they wanted to take her with them.

Yet would she fare any better trying to make it out of the city, through the forest, and back to civilization alone?

"Kestrel, you were really smart back there in the portal," Durwyn said. "We could sure use your help."

As if she had a choice. Get killed here or get killed trying to leave here. Nonetheless, if she was stuck on this suicide mission, there was one thing she wouldn't tolerate. She looked up at Corran. "No more insults from you."

"Agreed."

She glanced at Durwyn and Ghleanna. "All right then."

Ghleanna responded by suddenly raising her palms and hurling a spell at her. Kestrel dived to the ground. "What the—"

A burst of light appeared about ten paces behind her, followed immediately by an inhuman cry. A hideous creature stumbled out of the shadows, clutching at its eyes. The thing appeared to have once been human but now was a disfigured shell of its former self. Sharp, elongated teeth protruded from its mouth like fangs; the nails on its withered hands had grown into talons. Its dried-out flesh, visible through tattered clothing, hung tight on its bones.

"A ghoul!" Corran drew his sword and attacked. His first blow severed one of its skeletal arms. Black liquid spewed from the stump. Sightless, thanks to Ghleanna's spell, the ghoul could only blindly lash out with its remaining claw in defense.

Durwyn joined Corran's side and swung his battle axe. He hit the creature in the side. The ghoul moaned and swiped its talons at the guard.

"Don't let it touch you!" Corran warned. With a mighty swing to the ghoul's neck, the paladin made quick work of the weakened creature. Its head fell to the ground and rolled several feet. Kestrel was glad it stopped at an angle that hid its hideous face.

"I take it you've faced ghouls before?" Ghleanna asked Corran as he and Durwyn cleaned the ghoul's foul blood off their weapons.

The paladin nodded. "Several times. They're nasty creatures—their touch can paralyze. If you're killed by a ghoul, you'll become one too, unless it eats all your flesh first. They feed on corpses." He glanced at the dead adventurers and orcs. "It must have been attracted by the bodies. We should bury them before the sun fully sets, when the creatures will probably come out in droves. Where there's one there are sure to be more."

"Do we have time?" Ghleanna asked. "I'm almost out of spells, and we still need to find shelter for ourselves."

"I hate to leave them here unprotected," the paladin said. "These heroes died noble deaths—their remains deserve better than to become ghoul fodder."

Kestrel gestured toward one of the ruined buildings she'd studied earlier. "If we move the adventurers in there and leave the orcs out in the street, perhaps the ghouls will be satisfied with the easy meal." She expected Corran to dismiss the idea simply because she had suggested it. To her surprise, he agreed.

"We should also keep their equipment for our own use," she added. "It can't help them now."

He opened his mouth to say something but seemed to change his mind. "I suppose."

They distributed the goods amongst themselves. For the time being, Ghleanna carried the vials, planning to examine them later to see if she could identify their contents. Durwyn added several dozen arrows to his supply. Corran offered Kestrel an ordinary-looking dagger Loren had been carrying. "You seem to know how to use these."

"Thanks." She gestured toward the ring. "I'll take that too, if no one minds. It won't fit either of you."

"And it can be sold for a fair price when we return, right?" Corran said dryly. He glanced at the others, then tossed it to her. "It's yours."

She slid the dagger into a sheath on her belt and slipped the ring on her right middle finger where it wouldn't impede the dexterity of her dominant left hand.

They had just moved the last body into the makeshift crypt when a shout drifted out of another nearby building.

"Leave that alone! Hey—leave *me* alone! Scat! Scat, I tell ye! Git yer stinkin' carcasses outta here! Hey—*help!*"

They hurried off in the direction of the cries, following them to a well-fortified building that looked as if it might once have been an armory. A foul stench issued forth, one that reminded Kestrel of the undead bandit she'd seen last night beside Phlan's pool.

Within, they found a half dozen rotting, animated orc corpses in tattered clothing circling what appeared to be a peddler's wagon. Atop it, fending off the creatures with anything he could lay his hands on, perched a very irritated halfling. His leather armor seemed to deflect most of the zombies' claws, but a few scratch marks marred his arms and round, ruddy cheeks.

"Git back, I said!" He brained the nearest creature with a cast-iron frying pan, then tossed a basket over the head of another. "Whew! Ye need some perfume!" He unstopped a vial and flung its contents in the eyes of a third.

Durwyn moved to engage the undead beings, but Corran stayed him. The paladin stepped forward. "Foul creatures of darkness!" he called out in a commanding tone.

The zombies turned in the direction of his voice and staggered toward their new target, arms outstretched.

"Great," Kestrel muttered. Now the creatures were coming to attack them. At least these things moved slowly. Just as she was about to draw the twin daggers from her boots, Corran held a silver symbol of Tyr aloft.

"Begone!" he cried. "Trouble this man no more!"

The creatures moaned and tried to shield their eyes as they backed away. They shuffled jerkily toward a rear exit and out into the night. Within minutes the armory was free of their presence, though their odor lingered.

The halfling scrambled down from his perch and over to Corran. "Thank ye, sir," he said, removing his red knit cap and sweeping into a bow that revealed the start of a bald spot in the center of his thin brown curls. "Nottle's the name. Purveyor of the finest equipment and goods in all Myth Drannor." He straightened. "An' who might ye be?"

"Corran D'Arcey, Defender of Tyr. These are my companions, Durwyn, Kestrel, and Ghleanna Stormlake."

"Well met!" Nottle bowed again in greeting, then stooped to retrieve his merchandise. He hung the frying pan back on the wagon and picked up a quarterstaff from the floor. "Usually I can fend off the beasts m'self, but t'night they got m'staff away from me."

"This happens all the time?" Kestrel asked. "Why do you stay?"

"Business is good here, m'dear," he said. "Adventurers comin' and goin', all thinkin' they're gonna strike it rich, then discoverin' they ain't as prepared as they thought they were. That's where I come in. Actually, the place has gotten a little less dangerous lately—them dreadful alhoon and phaerimm creatures have left this part of the city. The baatezu, too. 'Course, now we have the drow and undead to put up with, so it's not exac'ly paradise. Say, are ye needin' anythin'? I'll cut ye a deal, seeing as Corran here saved my wagon just now."

"Drow?" Ghleanna asked.

"Indeed, m'dear. They mostly stay below, in the dungeons, but I've seen a few here on the surface. At night, a'course."

Kestrel shuddered. She'd never encountered a drow before, but she'd heard tales of the ruthless subterranean elven race. They were said to have dark skin, shockingly white hair, and no mercy.

"An adventuring band was killed today not far from here," Corran said. "Did you ever do business with them?"

"Athan's band? Sad thing, that—them gittin' killed. I hope they weren't friends of yers?" He lowered his voice to a conspiratorial whisper. "Word is, the scarred mages got 'em."

At the mention of scarred mages, a tingle raced along Kestrel's collarbone.

"Who are the scarred mages?" Though she asked the question, she wasn't sure she wanted to learn the answer.

"No one knows fer certain. We jes' started seein' 'em one day. I think they got somethin' to do with the goings-on at the castle. Dunno why they killed yer friends, but I might be able to find out." He paused, a mercenary glint creeping into his dark eyes. "That kinda information . . . it don't come cheap."

"They weren't our friends," Kestrel said. Corran looked at her sharply, probably ready to accuse her of betraying the heroes' memory or some nonsense like that, but she didn't care. This little guy was a talker, and if the ill-fated party had disfigured wizards after them, she didn't need word spread around town that friends of the dead adventurers had come to avenge them. "We just saw them lying in the street and wondered."

"Curiosity ain't generally healthy in Myth Drannor," he said. "But I owe ye for scarin' off those zombies, so if ye find yerselves needin' information, come to me. If I don't know the answer, I can usually find out."

"Have you heard anything about a Pool of Radiance?" Durwyn blurted.

Gods! If he hadn't been wearing armor, Kestrel would have kicked the big, dumb warrior for being so obvious.

Nottle scratched his head. "Can't say as I have." He pulled a canvas tarp over the wagon. "That some sort of landmark round here? You wanna to talk to the elves up at the shrine—coupl'a Mystra clerics, Beriand and Faeril. They can maybe tell ye more." He lifted his staff and muttered a word Kestrel couldn't discern, apparently securing his goods for the night.

The peddler turned back to the group. "The shrine's hidden in a big tree stump. Head down the street—ye'll see it." He patted the many pockets of his oversized vest, then reached inside one to withdraw a scroll. "Ye'll be needin' this. Study the word on it afore ye git to the shrine. That should git ye in."

Corran reached for the proffered scroll. "Thank you, Nottle."

The halfling paused before handing it over. "We're square now, right? Ye helped me, I'm helping ye, and that's the end of it."

The paladin appeared bemused, but Kestrel knew where Nottle was coming from. He didn't want to be in their debt. "Yep, Nottle, we're even," she said.

He released the scroll to Corran's grasp. "Best of luck to ye, then. An' remember, if ye find yerselves needin' any goods . . ."

⊛ ⊛ ⊛ ⊛ ⊛

They found the ruined shrine as Nottle described. An enormous tree trunk—easily as wide as any ordinary church Kestrel had seen in Faerûn's human cities—stood at the end of the road. Mystra's symbol, a circle of seven stars, had been carved into the bark, and a walkway had been hewn out of the wood about one story up. It wasn't much, as far as temples went, but at least the building was intact. Kestrel could not, however, discern an entrance to the shrine or any stairs up to the walkway.

Though they had all studied the scroll, they'd agreed Ghleanna should speak the password. The sorceress possessed the most knowledge of things magical and had elven blood besides. In her distrust of the arcane arts, Kestrel was perfectly happy to leave the task to the half-elf.

As they approached the stump, a deep, booming masculine voice rent the air. *"Tam-tamak!"* They all jumped, startled, at the thunderous enunciation. The word resonated as if one of the gods themselves had uttered it.

Before their eyes, the tree stump transformed into an exquisite celebration of Mystra. Intricate renderings of the goddess and other decorative carvings emerged from the bark. A wide staircase leading up to the walkway also emerged. At its head appeared double doors marked with Mystra's symbol. Ionic columns with flowing scrollwork flanked the opening.

They hastened up the stairs. When they reached the top, the doors slid open to reveal a small antechamber. The party had barely passed through when the wall sealed itself shut behind them, leaving them in darkness.

"Who enters Mystra's house?" demanded a strong female voice. Kestrel searched the darkness but saw no sign of the speaker.

"Travelers who respect the Lady of Mysteries and seek aid from her faithful," Corran replied.

A moment later, a ball of light appeared, illuminating the room and the woman who had spoken. She was an elf, with shoulder-length braided hair the color of pure gold and a round face dominated by the bluest eyes Kestrel had ever seen. Golden flecks within them caught the light, as did a medallion around her neck engraved with Mystra's circle. The armor of a fighter protected her sinewy body, and she carried herself with strength and confidence. Had she been human, Kestrel would have guessed her to have seen thirty-five or more summers, but she had no idea how old that would make the woman in elf years.

"Then welcome, friends," the elf said. "My name is Faeril. How came you to learn the password to this safe house?"

"From a scroll given us by Nottle the peddler."

The corners of her mouth turned up in a half-smile. "Then Nottle must think well of you, though I am sure you paid him dearly. Here you will find shelter, food, and if you need it, healing. We merely ask that you share the password only with those of good heart."

"A promise freely given," Corran replied.

Faeril bade them follow her and led them through a short passage into a room with a makeshift altar, a cook-fire, and half a dozen cots that Kestrel guessed had been pews at one time. "This used to be the shrine's sacristy, but now we use it for everything—worship, nursing, and daily living," Faeril explained.

The chamber *looked* like a room hewn out of a tree

trunk. Every surface was of wood—floor, walls, ceiling, furniture. The one exception was a pair of crystal cabinets etched with circles of stars. Though it appeared that the room had held windows at one time, the tree's outer bark had overgrown the openings. As a result, the shrine was well-fortified, but dark.

The cook fire provided the chamber's only light besides Faeril's free-floating orb. A moment's study revealed that it gave off no smoke. Kestrel suspected it was a magical flame, one that would heat food without burning down the shrine.

An older elf, perhaps the human equivalent of sixty-five, knelt before the altar but rose when the party entered. Unlike Faeril, he wore the simple garb of a cleric. A length of white cloth was wrapped around his waist and secured over one shoulder. His other shoulder and half his torso remained bare. He seemed to have begun losing muscle mass in his upper body, but his chest did not yet have the sunken appearance of an older man. The elf's graying hair flowed to his shoulders, and around his neck, barely visible beneath a pointed beard, he wore a medallion that matched Faeril's.

He took several steps toward them on bare feet. His eyes, dark as coal but warm as a summer rain, seemed to look not at the foursome but past them. After a moment, Kestrel realized why: The older cleric was blind.

"You are new in Myth Drannor, yes?" the holy man inquired. Though handicapped by blindness, he had a strong, self-assured voice. "I am Beriand, Mystra's servant. Welcome to our sanctuary."

The group answered the elves' inquiry as to whether any of the party needed healing, and gratefully accepted an invitation to partake of an evening meal. Kestrel was so hungry she almost could have eaten the Bell's five-day potluck soup. Almost. Fortunately, the clerics' vegetable stew looked and smelled far more appealing.

Corran and Durwyn removed their armor before the meal. Eased of the burden of its weight, they relaxed visibly. Even their faces appeared less strained. Kestrel took the opportunity to study the paladin. Sweat dampened his short dark hair, which had been trapped beneath his helmet most of the day. Though he appeared less intimidating without his armor, Corran was still a formidable figure. His carriage revealed a man confident of his place in the world. He moved about as if he had a right to be there— wherever "there" was at the moment, be it the streets of Myth Drannor, the pool cavern of Valjevo castle, or this temple to a god not his own.

Durwyn, by contrast, appeared ill at ease in the shrine. He moved as if trying to confine his large body to the smallest space possible, a trait she hadn't noticed when they were in battle or out of doors. Was it the temple, she wondered? Did he feel out of his element because this was a holy setting, or was he comfortable only in a combat environment?

The makeshift shelter had only three chairs, so the whole group sat in a half-circle on the floor as they ate. Beriand and Faeril sat in the center, with Ghleanna and Corran on one side of them. Kestrel and Durwyn sat on the other.

During the repast, the clerics explained how they came to be in Myth Drannor. "Few elves venture to this haunted city," Beriand said. "Since the year our race finally abandoned Myth Drannor altogether, our leaders have discouraged return, and the evil creatures who overtook its streets and dwellings did their part to deter all but the most stalwart—or foolish."

"Yet you came," Kestrel said between hungry mouthfuls.

"We were called," he responded.

"Beriand had visions that led us here," Faeril explained. "He saw Mystra amid the ruins of Myth Drannor."

"I believe it was a 'genesis vision'—an image sent by Mystra to summon us here, back to where our sect began." Though sightless, Beriand's eyes shone with devotion to his goddess. "Our sect was founded in this city centuries ago by a priestess of Mystra named Anorrweyn Evensong."

"Several months ago we journeyed here with six other clerics," Faeril said. "But we never reached Anorrweyn's temple. When we arrived at the city Heights, someone launched a huge fireball at our party. It killed all but the two of us."

Corran gasped. "Unprovoked? Who would do such a thing to holy men and women?"

"We still do not know," said Beriand. "We retreated into an undercity complex carved out long ago by dwarves, only to find the so-called 'dwarven dungeons' crawling with drow. Such an abomination would not be possible if the Mythal were functioning properly."

Kestrel set aside her empty bowl. "The Mythal? What's the Mythal?"

"The city's ancient protective magic," Faeril said. "Centuries ago, Myth Drannor's most powerful wizards—including your human Elminster—came together to weave a protective spell that encompassed the entire city like a mantle. We suspect, however, that of late it has become corrupted."

"I believe that is why Mystra summoned us here," Beriand said. "As elves, we are naturally attuned to the Mythal. Though the magical Weave remains strong, many of its threads bear a foreign taint. The contamination has worsened in the time we have been here."

Faeril offered more stew to the travelers. When Corran

and Durwyn accepted, she rose to serve it. "It has been rough going since our arrival," she said over her shoulder as she ladled the food. "We were forced to retreat to this shrine, and most days so much violence rocks the streets that we cannot leave. By day it is orcs, and by night, swarms of undead. But there are many here who need our ministry—we have saved many lives—and the Mythal must somehow be purified. So we stay." She returned with two more steaming bowls.

Corran thanked her as she handed one to him. "In your time here, have you heard any talk of something called the Pool of Radiance?"

Faeril glanced at Beriand, whose face betrayed no hint of recognition. "Only from another band of travelers like yourselves," she said. "They also seek it, but we had no information to help them."

"Athan and his band were allies of ours," said Corran, "but they were killed this day. Do you know what happened to them?"

Faeril gasped at the news. "These are ill tidings indeed. Athan was a fine warrior, one of the best men I have ever known."

Beriand's expression also saddened. "We had not heard—greatly we rue their passing. I know only that they had just come from the Room of Words, a chamber high up in the Onaglym, or House of Gems."

Kestrel wondered if the tales she'd heard of Myth Drannor's riches might prove true after all. A whole house full of gems? "What were they doing there?"

"They had recently found an item known as the Ring of Calling," Beriand said. "They believed it would grant them access to the city's acropolis—or the 'Heights'—but first they needed to break the ring's bond to its previous owner. They went to the Onaglym's Room of Words in hopes of finding a command word that would free the ring from the skeletal arm on which they found it. I do not know whether their research proved successful."

At Beriand's mention of a ring, Kestrel removed her newly acquired one and put it in the cleric's hand. "We found this on one of the adventurers. Is it the Ring of Calling?"

He shook his head immediately. "Alas, no. The Ring of Calling is mysteriously bonded to the skeletal arm of its last wearer. No amount of physical force, nor any of the magic Athan's band attempted, could remove it." He gave Kestrel's ring back to her. "Did you find any such ring?"

"No."

He sighed. "Then I can only assume that whoever killed the party now has the ring, and searches for the enabling word themselves."

"Back in the Room of Words?" Ghleanna asked.

"That is the most likely place to find it," said Beriand. "The chamber is a repository of books containing words that power magical items. When Coronal Eltargrim Irithyl opened the elven capital city to other races, the dwarves came despite their distrust of magic. But later, when they built the House of Gems as their stronghold, they created the Room of Words to feel more empowered over the city's many magical devices." Beriand chuckled. "They thought if they could just collect all the enabling words in one place, they could somehow protect themselves."

Kestrel didn't think the dwarves' idea sounded all that silly—at least it was *some* action against the mysteries of sorcery.

"Why did Athan's band need the ring to reach the Heights?" Durwyn asked. "Couldn't they just walk there?"

"The wars that brought down Myth Drannor left the city's surface in such ruin that many sections are cut off from one another by huge piles of rubble from collapsed buildings and walls," Faeril said. "We are now in a section called the Northern Ruins; the Heights holds the Speculum, Castle Cormanthor, and other important buildings. The only way to move between the districts is through the undercity created by the elves and dwarves over the centuries. The Ring of Calling can unseal a door inside the dwarven dungeons that leads to the Heights."

"It sounds like our first step is visiting this Room of Words," Corran said. "If we're lucky, we'll find the band's killers there searching for the ring's enabling word and we can get the ring back from them."

No, if we're *lucky,* they will be long gone and we'll have to abandon this futile quest and go home, Kestrel wanted to say. Luck, however, didn't seem to be on her side these past few days.

"How do we get to the House of Gems?" Ghleanna asked.

"Through the dwarven dungeons," Beriand responded. "They connect to an isolated tower in the House of Gems. The tower is sealed from the outside, so the dungeons are the only way in. I must warn you, though—the undercity corridors are filled with orcs and undead. In fact, so many of the creatures were using the dungeons as a highway to this part of the city that I sealed the entrance. Rest here for the night to refresh your strength before challenging their numbers."

"In the morning, we will direct you to the doors," said Faeril. "Beriand sealed them with the Glyph of Mystra. Before you leave, study the book lying open on the altar. It contains the Word of Mystra, a command so powerful that it can be learned only through study, not by simply hearing it. Knowing the Word of Mystra will grant you entry through any portal marked with the goddess's symbol. Doors marked with other glyphs, however, require different words of opening."

Words of opening. The Mythal. Magical gates. The

Ring of Calling. As Kestrel lay on her cot that night, her head swam with it all. This morning, her sole thought had been leaving Phlan. Well, she'd left it all right—and now only hoped to get back alive. How had everything spun out of her control so quickly?

Damn Nat's firewine!

CHAPTER THREE

At sunrise, supplied with directions and rations from the clerics, the foursome left the elven shelter and hiked to the entrance of the dwarven undercity. Dawn proved a good time to travel the city's surface—the sunlight chased away undead wanderers, while the hour was too early for much activity on the part of humanoids. The few orcs they did spot en route were easily avoided.

The daylight, however, did little to lift the pall that lay over the ruined city. An aura of tarnished greatness hung about Myth Drannor, its former dignity reduced to rubble along with its structures. Everywhere Kestrel looked, flawed beauty met her gaze: crumbling arches, cracked columns, decapitated statues, dead or dying trees. The tales she'd heard of the fallen elven capital had described treasure there for the taking by anyone brave enough to face its new denizens. However, even to her rogue's sensibilities, looting this city seemed less like robbing from the rich than stealing from a cripple.

The party spotted the double doors inscribed with Mystra's star symbol. They approached slowly, this time anticipating the thunderous Word of Opening rending the air.

"Aodhfionn!"

The command, as yesterday spoken by the mysterious otherworldly voice, roared like the surf pounding on the shore. Kestrel started at the force as vibrations echoed in the air. Hinges too long in need of oil protested strenuously. The doors to the undercity swung open to reveal a dark corridor.

Smooth, perfectly planed rock walls lined the ten-foot-wide opening. Within, narrower passages broke off in three directions. Lit torches punctuated the walls at fixed intervals, confirming that some sort of humanoid occupants passed through regularly. When she'd heard these dungeons were of dwarven construction, Kestrel had feared she and the others would have to stoop to move through them. Fortunately, the ceiling was at least six and a half feet high. Durwyn might have to duck in places to keep his helmet from scraping the roof, but otherwise it appeared that the foursome would find their movement generally unhindered.

Kestrel waited for someone else to enter first. She might have agreed to accompany these misguided do-gooders on their suicide mission, but she had no plans to stick her neck out an inch further than she had to. She'd do what she could to keep the party alive and intact—thus improving her own chances of survival—but her commitment ended there.

"Go ahead, Corran," she prompted. The holy knight

seemed to have appointed himself the leader of their little group anyway. "I'll be right behind you."

"I assume that's supposed to reassure me," he said, "but I can't help wondering if I'll feel a knife in my back."

Don't tempt me, she thought. Aloud she said, "Only if you keep us standing here much longer. The sooner we go in, the sooner we get this over with."

"Let us enter, then." Sword in hand, Corran strode forward into the flickering torchlight. "May Tyr guide our steps—and our hearts."

"Whatever."

The two women entered after the paladin, with Durwyn bringing up the rear. Corran chose the path that broke off to the right. Kestrel thought they should have paused at the fork and listened for clues to what lay ahead in each direction, but she didn't care enough to speak up, and she didn't feel like arguing with him this early in the morning. If he wanted to believe that his god guided his steps, that was fine with her—she just wished he and Durwyn would make less noise clanking around the stone corridor in their armor. They must have alerted the entire undercity population to their presence already.

When they reached the third fork, she couldn't hold her tongue anymore. "Do you have any idea where you're going?" she asked.

He stopped, turning to face her. "Do you?"

"No, but it might help to listen ahead instead of just parading through." No sooner had she spoken than she thought she heard a voice murmuring in the passage to their right.

He opened his mouth to respond, but she covered it with her hand. "Hush!" She cocked her head, trying to make out the words.

"What do you hear?" Ghleanna whispered.

It was a low, guttural voice. An orc? Probably, but she

wanted to find out for sure. "Wait here." At the mage's raised brows, she added, "I won't go far."

She crept down the right passageway, moving soundlessly and keeping to the shadows created by the flickering torchlight. After a few dozen yards, she still couldn't see the speakers—she'd determined there were two of them—but she could hear them clearly, and the low rumble of many voices still further down the corridor.

"Ugly wizard need more guards. Blood Spear Tribe come today. Meet here later."

"Broken Skull Tribe show who boss."

"No! Ugly wizard say no fight each other."

They were orcs, all right. Either that, or the stupidest-sounding humans she'd ever overheard. She padded back to the fork, then trod about thirty yards down the other passage. She held her breath and listened closely but heard nothing but the crackle of torches. She returned to the group.

"A couple tribes of orcs are gathering in the right passage," she said, deliberately leaving out the mention of the "ugly wizard"—one of the scarred mages they'd heard about? Knowing Corran, he would want to confront the spellcaster immediately. "I vote we go to the left."

The others concurred. They headed down the left corridor, passing several solidly built wooden doors inscribed with glyphs—all of them different, none of them recognizable to anyone in the party. Kestrel tried to pick the locks of the first two doors, but discovered them magically, not mechanically, sealed.

"They must require those other Words of Opening the clerics talked about," Durwyn said.

"You think?" Kestrel retorted. Leave it to Durwyn to state the obvious.

Several hundred yards farther, they came upon a doorway that glittered in the torchlight as they approached, as if it held a door of glass. When they reached it, they discovered the surface thick with frost and crystals.

Ghleanna extended her hand to touch the surface. "It's ice. A solid sheet of ice."

"Strange," Kestrel said. "I wonder what's inside?"

Durwyn hefted his axe. "Let's find out." Before Kestrel could stop him, he swung the axe so hard it created an ear-splitting crash that echoed throughout the passageway. A huge web of cracks spread across the ice from the center of his strike. A second blow sent large chunks of ice flying into the room beyond.

Kestrel grabbed his arm before he could swing again. She fought to keep her voice muted. "What in the Abyss are you doing?" she hissed. "Every orc in this dungeon will hear you!"

Confusion spread across Durwyn's features. "I thought you wanted to—"

"He might as well finish now," Corran said. "One more blow, and we'll be able to get through."

Durwyn looked to Kestrel as if for permission. Corran was right—if breaking through was going to attract attention from the orcs, the alarm had already sounded. She supposed it was even possible that they were far enough away that the orcs wouldn't be able to determine the origin of the noise. Besides, for all they knew, the path to the House of Gems might lie beyond this frozen doorway. She shrugged her reluctant assent.

The warrior struck a third time, shattering enough of the door to create a man-sized hole. They kicked aside hunks and shards of ice, then grabbed a torch from one of the wall sconces. Corran thrust it through the opening and peered in.

"It's a small room," he said. "Maybe ten or twelve feet square. Looks like there's no one inside." He crawled through, followed by the others.

Once inside, Kestrel shivered with cold. In the center of the room—taking up most of the room, in fact—was a large circular rune inscribed on the stone floor. Its intricate knotwork pattern was outlined in white frost. In the center, about waist-high, floated a golden sphere encrusted with icicles.

She crossed to the levitating sphere, withdrew one of her daggers, and prodded it. The sphere did not move. She tapped harder, but her effort yielded only the clank of steel against ice. Finally, she put the dagger away and pushed against the sphere with all her strength. It felt as icy as it looked, but it would not budge.

"Let me help," Durwyn offered. The big warrior threw all of his weight against the floating object, but it remained just as firmly in place.

"I give up," Kestrel said. She glanced at their other companions. Ghleanna knelt at the edge of the rune, closely examining it. Corran stood facing one of the walls, his back to the group.

"Ghleanna, what do you suppose this is?" the paladin asked.

The mage approached, as did Kestrel and Durwyn. The wall held an engraved formation of four diamond shapes arranged in a column, with a vertical line bisecting them. A ruby was embedded in the lowest point of the bottom diamond.

"I've never seen its like before," Ghleanna said.

Corran traced the edge of the ruby with his index finger. "I tried removing the gem, but it's wedged in there pretty tight."

"Not exactly your area of expertise, I imagine," said Kestrel. "Let me try." She removed a pointed metal file from one of her belt pouches and tried to insert it between the gem and the wall to pry out the ruby. Despite her best efforts, the stone remained firmly in place—now surrounded by scratch marks.

"Apparently not your area of expertise either," Corran remarked.

She shot him a dirty look. The failure of her thieving skills bothered her enough—she didn't need Sir Self-Righteous rubbing it in. "It must be magically frozen in place, like everything else in this room," she said stiffly. "Otherwise I would have had no problem removing it."

Ghleanna offered to use sorcery in hopes of learning more about the room, but all agreed her spells were better saved for whatever lay ahead than to merely satisfy curiosity. "I'm sure this room isn't the only mysterious thing we'll encounter in Myth Drannor," Corran said.

Kestrel hoped the others proved this benign.

☙ ☙ ☙ ☙ ☙

After a while, the party entered an area of the dungeons that appeared less frequented by the orcs. Fewer torches lined these walls, and many of them had sputtered out or been extinguished. The light became dim enough that Corran removed one of the unlit torches from its sconce, lighted it off the next burning torch they came upon, and carried it with them. Soon, the passageway's illumination grew so bad that the others followed suit.

As they neared a chamber with an open doorway, a sudden voice from within startled them. "Light? Oh—whoever you are, I beseech you! Please bring your light this way!"

They exchanged glances, knowing that their torches would reveal them to the speaker well before they could see him.

"A trap?" Kestrel mouthed.

"I don't think so," Corran responded softly. "If he means to ambush us, why alert us to his presence?" More loudly, he called out, "We're on our way."

Corran entered the chamber first. "Oh!"

"What?" Kestrel darted in after him. "Oh!" she echoed. "Well, I'll be damned . . ."

In the corner of the room stood a man—or at least, half a man. He looked ordinary enough from the torso up, with a medium build, long brown hair, and penetrating dark eyes. From the waist down, the unfortunate fellow was embedded in an enormous boulder. His body appeared to simply end, consumed by the rock.

Behind her, Kestrel heard Durwyn and Ghleanna enter. The warrior gasped. "What happened to you?"

"If you can believe it, a lovers' quarrel," the man responded. "I was exploring these dungeons with my fiancée, a fellow sorcerer, when we fell into an argument. The subject was so trivial that I can't even remember what the fight was about, but in the heat of the moment I renounced my love for Ozama. She flew into a rage and cast a spell that sealed me in this boulder until I solved a riddle:

> A quest of love
> Ends with me,
> Yet I am made
> Endlessly.
> If I drop,
> I say my name,
> If I touch rock,
> Freedom gain."

Kestrel nearly snorted. "That old thing? Your sweetheart changed the ending, but the first half of it must have circulated through half the taverns between here and Waterdeep last year."

"And all the courts the year before," Corran added.

The man's face lit up, his eyes darting from one party member to the next. "Do you really know the answer?"

"A ring," Durwyn said.

Kestrel crossed the room and tapped her silver ring against the rock. A mighty *crack!* rent the air as the boulder broke into pieces. The long-trapped wizard immediately fell to his knees, his legs unused to supporting his weight.

"A ring," he murmured, rubbing the atrophied muscles of his calves through the fabric of his purple robes. "So much lost time over such a simple answer." He remained absorbed in his own thoughts, an expression of regret settling onto his angular face. His musings, however, lasted but a few moments before he left the mournful thoughts behind and addressed the foursome. "My name is Jarial. Words aren't enough to thank you for releasing me."

Corran introduced the party, then asked how long Jarial had been trapped in the boulder.

"Since the Year of the Arch—1353 by the Dale calendar," he said. "What year is it now? There's no way to tell time in here."

"The Year of the Gauntlet. 1369." Kestrel soberly studied him. Even though Jarial was a sorcerer, she felt sorry for him wasting so much of his life trapped alone in the darkness. He appeared only twenty or so, but he had to be much older. And the riddle that had imprisoned him had become so common while he endured endless isolation— even Durwyn had known the answer! "You mean this Ozama woman just left you down here for sixteen years and never came back?"

"I believe she meant to return," Jarial said. "Something must have happened to her. She was angry but not vindictive enough to leave me here forever. We came here in the first place seeking a magical item called the Wizard's Torc, said to lie in the lair of a dark naga somewhere in these dungeons. I fear she continued looking for it alone and met with misfortune."

"Or found it and left you here to rot while she kept it

for herself," Kestrel said. "How *did* you survive, anyway? I mean, excuse me for asking, but why didn't you starve to death, or get killed by the creatures dwelling down here?" She noted that his jaw was not even roughened by stubble, nor his clothes frayed by sixteen years of constant wear.

"Ozama's spell kept me safe from the ravages of time and enemies," Jarial said. "Though I did begin to fear I would go mad. At first, of course, I pondered the riddle every waking moment. When no solution came to me, I shouted myself hoarse calling for help. That attracted the attention of some of the undercity's more unpleasant residents, who offered no aid but found it entertaining to come in here and torment me."

Jarial's little-used voice sounded scratchy. The poor man was probably parched. Corran offered him some water, which the mage accepted gratefully.

"You're a sorcerer," Kestrel prodded. "Couldn't you use magic to free yourself?"

"Believe me, I tried! After going through all the spells I knew, I started devising new ones." Jarial smiled ruefully. "Though I had the satisfaction of using some of my mocking antagonists for target practice, I still couldn't gain my freedom." He continued kneading the muscles of his legs, trying to rub life back into them.

"After giving up on using sorcery to free myself, I spent probably another year just saying aloud every word I could possibly think of, hoping to accidentally stumble on the answer. Obviously, that strategy proved ineffective as well. Eventually, I stopped bothering to even use magic to light this room. I'd just consigned myself to spending eternity here, alone in the darkness with only my own thoughts for company." The lonely sorcerer tried again to rise, but his legs remained too weak to support him.

"Here, drink this." Ghleanna offered him a small vial of

bluish liquid, one of the potions they had found on Athan's band. Faeril had identified it as a healing potion made of blueglow moss, a local plant renowned for its curative properties but now in short supply. "You'll never manage to massage away years of disuse."

Jarial swallowed the dose and within minutes was able to walk around the chamber. When his stride had steadied, he held the foursome in his gaze. "I can't thank you enough," he said. "What quest brings you to these dungeons? You must let me aid you."

Kestrel laughed humorlessly. He was welcome to take her place.

The band, now five in number, continued through the maze of passages. Jarial thought he remembered the location of a stairway that led up into the hill of the acropolis, so at his suggestion the party backtracked to a previous fork and headed down a different corridor.

A few yards down, light spilled out of a doorway. Within, they heard sounds of shuffling and sporadic muttering as if someone were talking to himself. Kestrel snuck ahead and peered inside.

Nottle the peddler bent over an open trunk, rummaging through its contents. "An' what's this? Ah, yes! Dwarven weapons always fetch a good price."

Kestrel blinked. The peddler was foraging through the dungeons as casually as if he were shopping in Phlan's marketplace. Was the little guy trying to get himself killed? She motioned to the others to join her, then entered the chamber. Engrossed in his scavenging, the halfling didn't even notice her.

"Nottle, what are you doing here?"

"Yiaah!" The peddler jumped about a foot. The short

sword he'd been holding clattered back into the chest. "Jeepers! Ye scared me!"

"Worse things than us could stroll into this room," Kestrel said as her companions entered. "How did you get in here?"

"I saw ye folks unseal the door, and I follow'd ye in. Them elven clerics mean well an' all, but thanks t' them I ain't been able to git in here fer weeks—all the good stuff's nearly gone."

The paladin shook his head in disbelief. "You're telling us this whole dungeon complex has been plundered in a matter of weeks?" Corran asked. "By whom?"

"Everyone!" Nottle retrieved the short sword he'd dropped and added it to the collection of booty he evidently intended to abscond with. "Since them horrible phaerimm and alhoon have been run outta this part o'the city, all sortsa creatures come here to loot their old hoards. Why do ye think there's so many orcs about? It's a great time to be a scavenger!"

"Aren't you afraid for your safety?" Ghleanna asked.

"No more'n usual." The peddler struggled into his overstuffed pack and picked up his lantern. "A bit o'danger comes with the trade. If I wanted to play it completely safe, I'd open a borin' little shop in Waterdeep. 'Sides, the orcs're some o'my best customers, so they pretty much leave me alone."

"Orcs aren't the only things haunting these passageways," Jarial said. "I've seen zombies and—"

"Oh, I can handle a few zombies." Nottle headed for the door. "Nice chattin' with ye folks again. Let me know if ye need anythin'!" With that, he was gone.

All five of them stared after the peddler. "He's going to get himself killed," Durwyn said.

Kestrel shrugged. "Better him than us." In a way, she envied the halfling. Were the need for stealth not so great on this misguided mission of theirs, she would have enjoyed looting these ruins right along with Nottle. But she could ill afford the noise of carrying too much plunder.

As they filed out of the room, Kestrel heard Durwyn whisper to Jarial, "What's an alhoon?" She'd wondered the same thing herself at Nottle's first mention of them but hadn't wanted to admit ignorance.

"An undead mind flayer," the mage said. "Horrible creatures with heads that look like an octopus. Between their psionic powers and wizard spells they're deadly opponents."

"And the phaerimm?"

"Extremely powerful magic-using creatures, nearly all teeth, claws, and tail. I saw plenty of them—and alhoon—in the time I was trapped down here, but as the peddler said, they just up and disappeared one day. It must have taken something awfully strong to drive them away."

Kestrel didn't want to dwell on what that "something" might be. If it was the same creature—or creatures— responsible for creating the new Pool of Radiance, their mission was even more futile than she'd thought.

They headed farther down the passage, ducking into rooms as they continued their search for a way up and out of the dungeons. Many of the rooms stood empty or littered with broken furniture, while others—probably the former lairs of the alhoon and phaerimm—held ransacked chests or similar signs of already having been visited by scavengers such as Nottle. As in the region where Jarial had been trapped, the torches along the wall of this new area became sparser, until they reached a zone where there were none at all. Though each of the explorers held a torch, the flames did little to illuminate their surroundings. A pall of preternatural darkness cloaked this sector of the dungeons.

They came upon a room that seemed to serve as an antechamber to a larger complex. Several doors in the back and side walls stood open, and the party entered one to find themselves engulfed in nearly total darkness. The flames of their torches cast little more light than candles.

"I don't recognize this area at all," Jarial said. "We must have made a wrong t—"

"Hush!" Kestrel interrupted him. She held her breath, concentrating on a sound she heard echoing from the stillness. *Rattle. Scrape. Rattle.* The noise seemed to come from a room off to their right.

Rattle rattle. Scrape scrape. Rattle rattle.

"I hear it, too," Ghleanna whispered.

Clack. Clack. Clack clack.

Corran's hand drifted to his sword hilt, but suddenly stopped. He sucked in his breath. "It almost sounds like—"

A white shape shuffled into view, its grinning head and gangly limbs a stark contrast to the blackness beyond. Clattering erupted as a sea of others appeared behind it.

"Skeletons!" Durwyn leapt forward, swinging his battle-axe in a wide arc that shattered the skull of the nearest foe.

"At least a dozen of them," Corran called out as two creatures armed with swords closed in on him. He left his own sword in its sheath, reaching for the warhammer on his back instead. In a single movement, he brought it around and smashed the sternum of the first skeleton. It crumpled into a pile on the ground.

The creatures were closing in fast. There had to be more than a dozen, but in the poor light Kestrel couldn't determine where they were coming from. She grabbed her club from her belt and snapped her wrist to extend the weapon to its full length. Her daggers would do no good against a mass of walking bones with no flesh to pierce.

A sudden flare issued from Jarial's fingertips, sending a

sheet of flames shooting toward a group of skeletons. Within seconds, the blaze consumed three of them and caused two more to fall back. Distracted by the spell, Kestrel almost didn't hear the rattling bones approaching behind her. She spun around, automatically swinging her club. The baton struck the lone skeleton hard enough to knock it off balance. She seized the advantage and struck again, knocking its weapon out of its grasp. Her third strike bashed in its skull.

She glanced back at the others. Corran had dispatched several skeletons, but for every one that fell two more surged in. Both warriors were heavily engaged now, shielding the more physically vulnerable sorcerers. As she watched, Durwyn swung his axe in a powerful arc that sent the skulls of two creatures flying at once. Their headless remains clattered into a pile at his feet. He kicked the bones aside and pressed forward to attack another foe.

A flash of steel caught her eye, alerting her just in time to an advancing opponent. Was it the flickering torchlight, or had this collection of bones yellowed with age or decay? Its sinister grin held no teeth, and cracks appeared along its clavicle and pelvis. The creature swung its sword in a jerky motion that Kestrel easily parried. She then struck the frail hipbone with all the strength she could muster. The brittle pelvis shattered.

The skeleton, now in two halves, collapsed. The fall alone sent several ribs skidding across the floor. Its legs fell still, but the creature propped its torso up on one bony hand and swung its sword with the other, trying to cut Kestrel's legs out from under her. She jumped to avoid the sweeping weapon and landed on the weakened collarbone. It snapped under her weight. A final blow from her club kept the creature from rising again.

She had just finished off this latest foe when she saw Corran cast aside his torch. A moment later, a flash of metal in his left hand caught her attention. His holy symbol. Did he hope to repel the skeletons as he had the zombies last night? The creatures were coming at him too fast to give him a chance.

A crazy, desperate idea entered her thoughts, and she acted before she could talk herself out of it. She dove to the ground and rolled into the skeletons. The creature nearest Corran crashed to the floor. Before it could recover its feet, she swung her club and caught another skeleton in the knees. It fell on top of the first and caused a third to trip over their sprawled bones. Kestrel scrambled out of the pile. They were down but not defeated, providing Corran with only a small window of opportunity.

It was all he needed. "By all that is holy, begone!" he cried, holding Tyr's symbol aloft.

At the paladin's shout, the skeletons nearest him retreated. At the same time, light burst from the head of Ghleanna's staff, at last fully illuminating the room.

Nine skeletons—those Corran had repelled—circled the room's perimeter, keeping as much distance as possible between themselves and the paladin as they attempted to reach the exits. Two more yet advanced, while the three Kestrel had felled clumsily tried to disengage themselves from each other.

The sudden brightness startled the skeletons enough to give the explorers the initiative. Kestrel easily finished off the three fallen creatures, methodically bashing each skull. Ghleanna smashed her quarterstaff through the spinal column of one of those advancing, while Durwyn arced his axe to crush another. He and the paladin then set about picking off the retreating skeletons.

A low moan behind her caused Kestrel to spin around again—and add a groan of her own to the chant as an all-too-familiar smell greeted her nostrils. "Zombies!" she called out. Five of the creatures shuffled into the chamber from the door through which the explorers had entered. She tossed her twin daggers at the first walking corpse, then reached for the blade she'd retrieved from Loren's body. As she threw the unfamiliar weapon, it glinted in the magical light of Ghleanna's spell. The blade struck the creature's heart, causing it to crumple to the ground. She was out of daggers—she'd have to fight off the rest of the zombies with the club.

To her amazement, however, the nondescript dagger pulled itself free of the monster and flew back into her left hand. A magical dagger! She both thrilled and cringed at the discovery. A returning dagger could prove valuable, but magical weapons had been known to hold curses.

As the sounds of the skeleton battle died behind her, Corran's voice echoed off the chamber walls again. "Trouble us no longer!" The remaining zombies ceased their advance and attempted to escape. Kestrel threw Loren's blade at the creatures she'd already injured. No way were they shuffling off with her twin daggers stuck in them. Thanks to the weapon's boomerang power, she felled both foes. Corran and Durwyn took care of the last two zombies.

In the aftermath, Corran removed his helm and pushed sweat-dampened hair away from his eyes. He nodded toward the dagger that had once again found its way back to Kestrel's hand. "A magical blade. What will you call it?"

"Call it?" She wasn't even sure she would keep it—she would certainly use it conservatively until she knew she could trust its sorcery.

"Enchanted weapons deserve their own names."

Kestrel shrugged. "I've thought of it as Loren's blade up to now. I guess I'll continue to do so."

"Loren's Blade," Corran repeated. "A good name."

Kestrel studied the paladin as he cleaned and secured his own weapon. He might be an arrogant know-it-all, but the man knew how to fight. That little routine he did with the holy symbol was proving useful, too.

She'd sooner eat roasted zombie flesh than tell him so.

"Do you suppose we stumbled into their lair?" Ghleanna asked the group at large.

"Either that, or they may have been guarding something," Corran answered. "An exit, perhaps? Let's take a look around."

They poked through the room from which the skeletons had emerged, finding little more than rubble, and continued to explore the rest of the complex. Ultimately, they came to what appeared to be the main chamber. Bones lay strewn about, some human, some not. Unlike the animated skeletons they encountered earlier, these seemed to lie where their owners had died, earthly possessions still surrounding them. One of the skeletons yet wore a gray woolen cloak and a pair of snakeskin boots.

At the sight, Jarial caught his breath. "Ozama."

Kestrel turned away, allowing the mage a few moments of privacy in which to grieve his former lover's loss, or curse her for entrapping him, or whatever he wanted to do upon discovering her remains. She glanced around the room, noticing that the door opposite bore an unfamiliar glyph—two swirling circles drawn with a single line. The symbol was burned into the wood. A small barred window in the door looked into the next chamber, but from her vantage point she could see only darkness within.

She approached the door. Finding it sealed, she peered through the window but still couldn't see anything inside. She beckoned Ghleanna. "Can you cast the light from your staff into there?"

"Certainly." The mage came forward and lifted her staff toward the opening, but the darkness beyond completely swallowed up the light. Ghleanna frowned. "How strange. . . ."

"I'm afraid I'm a little shy," said a rasping voice from the blackness.

Despite its refined tone, the voice sent a shudder down Kestrel's spine, like the sound of fingernails on glass. "Who are you?" she asked.

"I might ask you that question," the mysterious speaker responded. The voice sounded male, but she couldn't be sure. "It is you, after all, who have intruded into my home."

Kestrel squinted, trying to make out a shape in the darkness, but could not discern even the dimmest outline. She did, however, detect a faint rustling, as of something sliding across a floor, followed by the clinking of metal.

Corran strode past Kestrel to stand before the window. "Please forgive the rudeness of my companion," he said, casting a scolding look toward Kestrel. "She's a little . . . uncultured."

Kestrel bristled, regretting that she had thought anything nice about the insufferable Lord D'Arcey a few minutes earlier.

The paladin then peered through the window himself. "We apologize for disturbing you—we seek only an exit from these dungeons to the Heights above."

"'Tis not a disturbance," the sibilant voice said. "Indeed, I welcome the diversion of visitors. This can be a rather solitary place."

The last *hiss* on the word "place" caused goosebumps to form on Kestrel's arms. She glanced at the dusty bones strewn about the floor. Had these visitors also provided a diversion? She ambled away from the door to give the dried-out bodies a closer look. At first she'd assumed the skeletons and zombies had defeated them, but now she wondered otherwise. An exchange of glances with Ghleanna revealed that the mage held similar suspicions.

"I imagine one could grow bored in such isolation," Corran said.

"Indeed, no," the voice said. "Lonely perhaps, but not bored. I have a hobby—a passion really—for collecting things."

"What kind of things?" Kestrel called out, looking at the unfortunate adventurers who had preceded them to this place. Lives? Souls?

"Oh, necklaces, amulets, torcs, chokers, neck rings, pendants, collars—just about anything that goes around one's neck."

Jarial's head, which until now had been bowed over Ozama's remains, snapped up. "Preybelish," he whispered.

Kestrel quietly moved to his side. "You know him?"

"I believe we've found the dark naga Ozama and I sought all those years ago," he said, his voice barely audible even to Kestrel. "The one said to possess the Wizard's Torc." His fingers stroked Ozama's cloak. "She must have died trying to get it from him."

"Yes, she did," the voice—Preybelish—hissed.

Kestrel's gaze darted to the door, then back to Jarial. "How could he possibly have heard you?"

Jarial drew his brows together. "I—"

"He doesn't know," Preybelish said. "But he does want to avenge his lady. Don't you . . . Jarial? As much as the little bird beside you wants to settle a score with a certain holy knight."

"What do you mean by that?" Corran asked.

Kestrel froze, not even releasing her breath. Could the naga read their thoughts? She dared not ponder the idea for fear of giving something away to the creature. Instead, she concentrated on the image of a topaz necklace she'd once seen in—and liberated from—a shop window in Waterdeep. It had fetched a handsome price, but she envisioned herself holding the piece of jewelry as if she still possessed it.

"Forget these temporary companions, little thief. You don't believe in their cause anyway," Preybelish said. "We could form a lucrative partnership. I'll give you fair recompense for that necklace or any other any neckwear you wish to sell me."

"What nec—" Durwyn began. Ghleanna hushed him.

"I might be persuaded to part with it," Kestrel replied.

"Good, very good. I shall unseal the door for you. Come in—alone—and we will bargain."

Kestrel looked to Jarial for guidance, all the while forcing her surface thoughts to remain on the necklace. The mage nodded, but gestured for her to stall. "All right," she said to Preybelish. "But I prefer to see who I'm doing business with."

As she spoke, Jarial slipped the snakeskin boots off Ozama's skeleton and held them toward her. "Magic," he mouthed. She shook her head in refusal. Her daggers were hidden in her own boots, and she trusted the blades more than any enchantment. After one more pleading look, the mage slipped the boots on his own feet.

"I'll dispel the darkness once you're inside," Preybelish said. The heavy wooden door creaked open.

She glanced at the others. Corran's hand rested on his sword hilt, ready to unsheathe the weapon at any time. Ghleanna's mouth moved in an unheard spell, her left hand drifting in a slow arc. Durwyn looked just plain confused, but he held his battle-axe ready.

"Let us bargain, then." Kestrel walked toward the door.

Just as she reached it, Ghleanna uttered a single word aloud. The darkness that had engulfed Preybelish's chamber immediately dissipated, revealing a large purplish-black snake with a humanlike face. Around his neck, supported by his inflatable hood, dangled necklaces, chokers, and other neckwear of varying lengths and ostentation. The naga's thick coils disappeared beneath a sea of coins and jewelry, but Kestrel guessed his body must extend at least ten feet. His eyes shuttered to thin slits in the sudden light.

Preybelish hissed, baring his long fangs. "You'll regret that, you foolish half-breed!" His tail, barbed and sharp as a razor, emerged from the treasure hoard and flicked violently, showering gold around the room and sending Kestrel diving for cover behind the decapitated marble head—and neck—of what had once been an enormous statue. Preybelish's attention, however, was focused outside his chamber. On Ghleanna.

A moment later, a jet of flame shot forth from the naga's tail straight at the female mage. Ghleanna howled as the entire left side of her body caught fire. She dropped to the floor to extinguish her clothing, rolling out of Kestrel's sight.

Corran, who had been standing a little too close to the doorway when the attack shot past, sucked in his breath as his armor—heated by the flames—seared his skin. Despite the obvious pain, he advanced on Preybelish, Durwyn close behind.

"I have to agree with the little bird," the dark naga said. His eyes were wide open now, sinister glowing yellow orbs. "I do so hate the company of paladins. So holier-than-thou."

Corran brought his sword down with enough force to cleave the snakelike creature in half. The attack, however, glanced off some invisible barrier, not even nicking a scale. "Vile serpent!" the paladin shouted in frustration.

Durwyn swung his axe. The blade found its mark, sinking into the naga's muscular body. Preybelish hissed and swung his tail, catching Durwyn in the chest and knocking him off his feet. Blood started seeping from a gash in the warrior's neck.

Kestrel looked through the doorway to see what Jarial was doing, but the wizard had disappeared from view. Was he attending Ghleanna? "Not now, Jarial," she muttered. "This can't be left up to me."

From her vantage point, she had a clear shot at the creature's back—or whatever one called the part of a snake's coils opposite the underbelly. Preybelish seemed to be focusing his attention and his mind-reading abilities on Corran at the moment. She withdrew her daggers from her boots but paused before throwing them. Once she hurled the weapons, then what? She'd accomplish nothing but angering the creature and drawing his attention back to herself. While Loren's Blade would return to her hand, she did not trust its magic.

The holy knight attempted another attack. This swing managed to bite into the monster's flesh, though it visibly slowed before impact. Preybelish uttered a string of foul epithets and thrashed his tail at the paladin. It hit Corran with enough force to knock a lesser man to his knees, but Corran caught his balance, his armor apparently shielding him from the tail's sting.

Durwyn lay slumped on the floor, unconscious. Though the gash in his neck bled, the flow was not profuse enough for such a large man to have passed out already. Kestrel looked back at the wicked barbs on the end of Preybelish's tail. Two of them dripped black fluid.

Poison.

The creature muttered arcane words under its breath—another spell. Where in the Abyss was Jarial? She let the daggers fly before the naga could finish his incantation.

The evil serpent howled in rage as the weapons drove into his flesh less than a foot from his head. Thick brown blood welled from the wounds. He twisted around to glare at her, fangs bared, yellow eyes blazing with pain and fury. "Don't you know that snakes eat little birds?" he hissed.

"Not this one." Kestrel managed to sound more confident than she felt.

Preybelish uttered a string of incomprehensible syllables, weaving another spell. Corran swung his sword again, this time striking the creature with full force. The naga, however, would not allow his concentration to be broken. He stared unblinking at Kestrel as his voice rose in pitch.

Her heart hammered in her chest as she tensed in anticipation of the inevitable sorcery. Would flames consume her, as they had Ghleanna?

Suddenly, an arrow materialized behind Preybelish and raced through the air to embed itself in the back of the creature's head. The acrid odor of burning flesh filled the room as acid ate through the naga's skin. Just feet away, Jarial appeared.

The naga screamed in rage, swinging his tail wildly. The barbed point caught Jarial's legs, knocking him down. Kestrel swore under her breath. Not Jarial too? Now two of their party were poisoned and a third badly burned.

Preybelish turned on Corran. "Don't even think about it," the creature said before the paladin so much as lifted his arm for the intended strike. The naga swung his tail once again, knocking Corran's sword out of his grasp.

Kestrel's mind raced. If they could only control that tail . . .

"Catch a naga by the tail?" Preybelish mocked, twisting around to fix her with his evil gaze. "What would you do once you got your hands on it?"

Behind the naga, to Kestrel's surprise, Jarial got back to his feet. The mage appeared winded but hardly scratched. She forced her thoughts away from the wizard, so as not to betray him to Preybelish's mind-reading powers.

"This!" Jarial said. He darted out his hand and touched creature's tail just below the barbed tip. The contact lasted only a split second, but it was long enough. Preybelish screeched inhumanly as the last quarter of his body went rigid and fell immobile to the ground.

The naga bared his fangs and spun his upper body to advance on Jarial, still possessing enough unparalyzed coils to reach the unarmored mage. Corran went for his warhammer but Kestrel was faster.

She leaped onto Preybelish's back, grabbed one of the many chains hanging from his neck, and twisted. When the chain closed around the creature's airway, she pulled hard. "Did you say you collect neckwear, Preybelish?"

Despite her effort, the naga managed to get enough air to begin hissing out the words of a final spell.

She braced her feet against the naga's spine and tugged with all her might. "Chokers, right?" Preybelish thrashed about so wildly that she had trouble retaining her grip. Corran hurried over to lend his strength. With the paladin's added power, the evil creature's eyes grew wide, his words of incantation becoming desperate gurgles as he fought to breathe. Kestrel threw her whole body into one final tug.

"Choke on this."

CHAPTER FOUR

Fortunately, the naga's poison did not prove lethal. Durwyn awoke from his drugged sleep just as Preybelish entered his final one. Within a quarter hour the warrior seemed none the worse for the battle, save the easily bandaged wound on his neck.

Ghleanna, however, was another story. She lay unconscious and badly burned on one side of her body.

Kestrel paled just looking at the injured mage. "How many of those blueglow moss potions do we have left?"

"Let me tend to her first," Corran said. He knelt at her side, removing his helm and gauntlets. Gently, he touched his hands to Ghleanna's damaged skin, closed his eyes, and bowed his head in prayer. Ever so slowly, as the paladin murmured words of supplication to Tyr, the half-elf's charred tissue healed.

Kestrel turned away. When Corran had repelled the zombies, she'd felt that his showy theatrics were meant to draw attention. Now, watching him lay on hands, she grew uncomfortable. His features and manner softened—the arrogance, the bossiness, the presumption were all set aside as he ministered to their injured companion. The sight deeply unsettled her. It revealed a side of Corran D'Arcey she did not wish to acknowledge.

Jarial approached, carrying Ozama's cloak. "I thought Ghleanna could use this," he said.

"I'm sure she'll appreciate it." Kestrel glanced at the woman rendered so vulnerable by the same magic she herself wielded. Corran still had a lot of healing to do. She turned back to Jarial and gestured toward Preybelish's treasure. "Let's leave them in peace and find that Wizard's Torc."

He regarded the naga's hoard reluctantly. "It doesn't seem important anymore. Certainly not worth the lives it cost—and almost cost." His lips formed a rueful smile. "Sixteen years trapped in a boulder has a tendency to alter one's perspective."

Kestrel could scarcely believe her ears. After all he'd been through, how could he not want the prize? "You're right—your lady did sacrifice her life in pursuit of the torc. Don't you think you owe it to her to retrieve it now that you have the opportunity?" Besides, it sounded valuable— if he didn't take it, she would.

A spark of interest returned to his eyes. "I suppose we should at least see if it's here."

By the time they emerged from the naga's lair with the magical necklace in hand, Ghleanna was up and around. Corran had done as much healing as was in his power, and one of the remaining blueglow moss potions had done the rest. Both she and the paladin appeared drained, however. The group elected to sleep a while in the relative safety of Preybelish's den, gnawing hungrily on dried provisions and taking turns keeping watch.

Their strength restored, they left the complex and returned to the maze of corridors. Eventually, they came upon a stairway leading up.

"Finally," Kestrel muttered. "I was beginning to think we'd never get out of this place."

"Don't start looking for the sun yet," Jarial said. "There are two dungeon levels built into the hill, so we have another stairway to locate after this one."

At least they were moving in the right direction. Kestrel nearly sprinted up the steps in her eagerness to make more progress exiting these tomblike corridors. She slowed, however, at the top of the stairs.

Light spilled out of a room about thirty yards down the passage. A grid of shadows on the floor revealed it was a prison cell with a door of wrought-iron bars. From within, a harsh male voice bellowed questions at someone whose replies Kestrel couldn't hear.

"Just give up the damn word, you cretin! We'll learn it eventually anyway!" The *smack* of someone being struck echoed off the stone walls. "Tell me what you know or I'll feed you to my master for supper."

The explorers exchanged glances. "Someone should sneak ahead and see what's going on," Corran said. Kestrel sighed. Given everyone else's skills at stealth, no doubt "someone" meant her.

She left the group hidden from sight in the stairwell and crept along the passage, keeping to the shadows as she neared the barred doorway. Though she moved silently, the interrogator spoke loudly enough that even Durwyn could have approached unheard.

Inside, a warrior sat on the floor. He was a sturdy

young man, no older than twenty, dressed in brown leather armor. His wrists and ankles were bound to one wall with chains. Six skeletons, armed with short swords as those downstairs had been, stood at attention on one side of the cell. It was the room's other occupant who made Kestrel suck in her breath.

A masked figure circled the prisoner. Though a red leather hood covered the interrogator's head and shoulders, holes revealed his eyes, mouth, and jaw. The hard cast of these features matched his voice. What Kestrel could see of his face was so devoid of kindness or any other humane emotion that it might as well have been carved from stone. He wore little other clothing: a loincloth, boots, and one bracer—all made of red leather that matched the hood—a wide studded steel belt, and a circular medallion on a neckchain. His athletic body, particularly his upper legs, bore menacing green tattoos in a weblike design.

The figure's most striking feature of all was his right hand—or lack thereof. In place of a normal human hand, the man bore a five-fingered reptilian claw. As the mutant human continued to hurl questions at the bound warrior, he scratched and poked the prisoner with his claw to underscore his displeasure.

"Perhaps a little sorcery will loosen your tongue. Shall I turn you into a rodent?"

Kestrel felt the blood drain from her face. This malevolent being was a *sorcerer*?

He struck the prisoner in the back of the head with his claw. The skeleton nearest them mimicked the movement, hitting the captive with the flat of its blade. The mage grabbed the fighter's hair and jerked his head up to look him in the face. "Who sent you here? What were your orders?"

"No one sent us."

"Liar!" He slapped him with his open hand. "You saw what we did to your companions. I'll give you one more day to come to your senses. If you put any value on your pathetic little life, you better start singing." He hit him once more.

Kestrel slowly backed down the corridor. It sounded as if the sorcerer were about to leave, and she didn't care to encounter him in the passageway. After the fight with the naga, she could happily live out the rest of her life without battling another spellcaster, and she intended to try.

She returned to the others. "There's one prisoner, a warrior. He's in chains. Used to be part of a larger group—it sounds like he's the only one left."

Ghleanna gasped. "One of Athan's band?" The half-elf's face brightened

"Possibly. He refused to tell who he works for or what he's doing here. But the—"

"We've got to free him!" Ghleanna said. "Is it Athan? What does he look like?"

"Who cares what *he* looks like? You should see the interrogator! He's some sort of sorcerer, a big guy with lots of tattoos. One of his hands is a claw!"

Corran looked at her as if she'd gone daft. "What do you mean, a claw? Is his hand shriveled?"

"No, I mean the end of his right forearm looks like it belongs on some other creature. Like a bird—or a dragon."

Corran raised his brows. "Oh." He digested this bit of information, then inquired about other guards.

"Six skeletons. The sorcerer sounds like he's leaving soon. I figure if—"

"Once he leaves, I'll take care of the skeletons. Durwyn, you try to break the prisoner's chains." Corran looked to the mages. "Unless one of you can get them open?"

Kestrel clamped her mouth shut. She'd been about to

suggest a plan of her own, but apparently Corran thought he was the only person capable of devising one.

"I'll have to look at how heavy they are, but I'm sure I can break them," Durwyn said.

"Good. Kestrel, you keep watch."

Keep watch? She ground her teeth, biting back a retort. The lowliest apprentice rogue could spring the locks on those irons. She'd mastered the skill as a child, when Quinn hadn't been quite fast enough to outrun some of the city patrols they'd encountered. Corran's arrogance made her want to spit. She hoped the high-handed paladin was the first to die when Durwyn's blows alerted the sorcerer to their activities.

The clang of iron signaled the sorcerer's departure. Kestrel watched as the threatening mage locked the door behind him and walked down the hall—thankful he went in the direction opposite from that where the party waited. Four skeletons stood sentinel outside the cell; the other two presumably remained inside with the captive.

When the sorcerer's light faded from view and they deemed him out of earshot, Corran led the group toward the cell. He held his holy symbol before him. "Leave us be!" he commanded the skeletons.

The creatures backed down the passageway about ten feet, afraid of Corran but apparently unable to abandon their post. The two inside the cell greeted the party at the door, thrusting their blades through the bars, until Corran repelled them, too. They retreated to the far corner of the cell.

"Who's there?" the captive called out.

Ghleanna's face fell. Apparently, the prisoner's voice wasn't the one she'd hoped to hear. "Friends." Despite her obvious disappointment, the half-elf injected a note of cheer into her tone.

Durwyn raised his axe to smash the padlock. Though

Kestrel had planned to let him bang on it til doomsday, she changed her mind: Her own survival depended on the party's. She extended her hand to stay the warrior's arm. "There's a quieter way."

"But Corran said—"

"Yeah, I heard him." Though Durwyn looked to the paladin for guidance, Kestrel didn't waste a second glance on either man. She was the best person for this job and she didn't care what His Holiness had to say about it. She withdrew her lock picks from their beltpouch and went to work on the padlock, which opened easily in her expert hands. Then she defiantly went inside the cell with Corran and the mages. Let Durwyn keep watch.

The captive looked up expectantly as they entered, hope flitting across his broad face. "Are you here to free me?"

"Yes." Kestrel knelt beside him and examined his irons. The shackles, too small for his meaty wrists, chafed the skin but had not yet broken it. "You're not magically bound, are you?"

"No—at least, I don't think so."

"Then I'll have you out of these in no time."

Ghleanna came forward and also knelt at the prisoner's side while Kestrel worked on the lock. "How long have you been held here?" The half-elf smoothed matted brown hair away from a nasty-looking cut on his forehead. "Are you hurt?"

"I'm fine. That sorcerer makes plenty of threats, but so far he's only smacked me around." Kestrel sprung open the wrist irons. He shook his arms to return the blood to his hands. "I believe I've been here two days or so. They knocked me out when they captured me, so I'm not certain."

"They?" Corran prompted from across the cell. He poked his head out the door to signal their success to Durwyn.

"The scarred mages. I'm not exactly sure who they are. Some sort of cult. You can't miss them—they all have one

78 • Carrie Bebris

mutated hand. My companions and I never learned what they were all about, but I think we got too close to finding out."

Kestrel shuddered involuntarily as she worked release the leg irons. There were more of the tattooed, clawed figures?

"Your companions—" Ghleanna began hesitantly. "Was a man named Athan among them?" Though the half-elf used a casual tone, Kestrel noted her grave expression.

The fighter had been watching Kestrel's progress on his chains, but now turned to Ghleanna with upraised brows. "You know Athan?"

Relief washed over her features at his indirect confirmation. She leaned forward excitedly. "I knew several in your band—Allyril and Loren as well."

"We came here to aid your party but arrived too late," Corran added. He offered the prisoner a hand as Kestrel sprung the lock on his leg irons.

Enlightenment spread across the prisoner's features. "You're the guards we tried to contact in Phlan! Thank the gods—there's still hope." He took Corran's hand and pulled himself upright. "My name is Emmeric. We doubted that magical gate would open, but desperation made us try. Did any of my companions survive?"

Corran shook his head. "We found four bodies."

"I didn't recognize any of them as Athan," Ghleanna added.

Kestrel studied the female wizard. The half-elf mentioned this Athan person repeatedly. Even now, her brows were drawn together in concern. Did Elminster's apprentice share more than a passing acquaintance with the missing adventurer? Was he a paramour? Of course— why hadn't Kestrel noticed before? Such a connection would explain the mage's eagerness to jump through that unstable gate and take up the fallen party's mission.

"There were six of us," Emmeric said. "I don't know what happened to Athan. The cultist who's been interrogating me hasn't mentioned another prisoner. I suppose he could have escaped alive, but the way those scarred mages were throwing spells at us, and other cultists—fighters—attacking . . ." He shook his head in resignation. "Even Athan couldn't have held them off forever. I hate to say so, but it's quite possible that there wasn't enough left of him to be found."

A stricken look crossed Ghleanna's features before she turned her face away. Oblivious to the half-elf's distress, the men continued their discussion. Kestrel decided to keep her suspicions to herself for now. The mage's relationship with Athan was her own business.

Emmeric confirmed that the cultists who attacked his party stole the Ring of Calling. While one of the sorcerers interrogated him to learn the ring's command word, a contingent was sent to the Room of Words to do its own research. "Our greatest failure," he said, his shoulders sagging, "was also losing the Gauntlets of Moander to the cult. From what I overheard before being isolated here, the cult's leader—an archmage named Kya Mordrayn—now possesses the gauntlets."

"Is she aware of their power?" Corran asked.

"Most certainly. Whoever these cultists are, they're the force behind the new Pool of Radiance. Knowing that the gauntlets can destroy the pool, Mordrayn keeps them with her at all times, or so I understand."

One of the skeletons in the cell clawed the wall, returning the group's attention to their surroundings. "We shouldn't tarry here," Corran said.

"Where are you headed?" Emmeric asked.

"The Room of Words. We hope to get that Ring of Calling back," Corran said. "Feel up to joining us?"

"I'll lead the way."

❦ ❦ ❦ ❦ ❦

The party found the topmost level of the dungeon crawling with lizard men and orogs. Though Emmeric had warned them en route about the presence of the humanoids, even he was surprised by their numbers. The creatures of both races seemed focused on a single task: systematically looting every abandoned lair in sight.

"Tyr's toenails," Kestrel swore as they observed an orog band from a hidden alcove. The blasphemy earned her a withering look from Corran. Good. She'd meant to goad him. "I've never seen so many humanoids in one place." The orogs looked like bigger, meaner—and unfortunately, more intelligent—orcs.

"I'm surprised the two races are operating as allies," Jarial said.

Emmeric shook his head. "I don't think they are. The orogs, I know, work as mercenaries for the cultists—a couple of them roughed me up to persuade me to talk, but I believe the lizard men were pillaging these caverns long before the cult showed up. They might resent the interlopers."

"I don't think they like each other at all," Durwyn announced. "Look at the way the orogs keep glancing at that group of lizard men over there. And the lizards watch them right back. Then each side whispers among themselves. They're like schoolchildren."

The guard's apt analogy surprised Kestrel. She hadn't credited the big man with such perceptiveness.

"Perhaps we can use their enmity to our advantage," Corran said. "They won't notice us if they're too busy fighting each other."

A smile broke across Emmeric's features. "I like the way you think. What do you have in mind?"

Corran turned to Jarial. "Was that an invisibility spell

you used back there against the naga?" At the mage's nod, he continued. "Can you cast that on any of us, or just yourself?"

"Any creature close enough for me to touch."

"Excellent." The paladin addressed the group. "Here's my plan. Jarial can use his invisibility spell on me. I'll move among the orogs and lizard men, getting close enough that if I speak they will hear me, but staying far enough away to make them think my voice is coming from a rival band. Then I'll utter a few insults to make the two groups turn on each other."

It sounded like a good scheme to Kestrel—it involved no risk on her part, and if it failed, she could spend the rest of this mission reminding Corran that it had been his idea. In moments, an invisible Corran was sneaking toward the nearest group of lizard men to put his plan into action.

"Look, Ugdag! Look at lizard slime." Though Kestrel easily recognized the voice as Corran's, he'd dropped it an octave lower than his natural timbre and covered his blue-blood accent with a gutteral rumble. The disguise proved convincing enough to fool the lizard men. Several of the scaly green beasts snapped their heads toward the orogs, webbed hands gripping the hafts of their spears more tightly. Unable to hear Corran's slurs, the orogs continued about their business.

"Lizards weak," Corran went on. "Hai! Too weak to fight orogs. Too weak to *serve* orogs!"

The reptilian leader of one band hissed. Hatred rimmed his red eyes. "Orogs full of swamp gas!" he cried, drawing himself up to his seven-foot height. His insult drew the attention of every orog in the vicinity. He shook his spear at them. "Orog clods! Shashiki!" The rest of the lizard men raised their spears as well. "Shashiki!"

"Lizard heads water-logged!" one of the orogs shouted in response. He strode forward, clawed toenails clacking on the stone floor, until he stood mere feet away from the lizard leader. Breath issued from his snout in angry bursts. The orog forces lifted their weapons. "Gagh-hai!" he cried, "Grabesh!"

"Graaabesh!" echoed the orogs.

"Shashiki! Kripp-kripp!"

The two races rushed toward one another, each determined to exterminate the other. In the confusion of battle, no one noticed the five visible—and one invisible—adventurers passing through.

☸   ☸   ☸   ☸   ☸

With Emmeric to guide them, they moved swiftly toward the entrance to the House of Gems. They slowed, however, as they passed an ice-covered doorway.

"Hey, that's just like the room we saw below." Durwyn ran his hand over the frosty surface. "With the frozen floating ball inside."

"There's a similar sphere in this room," Emmeric said. "We examined three such rooms—one on each level we explored. We never did figure out their significance."

They wound their way through the corridors until Emmeric stopped before a huge seal inscribed on the stone floor. Two small concentric circles lay within a larger one, with two arcs connecting the inner circles to the circumference. "From the description given us by the elven clerics at the tree shelter, we believed this is the Circle of Mythanthor," Emmeric said. "If so, the glyph protects a hidden door to the city surface."

"The one the Ring of Calling will enable us to access?" Corran's disembodied voice made Kestrel jump. Though she knew he was among them and her sensitive ears could hear his sounds of movement as they traveled, the paladin's continued invisibility unnerved her. She preferred to keep her antagonists, and her allies for that matter, where she could see them. Unfortunately, Jarial said the spell would remain in place for twenty-four hours, unless Corran attacked someone first.

"Yes, that door, but we never found the ring's enabling word," Emmeric said. "I don't know how it might be learned."

"What do you mean?" Ghleanna asked. "It wasn't in the Room of Words?"

Emmeric shook his head. "We searched thoroughly, but without success. When the cultists attacked us, we were on our way to visit the elven clerics to see if they could suggest another place we might look. Of course, during my captivity I never revealed that the command couldn't be found in the Room of Words—I wanted the cult sorcerers to waste as much time as possible conducting their own futile search."

Kestrel rolled her eyes. Could this quest become any more hopeless? "So let me get this straight—the cultists have both the Gauntlets of Moander and the Ring of Calling. Even if we can get the ring back we don't have the password. And if by some miracle we do somehow get to the city surface, we still don't know where the new Pool of Radiance is, or what this cult plans to do with it. Does that about sum it up?"

Ghleanna and Durwyn exchanged glances but did not speak. Emmeric appeared bewildered, but then he didn't know she'd never wanted to join this fool's errand in the first place.

The silence only provoked Kestrel further. "When are you people going to face reality? We can't beat these odds. If we keep this up, we're going to die trying."

Corran's voice penetrated the stillness. "I'd sooner die an honorable death than a cowardly one." She was glad the paladin remained invisible so she couldn't see the holier-than-thou look on his face. Self-righteousness dripped heavily enough from his voice.

"I'd rather not die at all, thank you."

"You have always been free to leave us, Kestrel."

Free to die alone trying to get back to civilization, he meant. It was not a true choice, and the paladin knew it. She glanced from one companion to the next, seeking a glimmer in just one pair of eyes that would reveal a like mind, a dawning of sense in one of these naïve do-gooders. None appeared. Obviously, nothing she said would convince any of them to give up their doomed mission.

"Are you quite finished?" Corran asked.

Oh, how she wished she could see the paladin's face— so she could smack off the smug expression she knew it bore.

❧ ❧ ❧ ❧ ❧

Emmeric, still in the lead, rounded a bend and quickly retreated, nearly bumping into Kestrel. "The entrance to the House of Gems is right around this corner," he said. "The cultists have posted guards, though."

"How many?" came Corran's disembodied voice.

"A cult sorcerer and maybe a half-dozen orogs."

Kestrel sucked in her breath. She'd rather face twice as many orogs than the cult sorcerer. Just the thought of that clawed hand—let alone the spells it could hurl—made her cringe.

"We can handle them," Corran declared. "We should focus most of our effort on the mage—he's the most unpredictable, and if the orogs are mercenaries they might flee once their employer is defeated. Durwyn, you and Emmeric fend off the orogs. Ghleanna, Jarial, and I— and Kestrel, if she cares to participate—will concentrate on the cult sorcerer."

Kestrel was sorely tempted to respond to Corran's barb by "declining to participate," but she let it pass for now. Later, when she had leisure for retaliation, she'd put the condescending paladin in his place.

Everyone readied weapons and spells. As one, they charged around the corner.

The cult sorcerer and his minions paused in momentary shock but soon recovered themselves. "Who are you?" the cultist demanded. "Depart from the House of Gems!"

"I'm afraid we can't do that," Ghleanna said as she released a spell. Three bursts of magical energy raced toward the evil wizard, all striking him in the chest. Before the injured spellcaster could utter more than a foul expletive, Jarial sent one of his magical acid-tipped arrows singing through the air. The missile struck its target squarely between the eyes.

"By the hand of Tyr!" Corran's voice rang out in warning. The paladin materialized as his sword impaled the mage. The cultist sunk to the floor, staring sightlessly through his red leather hood.

Kestrel, unused daggers still in hand, looked at the dead sorcerer in amazement. "Damn, that was fast."

The orogs, who hadn't even had time to close in, froze at a command from their leader. "Hey, you gubuk," he said to Emmeric and Durwyn.

"Gubuk?" Durwyn repeated.

"You soft-skin people. I parley with you. Stand. Stand and talk!"

The fighters turned for guidance to Corran, who nodded. "All right. Let us speak."

The two sides lowered their weapons and approached each other warily. "Orogs swore to protect ugly mage," the orog leader said. "If ugly mage dead, orog honor say, nothing to protect. No need to kill you gubuks. We go now. No hard feelings."

Kestrel had to smile at the creatures' simple logic. And pragmatic loyalties.

"A few questions first," Corran said. "What can you tell us about your employers?" Kestrel almost wished he hadn't asked—the rank smell of the orog leader's matted, hairy hide made her queasy. Or was that his breath?

The orog shrugged and tossed his head. His stringy, greasy hair didn't move. "Ugly mages full of lies. Make deal with orogs. Orogs walk dungeons, yes, find magic items. Mages promise lots of gold. But ugly mages no pay." He blew air through his snout. The noise seemed meant to signal disgust. "Today ugly mages say get small gubuk, put in box, they give big treasure. We take gubuk, put in box. Ugly mages not pay."

Ghleanna frowned. "Who was he—the small gubuk?"

"Garbage man. Lives in wagon—"

"Nottle." Kestrel groaned, shaking her head. Stupid scamp. Hadn't they warned him?

"Nottle, yes. That what ugly mages call gubuk. Oho, garbage man not like box! He talk and talk."

"Where is this box?" Corran asked.

"In old dwarf treasure room," the orog said. "Down in dungeon. Way, way down."

CHAPTER FIVE

"**Y**ou have *got* to be kidding!"

Kestrel couldn't believe her ears. Corran and the others wanted to drop everything to go rescue that hare-brained peddler. "We're here! At the House of Gems. We're right—" she gestured wildly at the door—"here!"

"Nottle's in trouble," Corran stated calmly, as one would address a stubborn child. "We must aid him."

"He's an idiot!" she sputtered. "We warned him about the danger. He ignored us. He deserves whatever he gets."

"Then I guess all of us better hope we never need your help."

Her fingers twitched. She wanted nothing more than to sink one of her daggers between the paladin's shoulder blades. How had he managed to make her the villain of the group? All she'd ever tried to do was inject a dose of reality into their starry-eyed plans to save the world all by themselves.

Emmeric cleared his throat. "Actually, I agree with Kestrel." Corran appeared surprised at the dissent, but the fighter continued. "We can't afford to waste time, not with the Ring of Calling so close."

"Thank you," she said. At least someone else in the party was showing some sense.

"But it isn't close," Corran said. "We're just hoping the cult sorcerers will be in the Room of Words when we get there. They might not be there yet. They might have been there and gone already. We don't know. We *do* know where Nottle is and that he's in danger. As men and women of good conscience—" he shot a pointed look at Kestrel— "we must aid the weak."

"And risk weakening ourselves and the success of our mission in the process?" Emmeric pressed.

"Tyr will look with favor upon us."

Kestrel rolled her eyes. "Tyr can kiss my—"

"Enough." Ghleanna released a heavy sigh. "In the time we have spent debating this, we could have traveled halfway to Nottle's prison. Let us make haste to release him and return here without further delay."

The group headed off. Kestrel, however, tarried. They had not searched the cult sorcerer's body for clues to the cult's activities—or valuables, for that matter—and she, for one, intended to get all she could of both.

Around his neck she found a bronze medallion on a leather strap. Etched into it was a symbol: a ball of flame with sinister eyes hovering above a four-pointed reptilian claw. She removed the medallion and stuffed it in one of her belt pouches, then assessed the rest of his body. The minimal clothing left few places to carry items, but she did find a thin key hanging from a chain on his belt. The end of the key had the image of a circle within an arch engraved on it.

"When I noticed you missing, I knew I'd find you here." Corran's voice did not surprise her. Though she could tell he'd tried to move silently, she'd heard him approach. "Are you nearly finished robbing the dead? The others are waiting."

She did not bother to look up from her task. Her back still to him, she slipped the key into a hidden sheath in her right sleeve. "I happen to be searching for clues to what this cult is all about—something you seem to have forgotten in your haste to save a half-witted halfling from himself."

"Uh-huh."

His tone of sarcastic disbelief pushed her over the edge. She whirled to face him. "What in the Abyss is your problem?"

He regarded her stoically. "My problem?"

She glared at him, her face hot with anger she could no longer hold in check. "You have done nothing but judge and insult me from the moment we met."

"You represent everything I abhor."

"How can I? You don't even know me."

"Are you not a thief? I have yet to encounter one who wasn't a selfish opportunist. Your behavior thus far has done little to change my mind."

Her behavior? She had been selfish to try talking the party out of a quest that amounted to a suicide pact? She had been opportunistic in helping them defeat Preybelish? Sir Sanctimonious would do better to examine his own conduct.

"I have yet to meet a paladin who wasn't judgmental and self-righteous," she snapped. "Seeing only my actions and hearing only my words, you presume to know my motives. Well, you don't know as much as you think you do, Corran D'Arcey."

He raised his brows patronizingly. "No?"

"No. You're a weak leader, a spiritual hypocrite, and a lousy human being." Expecting him to dismiss her reproof as he usually dismissed her, she tried to push her way past him.

He grabbed her arm, forcing her to stay. "It reflects poor breeding, Kestrel, to walk away in the middle of a conversation. On what do you base those criticisms?"

Why did his insults still hold the power to rankle? Their frequency should have rendered her immune by now. "You've appointed yourself the leader of this mission, yet you allow your prejudice to cloud your decisions, ignoring or underusing my skills to the detriment of the party." Despite her ire, her voice held steady. "For someone who professes humility in the service of his god, you have demonstrated precious little of it among your fellow mortals. And for someone who seeks to better understand the ways of the divine, you know very little about the human condition. I doubt very much that the third son of Baron Whoever-the-hell has ever wanted for anything or can comprehend what desperation can drive a person to do."

There—she'd said it all, and her heart hammered in her chest with the rush of having finally confronted him. To her delight, he looked as if he'd been slapped. She shook her arm loose, turned her back on him, and went to join the others.

❀   ❀   ❀   ❀   ❀

With minimal travel time, the party descended to the dungeon's lowest level and found the old dwarven treasury. The stone door stood ajar, its engraved glyph—a circle within an arch—desecrated. Through the graffiti, however, Kestrel noted that the original symbol matched that on the key she'd taken from the dead cult sorcerer.

A muffled voice, unmistakably Nottle's, came from within, promising riches in exchange for release. "Gems . . . I got a nice collection o'gems. Or if it's weapons ye want—"

"Oh, stuff a sock in it," responded another voice, this one gruff and just inside the door. A few low chuckles indicated that several men stood guard.

Durwyn nocked an arrow. After the surprisingly easy defeat of the mage upstairs, they'd decided to launch more conventional missiles during their initial volley and hold Jarial and Ghleanna's magic in reserve until they saw how many opponents they faced. Emmeric, armed with Corran's sword, fingered the hilt impatiently, eager to strike back at the cult for slaying his companions.

The paladin gripped his warhammer. He had not spoken to Kestrel since their confrontation. When she'd suggested that she sneak into the room after combat began—in an attempt to disguise their number and attack one of the guards from behind—a shrug had been the only indication that he'd heard her.

At Corran's nod, Durwyn stepped into the doorway and fired, a second shot quickly chasing the first. "One down—five more!" He jumped out of the way to let Corran and Emmeric charge past, then grabbed his axe and followed them into battle. Next, Ghleanna and Jarial entered.

Kestrel withdrew her twin daggers from her boots and waited in the corridor as sounds of combat erupted. She counted to sixty, then slipped inside.

It was a huge room, at least one hundred feet on each side, filled with chests, crates, and emptied sacks. Had Kestrel the time, her thief's mind would have loved to calculate the riches the chamber had held during Myth Drannor's peak. Now a more serious task occupied her attention.

The three warriors had engaged five guards in combat. A sixth guard lay on the floor, one of Durwyn's arrows through his heart. At first Kestrel thought their opponents were cult sorcerers, for they all had claws for right hands and wore red leather boots, loincloths, and bracers. These adversaries, however, had no hoods to hide their heads and shoulders, and she gasped at the sight of their deformed features. Their skin, though still flesh-colored, resembled a scaly reptilian hide from the tops of their heads to their upper chests, and their eyes burned red with battlelust. Where the scarred mages had tattoos to broadcast their cult affiliation, the fighters had three razor-sharp blades piercing each thigh. The guards wielded wicked-looking double-bladed halberds with spikes at their heads and hooks at their bases.

Durwyn battled two of the cultists. His second arrow protruded through the shoulder of one. He landed a blow on the arm of his injured foe, then managed to parry the other's strike. Corran also fought two opponents. His warhammer easily deflected the attacks that came his way, but he appeared unable to gain the offensive. Emmeric, though fighting with an unfamiliar weapon, seemed to be holding his own.

Ghleanna gazed balefully at one of Corran's adversaries, her fingers tracing ancient runes in the air. A moment later the sorceress uttered a single command word. The cult fighter shrieked, but Kestrel could discern no physical damage. His blows, however, lost their precision. When Corran's other foe caused the paladin to shift his position, the spellbound cult fighter swung wildly, apparently trying to hit anything within reach of his weapon.

He's blind, Kestrel realized. With one of Corran's opponents thus disabled, she darted around the room's perimeter to aid Durwyn. As she moved, she kept one eye on the unfolding combat.

Emmeric, gaining familiarity with the weight and balance of Corran's sword, backed his opponent against an open trunk. The cult fighter's calves bumped into the chest, knocking him off balance. As he struggled to regain his equilibrium, Emmeric seized the moment and scored a hit. The thrust opened a deep gash in the cultist's shoulder. Undeterred by the blood oozing down his arm, the fighter lunged forward to return the blow. Emmeric anticipated the strike but not the handful of diamond dust the fighter grabbed from the open trunk with his free hand and threw in his face. The distraction lasted only a moment, but that was long enough for the cultist to open a wound in Emmeric's sword arm.

A glance at Durwyn indicated that the large warrior still managed to fend off both of his opponents, so Kestrel elected to aid the injured Emmeric. She maneuvered behind the cult fighter, planning to stab him in the back. Just before moving in for her strike, she glanced toward Jarial and Ghleanna in the doorway to make sure they saw her and didn't inadvertently direct any magical attacks her way.

Her heart stopped.

Behind the door stood a hooded figure with the green tattoos of the cult sorcerers. The wizard's sinister gaze focused on Emmeric, his hands gesturing rapidly as his mouth formed unheard words.

"Cult sorcerer!" she shouted.

Her warning came too late. A crackle of electricity rent the air as a lightning bolt blasted from the wizard's fingertips to strike Emmeric. The bolt struck the fighter with so much force that he flew through the air and into the wall a good eighty feet away, the smell of burning flesh following in his wake. His scorched body dropped to the floor.

Kestrel took the dagger she'd meant to plunge between the fighter's shoulder blades and instead hurled it at the cult sorcerer. It buried itself in his stomach. The evil sorcerer looked up, surprised—but not stopped. As blood welled around the weapon and ran down his legs to pool on the floor, the cultist muttered the words of a new incantation. His gaze never left Kestrel.

Movement to her left, however, wrested her attention to a closer opponent. Emmeric's foe, alerted to her presence by the dagger that had sailed past his ear, now turned his attacks on her. She parried his blows with her other dagger, staggering under the force of his strikes. When a shout from one of the other cultists distracted him momentarily, she seized the opportunity to grab her club.

Even with Quinn's familiar baton, the cultist's hits came too quickly for her to manage any offensive blows. He laughed mockingly when she tried to strike back twice— and both times nearly lost her right arm to the cult fighter's superior weaponmastery. Meanwhile, she braced herself for the sorcerer's spell. When would it come? She dared not avert her gaze from the hideous visage of the cult fighter, even for a second.

Suddenly, a flash of orange light silhouetted her adversary. Beyond the fighter, a sheet of flames fanned the cult sorcerer. One of Jarial's spells. The evil spellcaster cried out in agony just as three bursts of magical energy materialized and sped toward her.

Searing pain tore through her right thigh. The wound burned, its sting worse than any inflicted by a mundane weapon. Kestrel sucked in her breath, waiting for two more.

Jarial's magic, however, had distracted the cult sorcerer at the moment he took aim. The other two conjured missiles hit her opponent, who yelped as both projectiles caught him in the back. She seized the momentary advantage and slashed his throat.

As the cultist sank to the ground, she quickly took stock of the situation around her. Durwyn had just felled one of his opponents. The other gasped for breath and swung his halberd with undisciplined desperation. The blinded fighter lay in a puddle of his own blood. Corran's remaining foe was backed against a wall. The three mages appeared locked in a sorcerer's contest, racing to see who could cast the next spell.

Kestrel hurled her second dagger at the cult sorcerer. The next spell would not be his.

The dagger caught the evil wizard in the calf. Kestrel muttered an oath under her breath. She was injured and tired. Her aim had been poor. The strike provided enough distraction, however, that the cult sorcerer lost his concentration, and Ghleanna completed her spell first. Bursts of magical energy hissed toward the injured spellcaster, at last finishing him off. Durwyn and Corran defeated their foes at about the same time, the paladin landing a blow on the head of his opponent and the warrior removing the head of his.

In the ensuing silence, they all took a moment to catch their breaths. Kestrel glanced around the chamber warily, half-expecting another cult sorcerer to leap out from the shadows. She couldn't even look at Emmeric's incinerated, broken body lying in a heap across the room. Gods, but she hated wizards.

Her leg burned where the cult sorcerer's missile had hit it. She bent over to examine the injury, anticipating a bloody open wound. Fortunately, her armor had slowed down the missile and thus prevented it from entering too deep. The magical energy appeared to have cauterized the area. Her thigh hurt like hell, but it would heal.

A single voice broke the stillness. "Uh . . . anyone still out there?" Nottle's muffled words came from a nearby cluster of strongboxes and crates.

"Yes, Nottle," Corran replied.

"Thanks be to Yondalla! I'm gittin' cramped in here. Lemme out!"

Kestrel left to the others the task of releasing the foolish halfling, instead making her way around ransacked coffers and trunks to Emmeric. Nottle had cost them a valuable comrade-in-arms and her a potential ally against Corran's tyranny. Only Emmeric had agreed that they could not afford this detour, a point he'd lost his life proving. Would the others listen to reason now, or would she eventually end up as dead as the fighter?

She tried to walk normally but found herself hobbling. Each step made the wound throb. Damn that sorcerer to the Abyss! Damn Nottle! Damn Corran, too—she blamed the paladin for the fact that they were down here at all.

Until she reached Emmeric's remains, she harbored a tiny, unrealistic hope that the warrior somehow clung to life. That hope evaporated as soon as she got a close look at him. His body was burned so badly that it scarcely looked human. Little flesh yet clung to his charred frame. She swallowed the bile that rose in her throat.

Movement behind her indicated that someone had followed her. Two someones, judging from the familiar sound of their footsteps. Corran and Ghleanna.

"Poor Emmeric," the half-elf whispered as she got a look the fighter. "I'd thought maybe . . ."

"Yeah, me too." Kestrel said.

The two women fell silent as Corran knelt over their fallen companion. The paladin gently untangled Emmeric's skeletal limbs and repositioned his body so that it appeared to rest more comfortably. Then he rummaged through a few open chests until he found a velvet cloth to drape over the fighter. Corran never spoke as he tended to Emmeric's remains. Did he feel guilty for dragging them down here, to the warrior's demise? Kestrel hoped so.

From the conversation drifting toward her, it sounded as if Jarial and Durwyn were having difficulty releasing Nottle from the strongbox in which the cultists had secured him. She sighed and limped toward them, her fingers already reaching for her lockpicking tools. Could any of these people survive without her?

"I'll smash it open with my axe," Durwyn said as she approached.

Nottle squawked. "An' smash my head, too?"

"That won't be necessary." Kestrel pulled the appropriate pick from her pouch. She tried to squat in front of the chest, but her injured leg screamed in protest. She wound up simply plunking her bottom down onto the floor. Before touching the lock, she looked up at Jarial. "I assume you've checked this for magical traps?"

"I didn't find any." The mage eyed her askance. "Are you injured?"

"I'm fine." Kestrel examined the lock for signs of mundane surprises. It appeared to be a simple padlock. The only unusual feature was a glyph engraved into the body of the lock. "Damn," she muttered. She'd seen a padlock like this once before—Quinn had nearly lost a finger to the blade that had sprung out of it. Different icon, but she'd bet it worked on the same principle.

Jarial leaned over her shoulder. "What?" Durwyn also bent down to get a closer look.

"I'm guessing this symbol's here for a reason. Use anything but the proper key to open it and something very bad happens." She glanced to Durwyn. "You did check the dead cultists for keys, didn't you?"

A sheepish expression crossed his face. "Uh . . ."

She rubbed her temples. "Why don't you do that before we go any further?" Durwyn immediately started rifling the corpses. Not much of a thinker, the warrior was great at following orders.

Nottle rapped on the lid of the strongbox. "What's takin' so long?"

"We're trying to make sure no one else gets killed saving your foolish hide," she said. The halfling sure had an irritating little voice. "You getting enough air through those airholes?"

"Yeah."

"Shut up or that will change."

Nottle fell silent. As Durwyn and Jarial searched the cultist's bodies, Kestrel studied the engraving on the padlock. She'd seen that circle and arch image before. It matched the glyph on the treasury door—and on the key she'd taken from the cult sorcerer upstairs.

"Never mind, boys. I think I've found it." She withdrew the key from her sleeve, and discovered that it slipped easily into the lock. The clasp sprung open. A moment later, the peddler was free.

"Finally! I thought I'd never git outta there." The halfling stretched his short limbs to their fullest extent.

"We told you this place was dangerous, Nottle," Corran said as he and Ghleanna rejoined the group.

"Yeah, I know. I couldn't resist. Scavenging's in my blood." He leaned toward Kestrel. "Surely you, m'dear, understand the lure of an old dwarven treasury? I suspect we're kindred spirits."

She didn't deny the allure but preferred to think she had more sense. She nodded toward the dead cultists. "I see this is a great place for making new friends."

He wrinkled his nose in distaste. "Nah, they weren't friendly at all. 'Specially when I wouldn't join their club."

Corran's brow rose. "They invited you to join their organization?"

"Well, not exactly—said I could make a 'great contribution,' but I kinda got the feelin' they were all in on some joke I didn't understan'. Not that I'd want t'belong to somethin' called the Cult of the Dragon. I don't like dragons. Though they have got nice treasure. Dragons, that is—I dunno about these folks."

Kestrel and the others exchanged glances, but no one seemed familiar with the cult's name.

"Did they tell you anything about their activities?" Corran asked.

"Nah. But I did overhear a thing or two. Once they shut me up in the box, they sometimes forgot about me and talked a little too freely. Since ye rescued me and all, I'll tell ye what they said without chargin' my usual price for information."

Kestrel smiled thinly. "How generous of you."

Nottle appeared not to notice her sarcasm. "These cult folks, they're the ones who killed yer friends the other day. They're also the ones who drove the alhoon and phaerimm outta this part o'the city."

"Their sorcerers are that powerful?"

"Their leader is—he's a dracolich!"

A shudder raced up Kestrel's spine. If an undead dragon was behind all these events, their quest was even more doomed than she'd previously imagined.

Durwyn scratched his head. "I thought Emmeric said the cult leader was an archmage. Some woman—Kya something."

"Perhaps they're working cooperatively," Corran suggested. "Nottle, did you overhear anything else?"

"Somethin' 'bout using some kinda pool t'make the dracolich stronger than he already is."

Everyone but Nottle exchanged apprehensive glances. "Does the pool have a name?" Ghleanna asked.

Nottle shrugged. "Don't know. They jus' kept calling it 'the pool.' It *was* a little hard t'hear from where I was sittin', ye know."

Jarial cleared his throat. "Can we talk about this en

route? Now that Nottle is free, we shouldn't tarry."

Corran nodded. "Jarial's right. This news only increases the urgency of our mission."

"Emmeric?" Durwyn asked.

"At rest," Corran replied. "Let us finish what he and his companions started."

⊛ ⊛ ⊛ ⊛ ⊛

Following a shortcut Nottle knew, they passed yet another ice-covered doorway on their way back to the Room of Words. "I sure wish we knew what those frozen rooms were about," Durwyn said.

"Perhaps they're related to the Rohnglyn," Nottle said.

"The what?"

The peddler shrugged. "Accordin' to rumor, some kinda magic transportation use t'connect all four levels of the dwarven dungeons. Rohnglyn, the elves called it. Years back, when the alhoon was still layin' claim t'these halls, they all got in some big feud an'one o'the beasts put an ice charm on the Rohnglyn. Froze the thing right in place, or so I hear."

"This device," Corran asked, "it would enable us to move between levels more quickly?"

"Instantly. So they say, anyway."

Corran pulled out his warhammer. "Care to help me make a few ice cubes, Durwyn?"

The two warriors smashed their way through the ice, revealing a room identical to the one they'd seen before—with one notable exception. The rune on the floor lay covered with ice stalagmites infused with colored lights. Elaborate icicles, many thick as tree trunks, hung from the ceiling, some of them fused to the lower ice formations in great columns of ice. As in the other room, a frozen golden sphere floated at about waist level in the center of the circular pattern.

Ghleanna tapped one of the ice formations with her staff. "Solid."

"Can you free it from the alhoon's spell?" Corran asked.

"We can try." She raised a brow at Jarial. "What do you think? Should we attempt to dispel the magic or counter it?"

"The alhoon are powerful spellcasters. I don't know if either of us has the experience to dispel such strong sorcery." Jarial circled the rune, running his hands along some of the icicles. "It looks like the sphere could withstand a fireball, which would probably melt some of the ice. . . ."

Ghleanna nodded pensively. "Perhaps if we all stood outside the chamber, a lightning bolt could break through the thicker ice formations."

As the two discussed additional possibilities, Kestrel noticed Durwyn shifting impatiently. The warrior concentrated on the icicle nearest him, his fingers absently stroking the haft of his axe.

Corran joined in the mages' discussion. "If you weaken the ice with your spells, I'm sure Durwyn and I could then—"

"Enough talk. We waste time!" Durwyn raised his battle-axe and swung at the closest icicle. The force of the blow sent a huge crack running along the ice from top to bottom. As it weakened, its center seemed to take on a bluish hue. Durwyn struck again, this time breaking through the formation. Embedded in the jagged layers of ice rested a thin blue shard that twinkled in the torchlight.

They all moved closer for a better look. "Well, I'll be pickled," Nottle said. "What do ye suppose that is?"

Jarial furrowed his brow in concentration. "It looks like . . . " He extended a hand, running his fingers along the crystal's edge. "It is. This is an ice knife, identical to one Ozama often conjured through spellcasting. Only hers wasn't blue."

"Borea's Blood," Nottle whispered.

"You've heard of it?"

The halfling's eyes glowed as he regarded the ice sliver almost reverently. "It's said that Borea's Blood—" He stopped suddenly, as if remembering himself. His eyes regained their usual mercenary glint, and he shrugged casually. "Jest a blue knife, that's all. Nothin' you folks would wanna lug around with ye." He reached toward it. "Here, I'll jes—"

"I don't think so." Kestrel batted away his arm. Obviously the knife had some value if the peddler took interest. "I'm sure lugging this around won't prove a burden to us at all." She grabbed the crystal and tugged, expecting it to remain frozen in place. To her surprise, the blue knife slid from the icicle as smoothly as a sword from its scabbard.

The moment Borea's Blood cleared its icy sheath, every shard of ice in the room immediately disappeared. The large ice formations vanished, while the broken chunks on the floor melted into small puddles. Only the blue crystal remained unchanged, resting coolly in the palm of Kestrel's hand. Above the rune, the colored lights danced like faeries on Midsummer Night.

"You did it—you unfroze the Rohnglyn," Durwyn said.

She regarded the fighter. Had he not taken matters into his own hands, they might have wasted an hour debating strategy. She was developing new respect for the quiet but dedicated warrior. "No, it was your no-nonsense approach that found the crystal in the first place."

At the compliment, the corners of Durwyn's mouth twisted in a self-conscious half-smile. He appeared unused to praise. "Now that it's thawed, how do you suppose it works?"

As in the room they'd entered earlier, the far wall of this chamber held a carving of four diamonds stacked right on top of each other, with a small gem—an opal—in the bottom-most point. Kestrel, Ghleanna, and Corran studied the pattern, while Jarial, Durwyn, and Nottle examined the floating golden sphere and the lights.

"Four diamonds, four dungeon levels," Ghleanna said finally. "I'm guessing the gem in that pattern indicates the current position of the Rohnglyn. The bottom diamond is the bottom level of the dungeon, and so on. Perhaps it's simply a matter of moving the gem to the level we want to reach."

"That tells it where we want to travel," Corran said, "but how do we activate the device?"

"I think that's what this sphere is for," Jarial said, poking at the globe. "Maybe once the opal is repositioned, we push or rotate the sphere."

"We'll never figure it out just standing here. Let's give it a try." Kestrel pulled the gem out of the wall and moved it up to the next vertex. "If Ghleanna's theory is correct, we should wind up one level above, in the room we entered before."

They all entered the dancing lights and moved to the center of the rune. Jarial reached toward the globe. "Ready?"

The moment he touched the golden sphere, the lights spun wildly about the perimeter of the rune, circling a half dozen times before returning to their usual state. The party waited expectantly, but nothing more happened.

"Maybe it's not as easy as we thought," Durwyn said.

Kestrel went back to study the diamond pattern again. She frowned in concentration. "Perhaps we need to do more than merely reposition the ruby."

"Ruby?" Ghleanna said. "It was an opal, was it not?"

Kestrel glanced at the sorceress in surprise. "You're right—the ruby was in the first room." She turned back to the pattern, now noticing the tiny scratch marks at the bottom of the pattern. "Here are the marks I made trying to pry it out."

Corran walked to the doorway and peered into the corridor. "Sure enough. We're back on the third level."

"Ha! That's a pretty good trick," Nottle said. "Gettin' around the dungeons will be a piece o'cake now." The halfling fairly skipped toward the door. "I'm gonna check on my wagon. See you folks later." He nearly exited before turning around once more. "Oh—if ye ever git tired o' toting around Borea's Blood, ye know where t'find me."

They watched him depart. "Let's get back to the House of Gems," Corran said.

Kestrel plucked the ruby out of the wall and inserted it in the topmost vertex. She reentered the dancing lights and nodded at Jarial. "Go ahead."

The wizard touched the golden sphere. This time the lights raced so quickly and flashed so brightly that Kestrel squeezed her eyes shut. She opened them a moment later, expecting to find herself in another identical room.

Not in the belly of a dragon.

CHAPTER SIX

The unpredictable Rohnglyn had landed them in an enormous oval-shaped hall. Elaborate murals and mosaics of dragons covered the walls, some studded with precious stones to depict gem dragons. Small round windows served as the dragons' eyes, allowing the first sunlight they'd seen in days to spill into the room. The hall's beams and columns were intricately carved in the same motif. Blue, red, green, and black dragon tails spiraled white pillars, while silver dragon claws cradled glowing orbs at fixed intervals along the walls. On the ceiling, two great wyrms—one red, one gold—were locked in eternal combat.

Corran fixed Kestrel with an annoyed glare. "This isn't the entrance to the House of Gems. What in blazes did you do?"

"Nothing! I just moved the gem to the top—I'm hardly an expert on this Rohnglyn thing, you know," she retorted.

"Obviously."

Durwyn turned in a slow circle, taking in their surprising new surroundings. "Where are we?"

Good question, Kestrel thought. Woven among all the dragon images were mysterious-looking runes and intricate knotwork patterns. The gilded railing along a second-floor balcony featured the most elaborate of these patterns. Similar designs were also set into the floor. Two rows of statues flanked the main walkway. These depicted sorcerers—some human, some elven, some of other races—all of whom appeared powerful, wise, and formidable.

"Wherever we are, this is a place of great magic," Ghleanna murmured. "Can you feel it surround us?"

After witnessing Emmeric's brutal death, magic was the last thing Kestrel wished to be surrounded by.

"Clearly, we've left the dungeons and are now above ground," Jarial said. "I wonder if we have stumbled into the Speculum—the old wizards' guildhall. When Ozama and I first came to Myth Drannor we saw the building perched near the castle in the city's Heights. It is shaped like a giant dragon curled around an egg. The hall we now stand in is large enough to constitute most of the dragon's body."

"It's so—still," Kestrel said quietly. Something about the room inhibited speech, making her reluctant to use any but muted tones.

"I imagine the protective magics cast in and around this hall long ago have kept it safe from the desecration overtaking other parts of the city," Jarial responded.

Durwyn stepped off the Rohnglyn rune. "As long as we're here, let's look around. Maybe the wizards left something behind that can help us."

Kestrel let the others advance well into the room before she left the security of the Rohnglyn, not needing to look at the familiar scar on her wrist to recall the nasty surprises sorcerers could leave lying in wait. The injury in her thigh served as ample reminder of magical treachery, though the pain had subsided enough that she no longer favored the leg.

Once she started exploring the hall, however, she became caught up in the striking architecture and detailed renderings of dragon and sorcerer alike. Each depicted wizard appeared frozen in the process of casting a spell. An image crossed her mind of all the statues suddenly coming to life and the sorcery that would be unleashed. She shuddered. Thank the Lord of Shadows, they were all just sculptures.

At the end of the hall stood an empty pedestal, apparently still waiting patiently for the statue it would never receive. It stood about three feet high and had a wider base than the others, with recesses curling around its side that looked almost like steps. Curious about the view the elevated height would afford, she used the footholds to climb up.

The moment her foot touched the top of the pedestal, a series of chimes sounded. The musical notes so startled her that she nearly toppled off, but she caught her balance just as a wavering image appeared before her. The image solidified into a large two-dimensional floating oval mirror. Kestrel wrinkled her brow as her reflection came into focus. She looked like someone who'd spent the past several days traipsing through dusty old dungeons and fighting for survival. What she wouldn't give for a bath!

Corran, Durwyn, Jarial, and Ghleanna all hastened to the pedestal. "How did you do that?" Durwyn asked.

Kestrel glanced down at the warrior. "I don't know—I just climbed up on the pedestal and this mirror appeared."

When she looked back at the mirror, she found her reflection fading until the surface became completely black. "Hey, what—"

A new image appeared, this one an unfamiliar face. It was a woman's visage: piercing ice-blue eyes set under perfectly sculpted brows, angular cheekbones, and blood-red lips. Her honey-colored tresses were wound into a towering coil studded with gems. Her neck and shoulders were bare.

Durwyn let out a low whistle. "Wow. Who is that?"

Even Kestrel had to concede the magnetism of the woman's beauty. It captured one's attention and would not let go, seducing male and female viewers alike. Yet Kestrel sensed something predatory about the unknown woman's charm, as if the stranger were a spider inviting her into its web. The thief's collarbone tingled, a sensation that surprised her—in all the danger she'd faced since coming to Myth Drannor, she'd not felt the intuitive warning signal until she gazed at this woman's face.

As they watched, more of the stranger's body became visible. The woman reclined against some kind of dark red, leathery, curved bolster or throne, her limbs carelessly draped over its sides. She wore a red leather bodysuit slit to the navel—and little else. Body piercings on her thighs marred the otherwise smooth lines of her long legs, which ended in a pair of high-heeled red leather boots. The piercings resembled those Kestrel had seen on the cult fighters. Was this woman involved in the Cult of the Dragon?

Soft wavering light emanated from a source Kestrel couldn't see, casting a warm but eerie glow on the white skin of the woman's face and arms. The mysterious figure pensively gazed at the source of the glow.

Pelendralaar, said a husky female voice, barely audible above a gurgling hiss-babble in the background. Though the enchantress's mouth had not formed the word, Kestrel was sure it had come from her.

"Child," boomed a deep masculine voice. A bright flash of orange light bathed the woman's face, then diminished. *The Pool has reached the port at Hillsfar.* She closed her eyes and tossed her head back, exposing the curve of her throat. Her lips formed a slow, wicked smile. *Can you hear the screams?*

Her unseen companion offered only a deep rumble in response. More flashes of orange lit her face. The woman's eyes opened. She turned her head and sat forward, gazing up and off to the side. *Something troubles you. Speak.*

"They are not fools," said the thunderous voice. "They will send their heroes."

The seductress nestled into her seat once more as she turned her gaze back to the source of the wavering glow. The view broadened, revealing a body of amber fluid lapping the ground nearby. *They will meet the Mythal. Our Mythal.* Another smile, this one more sinister than the last, spread across her features. She lifted her right arm and regarded her hand—not visible in the mirror—as if inspecting her manicure. *And then they will meet you.*

At the word "you," the view expanded. Kestrel gasped, a sick feeling spreading through her stomach. The woman had no right hand but an enormous reptilian claw, far larger and sharper than any they had seen on the cultists. She stroked her razorlike talons along the curve of her throne, eliciting a deep, low groan from the mysterious masculine voice. A moment later, Kestrel saw that the sorceress sat not against an object of mortal construction but a great red dragon. The beast, however, looked horribly withered and disfigured. Its skin was dried and tight against its too-visible bones.

It was not a dragon, Kestrel realized, but the animated

corpse of a dragon. The creature issued a final rumble, flames darting from its mouth.

The scene shrank, growing smaller and smaller until it appeared to be contained in a glass sphere the size of a child's ball. The sphere rested on a wooden stand atop a circular table. The glare of the dragon's flames illuminated several figures gathered around the crystal ball. Of them, Kestrel recognized only Elminster.

"Our heroes have already done well, taking up the fallen party's mission as their own. If only we could send additional help . . . " the great mage said with a weary voice. "But the corrupted Mythal prevents us. They must seize the power of the Mythal for themselves. Otherwise, Moonsea is lost, and the Dragon Coast, and with them all our hopes."

The other figures nodded in assent as the mirror faded to darkness, then disappeared altogether. Kestrel remained, unmoving, on the pedestal. A long minute passed before anyone spoke.

"I believe we've just had our first glimpse of Mordrayn," Corran asked.

"And her pet dracolich. What did she call him—Pelendralaar?" Ghleanna said. "It seems Emmeric and Nottle were both correct about the cult's leadership. The two are working together."

Kestrel hopped off the pedestal so she could converse more easily with her companions. "Mordrayn said the pool has reached Mulmaster. Do you think she means another Pool of Radiance has appeared, like the one in Phlan?"

"Elminster suspected the Phlan pool was an offshoot of a larger, main pool here—not separate bodies of water, but somehow linked." Ghleanna leaned against a statue of the notorious wizard himself, captured in bronze unleashing one of his human spells in the elven hall. "When he left

Phlan, he was on his way to Shadowdale to investigate tales of another offshoot there. If the pool has indeed reached Mulmaster, there is no telling how many other cities it might threaten. We must stop its spread, or we might not have homes to return to."

The mage's words chilled Kestrel. Until this point, she'd believed the Pool of Radiance was a menace confined to Myth Drannor and Phlan. She'd wanted to walk away and let those cities solve their own problems, figuring she'd just start over in a new town far from the Moonsea. But if the pool could replicate itself anywhere, was there a safe place in all Faerûn?

Durwyn shook his head as if to clear it of confusion. "I don't understand—how can the Pool of Radiance in Myth Drannor send tendrils of itself to cities tens of leagues away from here?"

"Maybe it has something to do with the Mythal," Corran said. "Beriand and Faeril told us it has been corrupted, and Mordrayn and Pelendralaar spoke of it as being theirs." He turned to Ghleanna and Jarial. "Suppose the cult gained control of it somehow. Could it enable the Pool of Radiance to expand in such a manner?"

The two sorcerers exchanged grim glances. "The Mythal is woven of ancient magic," Ghleanna responded. "Such powerful sorcery holds possibilities we cannot even conceive."

Kestrel glanced around the hall. They stood in a place of powerful sorcery, after all—perhaps the answer could be found right here. The runes on the walls were indecipherable to her, but maybe Ghleanna or Jarial could read them. Too, they had not yet explored the second floor. She peered up at the balcony. Several rows of bookcases, extending back as far as she could see, rested about two yards away from the railing. Scrolls and tomes neatly lined their shelves. A library? She pointed toward the balcony.

"The second floor seems to have a lot of scrolls and books. There might be a history of the Mythal or something."

They climbed the stairway. The moment they reached the top, however, a cold breeze blew over them. Out of nowhere, a figure materialized.

Rather, almost materialized. A solid wooden throne appeared, but the man seated on it remained translucent, the back of the chair showing through his form. Kestrel sucked in her breath. *A ghost.* Her heartbeat accelerated, adding to the sick feeling that still lingered in the pit of her stomach.

Weren't ghosts supposed to appear the way they did in life? If so, this man—an old elven sorcerer, from the look of his ornate robes and headdress—must have been ancient when he died. The spirit's gaunt face, sunken eyes, and bony limbs lent him a skeletal mien. He rested on a cobweb-covered oak throne as gnarled as he and seemed so deeply settled into it that Kestrel wondered if he had risen from it in centuries. On his lap he held a gold bowl filled with water, and his right hand rested on a grinning skull with glowing red eyes.

The spirit did not seem to notice the party. "Now foul water freezes the guardians," he muttered as he stared into the bowl. His voice had a tired, forlorn quality to it, as of one who has lived too long and seen too much, for whom immortality is more a curse than a blessing.

Kestrel and the others exchanged glances. She was in favor of backing right down the staircase without a word, but Ghleanna stepped forward. Before the half-elf could speak, however, the skull's eyes flashed.

"Do not disturb the Master."

Kestrel jumped. The skull had spoken!

"Here is the wise counsel you seek." The skull's feminine voice carried an eerie resonance, sending further chills down Kestrel's spine.

"How do you know that we—" Ghleanna began.

"Your coming has been foreseen."

Kestrel looked from the skull back to its "master." The ghostly wizard was a diviner, then—a seer. She had known her share of charlatans who earned their living telling fortunes for the gullible, but she'd never encountered anyone with the genuine power to foresee the future.

"Master Caalenfaire instructs you to seek out the spirit of the dwarf lord Harldain Ironbar," the skull said. "You will find him beyond the Circle of Mythan—but hold! You do not have the Ring of Calling!"

"No, we yet seek it," Ghleanna said. Kestrel didn't know how the sorceress had the nerve to address the skull, or even to stand so close to Caalenfaire.

"Master! Despair and woe! Your prediction has gone awry."

The ancient diviner stirred, but still appeared entranced. He never lifted his gaze from the scrying bowl on his lap. "What? Volun, what is this you say? Where are they? I cannot see them. I cannot hear them. The fools!"

"They are talibund, Master. They have left the Path."

Kestrel glanced at her companions to see whether they understood this conversation any better than she. The spellcasters appeared pensive, as did Corran. Durwyn looked absolutely bewildered.

"Volun, what is this 'Path' of which you speak?" Ghleanna asked. Kestrel noted that she gripped her staff tightly. Perhaps the sorceress wasn't as comfortable talking with the disembodied skull as she wanted the pair to believe.

"Master Caalenfaire had worked out a destiny for you—a path you should walk. For the eventual good of Myth Drannor, if not your own." Volun's eyes flashed rapidly. "Instead you have become talibund. Now you walk your own path, which none can see. May Tymora help us! This is an unsettling turn."

Kestrel edged closer to Jarial. "What's this word the skull keeps using—'talibund'?"

"I don't know," he whispered back.

"Talibund. The Veiled Ones," Volun said. "What soothsayers call those whose destinies cannot be foretold."

Ghleanna gripped her staff tighter and took a tentative step closer to the skull. "Is the warrior Athan talibund? Can your master say whether he still walks the path of the living?"

"Athan's path became veiled before even yours," Volun replied. "Master does not know his fate."

Disappointment flickered across the half-elf's face. With each dead end in her inquiries about the warrior, Ghleanna seemed to lose a little more of her spirit.

"Look, Volun," Caalenfaire said. "I have captured them in my bowl once more. Or at least, their shadows—the Veiled Ones will be writ into the Song of Faerûn."

"*Now* what is he talking about?" Kestrel muttered. Her nerves were too frayed to withstand much more of this mysterious speech.

"The Song of Faerûn is the great tale of the world, sung by the Bard of Kara-Tur at the close of the millennium. Master, tell us more about the Song!"

"Listen, Volun, and be amazed."

From the scrying bowl drifted the notes of a lute, soon joined by a feminine voice of such sweet perfection that Kestrel momentarily forgot her fear.

> *In Cormanthor did mage Mordrayn*
> *Speak spells of greed in Words of flame.*
> *With poison troth she soon unmade*
> *Proud treasure of the Silver Blade,*
> *And by her side, Pelendralaar,*
> *Their minds as one, come from afar;*
> *Dark creatures drown the city bright,*

The dragon's kin, the elf of night.
The Pool! The Pool! It grows, and yet
One small band against it set.

The bard continued the song, but her voice faded from hearing. Kestrel felt her anxiety returning.

"This is not what we had foreseen, Master! It gives me hope."

Durwyn stepped forward excitedly. "What happens next? How does the song end?"

Caalenfaire, apparently back in his scrying trance, did not answer. Durwyn looked at the skull hopefully. "Volun?"

"I will not tell you," Volun replied. "No mortals should glimpse their future. It is never happy enough, or long enough. Look at my master. Would you become like him? Do not seek out the future—it will find you soon enough."

"How do we return to the Path?" Corran asked.

"Return? You cannot. Do not even try." The flickering in Volun's eyes dimmed. "We will peer ahead as far as we can and give you such help as we are able, but if Master Caalenfaire could see you, perhaps others could also. People of power. Maybe it is better for you to walk alone in the dark—"

"Not quite alone," Caalenfaire murmured. "There is a hand over them, Volun. Whose hand, I cannot determine."

"Can you at least tell us something of the cult?" Ghleanna asked. "How can we succeed if we don't know who we're up against?"

The skull was silent, its eyes dark, empty sockets.

"Tell them, Volun," Caalenfaire said finally.

"The Cult of the Dragon is a secret society, four and more centuries old," Volun said, its eyes flashing red light once more. "Its founder was the madman Sammaster, a sorcerer who believed it is Toril's destiny to be ruled by dead dragons."

Kestrel had remained quiet until this point, not wanting to draw the attention of either the skull or its unsettling master. Now she felt compelled to question the outrageous statement. "Dead dragons? You said he was mad, but where in the Abyss did he come up with that idea?"

"From a passage in the oracle Maglas's book of prophecies, *Chronicle of Years to Come*."

Caalenfaire passed a hand over his scrying bowl. A distant, ancient voice echoed from within. "Nought will be left save shattered thrones, with no rulers but the dead. Dragons shall rule the world entire."

"Sammaster mistranslated the passage," Volun said. "He thought it said 'The dead dragons shall rule the world.' He founded the Cult of the Dragon to bring that prophecy to fruition."

"How do the cultists operate?" Kestrel asked.

The diviner stirred. He leaned back in his chair, but his gaze never left the scrying bowl. "Let the little bird come closer, that she may see."

Kestrel's heart slammed in her chest so hard that her pulse roared in her ears. Come *closer*? To an undead sorcerer? She'd never experienced a stronger impulse to turn tail and run. Somehow, she forced her feet to remain rooted to the floor as she glanced at her companions. Corran gave her a sharp look and jerked his chin toward the throne. She shook her head. No way.

Then she realized that the others waited for her to move forward. She would look the coward if she refused. Swallowing hard, she approached. Caalenfaire slid his left hand down the side of the scrying bowl so she could see into it, but otherwise he remained still. She peered into the water.

"The cult finds evil dragons willing to undergo the transformation into dracoliches—undead dragons," Volun said. As the skull spoke, an image appeared in the scrying bowl. A dozen cult sorcerers gathered around a blue dragon. The cultists performed some arcane ceremony involving the dragon and a large diamond. One of the cult sorcerers poured a potion into the dragon's mouth. Within moments, a glow appeared in the center of the diamond. As the glow strengthened, the dragon's skin shriveled and dried, its body becoming a corpse.

"In exchange for their mortal lives," Volun continued, "the dragons gain additional powers in their new undead state. They also win the cult's promise to help elevate them to world domination." The scene showed the archmage touching the diamond, uttering a few words, then touching the dragon's skeletal remains. The glow disappeared from the diamond as the dragon corpse jerked violently and rose, red flames flickering in its empty eye sockets.

Kestrel shuddered as the image faded away. She'd known the cult sorcerers were evil, but this kind of diabolical magic went beyond her comprehension. It made Caalenfaire and his familiar look downright approachable.

Well, not quite. As soon as she could politely do so, she backed away from the diviner's throne. "So this Kya Mordrayn person—she runs the whole cult?"

"The cult operates in cells," Volun said, "pockets of followers scattered throughout the continent of Faerûn. While each cell has its own leadership, the cult as a whole has no central power structure. The individual cells are too fractious to get along with each other. Such an organization necessarily attracts the unbalanced and power-hungry. Mordrayn is the archmage of a single, but strong, cell."

"And she's helping Pelendralaar amass enough power to take over the world?" Corran asked. "That's rather ambitious, isn't it? Even for a fanatic."

"She has unraveled the great Weave." Caalenfaire's voice held a disturbing note of resignation.

"Mordrayn and Pelendralaar use the powerful magic of

the Mythal to advance their goals," Volun said. "With such strong sorcery to aid them, Master fears they may actually succeed."

The diviner passed a hand over his scrying bowl, frowning. "Poison has reached the heart."

"Master Caalenfaire senses great evil deep within Castle Cormanthor. We believe this evil, whatever it is, helped contaminate the Mythal. Cleanse the Mythal and defeat the cult, and you might have a chance at destroying the evil that has overtaken the castle."

Kestrel stifled a groan. Cleanse the Mythal and defeat a bunch of insane cultists—as if doing so were as easy a picking a fat nobleman's pocket.

"Something troubles the little bird," Caalenfaire said.

Kestrel wished he would stop calling her that, but she wasn't about to tell him so. "This whole mission troubles me. 'Cleanse the Mythal.' 'Seize the power of the Mythal.' How are we supposed to take control of something we can't see or touch?"

Caalenfaire consulted his bowl once more. "The Path dims now. It twists." His voice seemed to span a great distance, not just the boundary of death but the march of time. "Still, the signs are clear. You must get up from under. Beyond the Circle, find Harldain Ironbar. You can enter his tower in the House of Gems only from the surface. Harldain is your ally. Heed well his counsel."

Volun's voice also seemed to be fading from the present. "To reach the Heights, you must unseal the Circle of Mythanthor. You have seen it—a great golden circle in the floor, in the uppermost part of the dungeons. You need the Ring of Calling to unseal the Circle. Master, look into your bowl. Can it tell you where the Ring of Calling lies?"

"I am looking. It is unclear. They are Veiled Ones now, and their shadow darkens anything they might touch or any place they might go. There are many possibilities. The

Tulun Wall . . . the Corridor of Salg . . . but first they should try the Room of Words in the Onaglym. Yes! But look—*Resheshannen*!"

"Master has spoken the Word of Oblivion. When you find the ring, use this word to release it from its once-proud bones. Wear the ring while standing in the Circle."

Ghleanna bowed. "We thank you, Master Caalenfaire and Volun. You have lent our quest new direction."

"The sword, Volun, the sword," Caalenfaire murmured. "Now that their path lies in shadow, they need it more than ever."

"Oh, yes—Master has a gift for you. Examine the scrying pedestal in the main hall. An arrow will guide you. And Master says the little bird should fear not Loren's Blade. It carries no curse."

Kestrel started at the unexpected announcement about the magical weapon she'd acquired from Athan's band. How had the diviner known she harbored doubts? The returning dagger had not even come up in conversation.

Caalenfaire seemed to have lapsed back into a trance, and Volun's eyes had gone dark. One at a time, the adventurers retreated down the stairs. Anxious as Kestrel was to depart, she hesitated to turn her back on the ghost and thus found herself the last one standing on the balcony. As she finally turned to go, the diviner's tremulous voice broke the stillness once more.

"The bird of prey feels under attack."

Kestrel froze. Why, oh why, had he singled her out? Slowly, she faced him. "I thought I was 'talibund.' What do you know of me?"

"You do not share the others' idealism. You speak uncomfortable truths. . . . I know something of that."

She grew warm, her hands trembling with nervous energy as if she'd been caught red-handed at some shady activity. Could the old ghost see straight into her soul?

"There is one in particular with whom you clash."

Corran. As if on cue, the paladin's voice floated up to them. "Kestrel?"

"Coming!" she called, not taking her gaze off the spectral wizard.

"Be of two minds but one heart," Caalenfaire said, his image fading from view and his voice seeming to echo from some far-off place. "Do not let conflict between you threaten your mission. It is too important." With that, the ghostly diviner and his familiar faded away altogether.

Kestrel paused to catch her breath before heading down the stairs. The apparition's words had left her feeling exposed, as if all her thoughts and emotions were on display for anyone to see. She shook her shoulders in an attempt to shrug off the sensation.

By the time Kestrel rejoined the others, they had already begun to examine the base of the scrying pedestal and had located a rune shaped like an arrowhead. Jarial had followed its point until he found a crack in the marble, which he'd traced to outline a secret panel. Kestrel tried to pry it off but ultimately had to give up and let Ghleanna cast an opening spell upon it.

Corran reached in and withdrew a gleaming silver long sword. He held the blade reverently, testing its weight and balance. The weapon seemed almost an extension of the paladin's own hand, so smoothly did it arc and thrust under his command. As Kestrel watched him swing the sword from side to side, Caalenfaire's final words echoed in her mind.

"'Tis a magnificent weapon—light but sturdy—the finest I've ever held." Corran swept the blade through the air one more time, then offered its jeweled hilt to Durwyn. "Care to test it?"

The guard hefted his axe. "Nay, this is my weapon. I'd hardly know what to do with a long sword."

Corran shrugged and offered the blade to Kestrel. Though she could defend herself with a sword in a pinch—hell, she could defend herself with a frying pan if she had to—her swordsmanship wasn't nearly worthy of such a weapon. "Keep it, Corran," she said. "You wield it much better than I ever could."

He gazed at the blade a moment more. "I shall call this sword 'Pathfinder,' that it may help us find our own way to defeat Mordrayn and the Pool."

They did not tarry longer. The diviner's cryptic hints and warnings had created a sense of urgency in them all. As the party headed back to the Rohnglyn, Kestrel fell into step beside Durwyn. "Little bird," he said absently.

"What?"

"Caalenfaire called you a little bird. So did Preybelish. I just realized why—they were referring to your name." He stopped and regarded her quizzically. "Why did your parents name you after a falcon?"

Kestrel stared at him. They'd just learned from a spooky diviner that a dracolich and some mad cultists were trying to take over Faerûn, and he was asking about her name? "They didn't."

"But a kestrel is a—"

"I know what a kestrel is," she snapped. "My parents didn't give me my name. I got it from the man who found me as a baby after they were killed." Her tone softened as she thought of Quinn. He'd been passing by the burned-out house and heard her hungry cries coming from the root cellar where her parents must have hidden her before brigands put arrows in their chests and set the cottage ablaze. "He said when he first saw me I reminded him of a falcon because he'd never seen such fierce eyes in so little a person."

She flushed, self-conscious at having revealed the personal story to a group of people she barely considered allies, let alone friends. Durwyn had caught her off-guard. No one had ever asked about her name before. As she looked away from Durwyn, she caught Corran regarding her pensively. Yes, she was a ragamuffin raised by a rogue stranger—she'd probably just confirmed every low opinion he held of her.

She noted Ghleanna's gaze on her also. The sorceress, however, regarded her not with condescension but with understanding. Her expression surprised Kestrel—the half-elf had seemed reserved until now, except on the subject of Athan. Perhaps her missing lover made her empathetic to the losses of others.

They reached the dancing lights of the Rohnglyn. Just before Jarial touched the golden sphere to take them back into the dwarven dungeons, Kestrel glanced up at the balcony once more.

Caalenfaire and Volun reappeared. For the first time, the diviner gazed at the party instead of into his scrying bowl, his face careworn but hopeful.

CHAPTER SEVEN

Outside the entrance to the House of Gems tower, the body of the cult sorcerer Kestrel and her companions had defeated lay undisturbed. Either the cultists had not passed through the door to the Room of Words since the party was last here or they had stepped over their comrade's body as if it were no more than a piece of litter.

To the group's surprise, they found the tower door unlocked. It opened into a single round room about thirty feet in diameter, a curved stone staircase spiraling up the far wall. The chamber was empty of furnishings or occupants.

"At last a lucky break," Durwyn said as he strode forward.

"Wait!" Kestrel grabbed his arm. The cultists

were no fools—and neither were dwarven engineers. She studied the circular room, noting a line of what appeared to be pockmarks rimming the stone wall at a height of about five feet. She knelt to retrieve one of the daggers from her boots but changed her mind and withdrew Loren's Blade instead. The magical dagger would better serve her purpose.

With a snap of her wrist, she sent the weapon hurling through the air at eye level. Dozens of darts came flying from the wall in rapid succession, shooting out of the holes on one side and into the holes opposite. The others gasped in surprise. Durwyn let out a low whistle.

Kestrel herself was so startled by the profusion of missiles that she almost forgot to catch Loren's Blade as it returned to her. "The darts flew too fast for me to see, but I'll wager they're spiked on both ends," she said. To prove her point, she threw the dagger again, with the same results.

"A perpetual trap," she explained. "There's no need to reset it once it's sprung. The darts can cross the room over and over until doomsday." Though Kestrel forced herself to adopt a nonchalant all-in-a-day's-work demeanor, inwardly she cursed every person under four feet tall who'd ever lived in this city. She admired the dwarves' engineering prowess—not one dart had missed its chamber—but damn, they made her life more difficult.

Durwyn rubbed the stubble on his chin. "So how do we get past the trap?"

On a hunch, Kestrel flung Loren's Blade across the room once more, this time four feet off the ground. Nothing happened, except that her weapon clanked against the wall and boomeranged back to her hand.

That was the secret, then. "The trap's designed to strike nondwarves—people taller than them." She addressed Durwyn primarily but extended her gaze to include the others. "As long as we stay close to the ground, we should be all right."

The party crawled single file through the booby-trapped chamber and made it to the other side safely. Corran started to speak, but Kestrel hushed him as she examined the steps for more unpleasant dwarven surprises. Though he bristled under the rebuke, the paladin held his tongue. She cast a discerning gaze at each tread and riser, running her fingers along the cold, smooth stone. Though she found no evidence of additional traps, her sensitive ears detected a faint shuffling sound above.

"Wait here," she advised the others. She silently crept up the stairs, stopping before she reached the top. From this vantage point, she could peer over the second-story floor and see most of the room while remaining hidden in the stairwell.

This level of the tower comprised a single room with shelves full of scrolls. Wooden cases similar to wine racks lined the wall, with each diamond-shaped opening holding its own roll of paper. The documents merited only a cursory glance, however—it was the dozen or so orogs in the chamber that arrested her attention. They occupied the center of the room, effectively blocking the stairs to the third story. The humanoids stood in perfect formation, their eyes blankly staring straight ahead. She studied the unit for a leader but didn't discern one.

A fly buzzed past Kestrel's ear, landing on her forearm. She brushed it off, but the pesky thing buzzed around her face again. "Shoo!" she whispered, batting it aside. The fly finally got the message and sped off to bother someone else.

She observed the orogs for a few minutes longer. The guards stood so still they didn't seem to breathe. They merely gripped their short swords, ready for combat. As she watched, the fly that had irritated her flew into the midst of the orogs and landed on one humanoid's snout, where it proceeded to dance around the creature's nostrils. Just watching the insect made Kestrel's own nose itch, but the orog didn't so much as flinch. He continued to stare straight ahead.

Kestrel returned to the group. In a hushed voice, she reported what she'd seen.

"Maybe we can parley with them as we did with those other orogs guarding the cult sorcerer." Jarial glanced up the stairs. "Do you think they would be willing to talk?"

"I'm not even sure they're alive," Kestrel responded. "I mean, the whole thing with the fly—"

"They might be under the influence of a charm," Ghleanna said. "Or in a state of suspended animation."

Corran rubbed his chin thoughtfully, his fingers stroking the rough stubble of the past three days. "If that's the case, can we figure out a way around them? We need to reserve as much of our strength and resources as possible for the cultists in the Room of Words."

"You all think too much." Durwyn grabbed his bow and nocked an arrow. "We waste time. We can handle a dozen orogs." He mounted the stairs.

Kestrel stared after him, surprised by his assertiveness. "Wait for me!"

The others followed close behind. As soon as Durwyn rose high enough in the stairwell to sight the orogs, he stopped and let the arrow fly. Another shaft quickly followed. Both arrows found their targets, felling a pair of humanoids.

The rest of the orogs started forward. Kestrel maneuvered around Durwyn and hurled her twin daggers at two of the creatures. Behind her, she heard Ghleanna utter the words of a spell.

Kestrel's first dagger struck an orog in the throat. He sank to his knees, then slumped over. Her second dagger, thrown with her right hand, hit its victim in the side. Though the blade had buried itself in his flesh, the creature's face didn't register the slightest discomfort. He continued his advance as if nothing had happened.

Ghleanna's incantation also had no effect. "These are no ordinary orogs," the sorceress said. "That spell should have put two of them to sleep."

The orogs closed in. Their movements lacked fluidity. Though they moved quickly, they jerked and lurched, as if they were marionettes on strings and someone else controlled their steps.

Kestrel hurled Loren's Blade at her wounded opponent. The magical dagger struck him in the chest. As the weapon returned to her hand, the orog kept coming. He was so close now that she could see the yellow stains on his long, canine teeth, smell the stench of the matted, coarse hair covering his unwashed body. Though the creature had been injured twice, his pale eyes retained their vacant stare.

She hadn't enough distance to throw Loren's Blade at him again. She reached for her club and hastened to one side so as not to be forced backward into the stairwell. A snap of her wrist extended the baton to its full length, but a simultaneous blow by the orog knocked the club out of her hand. It scudded across the floor among the clawed feet of the other orogs.

She gripped Loren's Blade tighter as her foe raised his sword for another strike. She'd have to parry with the dagger until she found another melee weapon.

Jarial released a spell. A fan of flames shot out from his hands, seriously burning the four creatures closest to him and singeing the hides of several others. Kestrel had hoped the fire would distract her opponent long enough for her to sink her dagger into him again, but he didn't so much as blink. None of the creatures did.

"Tyr preserve us," Corran muttered. Pathfinder in hand, he battled two orogs at once. The first lunged at the paladin with its blade. Corran's gleaming weapon easily disarmed the humanoid, sending the orog's short sword flying. It landed a few feet from Kestrel.

She retrieved the weapon and assumed a defensive posture just as her foe struck again. Sword fighting was not her forte, but the orogs didn't have to know that. She parried the humanoid's blows, giving herself a chance to become accustomed to the weapon before shifting to an offensive stance. Her opponent was strong and towered over her by at least a foot. When the opportunity arose, she would have to press her only advantage—superior agility.

Meanwhile, Durwyn's swinging axe caught her peripheral vision. The warrior had already defeated one opponent and now fought two more. Make that one more—another orog succumbed to his powerful strokes. The unfortunate mercenary, already burned by Jarial's spell, lost an arm to Durwyn's axe. He dropped to the floor without a sound.

So had all the fallen orogs, Kestrel realized suddenly. Except for her own companions' grunts of exertion and the clang of metal on metal, this was the most quiet battle she'd ever experienced. The humanoids fought and died without so much as a groan—a far cry from their usual whoops and calls of war.

More comfortable with her newly acquired weapon, Kestrel darted to one side. The movement forced her opponent to twist his body awkwardly to continue countering her strikes. The creature fought hard but mechanically, its swings and parries more the product of rote than battle fervor.

That blank stare was really starting to give her the creeps. There was definitely something wrong with these creatures.

Ghleanna swung her staff and hit Kestrel's opponent in the head, providing the opportunity the rogue had been looking for. Kestrel thrust her blade at an upward angle, catching the humanoid in the throat. The orog sank silently to the ground, its face never losing the blank stare.

When Kestrel glanced around, she saw that Durwyn had just dispatched the last of his trio of foes. Corran also had defeated three orogs with his new magical blade. As she watched, he lunged to catch another one—who had turned on Jarial—in the back. The creature remained standing, still as death, for a full minute, as if it hadn't realized it had been killed. Then it dropped as its comrades had.

As everyone caught their breaths, Kestrel retrieved her weapons. She studied the bodies of the orogs she had slain, then swept her gaze across all the orog corpses.

Not one of the creatures had bled.

"Uh, guys? Have you noticed—"

"No blood," Corran said as the realization hit him as well. He bent down to examine one of the orogs more closely. "The cult somehow drained the blood and life out of these creatures, leaving them animated corpses. Soulless."

Kestrel shuddered involuntarily. The more she learned about the Cult of the Dragon, the more she wished she could just walk away from this whole quest. Only the vision of all humanity wandering around in the orogs' soulless state kept her from making the suggestion. Instead, she turned her gaze to the stairs the bloodless humanoids had been guarding. At the top, the Room of Words waited. The Ring of Calling was only feet away—along with the cult sorcerers who would fight to the death to keep it.

❧ ❧ ❧ ❧ ❧

The party burst into the Room of Words so suddenly that the sorcerer holding the Ring of Calling dropped the skeletal arm in surprise. He recovered quickly, his fingers and lips immediately moving to form an incantation.

Kestrel's dagger prevented him from ever finishing it.

Once she saw the light of life leave his eyes, the thief didn't spare the dying cultist another glance. One down, five to go, and good riddance to the chump on the floor. She gripped her second blade and scanned the room for her next target.

Beside her, Durwyn released an arrow. The shaft whistled past her ear to embed itself in the heart of another cultist. The evil sorcerer's eyes widened beneath his leather hood. He gripped the shaft with his clawed hand and tried to yank the arrow from his chest, but his clumsy struggle only caused more blood to ooze from the wound. As the cultist gurgled something unintelligible, his gaze met Durwyn's—then took on the glassy stare of death.

Meanwhile, both Jarial and Ghleanna managed to unleash spells before the cultists could prepare any sorcery of their own. The half-elf's magic rendered one hooded sorcerer blind, while Jarial's sank an acid-laced arrow in the stomach of another. The wounded sorcerer screamed in agony as the smell of burning cloth and flesh filled the air. Tendrils of greenish smoke wisped from the hole in his gut. He stared at Jarial, his features forming a mask of hatred. His lips curled to spit out a foul-sounding, arcane curse. Then he began weaving a spell of his own.

Kestrel's heart pounded as the scarred sorcerer spun his retaliatory enchantment. The element of surprise had enabled the companions to kill or handicap four of the six cultists in the chamber. Though their odds had improved, victory still wasn't assured. Now they would have to rely on their wits and the strategy Corran had devised just before they entered the chamber. According to plan, the paladin would identify the band's most powerful sorcerer and—cloaked by Jarial's invisibility spell—disable him.

There was no sign of Corran yet, and the two unharmed cultists had overcome their surprise. One, the youngest-looking cult sorcerer she had yet seen, nervously stumbled over the words of an evocation that sent a burst of dark energy flying at Durwyn. The black flames struck the warrior in his bow arm. He dropped his bow and clutched his arm. "To the Abyss with your hellfire!" he cried. Pain flashed across his face, but for only a moment. His axe arm was still good, and with the discipline of a trained fighter he concealed his suffering and reached for his favored weapon. Axe in hand, he strode toward the wizard who had injured him. The scrawny young man backed up as the massive warrior neared.

When Kestrel's gaze landed on the other uninjured cultist, she caught him sneering at her. Judging from his more elaborate tattoos and the size of his claw, she guessed him to be the highest-ranking sorcerer of the group. The leader unleashed four black-flamed missiles. All at Kestrel.

She tumbled to the floor, but the sorcerous darts followed her. Pain ripped through her stomach, then her already-injured leg, with intensity that brought tears to her eyes. She curled into a ball in a half-coherent attempt to shield her chest and gut from the remaining missiles. The strikes seared her right arm, nearly forcing her to drop the dagger she still gripped in that hand.

"Bastard!" she spat as pain rocked her body. Her arm burned as if flames consumed it. She could barely control her hand.

The hooded cultist waved mockingly with his own mutated right hand. "Having a little trouble?"

Through an act of sheer will, Kestrel rolled to prop herself on her injured right arm. The smug sorcerer thought he had disabled her throwing hand. Arrogant troll—she'd show him. She blocked out the agony coursing through her limbs and transferred the weapon to her dominant hand. Then she met his baleful gaze. "Not as much as you." She hurled the dagger.

The blade should have struck his foul heart. Despite her injuries, her aim had been true. To Kestrel's despair the weapon fell short of its mark, instead sinking into his left calf. The wizard acknowledged the hit with no more than a hissed curse, then moved his hands in the sinister gestures of another spell.

She tore her gaze away from the evil sorcerer long enough to glance wildly about the chamber. Where in the Abyss was Corran? She saw no hint of the invisible paladin. Apparently he'd left Kestrel to battle the chief sorcerer by herself. "Damn you, Corran D'Arcey," she muttered.

An eerie babble of voices filled the air as all the spellcasters in the room uttered arcane words of individual incantations. Even the sightless mage was in the process of casting a spell—Mystra only knew where that magic would land. Durwyn, who had killed the hapless apprentice, appeared to have chosen the blind wizard as his next target. She only hoped the warrior's axe struck before the sorcerer's spell.

Jarial was locked in a spellcasters' duel with the acid-burned sorcerer. In the few seconds that Kestrel watched, the injured cultist released a retributive gout of flames at Jarial. Ghleanna and Jarial had agreed to avoid fire-based attacks out of concern for the many ancient books, scrolls, and maps in the chamber, but apparently the cultists had no such qualms.

Kestrel heard Jarial's cry as the flames licked his skin but had to return her attention to her own adversary. Corran had abandoned her. She would have to face the sorcerous leader alone. She still had one more dagger, Loren's Blade. She reached for its hilt at her waist.

And blinked. Was pain making her head swim? The sorcerer suddenly appeared blurry. Kestrel squinted and stared, but could not discern a steady outline—the cultist seemed to waver before her eyes. She gripped the magical dagger, eager to hurl it at the wizard but unable to fix a target.

The smell of burning paper met her nostrils as smoke drifted toward her. In trying to injure Jarial, the foolish cultist had set an enormous old tome ablaze. Its wrought-iron stand probably would keep the flames from spreading, but the book and the knowledge it contained were now lost forever.

The smoke obscured the cult leader's image even further. His shifting form seemed to be preparing yet another spell to aim at her. Kestrel groaned, her body already aching beyond anything she'd ever experienced. Despite the poor visibility, she couldn't just stand here offering the wizard target practice. She peered through the dense air and grasped her weapon, preparing to throw. She would have to trust her instincts.

Just as she was about to toss the blade, a familiar voice penetrated the haze. "By the hand of Tyr!" The wizard yelped and doubled over. Corran materialized, his new blade wet with fresh blood.

"About damn time!" she shouted.

With a cry of rage, the evil sorcerer released the spell he'd prepared for Kestrel onto Corran instead. His image still blurred, he appeared to touch Corran's arm for only a split second. Corran immediately staggered backward two paces, his face ashen and somehow drained of vitality.

With an evil grin the wizard straightened, now scarcely bothered by the wound Corran had opened in his gut.

A cold chill passed through Kestrel. The sorcerer had stolen some of Corran's life force! What other evil could this necromancer wreak?

They could not afford to find out. She flung the dagger. It soared through the air and struck him squarely in the chest. Corran followed the strike with one of his own as Loren's Blade flew back to Kestrel's hand. The sorcerer's eyes widened in pain and hatred, but he still did not die. Instead he began to utter the words of another incantation.

Kestrel prepared to hurl the magical blade again. Though the cultist's wavering image became increasingly hard to discern through the smoke, she thought she saw him glance at the floor off to one side. She followed the direction of his gaze. There, forgotten in the fray, lay the skeletal arm bearing the Ring of Calling. The chief sorcerer seemed to be moving toward it as he avoided another of Corran's blows.

Kestrel glanced at her companions. Jarial unleashed an incantation on his rival, sending another acidic arrow through the air to silence the sorcerer for good. Ghleanna also appeared in the process of casting a spell, this one at the leader. She squinted through the smoke, trying to fix her sight on him. Durwyn had just finished off the blinded mage and stood not far from the skeletal arm.

"Durwyn—the ring!" Kestrel cried. "Pick up the ring!"

Durwyn scanned the floor, spotted the arm, and rushed toward it. The cult leader's voice increased in volume, sounding as if he were nearing the end of the spell he wove. As Ghleanna spoke the final word of her own spell, his shifting image solidified. The cultist stood only feet from the ring. He uttered the final thunderous syllable of his spell and reached for the skeletal arm.

Durwyn snatched it first. The sorcerer shrieked in anger.

And disappeared.

❀ ❀ ❀ ❀ ❀

Knowing the cult sorcerer could return any moment with reinforcements, the party did not tarry in the Room of Words. Kestrel, Corran, and Jarial quickly downed blueglow moss potions for their injuries, and the band headed back through the tower to the dungeons.

They reached the Circle of Mythanthor—their gateway out of the dwarven undercity and up to the surface of Myth Drannor. Kestrel could feel the adrenaline pumping through her as they all gathered beside the golden circle on the floor. As much as she'd resisted joining this mission, she was swept up with the others in the excitement of at last completing the first stage of their quest. Finally, they could leave the dark dungeons behind them.

Durwyn handed Ghleanna the skeletal arm. She traced her fingertips around the Ring of Calling, lingering on the starstone gem. Then she tilted her chin up, closed her eyes, and spoke the Word of Oblivion in a steady, clear voice.

"Resheshannen!"

The bones crumbled to dust, leaving only the ring in the sorceress's hand. The white starstone sparkled in the torchlight as Ghleanna slipped it on her finger. "Come," she said. "Let us leave the darkness."

One at a time, they entered the circle. Ghleanna crossed the boundary last. The moment she stepped inside, a sphere of light appeared and hovered before them. It widened until it reached the size and shape of a doorway. Sunlight shone through from the other side, where Kestrel could make out the towering spires and elaborate architecture of the ruined but still impressive Heights of Myth Drannor. In the distance, the parapets of Castle Cormanthor rose toward the sky as if seeking release from the evil that gripped the fortress.

The city surface—and with it, Mordrayn and Pelendralaar—awaited.

BOOK TWO

Myth Weaver

CHAPTER EIGHT

As the party emerged into full daylight, Kestrel squeezed her eyes shut, then forced open two narrow slits. After days spent in the dim torchlight of the dwarven undercity, the sudden brightness of the sun's rays stung her eyes. Several minutes passed before she could open her lids wide enough to behold Myth Drannor's acropolis.

They entered the Heights at the base of a large statue of a wizard. The elderly elven spellcaster was half-enveloped in a finely-woven mantle, its threads seemingly swirling about him. He stood with his hands thrust skyward and his head thrown back, an expression of intense concentration or ecstasy—Kestrel could not tell which—etched on his face. The pedestal on which the statue rested bore the name "Mythanthor."

Behind them, the Speculum rose up in all its majesty and mystery. As Jarial had described, the structure was indeed shaped like a dragon. An enormous horned head dominated the main entrance, its jeweled yellow eyes glowering at all who dared enter the doors below. As Caalenfaire had told them, huge boulders and other piles of rubble blocked the entrance. Fore- and hindlegs projected out in high relief from the stone walls, and a curving exterior staircase formed the creature's tail and back. The mighty beast lay curled around a large "egg"—a domed room in the center of the building.

Next to the Speculum stood an amphitheater. Its seats, many of them crumbling from age or assault, rose fully half the height of the Speculum dragon in a half-circle that matched the curve of the dragon's tail. The stage was a large, but simple, white disc-shaped stone.

To the east lay the Onaglym, its intact state a testament to the unequaled engineering talent of the dwarves who constructed it so many centuries ago. While hundreds of Myth Drannor's lesser buildings lay ruined by the ravages of war or years, the House of Gems yet remained, a strong, silent sentinel to the changes wrought by time and mortal vanity.

Castle Cormanthor graced the highest point of the Heights. It rose up from the cliff on which it was built, its many graceful spires reaching higher into the sky than any others in the city. At one time, walkways apparently had connected the all spires to the main castle and to each other, but most of these had been destroyed or damaged beyond use. Those that remained looked like a precarious challenge to even an acrobat's sense of balance. The narrow spans, several hundred feet above the ground, had no rails, and nothing below to break one's fall.

Moments ago, Kestrel had flushed with a sense of accomplishment at managing to leave the dwarven dungeons at last. But now, scanning the center of Myth Drannor, she realized much more work lay ahead. They had to find Harldain Ironbar, the ally Caalenfaire had mentioned. They had a Mythal to cleanse, an archmage and a dracolich to defeat, and a pool to destroy. She stifled a sigh. "I suppose we ought to head back to the House of Gems?"

Corran glanced at the Onaglym, frowning at the wisps of smoke that still drifted out of the Round Tower. "I suggest we explore a bit before seeking out Harldain Ironbar. That sorcerer might come back to the House of Gems looking for us, and I'd like him to think we're long gone."

"So would I." Kestrel gingerly rubbed her right arm. Though healed of its worst injuries, her body still ached where the cultist's magical strikes had hit her.

They headed in the opposite direction of the Onaglym, to an area southwest of the Speculum. This part of the city lay in almost complete ruin. Its once-stable ground had become marshy, and now the stagnant water and damp air slowly completed the destruction that the wars had started. Large chunks of marble, granite, and crystal lay strewn about like dice from the hands of giants, their surfaces eroded by the elements and covered with green-gray moss and other vegetation. Few buildings retained enough of their structure to be recognizable as former dwellings, businesses, or temples.

One such ruin caught Kestrel's attention. A shell of white marble reached heavenward, the star symbol of Mystra etched into its largest remaining side. Mystra's sign was barely visible beneath the new symbols covering the crumbling walls. The name and image of Llash, a three-headed snake god, had been painted and scrawled all over the building in thick black lines.

Corran stopped in his tracks when he saw the sacrilege. "It's a mercy that Beriand's eyes cannot behold this," he said softly.

A light breeze stirred. From the ruined shrine came a sound like the whimper of an injured animal.

"Do you hear that?" Kestrel asked.

Ghleanna frowned in concentration. "Hear what?"

The sound drifted toward them again, this time resembling a crying woman. Kestrel glanced at each of her companions in turn, but all wore blank expressions. Could no one else hear that wail? "Never mind." She shrugged, trying to dismiss the unsettling feeling creeping up her neck. "It must be the wind whistling through cracks in the walls."

"Are you sure about that?" Jarial regarded her seriously. "If you think you hear something, Kestrel, we should check it out."

The vote of confidence surprised her. "All right, then. I think I hear something—or someone—crying inside."

They approached the shrine. The land surrounding it seemed particularly swampy. In fact, a large puddle of stagnant water had formed to one side of it. The closer they got, however, the more the hairs on the back of Kestrel's neck rose, until her collarbone tingled.

"Stop!" The party came to an abrupt halt as Kestrel peered at the puddle. Was it her imagination, or did the water have an amber glow to it? "Unless I'm mistaken, that's no ordinary water."

Jarial, the only one among them who hadn't seen Phlan's pool, edged closer for a better look. "We can't have found Myth Drannor's Pool of Radiance so easily?"

"I wouldn't stand so close if I were you," Kestrel warned. She recalled all too clearly the sight of the bandit's life being sucked away by a stray splash.

Ghleanna studied the puddle from a safe distance. "It's too small and too exposed to be the source of the cult's growing power. I suspect this is an offshoot, like the pool in Mulmaster. A spawn pool, you could call it."

From within the ruined shrine, Kestrel once again heard the soft cry. This time, the wind carried words to her: "Where are the followers of Mystra?" And this time, the others heard it as well.

"Is that the cry you heard before?" Corran asked. At her nod, he started toward the entrance to what remained of the shrine. "Who's there?" he called. "Are you all right?"

"Simply marvelous, my good sir," answered a new voice. Though feminine-sounding, it was a harsher voice than the one they had heard previously. "So kind of you to ask."

Corran stopped short just outside the doorway. He seemed about to speak, when he was interrupted from within.

"Oh, come now. Is that any way to greet two lonely ladies?"

"Forgive me." The paladin appeared to recover himself. He cast a deliberate glance toward the rest of the group, then returned his gaze to the hidden speaker. "I believe we may have a common acquaintance. Are you friends of Preybelish?"

At Corran's mention of the dark naga, Kestrel stifled a groan. Not more of the creatures? They'd had a bad enough time handling the first one.

"A distant relation of ours," responded a second sibilant voice. "Sadly, we have not seen our cousin in years. How is he?"

"Quite peaceful, when last I left him."

Kestrel turned to the others. If these nagas had the same mind-reading ability as Preybelish, the party would have to rely on Corran to keep them distracted while the rest of them devised a plan. She only hoped the pair remained unaware that the paladin hadn't arrived alone.

At least this time, they had an idea of what kind of attacks to expect. They needed to stay clear of the nagas' tails, while also avoiding any spells they might hurl. Jarial and Ghleanna whispered hurriedly about what sort of sorcery to use. In spare moments of the journey, they'd been working to expand their arsenal, developing new spells based on magic that opponents had used against them, and they were eager to try out some of the new incantations in combination with their old standbys. Kestrel gave one ear to them while keeping the other tuned to Corran's conversation.

"Have you seen any activity around the castle?" one of the hissing voices inquired. "We hear a dracolich has made his lair there."

"Really? Where within the castle?"

Kestrel had to give Corran credit for improving his subtlety skills. The paladin injected a casualness into his tone that he could not have felt.

"Inside a cavern, far below. From what we understand."

Ghleanna and Jarial settled on their spellcasting plan. Jarial murmured to Kestrel not to forget Borea's Blood, which she carried in a beltpouch. "Ozama's ice knife had the power to paralyze. The shard blade may have a similar effect—worth a try, anyway."

The sorcerers waved their hands, casting protective spells, including one on Corran, who, from his spot in the doorway, now chatted with the nagas about a marble idol of Llash, the snake god of poisons, that they had raised in the ruined shrine. When the mages were finished, they nodded in unison. Kestrel glanced around, lifting her hand, then brought it sharply down, signaling the attack.

Jarial and Ghleanna moved in first, each casting an offensive spell on a different naga. From Jarial's fingers a lightning bolt seared one of the creatures with electrical energy, lifting her off the ground and propelling her across the room to land at the base of the statue. Before the other naga comprehended what happened to her sister, Ghleanna struck her with the same fiery evocation that Preybelish had used against the half-elf.

Durwyn followed the magical attacks with a pair of arrows. He missed Jarial's naga, but Kestrel caught the creature between the eyes with a dagger. The beast's head thumped to the floor.

"One down!" Durwyn shouted. Already, Kestrel breathed a little easier.

Beside her, Jarial began a second incantation. The injured naga rose, parts of her charred purple flesh still smoking. Hatred seethed from her gaze as she took in the party. "Vile humans!" She started a spell of her own.

Just as Jarial seemed about to complete his casting, he suddenly flew back and sprawled facedown on the ground. A hole in his back welled blood.

Kestrel spun around. A third naga had stolen up behind them, unheard in the noise of battle, and struck the human sorcerer with her tail.

"Arrogant wanderers!" the creature hissed. "How dare you bring violence into our place of worship?" She swung her tail again, this time aiming for Kestrel. The thief ducked and rolled away from the giant snake, but the creature drew back its tail for a second attack.

"*Your* place of worship?" Corran sputtered. "You blaspheme a house of Mystra with your profane idol!" He grabbed his warhammer and swung it against the black marble statue of the snake god, breaking off one of its three heads.

"No!" The naga's tail dropped in mid-swing, her attention fully drawn to Corran.

The injured naga finished her spell, directing it at Ghleanna. Three bursts of dark magical energy sped toward the half-elf. When they came within a foot of her, however, they bounced off a shimmering barrier and harmlessly sputtered out.

"Llash damn you to the Abyss!" the thwarted creature swore.

Corran swung his warhammer at the base of the idol. The marble fractured, and the top-heavy sculpture wobbled. The paladin threw his weight against it, pushing it toward the monster. The idol tottered. Corran threw himself at the statue once more, this time toppling it onto the injured naga. It landed on her head with a mighty crash. The creature's body jerked spasmodically, then fell still.

"Llash! Aid your servant!" the remaining naga cried. Unable to tear her gaze away from the fallen statue, she seemed oblivious to the enemies surrounding her. She slithered toward the idol.

Kestrel took advantage of her distraction to hurl Borea's Blood. The ice knife caught the creature in the throat just below her head. The naga couldn't even scream before the paralyzing cold numbed her upper body. Her head fell to the floor, where Durwyn easily removed it with a stroke of his axe.

The moment he struck the death blow, a loud hissing commenced outside the ruined shrine. Not another naga? Kestrel didn't think so—this was a different sort of hiss, like that released by the last few drops of water in a pan boiled dry. She cautiously approached the doorway and peered out.

The amber pool was evaporating so rapidly that steam billowed into the sky. As the foul water dissipated, the land around it returned to health. Greenery once again graced the area surrounding the ruined shrine, and patches of blueglow moss appeared.

Kestrel turned to the others. "The pool's gone!" Then an idea struck her. "I'll be right back," she called over her shoulder as she dashed out the door. She dug up a patch of the healing moss and brought it inside for Jarial. Ozama's boots had saved him once again from the naga's poison, but the creature's barbed tail had inflicted a nasty wound. As Kestrel applied the moss to the sorcerer's back, the air in the ruined shrine suddenly chilled.

"Where are the followers of Mystra?" beseeched a forlorn voice. The sound seemed to come from above. They all looked skyward—to find their view of the clouds veiled by a translucent ceiling.

The ruined walls of the shrine seemed to be restored, but in a shimmery, intangible state. At the same time, the Llash graffiti faded. All around them, features of the former temple reappeared—statues, tapestries, ritual objects. The ghostly shrine looked as it had centuries ago, before war brought it to ruin.

"Those faithful to the Goddess of the Weave—are they no more? Where are the servants of Mystery?" The plaintive voice echoed throughout the spectral building, but the speaker remained unseen.

"There are many who yet serve you in our time, my lady," Corran called to the air.

Kestrel stared at him. "You think that's actually Mystra's voice?"

He shrugged. "Perhaps."

"Where are the followers of Mystra?"

Kestrel didn't believe they heard a divine call. Wouldn't a goddess, of all people, know where her followers were? As it was, the voice held such melancholy that she didn't think she could listen to it much longer. "Can we leave before whoever she is drives us mad?" She retrieved her weapons and went to clean them on the grass outside while Durwyn helped Jarial to his feet.

When she returned, Corran still cast a searching gaze heavenward. "She sounds so sorrowful," he said. "We should try to help her."

The sad voice stirred a response in Kestrel as well— not that she'd ever admit that fact to Corran. Unlike the quixotic paladin, she knew they couldn't afford any more tangential delays. "Like we helped Nottle? Look what that cost us."

The words came out more sharply than she intended. Corran turned his head away, but not before she saw a look of bitter regret cross his features. Apparently, the paladin felt the responsibility for Emmeric's death more keenly than she'd realized.

"All right, then," Corran said quietly, his back to them all. "Let us go."

❂ ❂ ❂ ❂ ❂

Injured, tired, and nearly out of spells, the party voted to visit Beriand and Faeril before returning to the House of Gems. Though the elven shelter lay out of their way, there they could find healing and a safe place to rest.

Kestrel hadn't apologized to Corran for her earlier barb about Emmeric, though her conscience pricked her. The delight she'd expected to feel at having discovered a way to wound him hadn't materialized. She felt more hollow than anything else. There was no satisfaction, she realized, in causing a companion the chagrin his unguarded response had revealed.

Faeril greeted them warmly upon their arrival. "You have been busy!" she said as soon as she saw them. "Already, we feel a change in the Mythal."

Corran acknowledged her with a bow. "For the better, I hope?"

"Oh, yes!" Faeril's face shone, some of the careworn lines having faded since they last saw her. "Come inside. You must tell us of your deeds."

Though eager to learn what the adventurers had accomplished, the clerics insisted on first tending to their injuries. The party was in sorry shape. While the blueglow moss and potions had relieved their immediate distress, Kestrel and Jarial yet moved stiffly. The wound Durwyn had received from Preybelish had not had time to heal of its own accord. Corran remained weakened from the cult sorcerer's life-draining spell—the paladin had refused to use his limited healing powers on himself lest a greater need arise before the day's end.

They shed their armor, grateful to be in a place of relative safety where they could rest and renew their strength. The elves tended the four wounded humans and also checked how well Ghleanna had healed under Corran's care after Preybelish's near-fatal attack. "I cannot even tell you were injured," Faeril declared. She turned to the paladin. "Your faith must be strong indeed."

Over a meal of roasted rabbit and hearty bread, Corran, Kestrel, and the others related their exploits in the dwarven undercity, ending with their ascent to the surface and their encounter at the shrine. "When the pool evaporated, a ghostly image of the intact temple appeared," Corran concluded.

Faeril gasped, her thick slice of bread dropping to her plate. "By Our Lady, you have seen Anorrweyn's shrine!" Her eyes shone with reverence.

"The shrine is one of several ghost buildings in Myth Drannor," Beriand said. "The wars destroyed many structures, but some were so sacred to the elves that they refuse to disappear completely. From time to time, under certain conditions, these buildings reappear intact. When you defeated the naga and destroyed the spawn pool, you must have triggered the temple's appearance." He paused to sip from his goblet. "Did you ever see the crying woman you spoke of?"

"Just heard her," Kestrel said, nibbling the last few shreds of meat off a bone. She hadn't realized how hungry she was until she'd started to eat. "'Where are the followers of Mystra?' That's all she said—over and over."

"How blessed you are—to have heard her voice!" Faeril exclaimed. She rose to pour more wine, beginning first with Durwyn's goblet and ending with Beriand's. Kestrel noted that she did not lift Beriand's cup to pour, as she had with the others, but brought the bottle to the sightless cleric's goblet.

"That was Anorrweyn Evensong, the founder of our sect," Beriand said. "When evil magic destroyed the temple during the fall of Myth Drannor, its head priestess also perished. So strong was her devotion to Mystra that her spirit remained on this earth to continue her work. Whenever the ghost shrine appeared, so did she." Beriand reached for his wine, his practiced hand going straight to the goblet. "For centuries after the temple's physical destruction, followers of Mystra would visit the site and use talismans to invoke the apparition and speak to Anorrweyn. But in the past two hundred years or so, Myth Drannor has become so dangerous that pilgrims stopped coming. I doubt anyone has invoked the shrine in over a century."

Durwyn frowned thoughtfully as he chewed his food. Finally, he spoke. "If the priestess shows up whenever the temple does, why couldn't we see her?"

"I suspect because there was no follower of Mystra among you."

"Anorrweyn's cry must be answered!" Faeril said. She pushed aside her wooden plate, her supper forgotten in her zeal. "Let me return with you and prove to the high priestess that Mystra still has followers in Myth Drannor. We cannot leave her spirit to think that the city has fallen entirely to the nagas who debased her sacred shrine."

Kestrel could tell by the expression on Corran's face that the paladin was about to take Faeril up on her offer. She shifted uncomfortably, pushing aside her own plate and drawing her knees up in front of her body. She had a feeling she was about to be labeled selfish again, but someone had to keep this mission on track. "Not that I don't feel sorry for your priestess and all," she began, trying to use more tact than she had previously, "but we have more pressing matters."

Corran turned toward her, his brows drawn in displeasure. Before he could speak, however, Faeril addressed her. "Anorrweyn can help your cause, Kestrel. I know she will!"

Beriand nodded his agreement. "Anorrweyn Evensong would prove a powerful ally against those trying use the Mythal for their own wicked ends. In life she was dedicated to the causes of unity and peace, and was among the city leaders most in tune with the Mythal. She may know of ways to cleanse it that we do not."

"In that case, we'd be honored to have you join us," Corran said to Faeril. Kestrel bristled. She'd been about to concede the point herself, but once again Corran had spoken for the whole party without consulting anyone. She began to feel less contrite about her earlier remark.

The others were apparently tolerant of the paladin's high-handedness. Ghleanna, in fact, extended the invitation to Beriand.

"Thank you for asking," he said, his voice thick with emotion. "I would like nothing more. But I know that a blind man would slow you down, and time is too precious, your mission too vital." He rose from the floor, leaning on his staff, and made his way over to his cot. "No, leave here tomorrow morn without me. When the cult is defeated and the Mythal restored, then shall I meet Anorrweyn Evensong."

❧   ❧   ❧   ❧   ❧

Long after the others retired, Kestrel remained by the fire, staring into the flames. Caalenfaire's words yet echoed in her mind, and she'd hardly had time to think about the whole strange interview since it took place.

Be of two minds but one heart. The diviner had looked straight inside her and seen the frustration building there. She missed the freedom of working alone, of deciding for herself the best course of action. She was tired of making nice with her companions, tired of compromising. Especially with Corran.

The others were tolerable. Durwyn didn't have the confidence to voice his opinion very often. Jarial, conscious of his status as the newcomer, didn't throw his weight around much either. Ghleanna usually had good ideas, and Corran respected the sorceress enough to listen to them. If only he'd show her, Kestrel, the same courtesy.

She raised her arms above her head and stretched. At times, the others' company seemed almost physically confining. When this quest was over—if she lived to see its end—she'd be on her own once more. She'd make her own choices again, do things her way. When she built up her fortune, when she finally had that easy life she craved, she'd be the one telling other people what to do.

Rustling near the cots interrupted her musing. Light footsteps followed, bringing Ghleanna into view. "May I join you?"

Kestrel didn't object. "Can't sleep?"

"Nay. My mind swirls with too many thoughts." The mage sat down cross-legged beside her.

She studied the half-elf. Ghleanna was a beautiful woman, combining the best features of her mixed heritage. The firelight glinted off the gold specks in her eyes and the highlights in her unbound golden hair. Kestrel could see the appeal the sorceress would hold for Athan, or any man for that matter. She wondered again if Ghleanna was romantically involved with the famed warrior. "Does Athan occupy some of those thoughts?" she asked boldly.

Ghleanna did not answer immediately, instead pushing a lock of hair behind one delicate, pointed ear. "Aye," she finally admitted, bringing her knees up and hugging them to her chest. "Athan is very dear to me. News of his death would wound me deeply, but this not knowing . . . I think sometimes it is worse."

Though Ghleanna had confirmed her suspicions, Kestrel floundered for a response. Since Quinn's death she'd made a priority of keeping others at a distance. She'd never had the need—or felt the urge—to offer words of support to anyone on any occasion. A minute lapsed, then two, until a reply no longer seemed necessary.

"The man who raised you—" Ghleanna began tentatively, breaking her gaze away from the fire to regard Kestrel. "Was he a good man?"

"He was." She grinned, more to herself than Ghleanna. "Not an honest man, mind you, but a good man."

"Does he yet live?"

Her grin faded. "Quinn died in a tavern brawl when I was twelve. Slipped an ace up his sleeve once too often." She glanced toward the cots, where the others all seemed to have dozed off at last. "I can only imagine what Lord D'Arcey would think about that."

Ghleanna flashed her a conspiratorial smile. "He shan't hear of it from me."

"Thanks." They lapsed into silence again. Kestrel felt as if she ought to return the other woman's show of interest. "What about your folks?" She prepared to sit through the tale of some aristocratic elven or human house—perhaps both.

"I never knew my parents, either," the half-elf said softly. "My mother died birthing me, and my father—well, he'd gone back to his human wife and son before I was born." Ghleanna returned her gaze to the fire, apparently finding it easier to avoid eye contact when talking about herself. "My uncle took me into his household, but he resented a 'half-breed' growing up alongside his elven children. 'Twas not until my human brother found me—after our father had died—that I felt I truly had a family."

Kestrel listened with surprise. She'd always found the ways of wizards so mysterious that she never considered the real, flesh-and-blood people beneath the robes. She'd assumed the half-elf boasted a pedigree similar to Corran's, one full of wealthy family members eager to pay for her magical training or anything else she desired. The rogue had never imagined Ghleanna's background could have a thing in common with her own.

The sorceress yawned and rose. "Dawn shall be upon us all too quickly, I think. Will you retire as well?"

"Soon," Kestrel answered. Ghleanna had given her much to ponder.

❖ ❖ ❖ ❖ ❖

At first light, the party set out for the southwest ruins. They entered the ghost shrine to hear Anorrweyn's spirit still repeating her lonely, sorrowful call.

"Where are the followers of Mystra?" The cry seemed to echo off the intangible walls.

Faeril stepped forward, holding out the medallion she wore around her neck. "Here, priestess! Mystra's faithful still walk this earth. I am Faeril, but one of Our Lady's many servants."

Goosebumps prickled Kestrel's arms as she waited to see whether the elven spirit would respond. The room fell unnaturally silent. No sounds from outside seemed to penetrate the spectral building, and those who stood within scarcely dared to breathe.

A faint scent stole into the air. Kestrel inhaled the musky perfume, searching her mind to identify the familiar fragrance. Gardenias.

Moments later, the slender figure of a woman appeared—at first dim and wavering, then brighter and steadier. A small nose, high cheekbones and a soft mouth set off the large turquoise eyes that dominated her heart-shaped face. Long, dark tresses cascaded over her shoulders, disappearing behind the silky fabric of her close-fitting green gown. Though an emerald ferronniere crowned her forehead, in truth Anorrweyn Evensong needed no adornment.

Kestrel absently ran her fingers through her short, boyish locks. The priestess's understated elegance made the rogue suddenly self-conscious of her own rough-and-tumble appearance. Kestrel knew that while she might have the dexterity of a cat, she'd never possess one-tenth Anorrweyn's grace. In the past, women like this gentle elf made her feel defensive, but somehow this spirit struck a chord in her.

"Faeril." The elven spirit smiled and extended her hand toward the cleric. Her fingertips came within inches of Faeril's face but did not touch it. "You are truly a daughter of Mystra?"

"Yes, priestess. Your sect has suffered hardship but yet survives."

"I had feared the spinning centuries had put an end to Our Lady's worship." Anorrweyn's gaze swept the group. "These are your companions?"

"Yes, priestess."

The spirit then studied the party one member at a time, briefly assessing each person as Faeril made introductions. When Anorrweyn's eyes met Kestrel's, the thief felt warmth and peace pass through her. "You are the heroes who freed the remains of my temple from the evil creatures who laid claim to it." Anorrweyn's voice had lost its melancholy timbre, and its tones now fell soft as spring rain. "How may I aid you in return? Speak quickly—my foothold in your time is light."

Corran removed his helm and genuflected before her. "The Mythal is in jeopardy, priestess. Evildoers have corrupted its magic and harnessed its power for their own diabolical ends."

"Yes, I feel them, even through the years. They have raised an abomination under the very seat of the coronal, an abomination that cracks stone and earth in its hunger." She extended her hand toward the paladin. "Rise, holy knight."

Corran obeyed. Though his large form physically dwarfed the priestess, it was she who exuded more presence. "They plan to overtake first Myth Drannor and then all Faerûn," Corran continued, "raising a dracolich to ultimate dominion over all."

If it was possible for a bloodless, incorporeal being to pale, Anorrweyn Evensong did so. "They cannot be allowed to succeed!"

"We have made it our mission to stop them," Ghleanna said. "But we have only an imperfect understanding of the Mythal. We come to you seeking knowledge."

"I will gladly share all I have. Please, sit and rest, as the Mythal's tale is one that spans centuries. I will tell as much as I can before my spirit slips back into the past." She gestured toward several benches that looked as if they'd been literally tossed into the corner. Broken legs and blocks of stone lay scattered around them. "I regret I cannot offer you better hospitality, but I believe you may find an intact seat or two in that pile."

They found three benches that appeared sound enough

to support the weight of six people. Corran and Durwyn positioned them in a half-circle. Kestrel and the others sat down—all except Durwyn, who repeatedly glanced over his shoulder at the entrance. "I don't want any more nagas to surprise us," he said finally. "I'll stand guard and listen from the door."

The fighter's absence left an empty space beside Kestrel. To her surprise, the ghost herself took that seat. Had Caalenfaire come so close, Kestrel would have jumped like a rabbit, but somehow she felt calm in Anorrweyn's presence. A fleeting look of envy passed over Faeril's features at Kestrel's proximity to Anorrweyn, but the cleric's own seat actually offered a better view of the priestess.

"The Mythal was woven in the Year of Soaring Stars," the spirit began. "The city's greatest wizards, most of them elves, came together to lay the Mythal. Working cooperatively, they wove a spell greater than the sum of its casters. Each chose a special power to infuse into the mantle, and each gave some of his or her life to engender it." The ghostly elf turned to Corran. "You wish to speak?"

Anorrweyn's perceptiveness impressed Kestrel—the priestess had not even been looking at him directly. "Yes," Corran said, appearing startled himself. "What kind of powers?"

"All kinds. Protections preventing certain types of magic from being used within the city. Interdicts to prevent undesirable races—such as drow, orcs, and goblins—from entering the city. The creation of amenities such as blueglow moss for the injured and a featherfall effect for the clumsy. These are but a few." The elven priestess glanced at the others as if checking whether more questions were forthcoming. Seeing no such indication, she continued. "The chief caster, Mythanthor, sacrificed his life to bring the Mythal into being. The weaving process consumed him body and soul. This sacrifice he made willingly, that by his death the Mythal and his beloved city would live."

Kestrel tried to imagine the fierce and selfless dedication of the wizard Mythanthor but found she could not. She'd never believed in anything strongly enough to give her life for it, and she doubted she ever would.

"The City of Song knew centuries of glory under the mantle of the Weave," Anorrweyn continued. "Ah, the beauty of those times . . . the Serpentspires, the Glimgardens . . . We floated on the air! But then the Armies of Darkness came." Anorrweyn's image flickered. "I hear their thunder, see their fire. . . . "

Faeril started forward. "Priestess?"

Anorrweyn hovered between planes, phasing in and out of the present. "My spirit slides back to those wicked days even as I tell their tale." Her image solidified but the priestess swayed. "The drums. Can you hear the drums?" She closed her eyes, frowning in concentration. "No, of course you cannot. I must tighten my grip on the present. Show me your medallion again, daughter."

Faeril knelt before the priestess and laid the amulet at her feet. The wavering ceased for a time. The cleric remained on her knees. "Prithee continue priestess, if you can."

Anorrweyn raised her hand to her temples, forcing herself to focus. "The Weeping Wars that ruined Myth Drannor damaged the Mythal as well. Many of its powers were lost or weakened. The surviving city leaders met in secret to devise a way to save the Mythal from further decay. After years of study and debate, they decided to create an artifact now known as the Gem of the Weave. Through this gem, the Mythal could be monitored and, as necessary, tuned. One person alone would be forever entrusted with the power and responsibility of using the gem to protect and maintain the Mythal.

"Our city engineer, Harldain Ironbar, secured an appropriate gem—a perfect sapphire—and the city's most powerful spellcasters created the Incantation of the Weave to bind the sapphire to the Mythal. But a communicant was needed, a person who would bind his or her spirit to the gem. Once again, a far-seeing elf came forward to sacrifice his life to protect what remained of this great city. Miroden Silverblade, a lord of House Ammath, willingly ended his mortal existence to spend eternity as a baelnorn—an immortal guardian. Now known simply as the Protector, he holds safe the Sapphire of the Weave, which he uses to commune with and tune the Mythal."

"It seems we should meet this Protector," Corran said.

Kestrel did not relish the thought of encountering yet another ghost. Anorrweyn wasn't so bad—the rogue might have forgotten the priestess was a spirit at all were it not for her translucence and her tentative hold on the present. However, the image of Caalenfaire in his scrying chair still gave her the shudders.

Ghleanna nodded in response to Corran's statement. "How well do you know the baelnorn?" she asked Anorrweyn. "If we seek help from him, will he aid us?"

"I know he would," the priestess responded. "Guarding the Mythal is his whole reason for being. Miroden Silverblade can use the gem to undo the corruption of the Mythal. That should help you drive out the evil that has invaded Myth Drannor."

"Can you take us to him?" Jarial asked.

"Alas, I cannot." A note of sorrow crept into the spirit's voice. "Once my spirit walked freely on this plane to continue My Lady's work. But vandals stole my skull from its resting place beneath this shrine. I cannot leave this ghostly building until it is returned. Forsooth, I can scarcely cling to the present." Her image flickered again, disappearing for longer beats of time than before. "Eltargrim—Coronal—

where are you? Shall the Tel'Quessir drown uncaptained in this dark sea?"

Kestrel found herself feeling sympathy for the trapped spirit. Anorrweyn's consciousness had survived her death only to see her mortal remains scattered about like so much litter. How horrible—to have pieces of one's body dispersed over ruins, while one's consciousness forever flitted between centuries.

"No, no—I must hold to the living moment a while longer." The priestess clawed at the air, fighting a temporal battle they could not witness. "Night falls again on the eve of my death. The spellfire comes. Listen, before I am caught in its blaze once more. . . . Seek out the baelnorn yourselves. He lives deep below Myth Drannor's surface, in the catacombs beneath Castle Cormanthor. Harldain Ironbar, whose spirit yet haunts the Onaglym, can help you gain access to the catacombs. Once inside, the baelnorn's lair is marked with the Rune of the Protector." She traced the symbol in the air. "To reach him, you must know the Word of Safekeeping: *Fhaomiir.*"

Corran rose and bowed once more. "We thank you for your aid, Anorrweyn Evensong. I but wish we could do more to help you."

"You can . . . " Anorrweyn's image flickered, disappearing for so long that Kestrel thought she would not return. Nonetheless, the strong-willed spirit fought her way back to the present one more time. "I believe my graverobbers were minions of a lich who dwelt within the catacombs. They may have taken their prize there. If you should happen upon my skull—"

"Of course," Corran said.

"I could then stand with both feet in this time. I could help you further." Anorrweyn smiled, the first smile they had seen from her. The expression lit her whole face with an angelic glow, sparking a response in Kestrel that caught the rogue by surprise. She wanted to aid the ghostly priestess, wanted to help this gentle, noble spirit obtain some peace as she faced eternity trapped on this earth.

"I promise you, priestess, we will do all we can," Kestrel said solemnly. "It would be our privilege to restore your skull to its sacred resting place."

The vow—the first words Kestrel had spoken since Anorrweyn appeared—pleased the priestess. Corran looked at her in astonishment, approval dawning in his eyes.

Kestrel rose and turned away from the paladin's gaze, intending to join Durwyn at the entrance. She didn't need Corran D'Arcey's approval, or anyone else's for that matter. Helping Anorrweyn just felt like the right thing to do.

A small cry from Faeril arrested her attention. Anorrweyn's form was fading from view, wavering and shimmering as it dimmed.

"Be not afraid, daughter," the priestess said. "I must leave you now. But return with my skull and I shall be stronger." Anorrweyn Evensong was but a faint outline now, rapidly disappearing altogether. "Trumpets cry . . . the tide rushes in. . . . Summon the armathors!"

With that, the elven spirit was gone. The scent of gardenias lingered.

CHAPTER NINE

The House of Gems resembled nothing so much as the dwarves who had raised it. Though the Onaglym was a large two-towered building, its stone construction lent it a dense, compact appearance, giving Kestrel the impression that nothing could ever budge—or even mar—the dwarven stronghold. Despite the wars that had rocked the rest of Myth Drannor, the fortress stood solid and strong, undaunted by the changes wrought upon the city around it.

Here they would find Harldain Ironbar, or so Caalenfaire had said. As both the diviner and Anorrweyn had mentioned the dwarven spirit— did all the ghosts in this town know each other?—visiting him seemed the next logical step of their mission. Besides, they needed to learn from Harldain how to enter the catacombs if they ever hoped to meet the Protector or locate Anorrweyn's skull.

The Onaglym's exterior betrayed no sign of cult sorcerers still occupying its Round Tower. In fact, with the exception of the cultists, the rest of the city's evil denizens seemed to give the fortress a wide berth. The dwarven meeting hall appeared to have escaped the looting and lairing that characterized most of Myth Drannor's surface buildings. After the trap the party had encountered while trying to reach the Room of Words, Kestrel could guess why.

They found the main door open, a fact that bothered Kestrel almost as much as the eerie rhythm, like a giant heartbeat, coming from within. *Pa-pum. Pa-pum.* It was an ominous greeting, to say the least. While the others speculated about the source of the faint noise, she spent twenty minutes searching the doorway for traps. Finally Corran, eager to investigate, simply walked through the entrance. He turned around, unscathed. "Sometimes a lucky break is just a lucky break, Kestrel."

She rolled her eyes. Sometimes. Not often. And based on previous experience, not in this fortress. Kestrel hung back as the others brushed past her into a small courtyard containing the statue of some long-forgotten dwarven hero. An archway led to a larger, open area beyond dotted with more statues.

Pa-pum. Pa-pum.

She scanned the walls, floor, and ceiling once again. Dwarves would not leave the front door—even the front door of a building they were abandoning as they fled the city—hanging open. The last one out would have closed the door and extinguished the lights. There had to be something she wasn't seeing.

Pa-pum. Pa-pum.

Corran cast an impatient glance her way. "Are you coming or not?"

Still suspicious, she relented. "Coming."

The moment she stepped through the doorway, an iron door clanged down behind her. Damn it all! How had she missed that? She let fly a stream of expletives against crafty dwarven engineers. "Lucky break, my arse! I told you it was too easy to get in here!" Before her companions could answer, she turned her back on them to study the iron door. She had a feeling they would be using a different exit.

Pa-pum. Pa-pum.

"Kestrel, we're inside now." Corran's voice grated on her nerves. "Let's find Harldain—I'm sure he can tell us how to get out."

"Just give me a minute!" she snapped. Corran was probably right, but the undiscovered trap had bruised her pride.

"Suit yourself. We're going on ahead."

"You do that." Arrogant, insufferable jerk . . . She heard him leave, heard the others following, all except Durwyn, whose presence she yet sensed, though some feet away. He waited quietly as she continued to examine the door.

Pa-pum. Pa-pum.

Less than a minute later, his voice broke the stillness. "Uh, Kestrel?" Durwyn spoke softly, probably afraid of irritating her further.

She tried to tamp down her annoyance and keep her tone even. "Yes, Durwyn?" From behind, she heard the warrior rattling around. He was closer than she'd thought. Good grief—was he deliberately scraping his armor across the stone floor? She tried to block out the noise and concentrate on her task, running her hand along the smooth iron door.

Pa-pum. Pa-pum.

"I'd turn around if I were you."

A sense of dread shot through her. She spun on her heel to face him.

And found herself looking straight into the eyes of a dwarf.

The statue in the center of the courtyard had come to life. The bearded champion, armed with a two-handed axe, stood between her and Durwyn. The dwarf stared at her, his expression inscrutable. She stared back as her mind raced. Should she slowly circle toward Durwyn? Say something to the animated statue?

Pa-pum. Pa-pum.

The dwarf winked. Mischief somehow twinkled in his cold stone eyes. Kestrel released the breath she didn't know she'd been holding and allowed the muscles in her shoulders to relax.

He leaped off the pedestal to attack.

The stone guardian swung his weapon in a wide arc meant to catch Kestrel in the midriff. Instinctively, she dropped to the floor and rolled to one side. The blade struck the door with a deafening *clang!* that left a dent in the iron.

She paled at the display of strength. A single blow from the dwarf could crush even Durwyn or cleave her in half. He came at her again, raising the axe high in the air this time.

She rolled once more, then jumped to her feet. The dwarf's axe struck the floor, sending rock chips flying. The ring of steel on stone echoed off the walls.

Pa-pum, pa-pum. The mysterious thumping continued, but her own heart beat double time. She noted that the statue's movements, though deliberate, were slow. Durwyn had moved forward to aid her, but she grabbed his arm instead. "Let's find the others!" She tugged on his hand, urging the big man to abandon the fight. If the dwarf followed them, at least they could face him with help.

They darted through the archway—only to discover an even worse scene. Corran, Faeril, and the two sorcerers were locked in combat with three more animated statues, and other figures nearby seemed to be stirring to life. Kestrel's gaze swept the fortress ward. At least two dozen dwarven sculptures were scattered about the grounds. They couldn't possibly fight them all.

Pa-pum. Pa-pum.

Across the embankment, another iron door stood open. If they could reach it and close it behind them, they would be safe from the statues—though with that strange, perpetual thumping noise ringing off the walls, who knew what lay on the other side? Kestrel heard the first dwarf catching up to them, and a swing from one of the other statues had just narrowly missed Corran's head. It was a chance they would have to take.

"There are too many statues!" she shouted, hoping the others would hear her over the sounds of combat. "We have to outrun them!" The sorcerers were launching their magical volleys from a distance. They should have no trouble dropping their attack to flee. Corran and Faeril, on the other hand, might require aid to disengage from combat.

"I've never retreated from a battle," Corran declared, parrying another blow. Kestrel was surprised his warhammer hadn't snapped under the force of the statue's strike.

Anger welled within her. Would Corran rather die than listen to her? Durwyn nearly jerked her off her feet as an axe whistled past her ear—the first dwarf had caught up to them. The blow struck a granite fountain, sending huge chunks of rock scudding across the ground.

"Abandon this one!" Durwyn called out. He pushed her forward, turning around to guard their backs. "Go, Kestrel! Lead the way. I'll be right behind you."

Would the others follow? She had no time to speculate. With a quick survey and a split-second decision, she darted across the ward.

Pa-pum. Pa-pum.

Durwyn shadowed her steps. He paused, however, to pick up a large chunk of granite, which he launched at the legs of Faeril's opponent. The statue tottered, ceasing its offensive just long enough for the cleric to break free of combat and join the retreat. Ghleanna and Jarial also followed.

They had to dodge the blows of several already-animated statues before reaching terrain where no guardians yet stirred. Kestrel steered as far as possible from statues that had not yet awakened, hoping to minimize the number of attackers. The likenesses were positioned, however, so that no intruder could bypass them all. Every hundred paces or so they awakened another one.

Pa-pum. Pa-pum. The thumping grew louder as they traversed the ward. Whatever was making that noise, they were running toward it.

At last, they reached the second iron door. As they ducked inside, Kestrel quickly scanned the interior for the source of the thumping sound. Spotting nothing, she turned around to see whether Corran had joined them.

"Damn him!" She could have spat nails. The paladin remained behind, stubbornly trying to hold his ground. Before she could stop him, Durwyn headed back to aid Corran. "Durwyn! No!"

The fighter could not return the way they had come, for by now the statues Kestrel's party had awakened were fully animated. He was forced to chose a less direct path, rousing new guardians in the process. He reached the beleaguered paladin just in time to block a strike that would have hit Corran from behind.

Damn Corran D'Arcey to the Abyss! His arrogance now endangered Durwyn as well. The statues were closing in on them—and those that weren't headed toward the door where Kestrel and the others stood watching.

Pa-pum. Pa-pum.

Durwyn shouted at his comrade, but the distance, the everpresent heartbeat, and the sounds of the stone dwarves' laborious movements prevented Kestrel from making out the words. Whatever he said, however, seemed to sink through Corran's thick skull. The two began to retreat, Durwyn leading them along a circuitous route past the last of the sleeping statues. A dozen stone dwarves approached from all sides.

Ghleanna muttered something. Kestrel, her attention divided between Durwyn's plight and the half-dozen statues marching her own way, missed what she said and asked her to repeat it. When she glanced at the sorceress, however, she realized Ghleanna was casting a spell.

A huge mass of sticky strands suddenly draped itself over most of the dwarves chasing Durwyn and Corran. The enormous spider web gummed up the statues' movements, impeding their pursuit. At the same time Jarial uttered a command of his own at the dwarves approaching the door. Their advance instantly slowed to a rate that would have looked comic had the danger they posed not been so great.

The two fighters still had to dodge the blows of four unaffected statues that blocked their path. As they darted past, one of the dwarves landed a strike on Durwyn's left arm, nearly severing the limb. The warrior cried out and gripped his arm to his side, but kept moving.

Pa-pum. Pa-pum.

Kestrel forced herself to watch their final approach but could not look at Durwyn's face. The agony she'd seen flash across it had been so intense it left her own knees weak. Blood streamed down his side.

Anger at Corran battled fear for her friend. *Her friend.* She hadn't thought of Durwyn that way until this moment, but she'd probably be dead right now if he hadn't stayed behind in the courtyard waiting for her. He'd been a faithful companion to her, to them all—which was why he was now injured. She regretted every unkind or impatient thought she'd ever had toward him.

The two made it to the door just as Jarial's spell wore off the nearest dwarves. Kestrel, Jarial, and Ghleanna swung shut the heavy door while Faeril immediately attended Durwyn. "Sit down," she said calmly, helping him to the ground.

Pa-pum. Pa-pum. With the door closed, the thumping echoed louder. Kestrel tried to block it from her mind as she knelt beside the injured warrior. Durwyn's face was pale—he'd already lost a lot of blood. His eyes held the steely look of someone trying to mask suffering.

She'd never felt this scared for someone else, not since Quinn had died. Instinctively, she reached for his good hand and forced herself to give him a wobbly smile. "We're lucky Faeril is with us. You're going to be fine." Eyes never leaving his face, she said to Faeril, "Tell me how to help you."

"Just keep doing what you're doing," the elf said gently, beginning her prayer of healing.

Behind her, Kestrel heard Corran approach. He cleared his throat. "May I assist?"

She looked up at him, her face hot. "I think you've done quite enough already." She had much more to say, but she didn't want to make a scene in front of Durwyn.

Remorse flickered across the paladin's features. "Perhaps I have," he said more to himself than to her. She wished he would just go away, but he remained, watching Faeril's ministrations.

Kestrel talked to Durwyn quietly while the cleric tended to him. The warrior was weak but lucid. "Thank you for watching my back earlier, in the courtyard," she said.

"I—" He paused as if choosing his words. "I know that I'm not the smartest guy in the world. I'm good with an axe, but I'm not so good at figuring things out. So when I find people smarter than me, I trust them to do most of the thinking. You've been right about a lot of things so far, Kestrel. When you said there was a trap, I believed you."

Durwyn's words heartened her. She hadn't been shouting into the wind this whole time, struggling in vain to be heard. Someone had been paying attention.

When Faeril finished, Durwyn's arm was fully healed. He rested awhile on the floor as the remainder of the party assessed their surroundings. They stood inside the main building of the fortress, in a great hall with numerous wooden tables, benches, and other furnishings all still in excellent condition. Even the tapestries on the walls, colorful depictions of dwarven artisans engaged in their crafts, seemed unaffected by age.

At the opposite end of the hall, two staircases led to the second floor. The periodic thumping sound, louder in Kestrel's ears now that Durwyn was out of danger, resonated off the stone walls. It repeated every minute or so, like the heartbeat of a man who refused to die. The noise seemed to come from above.

Pa-pum. Pa-pum.

They climbed the stairs to find a single large room—and Harldain Ironbar. Or so they assumed. A dwarven spirit occupied the center of the chamber. The middle-aged lord had apparently been a figure of some standing in Myth Drannor, judging from his thick fur cloak, ringed fingers, and the chain of office around his neck.

"I'd say that's Harldain, all right," Kestrel said. "But what's the matter with him?" The dwarf stood transfixed, his translucent image unmoving even under the party's scrutiny.

Ghleanna held two fingers up to the ghost's face, gliding

them back and forth as she watched his eyes. When she moved her fingers quickly, the eyes remained still. But when she moved them slowly, his pupils followed the movement. "He seems to be in a state of arrested animation," she said. "He can't move, but I'll bet he can hear us."

"Y . . . y . . . yes," the ghost said. Kestrel almost missed the single word, as the thumping noise had repeated at the same instant. The heartbeat sound was still louder up here and seemed to come from the other side of a door in the southwest corner of the room.

"He can speak!" Corran moved to stand directly before the spirit. "Are you Harldain Ironbar?"

No answer. The paladin repeated his question but still got no response.

"Let's try another question," Jarial said. Corran stepped aside so the sorcerer could face the spirit. "Anorrweyn Evensong and Caalenfaire sent us," Jarial told the ghost. "Do you know them?"

Still no response.

Kestrel thought they needed to get to the point. "How can we free you?" There would be enough time for other questions once the spirit could talk easily.

"P . . . u . . . mp."

"What did he say?" Ghleanna asked. His answer had coincided with the thumping noise again.

"It sounded like *pump*." Kestrel looked around the room. "But I don't see anything in here that looks like a—"

"Maybe he said *thump*," Corran said. "Perhaps that thumping sound has something to do with this."

Kestrel knew she'd heard a "p" sound, not a "th," but pointing that out to the paladin would require actually speaking to him. Still nursing her anger over Corran's pig-headed endangerment of Durwyn, she let his suggestion pass without comment. Besides, she had no better idea to offer.

Corran tried the southwest door and found it unlocked. When he opened it the heartbeat sound repeated, the strongest they'd heard it yet. "This way."

The door exited onto a small balcony with a narrow stairway leading up to the rooftop. They trotted along the fortress's battlements, following the rhythmic thumping noise, until they reached a similar staircase heading down. The steps deposited them in the stronghold's pumphouse, where the mechanical pump struggled to perform its duty. The slow *pa-pum* was the sound of the device fighting to draw water from the Onaglym's ancient cistern, which lay in a courtyard beyond.

"I knew he said *pump,*" Kestrel muttered under her breath.

Ghleanna wrinkled her nose. "What's that smell?" A putrid odor filled the air, as of rotting garbage. Or decaying flesh.

Kestrel raised her guard, remembering the zombies that seemed to appear whenever they'd previously detected such a stench. She heard no telltale shuffling of animated corpses, only the slow, laborious sound of the pump.

Faeril walked to the arched doorway that opened into the courtyard. "It seems to be emanating from—Oh, Lady of Mysteries, preserve us!"

The others rushed over. On the far side of the courtyard, the desiccated body of a human female hung impaled on a spiked pole. The former fighter had been disemboweled. In place of her organs nested a large membranous sac that pulsed and squirmed.

Kestrel's gorge rose. Anorrweyn's missing skull had seemed bad, but *this* . . . Was it the fate of all women in this city to have their remains defiled? She had to turn her head away from the sight. It was then that she noticed the unnatural color of the water in the cistern. The reservoir, which should have held clear rainwater, instead bubbled with murky brownish liquid. The water must have become polluted somehow through the centuries.

Or corrupted recently. Kestrel noted an amber cast to the fluid and closed her eyes against the realization dawning on her. They had found another spawn pool.

When she opened her eyes, despite her fervent wishes the abomination remained. "Uh, guys—"

"I just noticed it, too," Ghleanna said.

Corran and Faeril, meanwhile, had approached the corpse. Faeril gestured toward an insignia on the remains of the body's tattered clothing. "Sisters of the Silver Fire," she said. "This woman was a holy warrior dedicated to Mystra."

"Of your sect?" Corran asked.

"No, another, but I feel the loss as keenly." She studied the writhing sac in the fallen warrior's body cavity. "She appears to be infested by the eggs of some loathsome creature—and I suspect they are hatching. Jarial? Ghleanna?"

The sorcerers joined them. Kestrel and Durwyn followed a little behind. They heard Faeril say sadly, "I'd prefer a nobler death rite, but we haven't time."

The group stood back. Faeril raised her voice in prayer as Jarial hurled a ball of fire at the corpse. The blast incinerated both the fighter and the vile, squirming egg sac. When the last flames sputtered out, the sorcerer waved his hand over the ashes. A light breeze swirled them into a funnel, dispersing the ashes into the wind.

Kestrel watched the dust blow away, then turned her attention back to the pool. The insidious amber liquid was gone. Pure water once again filled the cistern. The pump resumed its normal pace, the mechanism sounding almost eager to get back to work.

At the edge of the reservoir lay the dead fighter's weapon, a gleaming sword with a red tinge to the steel.

Corran picked it up and handed it to Faeril. "Perhaps you can use it to avenge her death."

"With Mystra's aid, I shall."

They returned to the main fortress, where a liberated Harldain Ironbar awaited them. As they entered his chamber, the dwarf met them with a ghostly battle-axe in hand. "Identify yerselves!"

The paladin stepped forward, hands raised to show his peaceful intentions. "I am Corran D'Arcey. These are my companions Ghleanna, Jarial, Durwyn, Faeril, and Kestrel. We are come to free Myth Drannor of the evil that has overtaken it."

"So yer not part of that dragon cult?"

"Nay! In fact we are sworn to defeat them," Faeril said.

Harldain lowered his axe but continued to regard them suspiciously. Corran removed his helm and tucked it under his arm to allow the dwarf a clear look at his face. Following his lead, Durwyn did likewise. Harldain seemed to appreciate the gesture and studied his unexpected visitors.

"The priestess Anorrweyn Evensong advised us to seek your counsel," said Corran. "So did the diviner Caalenfaire."

"So you said earlier." Harldain rested the axe head on the floor and leaned on the shaft as if it were a cane. "Friends of yers, are they? Anorrweyn's a gentle soul, but that Caalenfaire—he gave me the shivers even before he was dead. The old sorcerer's never done me a bad turn, though, so I reckon if he and Anorrweyn are on yer side, then yer on mine. 'Bout time someone came to drive those dragon-lovin' vermin out of my city." He stroked his beard thoughtfully. "So, the priestess and the fortune-teller have teamed up, have they? Things must have gotten pretty bad while I was frozen there. I think that nasty water cloggin' the pump had somethin' to with it. Seems like polluted pools are poppin' up everywhere a glimmer of good remains in this city. Anyway, what have they sent you to talk to me about?"

"We need access to the catacombs," Corran said.

"Do you, now? Well, that's a simple enough matter to help you with. But what are they sendin' you down there for?"

"To find the Protector. We need to talk to him about the Mythal."

Some of the fire left Harldain's eyes. He let out a deep sigh. "They've gone and done it, haven't they? Those dragon worshipers, they've done somethin' to the Mythal." He shook his head sadly. "I'd always hoped that somehow we could use the Mythal to restore the City of Song to its former glory. But now . . ."

"You may yet," Ghleanna said gently. "If we act quickly to defeat the cult. We need your help."

Harldain nodded. "Yes, of course. Anything I can do." He stroked his beard again. "Dark elves have infiltrated much of the first catacomb level, so don't even try to use the main entrance—I'll send you a secret way. You'll have to face enough of 'em just to move deeper inside."

He crossed the room and pointed to one of the bricks in the wall. "That block is loose. Pull it out." Corran pried out the stone, revealing a hidden cubbyhole. "Now reach inside and get the stone that's in there. The key—take the key out, too. It's a passkey. It'll disable the statues downstairs, make it easier for you to leave."

Corran withdrew the key and a gem similar in appearance to the one set in the Ring of Calling. The gem sparkled with inner white light.

"That's a starstone," Harldain said. "Used to be that lots of folks in Myth Drannor had at least one. The starstones were set in different pieces of jewelry. When the wearer stood in specific locations, magical gates opened to different parts of the city. Helped a body get around faster."

Ghleanna extended her hand so Harldain could see the Ring of Calling. "Is this a starstone?"

"It is, indeed," the spirit confirmed. "That's one of the more common starstones. It got folks to the City Heights from various parts of town." Harldain gestured toward the sparkling rock Corran held. "That's a rarer stone. Belongs in a neckpiece called the Wizard's Torc. Sorcerers of the Speculum used the torc to open a secret entrance from the amphitheater to the catacombs. Restore the starstone to the Wizard's Torc and wear it while standin' on the theater floor—in the Circle of Ualair the Silent—and the door'll open for you."

Harldain's expression grew troubled. "Of course, you have to find the torc first—last I heard, a dark naga in the dwarven dungeons had the thing." He narrowed his brows at Jarial. "What're you grinnin' about?"

"You mean this torc?"

CHAPTER TEN

"Drow," Kestrel whispered, squinting in the dim torchlight.

Ghleanna rolled her eyes. "Not more of them?"

"Afraid so." Kestrel shared the mage's sentiment. This was the fourth such patrol they'd seen since entering the catacombs. The ebon-skinned, white-haired warriors seemed to swarm the undercity, their fierce war paint and lethally sharp halberds boldly declaring their right of occupation to anyone foolish enough to question their presence. Unlike the orogs Kestrel's party had observed in the dwarven undercity, the drow were a close-mouthed people. No stray snatches of conversation had revealed their purpose in Myth Drannor.

"If we double back and take that other fork,

perhaps we can bypass their encampment altogether," Corran suggested.

Kestrel shrugged, unconvinced. So far they'd successfully avoided detection by the dark elves, but their luck couldn't hold out forever. They'd been fortunate enough to escape serious combat with the all the undead creatures wandering about. Corran and Faeril had managed to turn away most of the shadows and zombies, and the cleric had even destroyed the skeletons they'd come upon with a single holy word.

As much as Kestrel disliked facing undead beings, she dreaded an encounter with the dark elves more. The drow had a reputation for cruelty toward their enemies—who, from what Kestrel understood, comprised just about everyone not drow. Even the unliving gave them a wide berth, lairing in separate parts of the dungeons.

They retreated down the rough-hewn tunnel. Once, Kestrel would have considered these dense subterranean warrens well constructed, but they couldn't help but suffer in comparison to the superior passages of the dwarves. Given their elven creators and their ancient age, however, the corridors and chambers remained in surprisingly good condition—from what she could see of them, anyway. The lighting was poor to say the least, with wispy flames barely clinging to widely spaced torches. She supposed they were lucky to have any light at all. Drow were known for their ability to see clearly in the dark, and the undead certainly hadn't lit the brands. The torches must be for the benefit of another mortal race. The cultists?

Corran led the group around a bend. A fork they'd passed previously lay just a few hundred feet beyond. Suddenly, the paladin stopped short—but not before a band of drow in the intersection spotted the party. "Hold!" one of them cried. "If you value your wretched lives!"

"They've nowhere to go, Razherrt!" came a voice from

behind them. "We heard their noisy clanking all the way down at our post."

Beshaba's bad breath! They were surrounded! Kestrel tensed, swearing silently at the Maid of Misfortune as she prepared to grab Loren's Blade and hurl it in a single swift movement should the need arise. Corran's hand rested on his sword hilt, while Durwyn gripped his axe more tightly. Faeril stood with hands on hips, her fingers inches from the hilt of her new sword.

"Humans. How such a primitive race has survived this long baffles the mind." The dark elf Razherrt laughed humorlessly as he approached. Six other warriors accompanied him. All wore black leather armor emblazoned with the symbol of a phoenix rising toward a dark green moon. Similarly marked bracers on Razherrt's arms set him apart from the others. Their patrol leader, Kestrel guessed.

The drow fighters pointed their halberds at Kestrel's party, but Razherrt held his weapon upright as if unconcerned by the possibility of any sudden moves by the lowly adventurers. His gaze swept the party, rapidly assessing each member, lingering on Ghleanna. "A half-breed. I see the People continue slumming."

The half-elf remained silent under the drow's insults. Corran, regarding the patrol leader warily, removed his hand from his weapon to indicate peaceful intentions. "We seek only to pass through."

A sneer crossed Razherrt's chiseled features. "You presume too much, human. The House of Freth does not appreciate vermin trespassing through its territory." As he spoke, he almost absently moved his hands in a series of gestures, as if he spoke in sign language.

"We did not realize the House of Freth laid claim to these halls."

Razherrt studied Corran with an intensity that Kestrel

thought would bore holes through the paladin's forehead. The leader of the other patrol said something in a language Kestrel had never heard before. Whatever he said, the statement elicited a low chuckle from Razherrt, who responded with several quick hand signals. The waiting drow warriors raised their blades.

"You find me in a good mood today, human," Razherrt said. "I deal with matters too important to waste time exterminating rodents. Get thee gone from my sight. No—better still, we shall escort you out of the Freth domain, so you do not 'accidentally' wander in again. Turn around."

Corran hesitated, apparently reluctant to expose his back to the drow.

Razherrt lowered the point of his weapon until it touched Corran's chin. "Are you hard of hearing or just simple? You have already trespassed on Freth territory— do not trespass on my patience."

The paladin turned, the expression in his eyes instructing the others to do likewise. Kestrel had rarely found herself so happy to travel in the middle of a party—as far away as possible from the drow on either end.

"Lead us to the stairs," Razherrt told the other patrol. "I don't know where our friends were headed, but they're going down now. We'll see how they like strolling below."

As they wended through the dungeons, they passed several more bands of drow at work clearing out various chambers. Apparently the House of Freth intended to stay for a while and make itself comfortable in Myth Drannor's underworld. Dark elves threw debris—and any other items they considered valueless—into carts for dumping in other parts of the dungeon. On one such cart, piled high with refuse, a skull rested as if carelessly tossed there. Was it Kestrel's imagination, or did a faint blue-white glow surround the skull?

Without warning, she was knocked to the floor from behind. Faeril sprawled on top of her.

"Get up, you sun-worshipping dog!" Razherrt kicked the cleric. "Are you too stupid to even walk?"

"I—I tripped." She caught Kestrel's gaze. *The skull,* Faeril mouthed before Razherrt gripped her wrist and jerked her to her feet.

So it was indeed Anorrweyn's skull! Kestrel couldn't guess how the cleric knew for certain, but at the moment she didn't have time to care. The skull lay about eight feet away, and they wouldn't be passing any closer. "My knee!" She rolled onto her side with a groan. "You landed on my knee, you bumbling fool!"

Faeril's expression clouded with genuine contrition. "I am sorry! Here, let me—"

"Oh, save it!" Kestrel awkwardly climbed to her feet and stumbled toward the cart holding the skull.

Razherrt's blade stopped her. "Where do you think you're going?"

"To lean against that garbage cart, if you don't mind."

"Kestrel, watch your tongue. You insult our hosts by not seeking their permission," Corran said. Was it a true rebuke, or had he also spotted the skull? "Pray overlook my companion's rudeness, Razherrt. If you'll let her pause a moment, I'm sure she'll give you no more trouble."

Kestrel balanced on one foot, as if she couldn't bear to put weight on her right leg. Razherrt stared at her, undecided. Her heartbeat accelerated as nervous energy coursed through her veins. "My apologies, sir. You know that humans are weak. Pain clouds my judgment."

She nearly choked on the sycophantic words, but they seemed to work. The drow raised the tip of his halberd. "A minute's rest. No more."

Kestrel stumbled to the cart and leaned against it, her fingers inches away from the skull. Anorrweyn's remains seemed to radiate an aura of calm, removing the anxiety she'd felt. Now she needed but a few seconds' distraction to snatch the skull from its disrespectful perch and drop it in a deep inside pocket of her cloak.

A series of chimes sounded across the room. All eyes turned in that direction—except Kestrel's. One of the sorcerers must have figured out her ruse. If not, she'd take advantage of the diversion no matter its source.

"What's that?" Razherrt glared first at Corran, then at the sorcerers. "Do you play games with us?"

"Perhaps it is a charm of the dungeons themselves," Jarial said. "Magic long sheltered the city above. Why should that not hold true for the city below?"

Razherrt grunted. "Get moving, all of you." He pointed at Kestrel. "You, too."

Kestrel rejoined the party, remembering to hobble. The uneven movement helped hide the bulge in her cloak.

❧ ❧ ❧ ❧ ❧

"Of all the insufferable—"

"We're alive and unharmed," Corran tossed over his shoulder. "And we retrieved Anorrweyn's skull to boot. Just count your blessings, Kestrel."

Kestrel found the paladin's condescension almost as galling as the Freth's arrogance. She simmered as they trod through the undercity's second level in search of another stairway leading down. "Well, I've had enough drow attitude for one lifetime, I'll tell you that. Primitive race, indeed! Razherrt can kiss my human—"

"Hush!" Faeril glanced around as if she'd heard something. "Did you—"

From out of nowhere, a huge ball of flame barreled down the corridor at them. Ghleanna immediately called out a command word and thrust her hand toward the accelerating flames. The blaze snuffed itself out, leaving only a few dying sparks scattered in the passageway— enough to illuminate the cult sorcerer on the other side.

Two drow bodyguards flanked the mage. As Corran and Durwyn moved to close in on the spellcaster, the dark elves immediately engaged them. The drow fought with mechanical precision, thrusting and parrying without so much as a grunt of exertion. Faeril tried to reach the sorcerer but wound up joining the melee instead, fighting by Corran's side.

The dark elves seemed utterly devoted to protecting the cultist. They could not, however, prevent Ghleanna and Jarial's magical attacks from reaching him. Kestrel decided to target the drow and leave the sorcerers to a spellcasting contest. She sent one dagger sailing toward each elven warrior.

Her aim held true. One blade struck its target in his side, the other hit Durwyn's opponent in his chest. Neither warrior cried out. She followed the double strike with Loren's Blade, hitting the first dark elf a second time. The dagger wounds did not seem to slow him down.

Kestrel had never seen combatants so fierce. Despite their injuries, the drow wielded their halberds with relentless vigor. The length of the weapon gave them an advantage over Durwyn's axe and the holy warriors' swords. Kestrel sucked in her breath. How could she fare any better with her club?

Durwyn's opponent backed him against a wall. Kestrel reached for her club, extended it with a flick of her wrist, then advanced on the dark elf. She managed to execute one hard hit to the drow's shoulder before he turned to engage her. Even with two-on-one odds, Kestrel felt at a disadvantage.

Meanwhile, flashes of light signaled the magical battle unfolding between the allied sorcerers and the cultist. Parrying the drow's blows, Kestrel could not spare even a glance to see who dominated that contest. *Please Mystra, let it be Jarial and Ghleanna!*

Suddenly, Kestrel's opponent collapsed to the floor. She looked up to see that the other drow had also fallen. The cult sorcerer lay with one of Jarial's acid arrows embedded between his eyes.

"As soon as the cultist fell, so did the drow," Jarial responded to the question in her eyes.

Durwyn prodded his former opponent with one foot. The body rolled over from the warrior's force, but otherwise did not stir. "He's dead. Just like that."

Faeril shook her head. "No, not 'just like that.' Look at these dagger wounds—there's no blood. I suspect these drow have been dead for some time."

"Soulless," Corran said. "Like the orogs."

Kestrel shuddered. Now that she had leisure to examine these dark elves more closely, they did look paler than Razherrt and his party had. They also bore a different emblem on their armor, two yellow chevrons bisecting eight red dots. She pointed to the symbol. "Do you think that's significant?"

"I suspect it indicates their House affiliation," Ghleanna said. "I noticed that Razherrt brushed his fingertips over his symbol whenever he mentioned the House of Freth."

"I guess these two belong to the House of Death," Kestrel quipped. No one laughed. Even to her own ears, the joke didn't seem funny. Only the gods knew how many legions of enthralled drow and orogs she and her companions might have to face before they completed their quest—if they ever did.

❧ ❧ ❧ ❧ ❧

The party spent the next several hours avoiding patrols of enthralled drow. They also came across additional soulless orogs and stumbled upon more than one lair of spectres in their search for the third level of the catacombs. Somehow, luck or the gods were on their side, and they suffered few injuries. Dead-ends and winding passages slowed their movements, but at last they found the path of descent.

Deeper in the bowels of the dungeons, travel became still more difficult. Huge chasms blocked their progress, forcing them to repeatedly backtrack and seek other routes through the claustrophobic tombs and prison blocks. They now wended through a narrow passage that seemed to go on forever. Kestrel wondered if they would ever find the Rune of the Protector that marked the entrance to the baelnorn's level.

"The passage seems to widen ahead," Corran said over his shoulder.

"About time," Kestrel muttered. It couldn't get much tighter—Durwyn's armored shoulders already threatened to scrape the walls.

They emerged in an enormous chamber but could enter only a few feet. They stood on an apron overlooking a drop-off so steep they could not see the bottom of the chasm. Kestrel kicked some loose rocks over the edge. She never heard them land.

Across the chasm stood a raised wooden drawbridge. She quickly scanned the nearby walls, floor, and ceiling for some mechanism to lower the drawbridge from their side but spotted nothing. She ran a hand through her hair, gripping the roots in frustration. "We are *not* turning around yet again."

"You don't have to," echoed a voice from across the chasm. A female drow warrior stepped out from behind the drawbridge. She held a long, jagged-bladed dagger as casually as another woman might carry a spindle. A top-knot secured her long white hair, exposing every angular line of her face. Sharp cheekbones, an aquiline nose, and hard-cast eyes appeared carved in stone. Worn, ragged armor revealed a body so muscular that Kestrel doubted this woman had a soft spot inside or out. Though the dark elf bore the same chevron symbol as the enthralled drow they'd encountered earlier, her skin had the healthy black color borne by Razherrt's band of living drow.

"Is that a threat?" Kestrel called back.

"Not yet." At a gesture from the woman, a ragged band comprising half a dozen drow warriors appeared behind her. "At present, we merely command parley."

Kestrel bristled at the word "command." The dark elves made Corran seem downright humble. After enjoying the House of Freth's gracious hospitality, she had no interest in chatting with more drow and was about to say so when Corran stepped forward.

"What do you wish to discuss?"

"Mutual interests."

Kestrel laughed humorlessly. "Your friend Razherrt didn't seem to think we have any."

The drow leader spat. "The House of Freth is no friend to the House of Kilsek. We seek the Freth's blood."

"We do not wish to become involved in a blood feud among the drow," Corran told the dark elf.

"Nor would we allow it! The House of Kilsek reserves for itself the honor of slaying our betrayers! I speak of a different enemy—the Cult of the Dragon."

Corran paused at that declaration. "What do you know of the cult?"

"More than you do, human! The Freth betrayed my kinfolk to the archmage and her minions. She uses a foul pool to trap my people's souls, then feeds their blood to a dracolich and enslaves their bodies. We despise Kya Mordrayn and her wicked cult even more than we loathe the traitorous Freth!" The drow's voice, which had risen to a fever pitch, suddenly turned cold as ice. "Hate is the song in our blood. It is all that lives in us now. We have sworn to release the souls of our kin into true death, even at the cost of own lives."

Corran studied the dark elf as she spoke, remaining calm in the wake of her passion. "What do you propose?"

"This chasm blocks your path. A cult sorcerer nearby blocks ours. He wields a magical device called the Staff of Sunlight—fatal to us but harmless to surface-dwellers. Agree to kill him, and I will lower the drawbridge. Claim the staff to use against the Freth—I care not. Just stay away from us."

Kestrel listened to the dark elf's proposal with growing wariness. Seven drow couldn't take on one sorcerer? When Corran looked to the group for opinions, she shook her head. "Either they're lying about how many cultists wait ahead or this sorcerer is more powerful than any we've faced so far. They're looking for spell fodder. After we take him on, they'll step over our dead bodies and continue on their way."

"I disagree," Corran declared. "His staff puts them at a disadvantage we won't suffer."

"So they say! Even if that's true, how do we know they won't betray us after we defeat him?"

Durwyn cleared his throat. "Kestrel's got a point. The woman said herself that dark elves aren't even loyal to each other."

"It does them no good to betray us," said Ghleanna. "We fight a common foe."

Irritated that Ghleanna sided with Corran, Kestrel listened to Jarial and Faeril's opinions and grew still more agitated. Except for Durwyn, they all favored the paladin. After their treatment at Razherrt's hands, how could they even consider allying with a group of dark elves?

"These drow are more concerned about their zombie kin than stopping the cult," she said, her voice rising louder than she intended. "Didn't you hear her? They want to release the Kilsek's souls, not battle Mordrayn. How does that help us?"

"Once my people enter true death, they will no longer pose a threat to you," the drow leader responded. "Know this: Before we're done I fully intend for the archmage to know the sensation of her blood draining from her body."

Kestrel studied the dark elf as intensely as she could across the gap. The drow leader stood proud and confident, apparently unperturbed by the rogue's scrutiny. "How do we know we can trust you?" Kestrel called. "You haven't even given us your name."

"Nathlilik, first daughter of the House of Kilsek. And you don't." She shrugged. "Accept our proposal or not, humans. You're the ones who need to cross this chasm."

The way Nathlilik used the word "human" as if it were a racial slur made Kestrel grind her teeth. She turned to Corran and the others. "To hell with them. We'll find another way across. I can use my grappling hooks to—"

"We accept," Corran called to Nathlilik. "Lower the bridge."

Kestrel gasped involuntarily. "But—"

"You're outvoted, Kestrel. And we can't afford for Nathlilik to change her mind while we waste time arguing."

So now her opinions were merely a waste of time? She fairly shook with anger at this latest example of the paladin's high-handedness. How dare he just shut her up? She glared at Corran, ready to unleash a stream of epithets when, entirely unbidden, Caalenfaire's final words entered her head. *Do not let conflict between you threaten your mission.*

With one final, very uncharitable thought toward Corran D'Arcey, she swallowed her ire. Nathlilik had begun lowering the drawbridge, and they needed to present a united front to the drow band. If anyone's egoism crippled their quest, it would be Corran's, not hers.

As they waited for the bridge to settle into place, Kestrel found herself standing off to one side with Ghleanna. Corran and the others were engrossed in watching the bridge mechanism. She studied the paladin as he bantered easily with Jarial and Faeril—even Durwyn. "Why do you all follow him so faithfully?" she muttered, half to Ghleanna and half to herself.

Ghleanna followed her gaze. "He inspires confidence."

Kestrel looked at the sorceress, puzzled. All Corran had ever inspired in her was frustration. "What do you mean?"

"When we go into battle. Just being near him—I am not afraid. Whatever odds we face, his presence makes me believe we can overcome them. I think it is because his faith is so strong." She met Kestrel's eyes. "Surely you feel it, too?"

Kestrel shook her head.

"Mayhap you have not let yourself."

Kestrel returned her gaze to Corran. To hear Ghleanna talk, the paladin had some aura about him that everyone could sense but her. As a rogue, she prided herself on her perception, on her ability to read people accurately. Had she allowed herself to become blinded? Even so, Corran had his own failings to work on, whether the others could see them or not.

The party crossed the bridge and came eye to eye with the dark elves. The Kilseks' faces held all the fierceness and arrogance of the Freths', but they also bore a weariness and desperation that hadn't been present among Razherrt's men. Perhaps Nathlilik told the truth after all.

As Kestrel passed the drow leader, their gazes locked. Nathlilik's red eyes burned with determination Kestrel knew she herself had never felt. "You really do hate the cult," she murmured.

"My lifemate, Kedar, is among those enslaved," Nathlilik said. "I *will* avenge him."

❂ ❂ ❂ ❂ ❂

They found the cult sorcerer exactly where Nathlilik had said to expect him.

They did not expect to find him dead.

"Ugh." Kestrel grimaced at the sight of the corpse. The cultist lay wrapped in a cocoon of sticky white strands with only his head and neck exposed. Bite marks covered his face and throat, leaving the flesh in shreds. The expression in his frozen eyes suggested he'd died a slow, painful death. "What got him? Spiders?"

"Some kind of wild creature." Jarial knelt beside the body to lift a long gold staff from where it had fallen near the sorcerer's body. "Whatever it was, it left this behind."

She crept closer for a better look. A G-shaped hook crowned the staff, within which a glowing yellow orb floated freely. "The Staff of Sunlight?"

"That's my guess."

Kestrel glanced around the rest of the room. A closed door stood opposite the one they had entered, and a table and chair sat in the corner. Several papers lay scattered on the table and floor. Ghleanna picked them up, scanning their content. "Most of these are useless notes, but this page is an order from Mordrayn. It says to eliminate the arraccat from the eastern section of the catacombs' third level."

"That's where we are, isn't it?" Durwyn asked.

Ghleanna nodded absently as she quoted from the order. "The creatures lair above the baelnorn and thus too close to our operations there."

Corran took the paper from Ghleanna's hand and studied it himself. "What's an arraccat?"

"I think it's a creature with eight eyes," said Durwyn,

his voice a bit higher-pitched than normal, "and eight legs with really sharp claws . . . and a wide mouth with wicked fangs. . . ."

Kestrel glanced at him in surprise, but his back was turned to her. "How do you know that, Durwyn?"

"Because I'm looking at one."

The arraccat hissed and sprang toward Durwyn. The fighter jumped out of the way, allowing the rest of the companions their first look at the creature. A cross between a spider and a cat, it stood nearly as tall as Kestrel and twice as wide. Brown fur covered its feline head, long tail, and oval arachnid body.

Just as quickly as it had arrived, it disappeared.

Faeril swept the room with her gaze. "Where did it—" Suddenly, two more appeared in the room. "Jarial! Ghleanna! Behind you!"

Ghleanna spun around, her staff cutting the forelegs out from under one of the arraccats. The creature buckled, then evaporated from sight. The other arraccat sprung at Jarial before he could strike it with the Staff of Sunlight, his only weapon at hand. The beast sank its fangs into his shoulder and disappeared.

The mage cried out in pain. "Their bite stings! I think they're poisonous!"

Kestrel grabbed her club and snapped her wrist. The weapon telescoped not a moment too soon—all three arraccats reappeared, this time behind Corran, Faeril, and Durwyn. She advanced on the closest creature, but a shout from Ghleanna stopped her. "Kestrel, look out!"

She spun to discover a fourth arraccat behind her. Green saliva—or was it venom?—dripped from its fangs. Four pairs of yellow eyes glittered menacingly in the torchlight through slit lids. Kestrel avoided eye contact, knowing that if she stared into those hourglass irises too long, she'd go dizzy.

The creature sprang. She grasped her club in both hands and struck it in the head, momentarily stunning it. No sooner did it disappear from sight than another took its place. The party fought at least six creatures now—the way they kept popping in and out, Kestrel couldn't keep track—and hadn't managed to land a fatal blow on any.

"Backs to the walls!" Corran yelled. "So they can't attack from behind!"

Kestrel fought off another beast and pressed herself against the door opposite the one they'd entered. No one had had time to check what lay on the other side, but at this point she didn't care. They had to get out of this room. The arraccats now outnumbered them, and more appeared each minute. No wonder the cult sorcerer had fallen prey to the creatures—they multiplied like rabbits.

She tried the door and found it locked. Damn her luck! She fumbled in her belt pouch, willing her fingers to find the right lockpick as she tried to fend off an arraccat one-handed. A moment later, Corran was at her side. "Open it! I'll cover you!"

The paladin's blade sliced through the creature and injured another in the time it took her to locate the tool she needed and open the lock. "Durwyn! Faeril!" she shouted over a nearby arraccat's hiss. "This way! Jarial! Ghleanna!"

One by one they backed over to the open door and slipped through to a small stairwell. Corran entered last. He slammed the door and fell against it, winded.

Several minutes passed in silence as they waited, arms ready, to see whether the arraccats would appear on this side of the door. None did. Jarial loosened his iron grip on the Staff of Sunlight and lowered its end to the ground. "I think we can relax."

Faeril examined Jarial's bite mark. The injury itself was minor, and Ozama's boots had once again protected him from the effects of poison. While the cleric bandaged the wound, Kestrel regarded Corran thoughtfully. The paladin might be an insufferable prig, but he'd seen to everyone else's safety before his own—unlike the debacle in the House of Gems courtyard. "I thought you never retreat from a fight?"

"Live to fight another day—isn't that how you rogues think?" He wiped the creatures' foul blood off Pathfinder and returned the weapon to its scabbard. "I'm beginning to believe that motto has some merit."

She hadn't time to contemplate his change in attitude, for Ghleanna summoned them excitedly. "There's a door at the bottom of the stairs, marked with the Rune of the Protector. The baelnorn cannot be far away."

CHAPTER ELEVEN

"Fhaormiir!"

The moment the party approached the door, the Word of Safekeeping boomed out of the air in a deep voice that reverberated throughout the stairwell. Adrenaline raced through Kestrel as the door silently swung open. Soon they would meet the Protector, and ask him to use the Gem of the Weave to undo the corruption of the Mythal. With the tide thus turned against the cult, perhaps she and the others would have a prayer of completing this mission alive. She did not want to consider their chances if the baelnorn refused their petition.

Expecting a long corridor, Kestrel was surprised to discover only a small antechamber. The room was empty, with a single pair of doors breaking up the smooth expanse of wall. The massive oak doors, however, took up nearly one whole side.

"Are we in the right place?" Faeril murmured. "I thought the baelnorn's dwelling—"

"Hush!" Kestrel closed her eyes to focus her sense of hearing. Muffled noises came from more than one place on the other side of the doors. A muted voice, the scrape of a chair, several low chuckles. She signaled to the others to remain still—and silent—while she investigated. Then she crept up to the doors and peered through the keyhole.

Her vantage point offered only a limited view of the room beyond. Flickering torchlight cast shadows on the walls—two figures standing, more sprawled in chairs around a table. She strained for a better view, but she could not see the people casting the shadows. From the relative size of the shadows, she guessed the erect pair to be closer than the seated individuals. She could hear them, male voices speaking in low tones.

"Still no word from Forgred's men, Lieutenant?"

"No, Captain."

"Or Gashet? Rubal?"

"No, sir. . . . She will not be pleased."

"Hrmph. She must learn patience."

Suddenly, a crackling sound rent the air. A gate, like the one that had transported the party to Myth Drannor, appeared in Kestrel's line of sight. It pulsed and snapped with light and energy. A bright flash lit the room. Then, just as suddenly, the gate disappeared.

Kya Mordrayn had arrived.

Kestrel stifled a gasp. The archmage appeared even more formidable in person than she had in the scrying mirror. She was a tall woman, approaching six feet, and her boots and upswept hair made her seem at least a foot taller. A stiff collar anchored two red leather shoulder pieces that extended like dragon wings on either side of her head. At her waist hung a pair of black metal gloves, with white symbols of an open skeletal mouth on each palm. The Gauntlets of Moander.

Mordrayn's monstrous right arm hung past her knee—until she raised it to point at one of the speakers who had fallen silent at her entrance.

What news, Mage Captain? As in the scrying mirror, Mordrayn did not open her mouth to speak. Her voice seemed to simply fill the minds of those who listened.

"The baelnorn remains locked away in the next room, Mistress. No one has entered."

The archmage nodded approvingly. *That is well. And the intruders?*

"We have not found them yet. But—"

Her brows drew together. *I grow tired of excuses.* The fingers of Mordrayn's human hand moved ever so slightly. The captain screamed as a blaze of light filled the room. The smell of burning flesh drifted through the keyhole, accompanied by a sickening sizzling sound.

Unable to see the captain, Kestrel kept her gaze on Mordrayn. As her servant shrieked in pain, the archmage remained stoic, even bored. When the screams ceased and the flames died out, one upright shadow remained on the wall. The seated figures appeared smaller, as if trying to sink into their chairs.

Mordrayn shifted her gaze to encompass the remaining officer. *You command now.*

"Yes, Mistress." The figure bowed his head, then raised it quickly. "Mistress—an idea."

The archmage had turned as if to leave but spun around at her servant's entreaty. She arched an eyebrow. *Speak quickly.*

"With your permission, I will unlock the doors."

The archmage gasped aloud. *Unlock them?*

"Yes . . . and be ready."

Mordrayn stared at her new commander a long time, flexing her talons as she pondered his proposal. Not a sound broke the stillness. Finally, she nodded in assent. *Plan wisely. Use the drow slaves as you see fit. And if you fail, pray that they kill you.*

The magical gate reappeared. A moment later, the archmage was gone.

Immediately, the commander spun to face the seated figures. "Get up, you maggots! Get moving! You—get everyone in here. . . ."

Kestrel backed away from the doors and returned to the others. "We've found the baelnorn—the cult is holding him captive here." As she described the scene she'd just witnessed, the sound of an enormous bolt sliding back indicated that the doors now indeed stood unlocked. "We haven't much time. They're mobilizing quickly."

Corran leaned on his sword, frowning. "How many are there?"

"Hard to say—I could see only shadows. A dozen, perhaps more. I suspect at least some of them are sorcerers, as the captain was one."

All eyes turned to the paladin, including Kestrel's. She'd never been involved in an out-and-out battle against an organized military force. For once, she was happy to let Corran take command. Was this the confidence Ghleanna had described?

Corran rubbed his temples, then mumbled a brief prayer to Tyr. "Okay, here's what we do."

❂ ❂ ❂ ❂ ❂

The cult forces were still organizing when Kestrel and her party burst into the room. The element of surprise won them a momentary advantage—long enough for Ghleanna to launch a fireball at the living warriors and

Jarial to use the Staff of Sunlight to weaken the enthralled drow assembled in the chamber. The combined effect created a burst of light so bright that even the surface-dwellers blinked.

The enslaved Kilsek staggered under the visual assault, cringing and covering their eyes. Kestrel picked off two of the weakened dark elves without even a struggle, slipping behind them in the bright light of day and sinking a dagger between their shoulder blades. Faeril sent two more to their final rest in the shock of the initial onslaught, her new blade glowing with holy fire.

At the sight of flames dancing around the steel, Kestrel glanced at the cleric in surprise. "I didn't know that was a magical weapon."

Faeril regarded the sword in awe. "Neither did I." She celebrated the discovery by plunging the blade into another dark elf.

Ghleanna had been assigned the task of subduing the commander, at whom she immediately launched a second spell. They'd all hoped the lieutenant would prove the only sorcerer among the cultists—the party had entered combat under the shield of protective spells, but their magical defenses couldn't hold out forever. Soon, Kestrel saw a sorcerous battle unfold out of the corner of her eye, with Ghleanna and the lieutenant launching magical volleys at each other.

Corran, once again cloaked by invisibility, was to help the half-elf slay the commander, applying steel to supplement spells. Kestrel saw no sign yet of the paladin, but her attention was focused on another drow opponent. The soulless dark elf moved his hands in the gesture-language of Razherrt and his followers. At the last second, she realized he was casting a spell. She dropped to the floor and rolled, trying to dodge his aim, but to no avail. A fan of flames burst from his hands, searing her side.

She yelped in pain but got to her feet, more determined than ever to save Nathlilik the trouble of releasing this particular Kilsek into true death. She hurled Loren's Blade at him, catching him in the throat. Beside her, Faeril's flame blade dispatched the last enthralled drow.

Meanwhile, six cult fighters charged Durwyn. Jarial appeared to launch a spell at them, but Kestrel saw no visible effect. She soon realized, however, that the fighters moved more slowly than they had before. Faeril rushed to fight beside Durwyn, while Kestrel maintained her position and sent Loren's Blade flying once more.

As Ghleanna unleashed a series of fire bursts, a cry of "Death to Tyr's enemies!" revealed Corran's whereabouts. Pathfinder penetrated the cult commander's defenses, striking a blow at the evil sorcerer's back. The combination of Ghleanna's spells and Corran's sword proved the mage's undoing, and before long he lay on the floor with the dead drow.

Ghleanna, however, suffered serious burns on her arms and face from one of the cultist's enchantments. Faeril, having just dispatched her opponent with a fatal strike to the chest, disengaged from combat to attend the half-elf. Durwyn had defeated two foes, leaving just three cult fighters blocking the entrance to the baelnorn's cell.

Kestrel noted the situation with cautious optimism. They could handle the remaining cultists—Corran and Jarial had already weakened two of them. Victory was all but assured.

Until the reinforcements arrived.

Without warning, a gate opened in the corner of the room. The additional forces the lieutenant had summoned earlier spilled out, surprised to find a battle in progress but ready to fight nonetheless. Cult fighters and countless enslaved drow entered the fight, filling Kestrel with despair. How could they possibly prevail against these numbers?

"Close the gate!" Corran shouted.

"How?" she shouted back. Even if she knew a way to physically shut a magical portal, too many foes stood between them and the opening.

Jarial darted off to the side, positioning himself directly across from the gate. He unleashed a forked lightning bolt straight at the portal. One branch stopped the flow of cultists streaming out by electrocuting those hapless individuals immediately within. The other branch hit the gate itself, sending a crackle of electrical feedback racing through the very fabric of the portal. The gate snapped and wavered and popped. Random zaps of energy ricocheted within its walls. In a great burst of light, it collapsed.

Kestrel had no time to appreciate the fireworks—too many cultists and drow swarmed the room. Three soulless dark elves had her backed into a corner from which she feared she would never emerge. She found herself unable to land a single offensive blow on any of them—parrying their strikes was the best she could do.

Another burst of sunlight issued from Jarial's staff, causing Kestrel's opponents and the rest of the Kilsek to stagger under the sudden brightness. She seized the advantage and brought her club down on one foe's skull with every ounce of strength she could muster. He slumped to the floor, but another dark elf took his place. The new opponent crippled her left arm with a retributive strike. Moments later, one of his comrades cut her legs out from under her.

Kestrel fell hard. She tried to push the pain from her consciousness, but it clutched at her mind like dark tentacles wrapping around her every thought. Her arm hung limp at her side, the broken bone protruding through her skin and armor. She transferred her club to her right hand and prepared to hold out as long as she could against the swarming dark elves. She called out, trying to draw someone's attention to her situation, but with their whole party so severely outnumbered she doubted anyone could help her.

This was it, then, the place where she would die—beset by undead drow in the bowels of Myth Drannor. She had always wondered.

She fended off two more blows but could not block the third. It slammed into her head, knocking her flat and blurring her vision. Did she still face three drow, or did six now surround her? Through the haze overtaking her awareness, she heard Faeril's voice rise above the din of battle. "By the grace of Mystra, I command thee to fall back!"

They were the last words she heard.

CHAPTER TWELVE

"**K**estrel? Kestrel!"

Faeril's voice drifted to her through a fog, stirring Kestrel to consciousness. Her battered body hurt all over, but her left arm ached so intensely that she almost lapsed back into oblivion rather than endure the pain.

Gentle fingers searched her throat for a pulse. "Thank Mystra, she's still alive," the cleric said.

"How bad is she hurt?" Was that Corran's voice or Durwyn's? Kestrel's head was still too cloudy to distinguish the male timbre, and she had not yet been able to force her eyes open.

"She's got a compound fracture in her left arm. I can heal that—it's her unconsciousness that concerns me most. I fear a serious head injury. Did anyone see when she fell?"

"Just before you turned the undead drow." *That* was Corran's voice. The other speaker must have been Durwyn. "She was surrounded by them. I tried to reach her, but—"

"We all had our hands full." Faeril grasped Kestrel's injured arm and—in movements that caused pain more excruciating than the break itself—reset the bone. Kestrel heard the cleric begin a prayer. In a few minutes the pain subsided, though it did not disappear completely. "That is all I can do for now," Faeril said. "I have exhausted my healing gifts for this day."

"Were it not for your healing spells during combat, none of us would have survived that battle," Corran said.

Faeril's ministrations, though limited, boosted Kestrel's strength enough that the rogue finally managed to open her eyes. She blinked rapidly, trying to focus her blurred vision. After a moment, her sight cleared.

Corran and Faeril knelt beside her, with Durwyn hovering close behind. The three of them had removed their helms, and all looked as if they'd journeyed to the Abyss and back. Blood spattered their armor and caked their hair. An ugly bruise had formed on Corran's right cheekbone, just above the stubble line of his four-day beard. Cuts covered Faeril's arms, including one long gash that ran from elbow to shoulder. Durwyn seemed to favor his left leg.

The burly warrior smiled as she met his worried gaze. "We thought we'd lost you," he said.

"Sorry to disappoint everyone," Kestrel said weakly. When she tried to sit up, Faeril had to support her. "Where are Ghleanna and Jarial?"

Corran glanced off to one side. "Resting. Both suffered terrible burns from cult spells. We were surprised to find Jarial still breathing after two fireballs hit him at once. I just stabilized him, but it will be some time before he—or any of us, really—is moving quickly."

Kestrel pushed the last of her mental fogginess aside, forcing herself to think clearly. "We've got to get out of here. Another gate could open any moment with more reinforcements."

The paladin nodded gravely. "I think that door over there leads to the baelnorn's cell. We haven't even had a chance to see whether it's locked. Feel up to examining it?"

With Faeril's aid, Kestrel got to her feet. Dizziness seized her, but she fought it off and stumbled to the door, praying to any deity who would listen that this would prove a simple lock. She couldn't analyze much more at the moment—not with the pounding headache forming behind her eyes.

They found the door unlocked. Within, an ancient elf sat in the center of the tiny boxlike room. Wrinkles surrounded his glowing white eyes, which assessed Kestrel and the others as they entered. Not a strand of hair remained on his pate, making his regal forehead look all the higher. His pointed ears and fingers seemed preternaturally long, even for an elf. Simple garments of brown homespun covered his shriveled, pale skin. Long arms hugged his knees to his chest in a defensive posture.

Yet for all the alterations wrought upon his physical form by age and undeath, the man once known as Miroden Silverblade still possessed such a puissant, vital presence that a full minute elapsed before anyone realized the baelnorn could not move.

Jarial leaned heavily on the Staff of Sunlight as he regarded the Protector. The mage's too-pink skin shone tight against the bones of his face. His eyelashes and eyebrows had been singed off altogether. "I believe he's magically bound," he said in a voice so scratchy that it pained Kestrel to hear it.

"Aye," said Ghleanna, who did not look much better.

"With an enchantment similar to one I used on you, Kestrel." Her blistered lips twisted into what Kestrel could only suppose was meant to be a wry smile. "The day we first met—remember?"

She remembered the incident, although that afternoon in Phlan seemed years ago. "Does that mean you can free him?"

"I believe I have enough strength remaining to try one spell." Ghleanna mumbled her incantation as she hobbled in a circle around the baelnorn. When she returned to her starting point, she extended one hand toward the guardian and uttered a final word.

The baelnorn unfurled like a morning glory in the sun, rising to a towering height. He was a tall man—well over six feet—made taller still, Kestrel soon realized, by the fact that he levitated about a foot off the floor. A noble calmness seemed to surround him, putting her at ease despite the fact that the party was in the presence of yet another undead denizen of the city.

"You have my deepest gratitude," the Protector said in a rich voice that belied his gaunt appearance. "But we are not safe here. Come." He swept his hand broadly. The room faded around them, and they found themselves in a large circular chamber. "Here, in my home, we may speak freely."

The apartment was comfortably, if sparsely, furnished. Soft light filled the room, though Kestrel couldn't determine its source. A wooden table and two chairs sat in one part of the chamber; a plush bedroll and plump cushions lay spread in another. A large section of the wall held shelves piled high with books and scrolls. Two massive trunks stood beneath.

Kestrel had expected the Mythal's communicant to enjoy more lavish quarters. To her way of thinking, gracious surroundings were a minimum trade-off for an eternity of constant vigilance. Yet the more she assessed the humble dwelling, the more it seemed a proper place for the baelnorn to guard the Sapphire of the Weave. Few would think to plunder such a simple abode in search of the priceless gem.

Opposite the doorway stood an ornate glass case containing a small, red velvet pillow. The pillow still held the impression of an item that had once rested upon it—surely the Gem of the Weave. The treasure, however, was nowhere in sight. Dread seized her. In the baelnorn's absence, had the cultists stolen the Sapphire? If Mordrayn had the gem, their quest was surely doomed, for Kestrel could think of no other means to cleanse the Mythal of the corruption that tainted it.

She tore her gaze away from the empty case to see whether the Protector had noted the missing item. He avoided her questioning look. Instead, he addressed the group as a whole. "Sit," he said, "and be well."

At a slight gesture from the baelnorn, Kestrel's headache immediately dissipated. A moment later the pain in her arm and residual aches from other injuries fled as well. She felt rested as if she'd slept for a week—better than she had since waking with that firewine hangover in Phlan before all this madness began. Looking around, she saw that the others also had been restored to perfect health. The men even appeared clean-shaven.

"I am Miroden Silverblade, known as the Protector for these past six centuries," he said, his tired but clear eyes studying the companions as keenly as they assessed him. "To whom do I owe my freedom? And what brought the six of you to that black corner of the catacombs?"

Corran introduced the party and described their activities thus far, concluding with Anorrweyn Evensong's suggestion to seek the baelnorn's aid. "She told us you protect the Sapphire of the Weave, and that you possibly could use the gem to reverse the corruption of the Mythal. But we didn't expect to find you held captive."

"Nor did I intend to become so." The Protector sighed heavily, the lines in his face settling deeper. "The cult imprisoned me because Mordrayn and Pelendralaar fear my influence over what remains of the Mythal. Since the Year of Doom, I have used my abilities as communicant to slow the decay of the city's mantle. As all that I once knew withered and died around me, I held fast to my belief that one day the Mythal would prove the key to restoring Myth Drannor to its lost glory. The cult thinks I still have the power to undo the corruption they have wrought upon the Weave."

Thinks. Kestrel's heart sank to the pit of her stomach. "You don't?"

"Nay." A stricken look crossed the baelnorn's features. He turned his back on them and floated to the empty case. His shaking fingers reached through the glass to caress the depression in the pillow. "They came. The Cult of the Dragon." His voice, so rich before, now warbled in the trembling tones of an old man. "I had . . . grown weak in my solitude. I succumbed when I should have stood fast."

Kestrel stifled a groan of dismay mixed with frustration. How could an artifact as important as the Gem of the Weave have been left in the care of someone too frail to protect it? Though the baelnorn had appeared formidable when they first discovered him, Mordrayn must have used her dreadful magic to take advantage of the guardian's true age. "They stole it from you, didn't they? Mordrayn and her minions?"

Silverblade yet stood with his back to them, hunched over the empty pillow. "Nay," he said brokenly. "I—" His hand slowly formed a fist, as if his fingers closed around the missing stone. He straightened his spine, lifted his shoulders. "I destroyed it."

Ghleanna gasped. "But how could you—"

He turned to face them, once more possessing the air of authority he'd momentarily lost. His hands no longer trembled, and he raised his chin. "Do you think I would let them have it? Do you think I would betray centuries of trust? I destroyed it!" His eyes challenged them to dispute the wisdom of his act. "The cult tried to steal the sapphire from me, and I annihilated it rather than allow the gem to fall into their clutches. I can no longer commune with the Mythal, for there no longer exists an instrument through which to do so."

The baelnorn's defiant tone discouraged anyone from questioning his decision. Besides, what would be the point? The gem was gone. Stillness filled the air—the sound of hope dying in the hearts of six weary adventurers.

Kestrel's shoulders slumped. Without the sapphire, how could they possibly touch the Mythal, let alone redeem it? She thought with irony of all the gems that had passed through her rogue's hands. She would have traded them all for this single stone.

That musing sparked another. She leaned forward as the notion took shape in her mind. "Can the gem be replaced?"

A fleeting expression of shock passed over the Protector's face, transposed so quickly into one of mere surprise that Kestrel wasn't entirely sure she'd seen it. "Replaced? I—I don't know. Such an undertaking has never been attempted." He paused, as if turning over the idea in his mind. "A new Gem of the Weave . . . We have nothing to lose in trying."

"Consider us your servants." Corran sprung to his feet. "Tell us what we can do to help. Do you need any special materials?" The others also rose.

"Only a gem," the baelnorn replied. "Harldain Ironbar provided the original sapphire. He can direct you to a new stone. But you also must find a new communicant."

Kestrel frowned. "Why? What about you?"

Miroden Silverblade shook his head wearily. "My time as Protector is over. A new Gem of the Weave requires a new guardian, someone who possesses the wisdom to guide the Mythal, the strength to survive symbiosis with the Weave, the power to keep the stone safe. And, of course, the willingness to spend eternity bound inextricably to the gem."

The party exchanged glances. Kestrel knew she sure as hell wasn't suited for such responsibility. None of them were. "Is there anyone in Myth Drannor who meets that description?"

"There is," the baelnorn said. "No mortal could withstand the Mythal's fire, but one exists who already knows the blessings—and curse—of immortality. Anorrweyn Evensong. The priestess is steeped in the lore of the Mythal, and her spirit has survived the trials of time and adversity. She would serve as the perfect communicant."

"We shall hasten to ask her as soon as we finish with Harldain," Corran said. "Assuming Anorrweyn agrees, how does she become bound to the new gem?"

"Once you obtain an appropriate stone, you must carry it up the spine of the Speculum to a focal point in the dragon's back. With the gem in place, the new communicant recites the Incantation of the Weave. Anorrweyn knows the words—she was present at the first binding. This spellsong bonds the chanter to the gem and attunes the gem to the Mythal."

"How will we know whether the ceremony succeeded?" Ghleanna asked. "Whether the Mythal accepted the new gem?"

"You will know."

Corran started to put his helm back on his head. "We have much to do. We'd best get started."

"Hold." The Protector looked as if he had something more to say but struggled over whether to reveal it. His gaze swept the group, then came to rest on the trunks that stood behind them. "Yes," he murmured, nodding to himself. "You need all the aid I have left within my power to give."

He went to the trunks, brushed dust off the top of one and opened its groaning lid. "In this chest lie some of Myth Drannor's greatest remaining treasures, items given me by the coronal himself to help me safeguard the Gem of the Weave. Though I have failed that duty, perhaps some item in here will help you succeed." Reaching inside, he called Corran's name. The paladin stepped forward.

"Are you trained to fight with a shield?"

"Aye, though I prefer to leave my left hand free."

"You might prefer it to hold this." The Protector withdrew an oval shield etched with white stars along its border. "This is a mageshield, designed to protect its user from death magic. Necromantic spells that hit this shield will bounce back at their caster." His expression darkened, his gaze clouding with memories he alone could see. "'Tis no less than those cult sorcerers deserve." Corran accepted the gift and bowed low, looking as humble as Kestrel had ever seen him.

Silverblade collected himself and turned to the others. "Ghleanna Stormlake." The half-elf walked to stand before the baelnorn. "Is that a magical staff you carry?"

"No, Protector."

"This is." He produced a six-foot wooden staff covered with ornate symbols and runes, most of them resembling flames and bolts of energy. "A spellstaff. Solid as oak, light as balsa. Use it as you would an ordinary quarterstaff. But should anyone send fire or lightning your way, the staff will absorb it. Tap it twice to release the energy at a target of your choosing."

Ghleanna's eyes shone with gratitude. "I have suffered terrible burns from fire magic these past days. I thank you, Protector."

More gifts followed: bracers of protection from paralysis for Faeril, a ring of regeneration for Jarial, a trio of bronze-tipped arrows for Durwyn.

"Finally you, Kestrel." Tremors raced up Kestrel's arm as the Protector lifted her right hand. The silver ring she'd inherited from Athan's band caught the light. "Do you know what this is you wear?"

She shook her head. "There's nothing special-looking about it. I thought it was an ordinary silver ring."

"On the contrary. You wear a mantle ring, a piece of magical jewelry crafted in the glory days of Myth Drannor. No doubt your ring earned its battered appearance from centuries of owners who engaged in dangerous missions like yours. The carvings have been worn until they look like mere scratches, but its power remains strong. This ring will shield you from injurious sorcerers' spells."

Kestrel thought of the magical hits she'd taken from the cultists and drow. "But it hasn't protected me from anything."

"Mantle rings must be worn in pairs. Its mate is probably lost to time." He opened his hand to reveal another silver band of the same size. This one had a smooth surface engraved with tiny runes. "Wear this ring on your left hand, and a dozen spells will wash over you harmlessly."

He dropped the ring in her palm. She stared at it, her intrinsic distrust of magic making her reluctant to put it on. Would she feel different? Would it have some other, unknown effect on her? She met the Protector's gaze and, at his commanding nod, slipped the ring on her finger. Nothing dramatic happened. In fact, within moments she scarcely noticed its presence.

"Now go," the baelnorn said, meeting each pair of eyes

one by one. His face held a look of desperation. "Save the Mythal. For if Mordrayn and the cult use it for the great evil they intend, the City of Song can never be redeemed."

CHAPTER THIRTEEN

"Back again, are you?" Harldain Ironbar greeted them as they entered his tower. "Did you find the old Protector?"

"We did indeed," said Corran. "Now we've another favor to ask."

"Name it."

Corran told the old dwarf about the sapphire's destruction at the baelnorn's hands and their need for a new stone. Harldain stroked his beard. "Well, I'll be damned." He shook his head as if in disbelief. "Centuries ago, when we mined for the sapphire, Caalenfaire advised me to secure three gems. He said we would need more than one to ensure the Mythal's survival. At the time, I thought he wanted some backups in case somethin' went wrong during the incantation ceremony.

But now I'll wager he saw this day comin'. Imagine that! Way back then."

"So you have another sapphire?"

"No. We couldn't find two perfect sapphires. Once we had the first, all others seemed flawed—the color was off, or they lacked clarity, or some such thing. So we mined an emerald and a ruby instead. The ruby was destroyed by the nycaloth when the Armies of Darkness swept the city, but we still have the emerald, down in the Hoard."

"The what?"

"The Hoard of the Onaglym Dwarves. Our private stash of treasure."

Kestrel felt her energy flag. "Don't tell me it's back in the dwarven dungeons." She couldn't bear the thought of still more backtracking.

"Nope. It's right below the courtyard. You know . . ." He cast a knowing look at Kestrel. "The one with your favorite statue."

Kestrel remembered the animated, axe-swinging dwarf only too well. Even with the passkey to disable it this time around, she'd given the stone guardian a wide berth when they arrived. "Where's the entrance to the Hoard?" she asked. "I searched the whole courtyard and didn't find any secret doors or hidden stairways."

"Did you check the statue itself?" He shrugged. "No matter. Even if you had, you couldn't get at the Hoard without the Ironbar."

Durwyn regarded the ghost in confusion. "Without you?"

Harldain winked and slipped a small baton out of a pocket in his robe. "No, this ironbar." He handed the object to Kestrel. It was an ordinary-looking rod about twelve inches long, half an inch in diameter, and—judging from its weight—made of solid iron. "There's a hole at the base of the statue. Push the rod into the opening to unseal the entrance."

They hastened back to the courtyard, where they immediately put the ironbar to use. A great grinding sound echoed through the courtyard as the statue slowly slid backward to reveal a shaft about twenty feet deep. Rungs embedded in the wall formed a ladder. At the bottom was a passage opening, but from their vantage point they could not see where it led.

Kestrel stared down into the blackness, then swung herself over the edge and scaled the ladder. When her feet touched ground, the passage flared with sudden brightness.

"What's that?" Corran called down.

She peered through the portal. The passage extended just three feet before opening into a large chamber lined with flaming torches. "Some sort of automatic lighting system. The treasure room's right here. You can come down if you want, but the doorway's only about four feet tall." She crawled through the entrance and let out a low whistle. "Wow! Get a load of this. . . ."

Her exclamation sent the party scurrying down the shaft for a look at the legendary Hoard of the Onaglym Dwarves. Durwyn elected to remain above standing guard, but the others soon joined her wide-eyed survey of the scene. Jewels by the trunkful, gold by the ton, exquisitely crafted armor and weapons all lined the room. In the center, surrounded by glass, a palm-sized emerald hung suspended in mid-air, slowly rotating in place, its facets catching the torchlight and sending deep green rays dancing along the walls.

Kestrel walked toward the glass. "That must be what we're looking for."

"Aye, that it is."

They all jumped at the sound of Harldain's voice booming

behind them. Without another word, the ghost approached the emerald, leaning on his cane as if it still supported the weight of a body. Though his hand penetrated the glass effortlessly as he reached toward the stone, he did not touch it.

"I wanted to see it one last time." His gaze caressed the gem reverently. "You'll not lay eyes on a finer emerald in all the Realms." With obvious reluctance, he tore his eyes away from the stone. "The dwarves of Myth Drannor kept this emerald safe all these years, awaitin' the need Caalenfaire foresaw. I now put it in your hands."

In one fluid motion, he raised his cane and smashed the glass. Thousands of shards fell to the ground in a circle around the gem, which still levitated and spun.

Undaunted by the sharp fragments, Corran crushed them beneath his armored feet as he claimed the emerald. "We shall defend the gem with our lives until a new Protector guards it."

"Let me help." Harldain crossed to a collection of prominently displayed armor and weapons. "These are the finest items our dwarven craftsmen ever produced, augmented by the spells of the coronal's best wizards for those who defended the City of Song in the Weepin' War. Rather than let such powerful articles fall into enemy hands, they were enchanted to return here if their bearers fell in battle." Harldain brushed his fingers along the edge of a breastplate that seemed to glow with inner light. His eyes held a far-off expression, as if he were remembering the soldier who last wore the piece. He cleared his throat. "They've been in this chamber ever since, and they aren't doin' anyone any good just sittin' down here," he said gruffly. "Take whatever you can use."

Kestrel gazed at the collection in awe, her eyes drawn in particular to a set of leather armor about her size, which looked more supple than a pair of ladies' kid gloves. Was it truly hers for the taking?

Harldain noted her admiration. "That suit will protect you much better than what you're sportin' now and let you move much easier. You'll think you're wearin' silk pajamas."

She laughed at the absurd statement—no armor could feel like that.

"Try it on if you don't believe me."

To her astonishment, she found Harldain hadn't been exaggerating. The pieces fit as if they'd been made for her and felt light as an ordinary shirt. "Take it," he urged. She couldn't argue.

The others each selected lighter, better protection than what they'd been wearing. Even the sorcerers found cloaks enchanted to repel enemy attacks. Durwyn, still standing watch above, was not forgotten—Harldain himself chose a suit of lightweight plate sized for the warrior's large build.

The ghostly dwarf had become increasingly gruff as they changed equipment. Kestrel thought it was because he didn't really want to part with the armor, but he revealed the true source of his anxiety as they departed.

"You're runnin' out of time," he said. "I can feel it. Find Anorrweyn and get that emerald to the top of the Speculum just as quick as you can. The cult's control of the Mythal is strong. The city is dyin' around us."

❂ ❂ ❂ ❂ ❂

The scent of gardenias manifested before Anorrweyn Evensong's spirit. Kestrel inhaled deeply. The sweet perfume soothed her frayed nerves as she waited for the priestess to appear. Would the ghost agree to serve as communicant? She fervently hoped so, for she didn't know what they would do if Anorrweyn refused.

A pensive silence hung over the group. Faeril had just finished some invocations to Mystra. Corran had joined her in the prayers, then offered a few of his own to Tyr. The events of the past several days had made it difficult for the paladin to perform his regular devotions, and he took advantage of this interlude to reconnect with his patron deity. The rest of the group, Kestrel included, had maintained a respectful quiet and used the time for contemplation.

Anorrweyn materialized moments after the telltale fragrance. She seemed less translucent this time, a little more solid. Her face bore a radiant smile. "You have found my skull."

Faeril knelt before her. "Yes, priestess. We've interred it with the rest of your bones in the grave outside."

"I thank you all. Now I may occupy this plane of time and better follow events of the present instead of forever reliving the past." The priestess made eye contact with each of them in turn, her eyes further expressing her gratitude. When her gentle gaze met Kestrel's, the rogue felt a sense of peace flood her soul.

With a gesture, Anorrweyn invited them all to sit in the half-circle of benches that still remained from their last conference. Kestrel found it curious that the ghost always sat down along with them, as if she too benefited from rest. Perhaps it was a habit carried over from her mortal days or an attempt to put them at ease in her undead presence. This time Anorrweyn sat beside Faeril, who regarded her idol with reverence.

"Did you also find the Protector?" the spirit asked.

"We did, priestess," Corran said. "But he could not help us."

Anorrweyn's eyes widened. She sat forward as if she hadn't entirely heard him. "Miroden Silverblade refused to aid your quest?"

"The Gem of the Weave is no more. The Baelnorn destroyed it to keep the cult from seizing its power."

"Impossible!" Anorrweyn shook her head vigorously, as if doing so could negate the truth of the statement. She rose and paced restlessly. "You are sure you understood him correctly?" She cast her gaze from one person to the next, but all gave affirmative nods.

"The Protector said he cannot commune with the Mythal because the sapphire no longer exists," Corran explained. "We found him imprisoned by the cult, who tried to steal it when they captured him."

Anorrweyn sat down once more. She seemed lost in thought as she stared though the doorway of the temple at the ruined city beyond. Several minutes passed in uncomfortable silence as the ghost remained in reverie and the mortals hesitated to disturb her. Faeril waited in rapt attention. Durwyn traced the handle of his axe with his thumb. Ghleanna picked lint off her cloak. When Kestrel turned her gaze to Corran, she was startled to find him regarding her. Surely her didn't expect *her* to do something? She frowned in question, but he looked away.

Were the others as conscious as she of time ticking away? Ultimately, it was the paladin who took the plunge. "Priestess . . . " Corran began tentatively.

Anorrweyn broke her trance. "My apologies. I hoped to sense confirmation of your news through my own, limited, attunement to the Mythal, but I cannot. These tidings deeply unsettle me. Either Miroden is mistaken about the fate of the sapphire, or he lied to you. I can think of no other explanation. The Protector's very existence is linked inextricably to the Gem of the Weave—that is what it means to be a baelnorn. If the sapphire was indeed destroyed, he would have died along with it." She frowned in puzzlement. "Did he say anything else?"

"He told us that a new Gem of the Weave could be

made, with a new stone and a new communicant. The replacement gem could be used to reverse the Mythal's corruption and free it from the cult's hold."

Anorrweyn's brows rose at the suggestion. Guarded interest danced across her delicate features. "This replacement gem—how is it to be created? Where are you to locate an appropriate jewel?"

"Harldain provided us with a new stone." Corran brought the emerald forward for Anorrweyn to see. Its color was a near-perfect match to the shade of her gown.

She reached toward the gem, caressing the air just a hair's breadth away above its surface. "An emerald this time. . . ." The jewel caught a ray of afternoon sunlight and held it, appearing to glow from within. Anorrweyn raised her eyes and met Corran's gaze once more. "And the new communicant?"

"The Protector thought that *you* might be persuaded."

Her eyes widened. "Me? I—" She fell silent again, apparently pondering the unexpected proposal. She glanced around the ruined shell of her temple, her gaze lingering on each small sign of destruction—the missing ceiling, wall cracks, rubble piles, vestiges of the nagas' occupation. Her face settled into an expression of sadness so intense it pained Kestrel to behold it.

"There is nothing left here for me," she said finally. "Of course I shall answer this new call to Mystra's service." She rose, her incorporeal form already starting to fade from view. "Since you have the gem, all that remains is to carry it to the top of the Speculum. There shall we attune the emerald. Pass through the Gate of Antarn to begin your climb up the dragon's back. I give you now my blessing, that the gate will open to admit you."

Anorrweyn closed her eyes and raised her hands over the party. In a low, soft voice she murmured the words of her invocation. Kestrel and the others bowed their heads to receive her blessing. Faeril dropped to her knees.

When the priestess finished, she lowered her arms and opened her eyes once more. "Farewell for now, my friends." Only the faintest outline of her figure remained, but her voice yet carried strong and steady, mingling with the heady scent of gardenias. "I shall meet you at the crest of the dragon's spine."

CHAPTER FOURTEEN

On previous visits to the Speculum, the party had not even noticed the Gate of Antarn. Under Anorrweyn's blessing, however, they clearly saw the solid pair of wooden doors that barred access to the building's winding exterior staircase. As soon as they neared the tip of the dragon's tail, the ancient oak doors creaked open to grant them entry.

Before proceeding, Kestrel cast a wary glance at the sky. "Let's be quick about this." Already, the sun dipped low. In an hour's time dusk would settle on the city. She'd no wish to stand exposed on the roof of the Speculum at all, let alone once darkness fell. Already, shadows gathered on rooftops and behind clouds.

The spiraling stone staircase proved narrow

and in poor repair. Ballistae had smashed many of the steps, leaving some sections impossible to surmount without Kestrel's rope and grappling hook. They climbed single-file, with Kestrel leading the way and Durwyn bringing up the rear. Kestrel repeatedly studied the sky, unable to shake the feeling that someone watched them from above.

"Do you see something?" Corran, immediately behind her, also raised his gaze heavenward.

"No. Not yet." She searched the clouds a moment longer. How often did Pelendralaar leave his lair to swoop through the skies? "This just seems too easy."

"Tell that to Durwyn." Even in his new lightweight armor, the big man was having trouble picking his way along the narrow, rubble-strewn staircase. He sent scree cascading with every other step. Kestrel observed the steep incline and smaller width of the stairs yet ahead— and the craters where steps used to be—and prayed the warrior would maintain his balance. Even she had trouble finding footing in some places.

Kestrel heard Ghleanna's voice call from behind Corran. "How do we find the 'focal point' the baelnorn mentioned once we reach the top?"

"No idea," Corran confessed, to Kestrel's surprise. She could not recall a previous instance of the paladin admitting to ignorance. "I'm hoping Anorrweyn will be waiting for us when we get there."

Kestrel paused and glanced around. They had climbed about a third of the way to the top and reached an elevation that provided a panoramic view of the Heights. Shadows dappled the structures below and grew longer with each passing minute. The setting sun also played tricks on her eyes—she could have sworn she saw movement on the ledge of a nearby building, but on second look she saw only grim statues perched watchfully along the rooftop. Gargoyles. She'd heard stories of the winged, horned beasts animating and taking flight, but she'd never put any stock in the accounts. Nursery tales, meant to scare children into staying indoors after dark. That's all she'd ever believed them to be.

She was starting to reconsider that opinion.

They climbed higher. The faint breeze that had tousled her hair now became a steady wind. The sun dipped behind the horizon, leaving only its upper hemisphere visible. Kestrel hated this time of day—twilight made the eyes play tricks. Were they halfway up the staircase, or further? Was that movement just now, off to the left? Though dusk could often prove a thief's best friend, right now she wished for full dark rather than the murky, ambiguous half-light.

She stopped once more and listened to the wind. She'd swear on Quinn's grave that she heard low, guttural voices followed by the flapping of wings. Was that too an illusion, a trick of the atmosphere? "Do you hear that?" she asked Corran.

The paladin never had a chance to answer.

A *woosh* from above was all the warning they had before a pair of gargoyles swooped down at them. Kestrel ducked instinctively, while Corran raised his shield to block the sharp stone claws that reached toward him. The creatures shrieked at the failure of their surprise attack, then circled for another run.

"What in blazes was that?" Durwyn asked.

"Gargoyles," Kestrel and Corran answered in unison. Kestrel glanced around wildly for cover, but there was none to be had—the party was completely exposed. Faeril began to chant a prayer-spell that Kestrel hoped would offer some protection. Ghleanna and Jarial, meanwhile, started muttering words of their own.

The gargoyles descended again. This time two more had joined their ranks. One swooped at Ghleanna just as she completed her spell. The creature suddenly went rigid, unable to control its dive. It crashed against the side of the building and smashed to bits that rained onto the ground below.

Two other gargoyles met the same fate. The fourth plunged toward Corran with both its claws outstretched. The paladin struck the beast with his warhammer, but the weapon glanced off without so much as chipping the stone. The gargoyle's claws lashed out but could not penetrate Corran's new armor.

Undaunted, the creature circled and dove once more. As its horns rushed toward the paladin, Corran grabbed Pathfinder. Glowing with magical light, the sword impaled the beast as its head struck the paladin's shield. The creature dropped to Corran's feet, where it took the combined strength of Corran and Durwyn to shove it off the stairs and send it tumbling to the ground.

Kestrel cast her gaze skyward as the fighters disposed of the body. She did not see any more of the creatures approaching, but the hazy gray light camouflaged the stone beasts so well that she couldn't be sure. "We've got to move faster," she said.

They climbed only a few steps farther when more wingbeats echoed through the air. Half a dozen beasts approached this time, each targeting a different person. Ghleanna released another spell, paralyzing three of the beasts and sending them plummeting to earth.

Two of the remaining gargoyles suddenly reared up as Jarial completed a casting. They hovered three or so feet away, advancing then retreating, as if they had forgotten what they were supposed to do. One of them uttered a guttural word that sounded like a curse in any language, and flew away. The other flew in confused circles.

The last gargoyle dived headlong into Durwyn. Though its horns did not penetrate the warrior's armor, the force of impact knocked him off balance. He struggled to regain his equilibrium, tottering precariously on the edge of the staircase.

"Durwyn!" Kestrel watched him in horror. They were well over a hundred feet above the ground—it would be a long fall, with a deadly landing. She willed the fighter to catch himself.

Faeril lunged toward him, trying to reach an arm and pull him to surer footing, but the guard lost his battle with gravity and toppled over the edge. Faeril managed to grasp only his ankle as he disappeared from view. Reacting quickly, Jarial grabbed her legs before Durwyn's weight could pull the cleric over the edge as well.

"I . . . can't . . . hold him . . . " Faeril's face turned red with exertion as she struggled to keep her grip. Several highly unladylike grunts followed. Every muscle in her arms and neck bulged.

Corran scurried to help, but before he could reach them the gargoyle swooped again. The paladin's blade rang as he struck the creature. Faeril, meanwhile, had turned purple. Her perspiring hands were sliding off Durwyn's armor. "I'm losing him!"

"Hang on!" Kestrel couldn't aid her—too many people were in the way, and the space was too narrow. She could help Jarial, who also struggled to maintain his grasp. As she grabbed Faeril's legs, she heard the sorcerer beside her muttering another spell.

Ghleanna also uttered another casting, this one directed at the remaining gargoyles. Both creatures suddenly ceased moving. Their wings fell still. Then, as had the rest of their pack, they dropped like rocks.

Corran reached Faeril and added his strength to hers. "You all right?" he called to Durwyn.

"I can't find a handhold," he shouted. "It's a sheer drop."

"Don't worry. We'll get you up somehow." After reassuring the warrior, he tried to help Faeril pull him to safety. His efforts, however, were thwarted by Durwyn's sheer bulk. Corran lowered his voice so only those still on the stairs could hear. "We can't get enough leverage to pull him up."

Kestrel felt her heart skip a beat. "I think Jarial is working on something."

Faeril released a groan. "Tell him to work faster."

A moment later, Jarial finished mumbling.

"Oh!" the cleric exclaimed. "Kestrel, Jarial . . . you can let go."

"W—what?" Kestrel stared at her in shock.

"I've boosted her strength," Jarial said.

Kestrel looked from him back to Faeril and reluctantly loosed her grip. Faeril rose to a crouch, some of the strain gone from her face. "Help me lift him," she said to Corran in a steady voice.

As the others watched in mute amazement, the cleric rose to her feet, bringing Durwyn's legs with her. Had she been taller, she could have lifted his whole body over the edge, gripping him by the ankles like a plucked goose. As it was, Corran guided the warrior's chest and head over the edge of the staircase while Faeril pulled him to safety.

"Damn . . ." Kestrel muttered. Magically boosted or not, she'd never seen a woman perform such an incredible feat of strength. Her voice was swallowed by the wind, which had changed direction and now carried a chill. The sun sank lower behind the horizon.

They continued up the stairs with as much haste as they could. Ahead, Kestrel saw a circle crowned by bony-looking spires. The dragon's spine, Anorrweyn and the Protector had called it, and now she understood why. The spindly arches looked like the vertebrae of a great beast. They rose toward the darkened sky, somehow untouched by the missiles that had bombarded the stairs. The circle had to be their destination.

The higher they climbed, the more the wind buffeted them about. By the time they reached the apex, their hair whipped about their faces and they had to shout to be heard. Lingering rays of sunlight streaked across the sky.

The party entered the circle with more desperation than reverence. Runes and intricate knotwork, similar to what they had seen inside the Hall of Wizards, covered the stone floor. About ten feet above, the bony spires arced toward a central hollow just large enough for a certain gem.

"Let's do this and get out of here," Kestrel said. Though she scanned the shadows, she saw no sign of the priestess. "Where's Anorrweyn?"

"We'll have to wait for her," Faeril said.

Out of the corner of her eye, Kestrel detected movement in the near-darkness. She turned, scanning the sky. More wings, and lots of them. "We don't have time to wait." She pointed. "There's a whole flight of gargoyles coming at us! Put the emerald in place!"

Corran hesitated. "We don't know the—"

"Just do it!"

The wind had become a gale, speeding the gargoyles closer each second. In the light of the dying sun, Kestrel could see a sinister gleam of hatred in their eyes. They hurled themselves at the party with frightening velocity.

Boosted by Durwyn, Corran slid the emerald into its setting. The gem caught the last ray of light just before the sun faded from view. The beam sparked a glow in the emerald that immediately radiated in a sphere so large as to encompass the entire Speculum in a pale green aura.

The gargoyles, too fast and too close to change their course, slammed into the intangible field. Their bodies bounced off the barrier like hail.

"Such creatures of evil deserve nothing less," said a soft voice behind them. Anorrweyn had materialized. Despite the force field, wind still whipped through the stone circle so hard that Kestrel and others had trouble staying on their feet. The ghost, however, appeared to exist in a state of perfect calm. Not a strand of her hair was disturbed.

Durwyn stared up at the green bubble surrounding them. "Is that the Mythal?"

"Nay, merely a force that protects us from predators whilst we conduct the incantation ceremony," Anorrweyn said. "Let us begin."

They parted to let her advance. When she reached the center of the circle, she offered a brief prayer to Mystra, then raised her hands toward the emerald and closed her eyes. *"Qu'kiir vian ivae, qu'kiir nethmet."* Her voice was barely audible.

Thunder rumbled in the distance. *"Ivae marat vand Cormanthor,"* Anorrweyn chanted softly. *"Mythal selen mhaor kenet. Qu'kiir vand tir t'nor."*

Anorrweyn's hair and gown fluttered gently, as if stirred by a soft breeze. *"Qu'kiir vian ivae, qu'kiir nethmet,"* she repeated, this time more loudly.

Kestrel shook off the words' hypnotic effect to edge closer to Ghleanna. "You speak Elvish, don't you?" she said just loudly enough to be heard above the roar of the wind. "What does she say?"

Ghleanna leaned close, but never took her eyes off the priestess. "The words are ancient, so my understanding is limited," she responded. "But roughly: Binding gem, awaken your light. Dance the weave of the Mythal. Bind it to me that I might drive corruption from our home."

Anorrweyn reached the end of the verse once more. *"Qu'kiir vand tir t'nor."* Another thunderclap boomed, much closer than the first. Without pause, she began again.

"Qu'kiir vian ivae, qu'kiir nethmet." The priestess tossed back her head, entirely given over to the incantation. She chanted the mystical words in a clear, strong voice that rose above the wind's howl. Her hair streamed behind her now, as if the natural forces of this plane finally touched her.

An enormous crack of thunder rent the air. Kestrel nearly jumped out of her skin as the echo reverberated through the night, but Anorrweyn never ceased in her chant. She shouted the words heavenward. *"Qu'kiir vand tir t'nor!"*

Slowly, Anorrweyn rose into the air as if drawn up by some unseen hand. When her fingertips touched the emerald, deep green light burst forth. The radiance spouted beyond the protective field and into the night sky, where it diffused into a wavery mantle of prismatic light that extended as far as the eye could see.

Kestrel gasped. Surely they gazed upon the Mythal itself.

The great Weave coursed with power beyond mortal comprehension, yet it was also a thing of overwhelming beauty. Strands of every hue interlaced in complex knot-work patterns that overlapped so tightly as to form an unbroken blanket of light and energy. The mantle enveloped the city as lovingly as a mother's arms encircle her child.

Yet as they watched, an oily blackness—darker even than the night sky—stole into the fabric of the Weave, oozing between its strands. The taint spread, appearing to open up gaping holes in the sacred shield. Beyond lay not the stars of the heavens, but nothingness.

Suddenly, bolts of black lightning arced through the mantle. They converged into a single charge that raced straight down into the emerald. Kestrel instinctively backed up, expecting the gem to explode into a thousand pieces. It pulsed and shook under the assault.

But it held.

Instead, Anorrweyn absorbed the electrical feedback. The force violently wrenched the spirit out of contact with the emerald. She flew backward, between two of the spires and beyond the circle. The wind abruptly ceased as the gem dropped onto the stone floor. Above, the vision of the Mythal evaporated.

"Priestess!" Faeril rushed after the ghost. "Priestess! Where are you?"

Anorrweyn was gone.

They left the circle and searched furiously, hoping to catch a glimpse of the ghost behind one of the spires, but no sign of her remained. Corran regarded the others soberly. "I fear that blast destroyed her."

Faeril choked down a sob and turned her face away.

"What do we do now?" Durwyn asked.

What, indeed? Kestrel fought back despair. It sickened her to think that Anorrweyn Evensong's spirit had been obliterated. The gentle priestess had touched a part of Kestrel's soul she hadn't known existed—had awakened in her the fledgling desire to do the right thing with no thought of personal reward.

Now she was gone. Apparently, that's where altruism got you in this world.

Damn this whole mission anyway. Misfortune dogged their every step, throwing new obstacles in their path before they could overcome the known ones. Now their path lay shrouded in more darkness than ever without the light of Anorrweyn's goodness to aid them. What had the noble spirit's sacrifice won? Kestrel reentered the circle and picked up the forgotten emerald. It twinkled in the starlight but appeared perfectly ordinary. She held it toward the sorcerers. "Did the ceremony take hold at all, or is this just a stupid piece of glass?"

Jarial and Ghleanna exchanged glances. The half-elf shrugged helplessly. "I have no idea."

The party erupted in debate over how to proceed from here. Corran wanted to infiltrate Castle Cormanthor in search of the pool cavern. Jarial suggested returning to Caalenfaire to see whether the diviner could learn more through scrying. Ghleanna thought a good night's sleep at Beriand's shelter would help them clear their heads and gain some perspective. Faeril was too beside herself over Anorrweyn's demise to voice an opinion.

Kestrel just wanted to get off the top of this building. There was no sign of the protective force field that had surrounded them during the ceremony, and she preferred to argue in a less exposed location. As she stood in the center of the circle, a faint fragrance caught her nostrils. A new calm washed over her. She inhaled deeply. Gardenias.

A moment later, Anorrweyn materialized before them. Her "body" appeared to have survived the ordeal unharmed, but her eyes bore a haunted look they hadn't held previously.

"Priestess!" Faeril cried. "Are you all right? What happened?"

Anorrweyn met each of their gazes. Her visage held the expression of one who has dire news to impart. "I could not commune with the Mythal. The Weave rejected my attempt."

Corran, whose face had become hopeful upon the ghost's reappearance, now addressed her with grim resignation. "The Mythal's corruption is too great to save it?"

The spirit shook her head sadly. "Worse. Another Gem of the Weave is already in use."

CHAPTER FIFTEEN

"Another gem?" Faeril exclaimed. "How is that possible?"

"Harldain gave us the only suitable replacement stone," Corran added. "At least, that's what he told us."

Anorrweyn's face clouded with disgust. "I doubt not the dwarven lord's word. It is the Protector who, I fear, plays a dangerous game with the truth."

Though the others looked at the priestess in confusion, a spark of understanding ignited in Kestrel. Anorrweyn did not speak of another replacement stone. "The baelnorn told us he destroyed the original gem—"

"We will see about that." With a sweep of the ghost's arm, a gate opened in the night air.

Beyond lay the torchlit lair of the Protector. "Come. Let us talk with Miroden Silverblade!"

The baelnorn appeared only mildly surprised by the party's abrupt arrival in his chamber. He set aside the book he'd been reading and rose to greet them. "Good eve, my friends." He looked each of them in the eye but could not meet Anorrweyn's gaze. "Priestess Evensong."

"I have known you many, many centuries, Miroden Silverblade," the priestess began. Though her tone was harsh, it softened. "In life and in death, our paths intertwined as we struggled to save the City of Song from evils mundane and arcane. Through the Opening, the Weeping War, the occupation by creatures of the Abyss—always have we been on the same side."

The Protector bowed his head as Anorrweyn continued. "Now that Myth Drannor faces its greatest threat yet, I fear our paths diverge. You have told these brave adventurers, who fight to save a city not their own, that you destroyed the Sapphire of the Weave. Miroden, I was present at the creation of the gem. I witnessed the Moment of Binding. I know that as you stand before me, the sapphire yet exists in this world."

The priestess touched her hand to the baelnorn's withered cheek. A tear wet her fingers. "You love this city more deeply than most of the People love their lifemates. What happened, Miroden, to make you betray your sacred duty as communicant? Where is the sapphire? Open your heart to me, old friend."

The Protector closed his eyes and pressed Anorrweyn's palm against his cheek. He sighed heavily—an anguished, heartrending moan—then tore his face away from her gentle touch. He crossed to the empty gem case and ran shaking hands over its surface. "I thought . . . I thought . . ." He extended his hands heavenward and dropped to his knees. "Mystra, forgive me!"

He collapsed, rocking on the floor as he hid his face from view. Anorrweyn laid her hands on the baelnorn's shoulders and whispered words audible only to his ears. He nodded, reaching up to grasp one of her hands. The priestess continued her gentle murmurings. After a little while, he nodded a second time and rose.

"It is with the deepest shame that I stand before you," the baelnorn said. His face seemed to have aged a century in mere minutes. "I allowed pride to blind me, and in so doing, I violated the sacred trust placed in me so many years ago." He paused and looked at the priestess. "Anorr-weyn's suspicions are correct—the Sapphire of the Weave still exists." The baelnorn lowered his head. "Kya Mor-drayn has it."

"That is not a cause for shame," Corran said softly. "You are but one person. She had a whole cult to help her steal it from you."

Silverblade raised his head sharply. A pained expression crossed it. "She did not steal it. I—I gave it to her."

Kestrel gasped. She was not the only one—all of them regarded the so-called Protector with shock. How could he have done such a thing? She wanted to shout a thousand questions and a hundred epithets but held her tongue. The baelnorn shut his eyes against their incredulous expressions.

"Continue, Miroden," Anorrweyn bade. "Tell us how it happened."

"When the archmage first came to me, she spoke eloquently of Myth Drannor's lost beauty and grace—of the silvertrees in the courtyard of the Maerdrym, of how the Windsong Towers brushed against the stars. Oh, how her words made me long for the old days, Anorr-weyn! Times so long past even the People have started to forget."

The baelnorn's eyes held a faraway expression.

"Mordrayn told me she had discovered a way to restore the City of Song to its former splendor. By using the Mythal to summon a Pool of Radiance, we could infuse new life into the city. The fading Mythal would grow strong once more, and Myth Drannor, in turn, would rise to greatness again."

The dreamlike trance faded as the Protector's thoughts returned to the present. He ran his fingers along the edge of the empty gem case. "She told me that the fate of Myth Drannor rested in my hands alone, and in my foolish pride I believed her. I did not ask the questions I should have asked." He met Anorrweyn's penetrating gaze. "I wanted so much for her words to be true, for myself to be the one whose faith and perseverance restored the city, that I did not probe into the details of her plan."

"I know that hope for the city's revival has sustained you through centuries of lonely isolation," Anorrweyn offered.

"That can never excuse my actions," he said. "I surrendered the Sapphire of the Weave—the treasure entrusted to me so long ago by more worthy lords than I—to Mordrayn. I taught her the incantation. Mordrayn contacted the Mythal and directed its ancient power to create a Pool of Radiance deep within Castle Cormanthor. Only afterward did she reveal herself as an archmage in the Cult of the Dragon. By the time I realized the horror of what I had done, I could not stop her. The pool brought life, yes— stolen life. It spawns tendrils of itself in other cities and drains the spirits of the living to fuel the tainted Mythal."

"A diabolical cycle," Corran said. "What is her final purpose?"

"I do not know." The baelnorn shook his head in bewilderment. "By Our Lady, this is not what I intended! I sought to redeem the City of Song—instead, I have damned it."

"Nay, Miroden," Anorrweyn said gently. "Hope lives. We have created a new Gem of the Weave."

Some of the anguish left his face. He gazed at the party in amazement. "You succeeded? Then you can undo some of the damage I have wrought. You must break Mordrayn's link with the Mythal." The baelnorn passed his hand in front of the wall. An opening formed, revealing a passage behind. "This tunnel leads to the castle. Find the sapphire. Destroy it by touching it while speaking this word: *Ethgonil*. It is the Word of Redemption."

Kestrel and the others hesitated, still trying to absorb all they'd heard. Kestrel felt she ought to be angry with the Protector for his betrayal, for setting in motion the events it now fell to her and her companions to stop. Yet, as she looked at the baelnorn's shriveled form, his face wracked with shame, she felt only pity.

"Make haste," Anorrweyn urged. "The cult cannot be allowed to poison the Mythal any further. I will return to the Speculum. When the sapphire is destroyed, I shall use the emerald to turn the Mythal's power against our enemies. Then you can seize the Gauntlets of Moander from Mordrayn to destroy the pool."

As they filed into the passage one by one, Kestrel stole a last glimpse at Miroden Silverblade. The elf lord who had for centuries defended the Sapphire of the Weave with strength and wisdom—who had willingly sacrificed his own life to protect the Mythal—once again huddled on the floor. Anorrweyn knelt beside him, drew his head into her lap and gently rocked the tortured spirit.

Kestrel felt she was observing grief too intense and private for an audience. She turned and entered the passage, leaving the ghosts to mourn in solitude. She and the others had no more time to dwell on the past.

Not if they were going to save the future.

BOOK THREE
——————The Arcane Cabal

CHAPTER SIXTEEN

"You can admit it any time now."

Corran's jocular tone took Kestrel by surprise. She frowned at the paladin as they stepped over the bodies of yet another soulless drow band. The winding passage beneath Castle Corman- thor was simply too tight to move the enthralled Kilsek aside after defeating them. "Admit what?"

"We were right to trust Nathlilik," the paladin said, muting his voice in case other patrols lurked nearby. "That Staff of Sunlight has proven invaluable."

She glanced at the sacred weapon in Jarial's grip. They'd encountered so many cult patrols since leaving the baelnorn that without the staff they would have exhausted themselves getting this far. "We would have found it anyway," she said with a shrug. "As for Nathlilik, if she had done what she promised and released all her kin into true death, we wouldn't even need the staff. She probably gave up and skipped town."

"Or got caught."

Kestrel followed Corran's gaze. Ahead, the corridor widened into a long, narrow chamber lined with prison cells carved into the rock like small caves. The pens, separated from each other by about six feet, stretched as far up the passage as Kestrel could see. In the closest cell, Nathlilik herself paced like a caged panther.

The drow leader stopped abruptly when she saw them approach. "We meet again, humans." She grinned mockingly, gesturing at her cell with a sweep of her hand. "Welcome to my new abode. Can I offer you tea? A glass of wine?"

Kestrel ignored her sarcasm. "What happened?"

"What do you think?" Nathlilik snapped. "The cult captured us. Killed all my men one at a time and fed their blood to the dracolich as an appetizer. I'm the main course—at least I was until you came along. What are you standing around for? Let me out."

Nathlilik's attitude made Kestrel's hackles rise. "I don't think I like your tone."

The dark elf barked a harsh laugh. "Don't expect me to beg, human. Not to you." She strutted to the corner and plunked down on the floor. "The cult has taken my lifemate. They've taken my men, and they've taken my weapons, but I'll hold my pride until the last drop of blood leaves my body."

Kestrel shrugged. "You do that." She walked past the cell, fighting the urge to turn around to see whether the rest of the group followed. If someone else wanted to free the arrogant drow witch, let them try to get past that lock. She knew exactly which tool it would require.

She heard Corran's footsteps behind her. "Kestrel . . . " he murmured.

"Corran, we haven't the time, and I haven't the inclination." She continued marching away.

"Wait!" Nathlilik cried.

Kestrel turned. To her amazement, the whole party had followed her lead. Nathlilik had watched all six of them pass her cell. "I've learned more about the cult's activities during my imprisonment," the dark elf said. "Free me and I'll tell you what I know."

"Tell us what you know, and we'll free you," Kestrel replied.

Nathlilik, clearly incensed at having lost the upper hand, hesitated. Kestrel waited. Finally the drow spoke. "In the upper part of the castle stands an enormous urn. The Vessel of Souls, they call it. That's where the cult keeps the spirits of all the creatures whose blood they drain. My kin are trapped in there. Kedar's soul is in there. Destroy the vessel, and the cult's enthralled slaves will trouble you no more."

"I thought that was your job," Kestrel said. "When we last saw you, isn't that where you and your band were headed?"

"The cult captured us before we could succeed. But we got as far as the Vessel Chamber—I've seen the wicked thing with my own eyes."

As much as Kestrel would have liked to leave Nathlilik to the cult's mercy—or lack thereof—she reluctantly opened the lock of the dark elf's cell. Nathlilik strode out of her prison without so much as a "thank you."

"We defeated a Kilsek patrol a hundred yards or so down the passageway," Corran said. "You can retrieve one of their weapons. Since we're on the same side, would you like to join forces?"

Kestrel's eyes widened. She found the thought of

spending any more time in Nathlilik's company abhorrent. Before she could voice an objection, however, the dark elf sneered. "Ha! Walk in the company of surface-dwellers? I'll take my chances alone." Without another word, she disappeared into the darkness.

The party stared after her. "That is one disagreeable woman," Durwyn declared.

They continued past the cell blocks, most of which stood empty. Apparently, the cult didn't hold prisoners long before using their blood to slake Pelendralaar's thirst. In the last cell, however, they found the crumpled form of a man passed out in the corner. He lay facedown, nearly naked, his blond hair matted with blood and his body covered with bruises. Whip marks swelled his back and oozed pus.

"Oh, by my Lady's grace!" Faeril cried. "Kestrel, let me in to help him!"

"Is he even alive?" Jarial asked.

Ghleanna dropped her staff and clutched the prison bars, peering intently into the dark cell. "He's a large man," she said softly. "A warrior. . . ."

The cleric started uttering prayers of healing while Kestrel struggled with the locks. There were several mechanisms, all more complex than the sole lock that had secured Nathlilik's cell. Apparently, this was one prisoner the cult wanted to keep.

She sprung the last lock and swung open the door. Faeril rushed to the captive's side, followed closely by Ghleanna. The sorceress touched his hair with a shaking hand. "It is Athan." She choked back a sob. "Oh gods, what have they done to him? Can you save him?"

"Mystra, lend me your light, that I may tend your servant." Instantly, Faeril's hands glowed with a soft blue-white light. The glow illuminated Athan's dark cell just enough for her to examine him. The cleric quickly assessed her patient, running her hands along his limbs and torso. She checked his head and neck, then with Corran's help gently rolled the warrior onto his side to better examine his chest.

Ghleanna watched Faeril in scared silence until she couldn't keep quiet any longer. "Well?"

"His pulse is weak, and he's barely breathing," Faeril said. "He's got a skull fracture and numerous broken bones—his right arm and hand, half a dozen ribs. His right leg is broken in two places, and both lower legs are smashed into pulp." She wrinkled her nose. "From the smell, I think gangrene has set in."

"But you can save him, right?" Ghleanna asked anxiously. "You can heal him?"

Faeril raised her gaze to Ghleanna's. "He is too badly injured for me to heal him fully. I think I can keep him from death."

"Do you hear that, Athan?" Ghleanna stroked a lock of his hair, her voice tremulous. "Faeril's going to help you."

Corran cleared his throat. "Can I assist?"

Faeril shook her head. "If you speak of laying on hands, let's see what I can do alone. We don't know what lies ahead—your healing powers may be needed later. But you can help me bandage his wounds." She turned to Kestrel. "I will also need your hands. Durwyn, Jarial, stand watch. This may take a while."

The cleric uttered a prayer-spell asking Mystra to heal Athan's gangrenous legs and lacerated back. "'Tis best to leave him unconscious until I can alleviate some of his pain," she explained to Ghleanna. When the decay was gone and the bone fragments fused, she beseeched the goddess to mend the other breaks in his leg and hand. Finally, she entreated Mystra to heal the warrior's head injury.

Athan's eyes fluttered open. He warily regarded the

unfamiliar faces surrounding him until his gaze rested on the sorceress. "Ghleanna," he whispered.

She took his good hand in hers and pressed it to her wet cheek. "Brother."

❧ ❧ ❧ ❧ ❧

Despite Faeril's care, Athan remained weak. The sight of his sister, however, appeared to hearten him beyond anything the cleric could do. His blue eyes quickly lost their glassiness, and the lines pain etched in his face seemed to fade as the minutes passed. After Ghleanna made introductions, he asked how she and the rest of the party had found him.

"Happenstance," she admitted. "Though I prayed you might still live, we had no way of knowing for sure."

He encompassed them all with his gaze. "I thank the gods you arrived when you did. After my last beating, I might never have awakened." He tried to rise but winced and settled back down against Ghleanna.

"Your ribs are broken," Faeril said. "I shall have to bind them, for your other injuries exhausted my healing powers. We'll also have to splint that arm." She opened a small pack and withdrew several rolled-up strips of cloth. "Kestrel, cut me several one-foot lengths from this roll." Corran, meanwhile, scouted around for some stray pieces of wood.

"The Cult of the Dragon has perfected the art of torture." Athan studied his right hand, flexing his fingers as if amazed to see them work once more. "You spend the first half of the interrogation afraid you'll die, and the last half afraid you won't." He glanced up to catch a stricken look cross Ghleanna's face. "You would have been proud, Lena—they never got a word out of me."

Corran returned with an extinguished torch and

Durwyn's axe. He measured Athan's forearm and chopped off the charred end of the torch to match its length. "What did they want to know?"

"At first, who had sent us and how much we knew about Mordrayn's plans." He inhaled sharply as Faeril grasped his injured arm and reset the broken bone. "Lately, though, all their questions have been about you folks. Of course, I had no answers to give them even if I wanted to—I didn't even know my sister was among you. All I knew, I gleaned from my captors' own questions. Your activities have agitated the whole cult."

The news brought a grin to Kestrel's lips. "Good. I hope we have Mordrayn's drawers tied in knots." She handed the lengths of cloth to Faeril and returned her dagger to its hidden sheath.

Athan's face became deadly serious. "Do not underestimate Kya Mordrayn. She single-handedly controls the Mythal now through some sort of gem and uses the corrupted ancient magic to expand the Pool of Radiance."

"Yes, we've seen evidence of the pool's expansion." Corran secured the torch shaft to Athan's arm to form a makeshift splint. "Spawn pools are popping up in random cities outside Cormanthyr."

"There's nothing random about them," Athan said. "Mordrayn and the dracolich are using the pool to drain the life force from key cities throughout the Realms. They intend to first gain control of the Heartlands' main trading and port cities—Phlan, Mulmaster, Hillsfar, Zhentil Keep. Once they achieve a strong foothold, they plan to expand their domination until the whole continent falls under their power."

When the splint was complete, Faeril and Ghleanna eased Athan into a sitting position so the cleric could bind his ribs. "If Mordrayn controls the Mythal and the Pool of Radiance, what does she need the dracolich for?" Kestrel asked. "Is she really doing this all just so he can rule the world?"

"Pelendralaar is her general." Athan groaned as Faeril wound cloth strips around his bruised and battered torso. "He masterminds all the cult's military strategy. The dracolich has already waged successful campaigns against the alhoon, phaerimm, and baatezu of Myth Drannor and has now started deploying forces outside the city. He crushed the first counterattacks of Mulmaster and Zhentil Keep."

Kestrel recalled the withered but massive beast they'd observed in the Speculum's scrying pool. He'd looked imposing enough from a distance. "Have you ever seen the dracolich in person?"

"I've been dragged before Pelendralaar and Mordrayn several times," Athan said. "Do not underestimate his power, either. Once the Mythal protected this city from foul races and creatures, but now Mordrayn uses its corrupted power to strengthen the dracolich. We'll never defeat him without breaking her hold on the Mythal first."

"We?" Ghleanna questioned. "Athan—"

"We aren't far from the pool cavern," the warrior continued. "It lies at the end of this passageway. That's where we'll find the two of them, the gem Mordrayn uses to control the Mythal, the pool itself—and the Gauntlets of Moander, hanging from Mordrayn's waist so that anyone who seeks to destroy the pool has to go through her first." The warrior struggled to his feet. In height and girth, he was Durwyn's match, but his remaining injuries lent him the awkwardness of a squire. "I'd like nothing more than to face them again with a weapon in hand—"

"Athan, not with your sword arm still broken."

The warrior smiled ruefully. "Ever the protective sister, Lena."

"Ghleanna is right," Faeril said. "You need more

healing before you could take on a wolf, let alone the arch-mage and her general."

"We can't just leave him here for the cultists to return," Corran said. "And for him to leave on his own with a broken sword arm . . ." He let the conclusion go unstated.

Faeril nodded. "I have considered this matter. Athan can recover at our tree shelter, speeded by Beriand's superior healing arts. With the group's leave, I will accompany him there to make sure he reaches it safely and to check on Beriand's welfare. Already I have been too long away from him."

Kestrel didn't like that idea at all. "You would desert us just as we prepare to confront Mordrayn and Pelendralaar?"

Jarial stepped forward. "Nay, I can accompany him. The party has another sorcerer—you are our only cleric. Your holy magic will be needed against the evil ahead. I will take Athan to the shelter, check on Beriand, and return as soon as I can."

If he could return. The sorcerer might very well get himself killed trying to return alone. But Kestrel couldn't think of a better alternative, and the whole party grew conscious of the fact that they'd tarried in one place overlong. They were lucky to have remained undisturbed thus far—they could not afford to spend more time in debate.

Ghleanna draped her cloak over Athan's broad shoulders and hugged her brother goodbye. "Easy, now," he chuckled. "Those ribs are still sore."

"Take care of yourself." The sorceress looked up at him with moist eyes. "Shall I see you again in this life?"

He kissed her on the forehead and smiled. "Count on it, Lena."

❧ ❧ ❧ ❧ ❧

The sound of lapping water echoed in eerie rhythm throughout the twisting passage. It hissed and burbled, a moaning chant that threatened to drive mad any who listened too long.

Kestrel shut her ears against the profane whisperings of the pool, retreating into a state of deep concentration she normally reserved only for the most complicated locks and high-stakes card games. Her collarbone tingled so badly it felt like a tuning fork. She did not need the familiar warning—she knew perfectly well how much danger she walked toward. The pool cavern could not be far now. Surely, just around that bend—

The sound of a female voice stopped them all short. A familiar, throaty voice. Mordrayn's voice.

"We have gates to get in and out of the cavern, Pelendralaar. The lowliest of our sorcerers can summon them. Why keep an outside entrance? It only makes us vulnerable, and we cannot afford any more mistakes." Her voice became a purr. "And I so enjoy your displays of strength."

The dracolich's deep rumble followed. "As you wish, child."

A second later, the passage shook with the force of an earthquake. Rocks and debris rained down, pummeling the party and thickening the air with dust. Kestrel held the edge of her cloak over her nose to keep from inhaling the dirt as she dodge the falling rocks, but a fit of coughing seized her.

Ahead of her, Corran lost his footing. He fell, narrowly escaping the path of a huge stone that slammed into the ground where he had just stood.

"Corran?" Kestrel shouted but could not hear her own voice in the din of the tunnel's collapse. Nor could she see the paladin. Had the rock hit him after all?

Suddenly, an enormous weight slammed Kestrel to the ground. Another boulder. White-hot pain shot through her legs from the knees down. She was pinned.

The explosion seemed to last forever. The few torches that lined the walls shook loose. They fell and sputtered out, immersing the party in blackness. Kestrel shouted again, but still the roar drowned out her words. Yet somehow, above the thunder sang Mordrayn's voice, laughing in wicked delight.

The sound wasn't nearly as bad as what followed. Once the debris settled, Kestrel called to her companions. Her unanswered cry echoed in the silence.

The silence of a tomb.

CHAPTER SEVENTEEN

She was trapped in the darkness.

Her legs were broken, her companions unconscious or dead.

Kestrel pushed at the boulder pinning her to the ground. It wouldn't budge. She leaned back, summoned energy from a place deep within herself, and tried again. She could not wobble the huge stone in the slightest.

"Dammit!" She choked back a sob of frustration and beat the rock with her fist, but succeeded only in bruising her knuckles. Damn it all! Every last, bloody moment of this whole damned quest.

She let the pain in, then—into her mind. She'd been forcing it back, but something had to drive off the despair that threatened to overwhelm her. A whimper escaped her lips.

"Kestrel?"

"Corran?" She'd never been so happy to hear another human voice. "Are you all right?" Her eyes, unused to the absolute blackness, probed the dark for some faint image of the paladin but saw nothing.

"I have a terrible headache—I believe I lost consciousness for a while there. What about you?" She heard him moving, his armor scraping against rocks and debris.

"I think my legs are broken."

"Keep talking so I can find you."

"Only if you talk back." Her spirit clung to Corran's disembodied voice like a lifeline. "I'm under a boulder—it fell on me, and I can't move it."

"It pinned your legs?"

"Just below the knee. I think they might be crushed." Her head suddenly felt very light. "I don't know—they hurt real bad for a bit, but now I don't feel them so much."

He seemed to move more rapidly. "Have you heard sounds from anyone else?"

"No."

He scuffled on some loose gravel. The sound was closer than she expected, and she felt the air move nearby. "Here." She reached out and caught his hand. It felt warm and strong in hers. She hadn't realized how cold she'd grown.

"You're freezing." He rubbed her fingers in his palms, then let them drop. "I'm going to see how big this rock is." She heard him shuffle around the boulder, running his hands over its surface. "If I can find somewhere to plant my feet for leverage, I think I can roll it off your legs. Here."

She heard more scuffling, followed by several grunts. Then, ever so slowly, the pressure lifted from her legs. Fresh pain seized her as blood coursed through the vessels.

Corran returned to her side. She flinched as his hands touched one of her legs, old defenses working reflexively. If the paladin noticed, he didn't comment as he methodically palpated her knees and shins. "Good news, Kestrel. The rock didn't crush the bones—I feel two clean breaks. With Tyr's grace, I can heal you."

"No." The word flew out of her mouth before she even had time to think about how foolish she sounded. She hated being injured, hated feeling vulnerable. That it was Corran who ministered to her now made it all the worse.

"Kestrel . . . I know we haven't gotten along well. Part of that is my fault. But right now I'm all you've got. Let me help you."

He was right, of course. Even if the others were alive, Faeril's healing powers were exhausted. If she wanted to get out of this cavern any time soon, she had to accept the paladin's aid. "Okay," she conceded.

She was grateful for the darkness as Corran laid his hands on her damaged legs and commenced his prayer to Tyr. Comforting warmth radiated from his palms and fingers, soothing away her pain and knitting her broken bones. As he prayed, she felt herself relax. The perpetual agitation he provoked in her subsided, replaced by reassurance. She might not bear any great love for Corran D'Arcey, but after all they'd been through together, she did trust him.

He finished his prayer and sat back. "How do you feel?"

"Good as new." She started to rise, eager to confirm that she could stand on her own, but Corran placed a restraining hand on her arm.

"Rest a while longer," he said. "Let your bones strengthen before you crash into something as you stumble around in the dark."

Reluctantly, she settled back down. He, however,

sounded as if he were starting to rise. "Where are you going?" she asked.

"To see if I can find the others."

"In the dark?"

"They may be alive but injured. I must at least try to locate them."

Kestrel thought the effort hopeless, but she could understand Corran's drive to try. It was the paladin in him—the helper, the healer. Faeril would have done the same.

The thought of the cleric sparked an idea. "Corran, when you heal people, you receive that power from your god, right? Just like Faeril?"

"Sort of." His tone questioned where she was going with this, but he continued. "In both cases it is divine power, but paladins and clerics channel it differently. Tyr grants me the ability to heal with the touch of my hands. Clerics heal through miracles—they petition their gods to answer prayer spells with divine magic, to heal and perform other wonders."

"Can you make your hands glow, like Faeril did?" She drew up her knees and hugged them to her chest. Perhaps it was the darkness, or the dread of being left alone, but she found herself warming to Corran's conversation.

"No. I suspect that is a gift specific to Mystra's faithful, for I have never witnessed it before." He paused. "I have seen Tyr's priests and older paladins produce a glowing ball of light through prayer. I've also seen seasoned paladins, like my father and older brothers, perform some of the miracles of clerics, but only after years of faithful service. Once they have proven themselves, Tyr thus empowers them to better do his work."

His father and brothers? "Is everyone in your family a paladin?"

He laughed. "Pretty much. The D'Arceys have served

Tyr for as many generations as we can remember. It's a lot to live up to."

No wonder Corran had such lofty notions about honor and justice. He'd probably been indoctrinated in the cradle and hadn't seen enough of the world to temper his idealism. At least, not when they'd met. Since coming to Myth Drannor, Corran had lost some of that naiveté. His personality still needed some work, but he no longer spouted about "fallen worthies" and never retreating from a battle. His experiences in this doomed city had indeed seasoned him.

Perhaps, she thought, Corran had served Tyr well enough to get them out of this living tomb. "Have you ever tried to perform a miracle?"

"Nay, 'twould be presumptuous!"

"Then how will you know when you've proven yourself?" Emboldened by the darkness, by her inability to see whatever expression—condescension? outrage?—his face held, she pressed on. "I don't pretend to know much about matters of faith, Corran. But if we die in this tunnel and Mordrayn succeeds at her plan, Tyr won't have any followers left on Toril because they'll all be dead. We could really use his help right now. If you're worried about sounding presumptuous, ask for something small—like a light."

When he did not answer immediately, she thought he'd dismissed her idea in disgust. A moment later, she heard his quiet, hesitant voice break the stillness. "Tyr, if this humble servant has found favor in your eyes, grant me light that I may see our path clearly."

A ball of brilliant light appeared in Corran's palm, nearly blinding Kestrel with its sudden brightness. She blinked rapidly until her pupils adjusted, then looked at Corran. The paladin gazed at the glow in wonder.

"He answered." Corran glanced up to meet Kestrel's

eyes. A smile, the first they'd ever shared, stole across his face. "He found me worthy. He answered."

❧ ❧ ❧ ❧ ❧

In the blaze of Corran's holy light, they found Ghleanna, Faeril, and Durwyn lying nearby, unconscious but alive. The brilliance woke Ghleanna almost immediately. The two others soon followed.

The tunnel's collapse had dropped tons of impassable rubble at both ends of the passageway, leaving the party in a cavern about a hundred feet long littered with piles of rock and dirt. They now stood at the far end, debating whether magic would blast through the rockslide or cause a further collapse. Corran and Faeril were optimistic, the others skeptical.

Kestrel shivered. She didn't care to experiment with sorcery but saw no alternative. They couldn't dig their way out, and if they didn't do something they'd starve to death—or perhaps suffocate first.

She shivered again. If she didn't know better, she'd say a draft crept along her neck.

Turning, she left the others to their debate and scanned the cavern. The tunnel walls were lined with debris, some of it piled quite high. A craggy hollow in one corner shadowed the ceiling from Corran's light. She picked her way over to that side and scaled the heap of stones.

"Kestrel, where are you going?" Corran called.

"Don't you feel that draft?" She crawled into the crevice. Sure enough, early morning light filtered through a hole not quite two feet in diameter. "Here! It's an opening to the outside!"

She reached up to grasp the edges of the hole and pull herself out. To her shock, she found her right hand grasped by a larger one. A moment later, familiar blue eyes peered down at her. "Need a lift?"

"Athan!"

With just one hand, he pulled her out of the cavern. They stood at the base of a cliff, with Castle Cormanthor looming high above them. The warrior appeared fully healed. No trace of injury or pain marred his features. He'd also shaven and washed away the dried blood and other physical evidence of the cult's torture. New armor— a suit she remembered from Harldain's hoard—made the strapping man appear even larger than he had before. A gleaming two-handed sword hung at his side.

"How did you find us?"

"By Mystra's grace, I think. I was skirting the castle base, seeking a way in, when I heard you call out just now. I never would have noticed that hole otherwise."

She looked around for some sign of the sorcerer. "Is Jarial with you?"

He shook his head. "Beriand has been fending off near-constant attacks in Faeril's absence. Jarial stayed behind to defend him." Kestrel noted that Athan now wore the ring of regeneration Jarial had received from the bael-norn. "He sent these along, too." Athan gestured toward the Staff of Sunlight and Ozama's boots lying at his feet.

The rest of the party appeared below. Athan lifted Ghleanna out next, giving his sister a proper hug—now that his ribs were healed—before helping Faeril squeeze through the narrow space. Durwyn had to widen the hole for himself and Corran to accommodate their broad shoulders.

Once all had emerged, Athan explained Jarial's absence to the others. "He said to give the staff to Faeril. Lena or Kestrel, I thought the boots would fit one of you best."

Kestrel nodded to the sorceress. "Take them." While Ghleanna donned the footwear and the cloak her brother had borrowed, Corran asked Athan whether he'd found a weakness in the castle's defenses.

"Nay," he replied. "The entrance is well guarded, and there's nothing here below. I'd hoped to sneak in, but I don't think it's possible."

Kestrel studied the fortress's exterior. Breaking and entering was something she knew a little about. A quick survey revealed their best option. One of the towers appeared to have no roof but rather sat open to the sky. They just needed to reach it.

She sighed and pulled out her grappling hooks. They had a long climb ahead of them.

❧   ❧   ❧   ❧   ❧

"You had to pick *this* tower?" Corran swung Pathfinder at the dragonlike creature swooping toward him. Instead of dodging the sword, the monster grabbed at it. Corran's quick stroke, however, left the creature clawing the air.

Kestrel dropped and rolled to avoid the clutches of another beast. "How was I to know there'd be a nest of these things in here?"

The party had tumbled into the open tower to discover the castle's former throne room. It was a large, cone-shaped chamber with a wide assembly area at its base. A long crystal staircase spiraled its circumference, leading to an observation platform. Once-elegant appointments—silk wall coverings, plush chairs and settees, and of course the coronal's golden seat itself—indicated that in times past the whole Elven Court might have joined the king in this room to enjoy its commanding view of the city. Now the sole occupants left to appreciate the panorama were the dozen or so winged beasts roosting within.

Kestrel had never seen creatures like these before. They had the horned heads, reptilian claws, and leathery wings of dragons, but the torsos and legs of humans. Red scales covered their bodies and snakelike tails. Their white eyes burned with malevolence.

Immediately, the creatures had taken flight, swooping down at the party. They launched an organized defense of their lair, communicating in a tongue that sounded like a series of hisses. While some attacked, others circled above, awaiting their chance.

Another beast swooped at Kestrel, targeting her weapon hand. A quick upward stroke gave the monster what it was after—Loren's Blade—but through the flesh of its underbelly. Its claws raked Kestrel's arm in retaliation but couldn't pierce the new armor Harldain had provided.

"Anyone know what these things are?" Durwyn launched an arrow. The shaft caught one monster in the side, eliciting a hiss.

"They're dragon-kin." Athan landed another strike on his nearest foe, rending a great tear in the creature's wing. "Allies of the cult. Be warned—they covet magical items."

Two dragon-kin swarmed Ghleanna. Or, more accurately, her spellstaff. She hit one of them with the staff, but the other beast reached out and grabbed the weapon in its razor-sharp talons. "That's mine, fiend!" she cried. The sorceress clung to the staff, digging her heels into the floor and entering a tug-of-war with the monster. She was no match for its brute strength, however, and the staff slid out of her grasp.

The creature darted off with the weapon. Ghleanna sent a sharp gesture and a command word after the beast. It spun around to look at her with wide eyes before dropping the staff and flying out of the tower. Three more dragon-kin in the vicinity joined the retreat.

"Ghleanna, whatever that spell was, keep 'em coming!" Kestrel called as another dragon-kin approached. Dark gray smoke puffed from its nostrils, stinging her eyes. She met its red-rimmed gaze and flashed Loren's Blade at the beast. "This what you want? Magic?" The creature lunged for the weapon. "Here!" She hurled it at the dragon-kin. The dagger struck true, then sailed back into Kestrel's hand. As the stunned beast stared at the oozing hole in its belly, Kestrel threw the blade again.

This toss caught the beast in its right eye. Black blood spurted from the socket and streamed down the creature's snout. The dragon-kin shrieked in pain and fury as it tried to swoop at her once more. With no depth perception, the creature crashed into the floor. Kestrel used the dagger for a third, final, strike in the back.

Free of opponents for the time being, she darted to the room's only exit. If the double doors were open—or secured with easily defeated locks—perhaps they could simply retreat from the remaining dragon-kin and reserve their strength for the more important battles ahead. She grasped the gold latch and tugged but could not even rattle the doors in their frame. Worse, the doors featured no ordinary lock. Magic had sealed them, and only magic could release them.

A battle cry from Durwyn drew her attention back to the action. The warrior fought two creatures on the dais that held the coronal's throne. Before Kestrel could reach him to lend a hand, Faeril moved in. The dragon-kin took to the air and circled.

While the cleric stood poised to strike with her flame blade as soon as one of the beasts swooped close enough, she reached out her hand to touch Durwyn's shoulder. "Mystra, I beseech you—strengthen the warrior Durwyn to better serve you." Just as she completed her prayer-spell, the dragon-kin attacked.

Durwyn swung his axe with such force that he lopped both claws off one of his opponents. The creature shrieked and soared out of range. Blood streaming from its severed limbs, it flew out of the tower and disappeared from view.

The second dragon-kin dived at the fighter in retaliation. Durwyn struck that creature as well, slicing off a wing. The beast crashed to the floor. It lay only a moment before it tried to rise, but the loss of its wing impaired its balance and the stone floor was slick with dragon-kin blood. The wounded creature slipped and slid in the slime. Durwyn picked it up and threw it into the throne.

The heavy dragon-kin landed so hard it dislodged the throne from its centuries-old resting place. As the great seat slid aside, it revealed a tunnel below.

Kestrel ran toward the passage, eager to investigate, but three dragon-kin also flocked toward the discovery. Another spell from Ghleanna disbanded them. They fled in fear, leaving only a few wounded comrades still engaged in combat. Durwyn made quick work of his grounded foe, then helped finish off the remaining creatures.

At last they were free to explore the surprise passage. "Nice work, Durwyn," Corran said as they all approached the dais. "Looks like you've discovered the king's emergency escape route."

The corridor was actually a narrow, spiraling staircase. At a word from Faeril, magical light illuminated the windowless stairwell. It continued down as far as their eyes could see, apparently untouched by either time or the castle's unsavory squatters.

"Well, either we give this passage a try or see if Ghleanna can magically unseal the double doors," Kestrel said. "I bet we'll encounter fewer cultists this way."

The party descended. They reached the bottom of the stairs to find a solitary door that offered no choice of direction. Kestrel pressed her ear to the wood. Beyond, she heard the sound of wings and the hiss-language of more dragon-kin.

Even worse, above it rose a horrible, mournful wailing. Thousands of voices joined in an unholy canticle of despair that howled like a wind storm.

The chorus of the damned.

CHAPTER EIGHTEEN

The Vessel of Souls radiated evil.

It was a thing of black magic, of life-taking, of soul-stealing. It looked every inch the accursed instrument it was. The vessel resembled a crystal chalice with a stem but no base. Images of tormented, eyeless faces adorned the sides of the cup, their black outlines standing out in high relief from the crystal.

Yet more horrifying than these representations of lost souls were the thousands of real spirits crying out for release.

The shadowy souls swirled in a red mist, their eyes blank, their mouths agape with their song of hopelessness. They rose above the rim of the cup in a great surge of spirit matter, only to be driven back down by the unseen force that held them captive. Their endless gyrations lent haunting rhythm to their wails.

The vessel hung suspended in the air, supported by three twisted steel beams as thick as Kestrel's waist. They formed a pyramid in the center of the round room, distributing the weight of the enormous urn to the edges of the chamber where the floor was made of stone. Directly beneath the vessel, a large circle of multifaceted glass lay inset in the floor. The glass caught the torchlight of the wall sconces and projected it up to the urn. As a result, eerie, undulating light bathed the chalice in a continuous profane baptism.

A score of dragon-kin and at least a hundred soulless drow guarded the Vessel of Souls. The lifeless dark elves stood silent and resolute in their watch, but many of the dragon-kin talked among themselves.

Kestrel closed the door as silently as she'd opened it and described the scene to her companions. "I saw no other doors to the room," she concluded. "Only a tall, narrow window with its pane blackened."

Corran rubbed his chin. "If we drop the vessel through the floor, we can destroy it and open up an exit at the same time." He looked to Durwyn and Athan. "If the three of us each take one of the supports and dislodge them simultaneously, the chalice should fall through the center of the glass."

Athan nodded. "I can manage it."

"Me, too," said Durwyn.

Corran next turned to Ghleanna. "Jarial's invisibility spell could prove a big boon. He didn't happen to teach it to you somewhere along the line, did he?"

Ghleanna grinned. "He did—and a few others."

"Excellent. Have you the power to render all three of us invisible?"

"Aye, and two others besides—"

Kestrel shook her head. "Just the warriors. We still have Mordrayn and Pelendralaar to face. We may need your spells more then."

"Are you sure, Kestrel?" Corran regarded her seriously. "We'll be relying on you, Ghleanna, and Faeril to hold off the dragon-kin and drow."

"We can handle them," Ghleanna declared.

Cloaked by Ghleanna's sorcery, the three fighters headed to their appointed positions. No one noticed their entrance, but one of the dragon-kin noted the open door. It raised a claw and gestured toward the remaining companions, hissing a word of alarm.

Ghleanna responded with a spell that sent the beasts into a state of confusion. Some of the dragon-kin stared stupidly at the sorceress, some wandered over to another part of the room, some actually began attacking each other. Eight dragon-kin took to the air, flying straight toward the trio of women.

Faeril, meanwhile, twice rapped the Staff of Sunlight on the floor. A burst of daylight issued forth, crippling many of the closest drow. Kestrel sent Loren's Blade and her other two daggers flying toward the nearest weakened dark elves. She eliminated two and injured a third—leaving a mere ninety-seven or so to advance on her. She prayed to any god who would listen that the warriors would destroy the Vessel of Souls quickly and that Nathlilik would prove correct in her belief that its destruction would eradicate the enslaved drow.

The dragon-kin swooped down to attack. Kestrel's armor resisted their claws, but Ghleanna did not fare as well. One of the beasts raked her face, turning her left cheek to bloody ribbons. The mage shrieked and clutched her damaged face, then responded with a volley of conjured missiles that hit the beast in rapid succession.

Through the corner of her eye, Kestrel saw Faeril inflict critical wounds on a swooping dragon-kin with only a word. The creature plummeted to the ground. After that, she lost track of what the others were doing as she fought her own battles against the remaining dragon-kin. One of them had her pinned against the wall. She used her club to beat off his swiping claws, all the while trying to score a hit with Loren's Blade.

Beyond, the weakened drow had mobilized. The first wave rushed in to join the combat against the intruders. One of them hurled a fireball at her. She braced herself for its impact, ready to feel the blaze sear her flesh, but miraculously, the flames passed over her like a gentle breeze. Her mind raced for an explanation until she recalled the mantle rings she wore. What was it the baelnorn had said—protection from a dozen spells? Corran and the others had better hurry.

Though the fireball passed over her without harm, it scorched her opponent. The dragon-kin shrieked and turned on the offending drow for revenge. As the two enemies fought each other, another dragon-kin moved in to attack Kestrel. She stole a look at the Vessel of Souls, still suspended in place. What was taking Corran and the others so long? Surely by now they'd had sufficient time to reach their stations. A second glance revealed slight movement of the nearest support beam. Thank the gods! The urn would drop any moment.

Suddenly, a loud *crash!* rent the air. The sound came not from the floor, where Kestrel had expected it, but from above. The dragon-kin, distracted, spun around, allowing her to plant Loren's Blade in her opponent's back and see for herself the source of the noise.

Shards of glass rained down from the chamber's window as a lone figure swung in on a rope. An angel of darkness, her face a mask of vengeance, swooped in to seize justice for the wronged and wreak retribution on the guilty.

Nathlilik.

The drow leader gripped the rope with only one hand. In the other she clutched a spiked mace, raised high. Blood running from cuts all over her body, her white hair streaming loose behind her, she sailed through the air toward the Vessel of Souls.

"Kedar!" she cried. "I do this for you!"

As the arc of her swing brought her directly above the urn, she let go of the rope. She dropped twenty feet to the vessel and struck the invisible force field with her mace. At the same moment, the support beams finally slid out of place. The Vessel of Souls, and Nathlilik along with it, plummeted.

It smashed through the floor, shattering the glass and continuing its descent. A deafening explosion sounded. Unholy shrieks and sobs filled the chamber, rising to a crescendo so intense that Kestrel covered her ears lest the cacophony of terror and torment drive her mad.

A whirlwind surged up through the jagged hole in the floor. Thousands of lost souls, their ghostly faces contorted with hopelessness, spiraled toward the ceiling. The cyclone snuffed out the chamber's torches, leaving only the pale natural light of the broken window to illuminate the room.

The funnel of damned spirits arched through the window. As it reached the open sky it flew apart, releasing the trapped souls to the gods. The horrible anthem of despair at last ceased.

Within, every drow in the chamber collapsed at once, their bodies turned to dust. At the loss of their allies, the remaining dragon-kin took to the air and fled. Only the companions remained.

In the hushed aftermath, Kestrel picked her way

through drow ashes and shards of broken glass to the edge of the circle. She peered down. Nathlilik's broken, lifeless body lay surrounded by fragments of the vessel she'd given her life to destroy.

Corran's disembodied voice broke the stillness. "Is she alive?"

Kestrel shook her head and backed away from the ledge in silence. She couldn't say she mourned the arrogant drow's passing, but she respected Nathlilik's sacrifice.

"Athan? Durwyn?" Corran called. "You still here?"

"Aye."

"Here."

"Then we haven't a moment to lose. Now that the drow have fallen, Mordrayn knows exactly where we are."

◉ ◉ ◉ ◉ ◉

"What word from Mulmaster?"

"The city is nearly depleted. Panic spreads throughout the Moonsea—soon all the Heartlands will be ours. What tidings here?"

"Intruders have toppled the Vessel of Souls. The Mistress is beyond irate. She says the pool shall be well-fed tonight—either with them or with us."

Kestrel smiled in satisfaction as she listened to the exchange between cultists. Though the news from outside troubled her, she delighted in the knowledge that they'd gotten under Mordrayn's skin.

After leaving the vessel chamber, the party had hurried to the ground floor of the castle and combed it for a route of descent to the pool cavern. Thanks to Pelendralaar's cave-in, none existed save this room—the castle's former great hall, now a magical way station for cultists. Four enchanted gates occupied the hall, one on each wall. Three were of ordinary size, while the last appeared three times the size of any Kestrel had ever seen. A cult sorcerer kept watch at the entrance of each gate, and several squads of fighters were stationed throughout the hall.

Kestrel and the others observed the scene from the corner of a gallery that ran the length of three walls. As they watched, cultists arrived through the smaller gates and entered the large one. A few, like the fighter they'd just overheard, stopped to talk with the cult sorcerers standing guard. From the conversations, she surmised that the small gates all led to points outside Myth Drannor, while the main gate led to the pool cavern.

She gazed at the smaller gates longingly. Beyond lay the outside world. What an easy thing it would be to sneak away from the party and dart through one of those gates, out of Myth Drannor and away from this impossible quest. A few short days ago, she might have done that very thing.

But—independent of the fact that the cult's plan meant no safe place existed to run *to*—she found she could not abandon her companions now. She felt a responsibility to them and to their mission. Her mission. The fate of the world as they knew it rested in their hands. For once in her life, she was part of something greater than herself. She would not back away.

When they were finished, when they had defeated the cult and destroyed the pool, then they could use those smaller gates to leave Myth Drannor. They could go home. She could collect her cache—perhaps even a reward from Elminster—and set herself up for a life of ease. After all this, she'd earned it.

With new conviction, she assessed the situation once more. Somehow, they had to pass through that main gate. "Ghleanna, perhaps now would be a good time for those remaining invisibility spells," she whispered. Corran, Athan, and Durwyn remained unseen. "Cloak yourself and Faeril—I can sneak past the guards."

Ghleanna, her clawed face partially healed by a blue-glow moss potion, shook her head. "I have developed a modified invisibility spell of my own. We can all pass through unseen."

"First we must close the other gates," Corran said, "to stop the influx of cultists."

"If we do that, how will we ever get home?" Kestrel wished she could see Corran's face and not have this conversation with a disembodied voice. "After we stop Mordrayn, and . . . " She caught the expression in Ghleanna and Faeril's eyes.

None of them were going home.

"You've been saying all along that this quest is suicidal," Ghleanna said gently. "I think we must face the possibility that in destroying the pool, we may also—"

"No!" Kestrel shook her head vehemently. "I won't accept that." She *couldn't* accept it—her survival instinct was too strong. "I know what I said before, but I don't intend to die a martyr's death. We are going to confront Mordrayn and the dracolich, we are going to annihilate that damnable pool, and then we are walking out of here alive. Do you hear me? Alive. All of us."

Her new-found optimism surprised Ghleanna and Faeril. In truth, it surprised her, but she had worked hard to get to this point, fought harder than she'd ever fought for anything in her life. No one—not Mordrayn, not Pelendralaar, not every member of the whole despicable cult—was going to rob her of telling this tale in her old age.

A strong, unseen hand touched her shoulder. "Let us leave one gate open, then," Athan said, "to go home."

❧ ❧ ❧ ❧ ❧

Ghleanna's forked lightning bolt stunned the sorcerer standing guard and collapsed one of the small gates in a crackling implosion of electricity. All eyes turned to the bolt's point of origin just in time to see a second bolt race forth to disable the gate opposite and shock that guard as well. The bolts seemed to spring from thin air—Ghleanna's improved version of Jarial's spell enabled her to remain invisible while spellcasting.

Kestrel rejoiced in the gates' easy destruction. At last, events were going their way. All that remained was to quickly dart through the main portal and into the pool cavern, then collapse the portal behind them. The party could worry later about how to return to the great hall to exit through the remaining gate. For now, they preferred to protect their backs from the arrival of reinforcements as they confronted the archmage and dracolich.

By this point, Faeril and Durwyn should have reached the other side of the main gate. The invisible pair was to pass through before Ghleanna's spells drew attention to the party's presence. Corran and Athan flanked the sorceress, in case Ghleanna's untried invisibility spell exposed her during casting after all. Kestrel was stationed at the main gate in the event its guard got any ideas about closing the portal before the whole party passed through. Each of her unseen companions was to sound a low whistle while entering to alert her to their movements.

It was a perfect plan. In theory.

The cultists, however, didn't cooperate. The cult sorcerer guarding the main gate immediately unleashed a spell aimed at Ghleanna—or at least, where one would assume she stood while summoning the lightning bolts. Kestrel prayed that her companion had moved in time to avoid the spell. To her horror, the half-elf materialized a moment later, unharmed but fully visible. The cultist's spell had counteracted hers.

A squad of cult fighters advanced on Ghleanna as the two remaining gate guards prepared to sling more magic at her. Kestrel sneaked up behind the closest sorcerer and slit his throat. Something slipped from his hand—a crumpled roll of paper. She let it drift to the floor, more pressing matters drawing her attention.

Seeing a fatal knife slash suddenly open in his comrade's neck, the final sorcerer diverted his spell at the last second to aim it at Kestrel. She used the cultist's body as a shield, letting the corpse absorb the enchantment. The body disintegrated in her hands.

She looked up from the dust to see Ghleanna hastily retreating toward her. Corran and Athan—exposed to sight by their strikes against the closing cult fighters—followed close behind. Ghleanna flung a final spell at the cult sorcerer before diving into the gate.

Her fireball sped toward the guard, but at the last moment veered away into the gate. The portal immediately imploded, disappearing in a puff of smoke.

They'd lost their way home.

Cursing, Kestrel dropped to the floor in time to avoid the sorcerer's next attack. How was it that he could see her? His spells were aimed with deadly accuracy. As a crackling finger of magical energy sped across the room, she realized she was not his target at all—he was aiming at the gate.

The enchanted bolt struck the portal. She rolled away as sparks flew and electrical feedback seized the opening. The gate collapsed.

Damn it all! Dread swept through her. Everything was falling apart. Half their party was on the other side of that gate, including both their spellcasters. Kestrel didn't know whose predicament was worse: those now in the pool cavern facing Mordrayn alone or those left behind with all these cultists.

Corran and Athan still battled their way toward her. She glanced wildly around the room in search of a likely exit. As she tried to rise to her feet, her left hand slid on something—the piece of paper the sorcerer had dropped.

Damn that cultist to the Abyss, anyway! Damn them all. She picked up the paper, crumpled it in her hand, and nearly hurled it in frustration before two words caught her eye: *Summon Gate*. It was a scroll, a magical scroll with the incantation to open the gate once more.

And Ghleanna was gone.

Kestrel looked to Corran. Could the paladin work one of those miracles he'd talked about and somehow cast the spell off this scroll? Beyond him, she saw the cult sorcerer prepare to throw more magic. Corran and Athan approached but not quickly enough. Another squad of cult fighters closed in.

She glanced at the paper once more. There was no one to read the incantation in time. No one but her.

Her voice shaking with desperation, she uttered the first few words. When no pillar of magical flame consumed her for presuming to work the arcane arts, she continued. Corran and Athan edged closer—as did their foes. The cult sorcerer raised his hands and pointed a sinister finger at the warriors.

She read faster, her tongue tripping over the unfamiliar syllables. Suddenly, a ball of light burst into being and grew steadily to the size of a door. She'd done it! She'd opened the gate.

"Corran! Athan! Now!"

The warriors heard her cry and retreated toward her. As the cultist unleashed his spell, the three of them dove into the portal.

The gate collapsed.

CHAPTER NINETEEN

She couldn't breathe.

"Kestrel? Is that you?" Corran rose, lifting his heavy bulk from where he'd landed on top of her. She struggled to inhale some air. His weight had knocked the wind right out of her lungs.

"Y . . . es."

Though she could barely gasp out the word, she would not have spoken louder if she could. They'd spilled out of the gate just as it imploded and wound up sprawled in the corner of a dank, earthen room. No cultists occupied this small antechamber, but she could hear hundreds of voices chanting nearby.

"Thank the gods you all made it here," said another familiar voice. Ghleanna picked up Corran's shield and handed it to the paladin. "We had begun to fear we'd have to take on the archmage alone."

"We?" Athan asked. "Faeril and Durwyn are here as well, then?"

"Right here," responded Faeril's disembodied voice. Durwyn also spoke up, though both invisible speakers used muted tones.

Kestrel passed her hand in front of her eyes to test the sorceress's spell. Fortunately, she too remained invisible. With a deep breath, she rolled off her stomach, sat up, and assessed their surroundings. The rough-hewn room appeared to have once served as the entryway to a vast chamber beyond. The pile of rock and rubble on one end suggested that they'd arrived on the other side of the cave-in Pelendralaar had caused earlier. Through the sole doorway drifted a monotone mantra droned by countless voices.

Above it, in macabre counterpoint, rose an all-too-familiar babble of lapping water. The Pool of Radiance.

Kestrel's collarbone vibrated in time with the sinister chant as she crept to the doorway. Corran approached even more cautiously, taking care to stay as hidden as possible. The sight that greeted them stole her breath once more.

The antechamber opened into a vast cavern. The floor of the cavern was well below the antechamber, joined together by a long slope. At the cavern's center lay the Pool of Radiance. Amber light infused its water, which gently lapped its banks in a peaceful motion that belied its lethal nature. Hundreds of cult sorcerers and fighters lined the pool's perimeter, their squads assembled with military precision.

At the far end of the cavern, on a recessed ledge overlooking the pool, stood Kya Mordrayn. The Gauntlets of Moander hung from a belt at her hips. Beside her, a stone pillar rose out of the ledge to about waist level. The

Sapphire of the Weave rested atop it, pulsing with brilliant blue light. The illumination dappled the cavern walls and bathed the archmage's face, lending it a deathly paleness that contrasted sharply with the expression of intense concentration she wore. Her eyes stared unblinking at the gem as she cupped it with her dragonlike claw.

Mordrayn was locked in communion with the Mythal. Tiny blue-white flames danced around the edges of the Sapphire, bathing the gem in supernatural fire. The flames also licked Mordrayn's claw, but the archmage either did not feel their heat or could not respond. She stood entranced by the sapphire's aura, her mind one with the Weave.

There was no sign of the dracolich Pelendralaar. Yet.

Kestrel listened closely to the sounds emanating from the cavern. The sapphire—at least, she thought it was the gem from this distance—emitted a low hum. The cultists droned in time with the stone's pulsations. Though Kestrel couldn't distinguish the arcane words, they resonated with blasphemy.

She backed away from the opening, her heart racing. This was it—their only opportunity to destroy the Pool of Radiance. There would be no second chances.

"We are so outnumbered I don't even want to think about it," she said as she and Corran returned to the others. "The cavern is filled with cultists. And all of them stand between us and Mordrayn."

Corran removed his helm. He ran a hand through his dark locks, grasping the roots at the back of his head and closing his eyes. He looked as weary as Kestrel felt.

"We need not defeat them all," said Ghleanna. "We just have to get someone on the ledge to touch the sapphire and speak the Word of Redemption."

"Destroying the gem is only our first objective." Corran opened his eyes and let his hand drop to his side.

"Afterward, we still need to defeat Mordrayn to get the Gauntlets of Moander and destroy the pool."

"Not to mention deal with the dracolich if he makes an appearance," Kestrel added. Her collarbone tingled so much she could barely stand still.

"He will," Athan asserted. "If Mordrayn summons him or we harm her, he will come."

Corran knelt and traced a representation of the pool cavern in the dust, marking the positions of the pool, Mordrayn, the sapphire, and the cultists. "Ghleanna is right about the gem being our first priority. We must create a distraction to enable one of us to get up on that ledge. There's a section of dry floor between the pool and the ledge wall." He glanced up from his tracings. "Kestrel, do you—"

He stopped short, staring at her. She squirmed under his scrutiny. "What? What is it?"

"Your invisibility is wearing off."

Kestrel looked down at her body. It appeared translucent, like those of Anorrweyn or Caalenfaire, but solidified more each second. A glance at the others showed Faeril reappearing as well. Only Durwyn—cloaked by the original invisibility spell, not Ghleanna's modified version—remained unseen. Kestrel swore under her breath.

"No matter," Corran said calmly. "Better now than unexpectedly during battle. We'll work around it."

Somehow, in the face of everything, Kestrel found Corran's matter-of-fact tone reassuring. For all their differences and the grief he'd given her, the paladin had proven himself a valuable comrade-in-arms. She wondered if the party ever would have made it this far without Corran's steadiness and faith in their cause. Certainly not if it had been left up to her.

Corran drew an X in the dust. "We are here. I suggest five of us create a distraction in this part of the cavern—"

he traced a circle—"while one person skirts the perimeter and scales the wall to reach the gem."

At the party's nods of agreement, Corran continued. "This room provides both cover and a good view of the cavern. Faeril and Ghleanna, cast as many spells as you can from here until the range of your remaining magic forces you to move to more exposed ground. Athan, Durwyn, and Kestrel, once the cult realizes where the magic is coming from, the spellcasters will need your defensive help. With luck and Tyr's favor, I will have reached the sapphire by then."

Kestrel frowned. Corran darting through cultists and scrambling up a wall? She was far better suited for the assignment than the brawny paladin. Once again he was underusing her skills. "Corran, that ledge is at least forty feet high. I'm smaller and lighter, not to mention more experienced at this sort of thing. I can scale it in half the time it would take you."

"That's true." His gray eyes met hers. "But Mordrayn will be waiting for whoever reaches the top."

Well, of course she would. That went without—

Kestrel's thoughts stopped abruptly as she realized the paladin's motive. He was taking the most dangerous assignment upon himself. Looking back, she realized that many of their arguments had arisen because he had tried to sacrifice his own safety first.

"I know she will," Kestrel said. A week ago she never would have volunteered for the job, never would have put herself at greater risk than she had to—certainly never would have offered to face an evil archmage alone. Still they could not fail, and she knew in her heart that of them all, she had the best chance of reaching the sapphire. "This is my battle, too. Let me fight it to the best of my ability." As she spoke, her collarbone vibrated so hard it ached. Had she just written her own death sentence?

Corran searched her face for a long moment. Respect lit in his eyes. "All right, then."

At his words, the tingling in her collarbone subsided, and with it her fear. Courage washed over her, chasing away the shadows of self-doubt and cynicism, filling her with the belief that victory was indeed possible. Despite the incredible odds, they might just pull off their mission.

She regarded the paladin with a mixture of surprise and new understanding. This must be the aura of which Ghleanna spoke—the reason the others had followed Corran almost without question from the beginning. The sorceress had been right. Until now, Kestrel had never allowed herself to feel it.

Their circle broke up as each person made individual preparations. Ghleanna readied her spells, Faeril and Corran offered devotions to their gods, Durwyn arranged his arrows near the doorway for easy access. Athan paced impatiently, eager to wet his sword with cult blood.

Kestrel withdrew a small pouch and sprinkled white powder onto her hands. The chalk would help her maintain her grip as she scaled the wall. Her rope and grappling hook hung from her belt, but she hoped to find enough natural holds in the rock to free climb. Mordrayn might be entranced now, but once the sorcerers set off their fireworks, Kestrel didn't want to risk the archmage kicking her grappling hook loose while she dangled from a rope.

She went to the doorway once more and studied the cavern, plotting her course. Fewer cultists gathered on the west side of the pool, but approaching the ledge from that direction required her to leap over a stray arm of the vile amber liquid. The east side held no water trap but twice as many human obstacles. She would dart west.

Behind her, Corran drew near. "Don't let even a drop of the pool touch your skin," he cautioned.

She gazed at the insidious lake, recalling the horrible fate of the bandits she'd observed in Phlan. "I've seen what it can do."

He leaned on his sword and cleared his throat. "I was thinking . . . perhaps I should follow you to the ledge. In case the cultists spot you. And so that when you face Mordrayn—"

"No." She turned toward him, struck by the look of genuine concern she discovered in his eyes. "You will slow me down, Corran. Or attract attention." Besides, she preferred to work solo—at least, she always had before. As tempting as she found his offer to cover her back, she shook her head. "If I'm to succeed, I must do this alone."

Reluctantly, he nodded his agreement. "After you destroy the sapphire, the rest of us will close in as quickly as we can."

Quickly enough to save her from a cruel death at the archmage's hands? Standing here with the paladin, she actually believed it was possible. "I'll see you there."

"Take care, Kestrel."

She shrugged. "Always do." But as she walked away, she cast one last glance at her former adversary. "Corran," she called. The paladin turned. "You, too."

❂ ❂ ❂ ❂ ❂

Kestrel slipped out of the antechamber and slunk into the nearest shadows. Though Ghleanna had cast a hastening enchantment on her, she crept down the slope slowly, relying on stealth instead of speed. Once she reached the outer wall of the cavern she stuck close to it, darting from shadow to shadow as she made her way toward the ledge. And Mordrayn.

The cultists' chanting muffled her movements. She realized, after she reached the cavern floor and could observe them more closely in the dim light, that only some of the cultists were participating in the Mythal ritual. The sorcerers all had their eyes on the Sapphire of the Weave as they repeated their profane mantra. The cult fighters, however, who comprised at least half the assembly, stood quietly on alert. She would have to proceed very cautiously as she wended her way past their ranks.

She paused and pressed herself against the wall. She'd traveled about a third of the distance to Mordrayn's ledge and had another third to cover before reaching the arm of the pool that obstructed her way. All the cultists had gathered on this side of the tendril, so once she passed that obstacle she'd have a clear path to the ledge. First, however, she had an army of dragon-worshipers to avoid.

She glanced up at the antechamber. Good—her companions betrayed no hint of their presence. She knew Durwyn, still invisible, watched her progress from the doorway. Faeril and Ghleanna were to initiate a distraction when she reached the pool arm, unless she had need of it sooner. With so many eyes focused on the sapphire, even she couldn't climb all the way up the ledge unnoticed.

The pool hissed louder down here, a sinister murmur that sounded almost sentient. By the gods, she couldn't wait to stop those foul whisperings from entering her ears. Still hugging the wall, she continued her surreptitious journey.

Ahead, three cult fighters leaned against the cavern wall, engaged in low conversation. She couldn't make out their words, and she didn't much care—she was more concerned about getting around them. She studied the shadows dancing across the cavern floor. There was no good route, but she found one that might work. If she was very lucky.

With a deep breath, she stepped away from the wall and into the pulsing blue light of the sapphire. She walked quickly and silently, hoping the combination of her speed and the strobe effect of the gem's light would play tricks on the cultists' eyes and obscure her exact position.

It didn't.

The trio raised an alarm. Kestrel didn't wait to see what happened next—she ran for all she was worth. Magically sped by Ghleanna's prior incantation, she practically flew past the cultists as the sorceress's lightning bolt streaked across the east side of the cavern to strike a cluster of unwary cult mages.

She'd expected the chant to stop abruptly after her party's initial strike, but many cult sorcerers were so absorbed in the Mythal ritual that a second attack hit before all the dragon-worshipers mobilized. Fortunately for Kestrel, most of the cultists focused their attention on finding the source of the magical attacks. Units of fighters hurried around the edge of the pool, trying to reach the west side to uncover the renegade sorcerer in their midst. Those cultists on the target side, meanwhile, scurried out of the line of fire.

The resulting pandemonium enabled Kestrel to get nearly to the pool tendril before anyone else noticed her.

"You!" a cult sorcerer cried, his voice all but lost in the din. He pointed his sinister claw at her and unleashed a cone of swirling white vapor.

Kestrel tensed as the funnel enveloped her, but she felt no harmful effects. With a grateful thought for the baelnorn, she rubbed her thumb over the band of one of her mantle rings and hurried on.

As fire and ice, poisoned gas, and conjured missiles soared and billowed through the air, Kestrel lost track of which spells were cast by her friends and which were retributive strikes. She just did her best to ignore the chaos erupting around her and focused on reaching the ledge. Mordrayn remained locked in communion with the

Mythal, oblivious to the mayhem that had overtaken the cavern. The blue aura, undisturbed by mortal turmoil, continued to surround the archmage and the sapphire.

She reached the pool arm—a slough, really, an extension of the main pool filled with watery muck. From the foul smell that greeted her, she wondered if the gray sludge comprised the remains of victims tossed into the wicked pond. The slough was about six feet across. With her running start, she should have no trouble leaping its breadth. She boosted her speed in preparation for the jump.

And landed on her face.

"Going somewhere?" The cult fighter who'd tripped her emerged from the shadows as she rolled to her feet and scrambled for a weapon. The enormous man towered over her, swiping his claw through the air like a second weapon. She snapped her club to its full length and swung it up just in time to block his first sword thrust.

He brought the blade around to strike again. Still under the hastening effects of Ghleanna's spell, Kestrel managed to block the second blow with her right hand while freeing Loren's Blade from its scabbard with her left. She hurled the dagger at her opponent. It caught him in the shoulder, then returned to her hand.

Enraged, the fighter attempted another blow, this time aiming for her throwing arm. The strike hit. Her armor saved her from injury, but Loren's Blade slipped from her grasp. It clattered to the ground, landing at the cultist's feet. The fighter kicked the offending weapon out of his way. It scudded across the floor toward the pool slough.

Kestrel leaped, trying to catch it in time. She missed by inches. The dagger slid into the mire and sank from view. Damn it all! The magical blade had become her favorite weapon.

She barely had time to gain her feet before the cultist

struck again. Ghleanna's spell was wearing off. Though she managed to parry the fighter's blows, he slowly maneuvered their duel until he stood between her and the slough. Now even if an opportunity to break away from combat presented itself, she could not simply run for the ledge—she would have to fight her way past him. Worse, with the slough at his back instead of hers, she was left exposed to other opponents.

He brought his blade down once more. She gripped her club with both hands, one on each end, to block the strike. The iron baton vibrated with the force of his blow. He swung again and again. Pain shot through her arms as she fought a losing battle against his superior strength.

He raised the weapon for another hit. She brought the club up to parry, but he suddenly kicked her instead. The stomach blow knocked her to the ground. Her club fell from her grasp.

She scrambled backward, hand flailing as she desperately tried to find her weapon. The cultist kicked her again as if for good measure. She heard her ribs snap, felt pain shoot up her side. Then her foe leaned back, raising his sword for the killing blow.

Turnabout was fair play. With all the force she could muster, she sprang off her hands to plant both feet in his groin. The surprise move, coupled with his shifted center of balance, proved enough to knock him over. He fell backward.

And screamed.

The watery mire of the pool caught him in its deadly embrace. In seconds, it sucked his withering form under the surface, leaving only iridescent bubbles in his wake.

Kestrel's abdomen and side throbbed, but she had no time to dwell on it. Spotting her club a couple feet away, she snatched it up, ran back to the slough, and leaped. She landed hard on all fours, her broken ribs screaming at her.

Not a graceful landing, but she'd made it across. Now only a wall stood between her and the Sapphire of the Weave.

Magical effects continued to explode and zoom through the air. A haze of smoke and other matter developed, blessedly obscuring vision. She could follow the sapphire's glow like a beacon while the haze cloaked her from others' sight.

She ran to the wall, her injured ribs protesting each step. She wanted to throw up. Maybe that's how she'd defeat Mordrayn, she thought darkly. She doubted the archmage would anticipate an attack like that.

Between the haze and shadows, she couldn't see the wall's surface well enough to judge whether it offered sufficient natural holds for free climbing. She tore her rope off her belt and tossed the grappling hook up to the ledge. The last time she'd glimpsed Mordrayn, the archmage had been as entranced as ever. She had more to fear from cult missiles and magic than from the evil sorceress herself. Or so she hoped.

She tugged on the rope to ensure the grappling hook's grip, then began her ascent. How were her friends faring? She couldn't dwell on their fate right now. She had to concentrate on reaching the sapphire.

Hand over hand. Hand over hand. Her arms ached with exertion and her ribs with each breath, but the familiar movements helped focus her ricocheting thoughts. The Word of Redemption. *Ethgonil.* She had to get close enough to speak it. She was almost there.

She reached the top and rolled onto the ledge. A glance at Mordrayn revealed that the archmage was still locked in communion with the Mythal, unmindful of all else. Blue-white flames shot up from the Sapphire of the Weave and danced around her, licking but not burning her skin. What was it the baelnorn had said—mere mortals cannot withstand the Mythal's fire? What did that make the archmage?

What would happen to her, Kestrel, when she touched the fiery gem?

It did not matter. Without further hesitation, she reached forward and placed her hand on the stone.

"*Ethgonil!*" Though her mouth formed the word, the voice that boomed through the cavern was not her own. It was an ancient voice, one that had existed before time began and one that would survive when time ceased to be. Everyone in the cavern—friend and foe alike—stopped their actions, their attention riveted to the ledge.

A floating ball of brilliant white light appeared. As Kestrel shielded her eyes from the glare, the ball expanded and opened to reveal a portal. A moment later, the baelnorn appeared. No longer the tragic figure they'd left behind in the catacombs, Miroden Silverblade stood tall and proud. He held his head high, his face a mask of righteousness.

His gaze met Kestrel's. "For you!" He thrust his hand toward her, then swept his arm toward the back of the cavern. Immediately, her pain vanished. At the same time her vision blurred—or something intangible obscured it. She viewed Silverblade as if watching him underwater.

The baelnorn's sweeping hand formed a fist. "For Myth Drannor!" He raised his arm high above the sapphire, then smashed his fist into the gem.

The Protector exploded in a burst of fire. In less than a second, both he and the sapphire were utterly consumed by the flames.

Kestrel instinctively leaped away from the pyre and curled into a defensive ball, but the flames burgeoned to overtake the whole ledge. She cringed as the deadly blaze raced toward her, preparing for a swift death. Miraculously, the flames did not touch her. She found herself protected by an invisible sphere that held the fire and heat at bay.

The inferno spouted outward like a tidal wave to fill the cavern. Cultists screamed and tried to outrun the blazing swell of holy fire, but the conflagration would not be cheated of its due. The flames rolled forth, consuming everyone in their path. Shrieks and moans echoed off the stone walls until they, too, drowned in the roar of the holocaust.

Then there was silence.

Kestrel looked out upon the destruction wrought by the baelnorn's self-sacrifice. The cult legions had been incinerated where they stood, leaving only mounds of ashes in their place. Hesitantly, dreading what she expected to see, she raised her gaze above the dust to the back of the cavern.

Movement. Her shoulders sagged in relief. Her friends had survived, shielded as she had been by the Protector's spell.

Below, the Pool of Radiance lay placid as ever. Steam rising from its amber surface offered the only hint that it had been disturbed in the slightest by the baelnorn's act of retribution.

Beside her—

"You little bitch."

The horrifyingly familiar voice broke the stillness with an edge that could cut glass. Kestrel's blood froze in her veins as she turned to look at a face whose fury burned hotter than the inferno just past.

There remained one cultist the baelnorn hadn't destroyed.

CHAPTER TWENTY

Kya Mordrayn's eyes blazed with hatred. Protected by the Mythal's aura, she had survived the baelnorn's cleansing fire unscathed. The archmage lifted her long reptilian arm and pointed a talon at Kestrel's heart. "Think you that I will allow one scrawny chit to undo a plan decades in the formation?"

A thin green ray shot out from Mordrayn's talon and raced straight at Kestrel. The thief instinctively ducked behind the stone pillar. The ray struck the pillar and instantly reduced it to dust.

Kestrel swallowed hard. Though Mordrayn wore only a flowing black cape and a red leather bodysuit split to the navel, it was the rogue who felt unprotected. Gods, but she hated wizards!

Before she had time to react, Mordrayn unleashed a second ray—this one red—from her mutated fingertip. Kestrel rolled out of its path, but the ray altered its course to stay on target.

When it struck, she felt a mild vibration, nothing more. Thank Mystra for those mantle rings.

The archmage sneered. "Your paltry protections cannot spare you forever." She spat the words out of her mouth.

Kestrel stared at Mordrayn, still dumbstruck in the presence of the sorceress. She realized that Mordrayn was actually speaking—not using her mind's voice, as they'd witnessed previously. Was this a sign that her connection with the Mythal was indeed broken?

Have faith. Anorrweyn's gentle voice entered Kestrel's thoughts. *Even now, I am one with the Mythal and work to turn its power against our enemies.*

That's all very well, Kestrel wanted to answer, but what do I do in the meantime? As if in response, she heard her companions hurrying toward the ledge from the back of the underground chamber.

Mordrayn lifted her claw once more, this time pointing it into the cavern. "We'll see if your friends are so well protected." She aimed her hand at Athan, who led the advance. "Back for more of my attentions, Athan? Some men just can't get enough." A bolt of lightning raced from her talons to strike him. The vigorous fighter staggered under its force but did not fall.

The bolt did not stop there. It arced to Corran, then Durwyn, catching all three men in a chain of electricity. When it reached Ghleanna, however, her spellstaff absorbed the charge. Ghleanna tapped the staff twice on the ground to send the bolt streaking back to Mordrayn herself. The electrical charge left a hideous burn on the cult leader's scantily clad chest.

The archmage screeched in outrage. "I'll pry that staff out of your dead hand!" She threw her head back and shouted in a voice that echoed off the stone walls. "Pelendralaar!"

Kestrel finally shook off her fear. Three of her companions were injured because she'd stood here like a half-wit and let Mordrayn get the upper hand. With passing regret for her lost magical dagger, she drew her twin blades from her boots. Their familiar hilts felt comfortable in her palms. She hurled the blades at the archmage.

They bounced off an invisible shield and fell harmlessly to the ground. She uttered a stream of curses—would nothing go right for her? Two more weapons gone and all she'd managed to do was capture Mordrayn's unwanted attention once more.

The archmage turned her baleful gaze on Kestrel. "What an annoying little gnat you are." She raised her dragon claw again. Kestrel prayed her mantle rings could withstand the continual assault.

Ghleanna's spell, however, was faster. The half-elf passed her arm in an arc, then pointed at Mordrayn. A blast of swirling ice crystals sprung from her hand. The frigid air formed a cone that enveloped the cult leader. Mordrayn let fly a string of foul epithets as she shook with cold.

"Not dressed for the weather, Kya?" Athan goaded. The knight's hair yet stood on end from the shock of Mordrayn's lightning bolt. He neared Kestrel's rope—somehow spared by the Protector's holy fire—and a moment later was lost to Kestrel's view. The rope grew taut. He was ascending. Corran followed close behind.

"Perhaps this will warm her." Faeril opened her palm to loose a searing ray of light. The beam sped straight toward the archmage. A mere foot away from her, however, it sputtered out.

Mordrayn laughed, a spine-tingling cackle devoid of cheer. "A child's spell!" She swept her dragon arm broadly. "Let me show you how grown-ups play."

A cloud of greenish-yellow gas formed in front of her, rapidly growing until it reached some thirty feet in width and brushed the recess ceiling. The fog's noxious odor left Kestrel nauseated by its proximity—she dreaded its effect on anyone who breathed it directly. Mordrayn curled her red lips into a perfect O and, with a small puff of air, sent the cloud drifting off the ledge toward Kestrel's companions.

Before the gas reached him, Durwyn released an arrow. It was a blind shot, as he couldn't possibly see the archmage clearly with the cloud between them, but it whistled through the air directly at Mordrayn. Like Kestrel's daggers, it struck an unseen barrier before it reached the archmage.

Kestrel again cursed the cult fighter who'd destroyed Loren's Blade. Mundane weapons could not so much as scratch Mordrayn with that barrier in place. She scanned the ledge for something—a sliver of the shattered sapphire, perhaps—some makeshift weapon with a little magic in it that she could use to attack the sorceress.

The memory of another blue shard stirred her thoughts. Borea's Blood. She'd all but forgotten the ice knife from the frozen Rohnglyn in the dwarven dungeons. She withdrew Borea from her beltpouch.

Coughing spasms seized her friends as the foul cloud reached them. Athan's bark came from nearby—he must be close to the top of the rope. Unfortunately, Kestrel wasn't the only one to notice his proximity. Another green ray shot from Mordrayn's talon, disintegrating the rope. Moments later, the clatter of armor sounded below.

Mordrayn chortled. Her glee vanished, however, when Ghleanna's voice rang clearly through the virulent mist. Ozama's boots had spared her from the poisonous fumes.

The archmage cocked her head, listening to the words of the half-elf's spell. "What's this?" she mumbled, frowning in concentration.

Kestrel clutched Borea's Blood, afraid it would slide right out of her sweating palm. If she could penetrate whatever invisible barrier blocked their missiles, the archmage's revealing attire left numerous critical areas vulnerable to attack. Its only useful feature was the stiff leather collar around Mordrayn's neck. Her chest, her stomach, her upper back—all lay exposed. And those heels! Kestrel hoped the woman would trip over them.

Mordrayn apparently recognized Ghleanna's incantation and commenced a counterspell. Kestrel took a deep breath. It was now or never.

She made a running leap at the archmage, knocking her to the ground as she plunged Borea's Blood into her stomach. Mordrayn's eyes widened in shock. Black blood welled out of the wound until the ice knife glowed white, freezing the blood and surrounding tissue. Kestrel yanked the weapon out and prepared to strike again.

Mordrayn, though, recovered more quickly than Kestrel expected. With an inhuman shriek, the archmage raked her enormous dragon claw down Kestrel's face.

Searing pain ripped through the rogue's cheek and neck. Kestrel rolled away, somehow maintaining her grip on Borea's Blood. Within moments, the fire gave way to an icy numbness. She couldn't feel her face. She couldn't lift her hand.

She couldn't move at all.

Mordrayn rose. Kestrel lay helpless as the towering archmage wordlessly drove her stiletto heel through the thief's right palm. As she heard bones crack and saw the heel pierce her hand from front to back, she found herself grateful for the paralysis. At least she couldn't feel Mordrayn's torture.

A sound arrested the cult leader's attention. From what Kestrel could see, the cloud had evaporated. If her ears judged aright, both Athan and Corran now scaled the wall, still trying to gain the ledge.

Another arrow whistled through the air. Mordrayn ignored it—to her detriment. When the shaft embedded itself in the archmage's thigh, Kestrel recognized it as one of the bronze-tipped bolts Durwyn had received from the baelnorn.

Fresh anger distorted Mordrayn's features. She snapped the shaft in half and flung the fletched end aside. The remaining half protruded from her leg, blood oozing around it to streak down the length of the limb. She tried to step forward, but the wounded leg buckled. She flailed to catch herself from falling. "Damn you all!" she screamed. With a wave of her hand, a volley of conjured arrows sailed back at Durwyn.

The archmage might still have her magic, but she was losing her composure. Unfortunately, Kestrel hadn't any means of using that observation to her advantage. She could only hope the others also saw that Mordrayn was unhinged.

Athan at last reached the top of the ledge. He immediately rushed Mordrayn, but pulled back about ten feet away. He tried again to close in, but was once more repelled by an unseen force. The archmage cackled in wicked delight. "You're just longing to touch me, aren't you, darling?"

The sickened look that crossed Athan's face made Kestrel wonder about the extent of the torture he'd suffered at Mordrayn's hands, but the warrior recovered quickly. "Only with dwarven steel."

A cry from Faeril ended the exchange. "Lady of Mysteries! Visit your divine fire upon this creature who corrupted your golden Weave!" At the cleric's summons, a column of fire descended from directly above Mordrayn, enveloping her in flames.

As the sacred blaze seared the onetime communicant, Corran cleared the ledge. He crossed to Kestrel quickly and applied his hands to her torn flesh. His voice wrapped her in a prayer of healing. When he finished, he met her gaze. "I have healed your wounds, but I cannot remove paralysis by laying on hands."

She stared at him hard, willing him to somehow understand her thoughts. *Try, Corran. Try for one of your miracles.*

He sighed. As if he'd heard her, he closed his eyes and made a second supplication to Tyr. A moment later, Kestrel waggled the fingers of her right hand. She could move once more. The paladin shook his head in amazement. "By Tyr's grace . . . "

They hadn't time to celebrate. The pillar of holy flames sputtered out, revealing a Mordrayn badly burned but still standing. Running blisters covered her withered skin. Her singed hair, what was left of it, had come unbound and floated wildly about her head. She fixed Faeril with a feral gaze. "You will follow *my* bidding now, worship at *my* altar!" The archmage barked out an arcane command.

At first, it appeared that Mordrayn's spell had no effect on the cleric. She merely stared, unblinking, at the archmage. A moment later, Faeril pointed a finger at Athan. "Hold!"

The warrior froze in place, both arms raised in a futile attempt to break his sword through the barrier Mordrayn had established. Kestrel gripped Borea's Blood. She'd penetrated that barrier once—she could do so again.

Durwyn launched another arrow at Mordrayn. The cleric turned on him. "Hold!" He, too, froze where he stood. One hand held his short bow, the other hung suspended in the process of reaching back for another bolt.

The bronze-tipped arrow struck Mordrayn in the shoulder. The archmage, her eyes blazing with the fever of the insane, did not even notice. She wheeled on Corran. "You next!" She raised her dragon claw to shoot a thin red beam of light at him.

The paladin raised his shield, positioning it to shelter both himself and Kestrel. The ray struck the shield squarely and bounced back straight at Mordrayn. "No!" she screeched. The beam hit her in the chest, knocking her to the ground.

For a fleeting moment, Kestrel thought the witch had been defeated by her own magic, but Mordrayn climbed to her knees and aimed her talons at Corran once more. Laboring for breath, she uttered the ancient words of another incantation.

From below, Kestrel heard Ghleanna's voice also raised in spellcasting. When the half-elf fell silent, Mordrayn's speech changed. Her words became inarticulate babbling, sounds more primitive than the language of the basest humanoids. She spun about, looking from one party member to another with dilated pupils, snarling like a trapped animal. Her claw lashed out wildly at each person she faced.

Whatever Ghleanna had done, it broke Mordrayn's hold on Faeril. The cleric shook her head as if to clear it, then called out a command to free Athan and Durwyn from her spells.

Athan, however, still couldn't draw near Mordrayn. Corran leaped up to engage her. He scored two hits on her dragon arm but could not sever it.

Kestrel saw her opening. With Corran keeping the paralytic talons at bay, the thief darted forward. She raised Borea's Blood high in the air, then plunged it with all her strength into Mordrayn's black heart.

The sorceress's eyes widened in sudden sanity. She sank onto the stone floor as choked, gurgling sounds issued from her throat. "No . . ." she finally managed to gasp out. In the distance, a rumbling commenced. Cracks split the rocky cavern base, from which dancing orange firelight spilled.

Suddenly, ebon tentacles and a host of dragon claws rose out of the floor. They wrapped themselves around Mordrayn's limbs and torso, pulling her into the rock itself.

"No! Not yet!" She struggled against their grasp, demons and her own horror seizing her with equal strength as payment came due for an ancient bargain. "No! Pelendralaaaarrr!"

Her cry, like the rest of her, was swallowed up by the earth.

Only the Gauntlets of Moander—divine artifacts unfit to accompany Mordrayn to her new abode—remained. Corran stepped forward and lifted the gloves from the floor. He offered them to Athan. "I believe Elminster entrusted these to your care."

Athan donned the metal gloves. The mouth images on their palms opened wide as the gauntlets stretched to conform to the warrior's large hands. "At last," he said. "Now it but remains to use them."

Strangely, the thundering continued. It grew louder, until vibrations shook the whole cavern. Ghleanna peered at the cavern roof. "Not another cave-in?"

Before anyone could respond, the noise rose to a deafening crescendo. Kestrel fell to the ground, knocked off balance by the strength of the tremors. Rocks and rubble broke away from the east wall of the cavern and splashed into the Pool of Radiance. Then the whole wall gave way. An overpowering roar echoed through the chamber.

Pelendralaar had arrived.

CHAPTER TWENTY-ONE

The mighty dracolich filled the pool cavern. His body easily extended a hundred feet, his spiked tail another eighty. He stretched his tattered, leathery wings halfway to the ceiling, draping Faeril, Ghleanna, and Durwyn in his long shadow. He towered over them, not quite close enough to snap them up in his jaws. The trio froze in terror, rendered helpless by the very sight of the living dragon corpse.

Behind the beast, cool air and starlight filtered into the cavern through dust that had not yet settled. In his rush to answer Mordrayn's summons, Pelendralaar had burst right through the cliff face. When he saw Athan wearing the Gauntlets of Moander, he realized he'd arrived too late.

Red flames burned in his empty eye sockets. The dra-colich opened wide his jaws in a bellow of rage. "Arrogant hatchlings! You know not what you have done!" Puffs of smoke escaped through rows of razor-sharp teeth. "But you shall pay for it."

The frightful fire-breathing creature inhaled deeply. Were Corran not so near, Kestrel knew fear surely would seize her as completely as it had her friends below. Forti-fied by the paladin's aura, she was able to dive to one side before flames burgeoned from the dracolich's mouth.

Pelendralaar blasted his burning cloud straight at Athan. Heat licked Kestrel's limbs, searing her skin as she tumbled away from the vicinity. Her body sweated beneath the leather armor, but it was protected from further harm.

She rolled until she reached the recess wall. Two hard objects jabbed her from beneath. Her daggers. They must have landed here when she threw them at Mordrayn. Gratefully, she grabbed the weapons and assumed a defen-sive posture as she cast a wary look back at the dracolich.

Pelendralaar advanced toward the ledge, ignoring the fear-stricken adventurers on the cavern floor. Somehow, Faeril managed to shake off enough of her dragonawe to cast a prayer-spell beseeching Mystra to imbue them with courage. Apparently, the Lady of Mystery granted the cleric's petition, for Ghleanna and Durwyn recovered their composure. Durwyn reached for another arrow.

Faeril's prayer and its results went unnoticed by Pelen-dralaar, whose sinister gaze focused on Athan alone. The fair warrior had been badly burned and lay unmoving on the floor. Kestrel saw that his chest yet rose and fell—life remained within him.

Corran, also burned, crawled toward the fallen hero. Even as the dracolich neared to finish off Athan, the pal-adin laid his hands on Ghleanna's brother and spoke words of healing. Athan stirred.

Pelendralaar growled.

From below, a ghostly, oversized warhammer sailed through the air to strike the dracolich's head. With a hiss, Pelendralaar turned his menacing gaze on Faeril. He lifted his claw to swipe at her and was struck in the underbelly by a bronze-tipped arrow.

Kestrel took advantage of the distraction to scurry over to Athan and Corran. Athan had recovered much of his strength, but the paladin looked ready to collapse. "I've healed him as much as I'm able," Corran croaked out through blistered lips and a throat parched by heat. "Tyr answered my prayers beyond my imagining."

"You should have saved some of those healing powers for yourself." Kestrel pulled her last two blueglow moss potions from her beltpouch. "Drink these." Corran accepted one vial but pushed the other away. "Both of them," she admonished. "No arguments." Athan voiced his agreement.

Pelendralaar swiped his claws at Durwyn. At a word from Ghleanna, the burly fighter suddenly moved with lightning speed, easily dodging the knifelike talons. The dracolich jerked his head at the sound of the mage's voice. "Your sorcery is nothing to what my queen's was." He fixed his gaze upon her and uttered a string of arcane syllables.

Bursts of magical fire raced toward the half-elf, but a shimmering barrier surrounded Ghleanna, repelling the missiles. Durwyn, meanwhile, landed an axe blow on one of the creature's claws.

Athan rose to his feet, anxious to reenter the battle. Corran too, now partially restored by the potions, looked for an opportunity to strike the dracolich. "Our swords can't reach him from up here," the paladin said. "And we're vulnerable to another breath attack. We have to get off this ledge."

Kestrel soberly assessed the steep drop. They'd kill themselves jumping, but she didn't relish the idea of a slow climb down with her back to Pelendralaar. "We have no choice but to scale the wall," she said finally. "Durwyn's got the beast distracted—this may be our only chance." She headed for the ledge and prepared to descend. Corran was right behind her, but Athan remained where he was.

"Go ahead," Athan said, his eyes on Pelendralaar. "I've got another way down."

Kestrel exchanged quizzical glances with Corran but had no time to ponder Athan's plan. She slipped over the edge and scurried down the wall as fast as she could.

The dracolich batted at Durwyn like a kitten trying to catch dust motes. Faeril struck him with the spiritual hammer once more. With a roar, Pelendralaar twisted his long neck to capture the cleric in his sight. His mouth opened wide and rushed toward Faeril. Mystra's servant stood her ground.

Just as his jaws were about to snap around her, Faeril shouted a command. Brilliant sunlight streamed from her staff. The dracolich howled as the pure rays eclipsed the unholy fire in his own eyes. The cleric thrust the weapon into his jaws, wedging them open. Thus disabled, the dracolich could neither bite nor speak—nor cast spells.

Pelendralaar's whole body thrashed as he tried to shake loose the staff. He tossed his head wildly. Tendrils of foul-smelling smoke curled up from patches on his body where his undead flesh smoldered in the sunlight.

An evocation from Ghleanna draped an enormous, sticky web over Pelendralaar's forelegs. Each time he raised his claws they became more enmeshed in the webbing. Unable to bring his forelegs up to his jaws, he tried lowering his head to meet the limited range of his claws and mired his snout in cobwebs. He flapped and twisted at the edge of the Pool of Radiance.

Kestrel, now safely on the ground with Corran, dashed out of harm's way as Pelendralaar's flailing brought him near the ledge where Athan yet stood. The dracolich beat his wings, scraping the ledge with the leathery appendages. Before Kestrel realized his intent, Athan leaped forward and grabbed hold of one of the wings.

Pelendralaar buffeted with new violence, now trying to throw off Athan. Somehow, the fighter held on. He gripped the wing with one hand while hacking at it with his sword in the other. Kestrel marveled at the feat of strength. Perhaps the gauntlets lent him magical aid—they and the spell Ghleanna had just uttered.

Durwyn backed away from the web ensnaring Pelendralaar's claws and switched to his bow. He sank several bolts into the creature's writhing neck, while Faeril struck him in the head with her spiritual hammer. Kestrel added one of her daggers to the assault, hurling a perfect strike in the dracolich's underbelly. Corran attacked the beast's tail, dodging its whiplike snaps.

In desperation, the dracolich breathed his fire once more—this time at his own limbs. The web fell apart, freeing Pelendralaar's head. Though the flames had billowed against the dracolich's skin, he'd suffered no damage from them.

The Staff of Sunlight, however, had. The inferno that blasted from the creature's lungs burned hot enough to melt metal. The staff bent into a U as Pelendralaar slowly clamped his mouth shut. Its light faded away, then disappeared altogether as he swallowed the precious weapon.

Though the dracolich triumphed over the staff, the flickering flames did not return to his eye sockets. The holy rays had rendered him sightless.

Nonetheless he could still feel the sturdy warrior clinging to his wing. Pelendralaar twisted his long neck, trying to catch Athan in his sharp teeth. The fighter braced his sword arm. When the dracolich darted his head toward

Athan, the warrior used the beast's own momentum to drive his blade into Pelendralaar's snout.

With a roar of pain and rage, the creature jerked back its head.

The fighter, still gripping his sword, was torn from Pelendralaar's wing and now dangled from the beast's snout. He clung to the hilt with both hands as the dracolich thrashed his head from side to side, but could not maintain his hold against such violent force. He went sailing through the air, straight toward the Pool of Radiance.

"Athan!" Ghleanna screamed.

Faeril sent her ghostly hammer racing toward Athan with lightning speed. The weapon struck him just hard enough to alter his course. He landed in a heap at the edge of the pool.

Immediately, light burst from the mouths of the gauntlets. The beams arched forth to strike the pool, infusing its depths with a pure white glow. As the blessed light met the pool's tainted amber radiance, the water churned and roiled.

"The pool is dying, Pelendralaar!" Corran cried. "You shall soon follow!"

Athan, too? Kestrel gazed at the brave fighter. He had not moved since crashing to the ground. With the dracolich standing between him and the rest of the party, Faeril could not reach him with her healing magic.

"I have no intention of falling to a pathetic handful of mortals," the dracolich rumbled. Though still fierce, his speech had lost some of its strength. The blinded creature swiped his claws toward the sound of Corran's voice. His talons whistled past the paladin but struck another target—Durwyn.

The force of Pelendralaar's blow knocked the burly warrior to the ground. Despite the lacerations oozing blood down his entire right side, Durwyn tried to rise. He struggled, then sank back to the floor, his arms going limp. "I can't feel my legs," he gasped. "I can't—"

Move, Kestrel finished silently. Apparently, Pelendralaar shared Mordrayn's paralytic touch. Or vice versa. While Faeril dodged her way to Durwyn's side, Kestrel sent her last dagger soaring toward the beast. The trusty blade scored another strike to his underbelly.

He hissed and lunged toward her with open jaws, but they met only the acid-edged heads of a volley of magical arrows—courtesy of Ghleanna. "That's for my brother," she spat.

In response, the dracolich spewed another gout of flames. The sorceress held forth her spellstaff, drawing the heat and fire into the enchanted wood. The staff glowed red with the intensity of the attack it had absorbed. White smoke wisped from its runes. Ghleanna tapped the staff twice on the floor.

The flames spilled out and raced toward the dracolich. The great beast raised his head and laughed. "You think my own fire can harm me? Foolish hatchlings!" He swept his tail in a wide arc.

Kestrel ducked, letting the tail breeze over her head. Corran and Ghleanna did likewise. She noted that for all the creature's bluster, the swing had less energy than before. They—and Anorrweyn, working from afar?—were wearing Pelendralaar down.

The gauntlets, meanwhile, weakened the pool. The whole lake was infused with white light now, bubbling and rolling like a pot set to boil. Steam rose in the cavern, lending the air a humid thickness. The cavern smelled of sweat, fire, and blood.

Kestrel pushed damp locks off her forehead and reached for her club. She'd no desire to employ such a close-range weapon against the dracolich, but it was the only tool she had left.

Pelendralaar, however, would not give her the opportunity to use it. The dracolich beat his wings rapidly, trying to take flight. Did he seek to escape or attack from above?

As the creature rose in the air, his tail snaked down behind him. Corran dropped his shield and ran to the tail. He grabbed it just as its end was about to slip from reach. The paladin dangled one-handed for a moment, then sheathed his sword and began to climb the tail as if it were a rope.

Pelendralaar swung his tail like a pendulum, trying to dislodge Corran, but each sway threatened his equilibrium as he struggled to hover in the cavern's close quarters. He didn't have room to properly spread his wings, and Athan had significantly damaged one of them before being flung aside. Corran climbed higher, using the tail's spikes as a ladder.

"Hang on, Corran. Hang on," Kestrel whispered. Ghleanna sent another barrage of acid arrows to distract the creature. Durwyn, now restored by Faeril, also launched bolts at the beast. The missiles struck Pelendralaar in the neck and upper body. Faeril dashed to Athan's side now that the path was clear.

Though Kestrel could smell the acid burning through what was left of the dracolich's skin, the beast ignored it. He kicked with his hindlegs, but could not quite reach the paladin. Furious, he shot a series of magical bursts at Corran. Those hit but did not deter Tyr's knight.

Corran scaled farther up the dracolich's body. Kestrel held her breath each time he touched another spike—one scratch and the paladin would become paralyzed and tumble helpless to the ground. As Ghleanna released a third volley of arrows upon the creature's head, Pelendralaar awkwardly maneuvered himself until he was directly over the Pool of Radiance.

As the pool boiled below, Corran reached Pelendralaar's back. When the beast twisted his neck to snap up the paladin in his jaws, Corran was ready. With an upward thrust, he drove his sword through the underside of the creature's jaw and into his skull. "I smite thee in the name of Tyr the Just!"

Pelendralaar threw back his neck, then dived headlong toward the bubbling pool. The paladin rode the creature like a runaway horse. The two plunged into the frothy water and disappeared into its depths.

"Corran!" Kestrel ran to the pool's edge. She and the others peered into the cloudy water but saw no sign of him.

Suddenly, the center of the pool spouted. Kestrel's heart stopped as a fully restored Pelendralaar shot into the air—without Corran.

"I live again!" the dracolich shouted in triumph, buffeting his wings as he hovered near the ceiling. Flames flickered in his eyes once more. He celebrated his restored strength with a mighty roar.

Steam poured from the pool below, filling the cavern with sultry fog. The boiling water hissed and popped. Before their eyes, the waterline dropped—one foot, ten feet, a score and more.

The vapor surged up at Pelendralaar. The creature's bellow quickly dissolved into a choked gasp. His tail crumbled to powder, his legs next. When his wings disintegrated, the rest of him plummeted into the basin.

The dracolich exploded in a cloud of dust on the dry pool floor.

CHAPTER TWENTY-TWO

White mist filled the cavern. It swirled and danced, propelled by the cool breeze that drifted in with the early dawn light from the hole in the chamber wall. Kestrel could barely make out the faces of her friends, though all sat mere feet away.

All but one.

Kestrel felt Corran's absence more strongly than she'd ever imagined possible. She'd said all along that this mission was suicidal, told the paladin repeatedly that they faced insurmountable odds, that they couldn't go up against an arch-mage and a dracolich, and live to tell about it.

She hadn't wanted to be right.

In the end, Corran had proven himself a man of integrity. A man who not only spoke about honor but lived it—and died for it to preserve what he held dear. A man worthy of the title "paladin."

He had died a horrible death. Kestrel could not close her eyes without seeing the bandits in Phlan, the cult fighter in this very cavern—how the pool had first consumed their spirits, then their bodies. She wondered where Corran's spirit was now. With Tyr? She hoped so.

She moved several paces away from the group, seeking solitude, but she still could hear the others speaking in low tones. Faeril. Ghleanna and Athan. Durwyn. Though the latter three spoke of returning to Elminster—and from there, home—all used the muted tones of a funeral service. Corran's loss hovered in everyone's thoughts.

Faeril approached to offer her curing magic. Kestrel yet suffered burns from the dragon's fire but motioned the cleric away. "Treat the others first." She wasn't in the mood for ministry.

"I already have."

With a sigh, she submitted to Faeril's healing. As the cleric prayed, Kestrel stared into the swirling fog. Her mind was full, her heart heavy.

A pale green light appeared in the mist, far away at first, but growing closer. A figure emerged—a tall, slender woman with a heart-shaped face. She floated a foot off the ground and brought with her the scent of gardenias. Anorrweyn.

In her arms, she carried Corran's limp body.

Kestrel swallowed the lump in her throat. She and the others rose as the ghost approached. The mist clung too closely to the paladin for Kestrel to see his face—to see what his immersion in the Pool of Radiance had done to him. The priestess gently laid him on the ground.

"Is he dead?" Kestrel knew he was, but she had to hear the words.

"Nay," Anorrweyn responded. "Only sleeping."

Kestrel gasped. "Really?"

"Truly, Kestrel." The priestess smiled. "He never entered the foul water of the pool but landed safe in the Weave's embrace. See? Already he stirs."

The mist around Corran cleared. He rolled his head to one side, consciousness returning. Kestrel saw that he had been restored to perfect health—even the lines of care etched into his face by recent events had faded.

"I leave him in your keeping now," Anorrweyn said. "I must return to the Emerald, and continue to undo the corruption wrought by Mordrayn upon the Mythal. There is much work to be done." Behind her, a glowing ball of blue-white light appeared and expanded to become a portal. "I leave you with one final gift: this scroll. On it you will find the Word of Farewell. It will open a gate home for you. Speak it soon, for once the Mythal is more fully restored, gates to the outside will no longer open."

The priestess handed the paper to Kestrel. "Take care, my friends. And thank you." With that, she was gone.

Slowly, Corran's eyelids fluttered open. He blinked, giving his pupils a chance to focus, and propped himself up on one elbow. His gaze swept the cavern before meeting Kestrel's. "Pelendralaar?"

She smiled. "Dust."

He released a deep breath. "And the pool?"

"Destroyed."

The others crowded around, eager to describe the dracolich's final moments for Corran and hear what he remembered of his plunge. Kestrel hung back, letting Ghleanna and Durwyn tell the tale of the party's triumph to the leader they'd followed from the start.

Their quest was over. At last, she could go her separate way, resume the solitary path she'd walked before all this madness began. She could collect her cache in Phlan—provided it was still there—and move on. There was always another city, always another heist or con game. Soon, the easy life she'd struggled all her years to attain.

Somehow, that life no longer seemed like enough.

She glanced at her companions. Faeril was saying goodbye, preparing to return to Beriand and aid Myth Drannor's guardians in rebuilding the city. The other four spoke of reporting to Elminster, then helping the Moonsea's port cities recover from Mordrayn and Pelendralaar's reign of terror.

Once they all passed through the gate to Phlan, she had a choice to make. She could walk away and put this whole harrowing ordeal behind her. Or she could join Corran, Athan, Ghleanna, and Durwyn in their effort to right the wrongs of the cult.

Kestrel sighed. Her cache could wait a little longer.

There was much work to be done.

Venture into the
FORGOTTEN REALMS
with these two new series!

Sembia
GET A NEW PERSPECTIVE ON THE FORGOTTEN REALMS FROM
THESE TALES OF THE USKEVREN CLAN OF SELGAUNT.

Shadow's Witness
Paul Kemp

Erevis Cale has a secret. When a ruthless evil is unleashed on Selgaunt,
the loyal butler of the Uskevren family must come to terms with his own
dark past if he is to save the family he dearly loves.

The Shattered Mask
Richard Lee Byers

Shamur Uskevren is duped into making an assassination attempt on her husband
Thamalon. Soon, however, the dame of House Uskevren realizes that all is not
as it seems and that her family is in grave danger.

JUNE 2001

Black Wolf
Dave Gross

The young Talbot Uskevren was the only one to survive a horrible
"hunting accident." Now, infected with lycanthropy, the second son
of the Uskevren clan must learn to control what he has become.

NOVEMBER 2001

The Cities
A NEW SERIES OF STAND-ALONE NOVELS,
EACH SET IN ONE OF THE MIGHTY CITIES OF FAERÛN.

The City of Ravens
Richard Baker

Raven's Bluff — a viper pit of schemes, swindles, wizardry, and
fools masquerading as heroes.

Temple Hill
Drew Karpyshyn

Elversult — fashionable and comfortable, this shining city of the heartlands
harbors an unknown evil beneath its streets.

SEPTEMBER 2001

FORGOTTEN REALMS

THREE OF THE MOST POPULAR
FORGOTTEN REALMS
AUTHORS TELL THE STORY
OF FAERÛN'S GREATEST KINGDOM
—AND ITS GREATEST KING.

The Cormyr Saga

CORMYR: A NOVEL
Ed Greenwood & Jeff Grubb
A plot to poison King Azoun IV brings the kingdom to
the brink of disaster.

BEYOND THE HIGH ROAD
Troy Denning
With the threat from within at an end, Cormyr faces an even
greater threat from the barbaric Stonelands, and a princess
begins to understand what it means to rule a kingdom.

DEATH OF THE DRAGON
Ed Greenwood & Troy Denning
Plague, madness, and war sweep through Cormyr and the people
look to their king for salvation. Only the mighty Azoun has any
chance to defeat the horror that will change Cormyr forever.